WINDY CITY SERIES
BOOK FOUR

LIZ TOMFORDE

LIZ TOMFORDE

Play Along

**HODDER &
STOUGHTON**

First published in Great Britain in 2024 by Hodder & Stoughton Limited
An Hachette UK company

The authorised representative in the EEA is Hachette Ireland, 8 Castlecourt
Centre, Dublin 15, D15 XTP3, Ireland (email: info@hbgi.ie)

12

A CIP catalogue record for this title is available from the British Library

Paperback ISBN 9781399728614

Typeset in Plantin Light by Hewer Text UK Ltd, Edinburgh
Printed and bound in Great Britain by Clays Ltd, Elcograf S.p.A.

Hodder & Stoughton policy is to use papers that are natural, renewable
and recyclable products and made from wood grown in sustainable
forests. The logging and manufacturing processes are expected to
conform to the environmental regulations of the country of origin.

Hodder & Stoughton Limited
Carmelite House
50 Victoria Embankment
London EC4Y 0DZ

www.hodder.co.uk

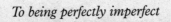

To being perfectly imperfect

Playlist

Love On the Run – Sons of Zion feat. Jackson Owens	2:57
Drunk & I'm Drunk – Marc E. Bassy	3:56
Obsessed – Mariah Carey	4:02
You Got It – Jamieboy & Myles Parrish	3:36
Lose Control – Teddy Swims	3:30
Bad Side – iyla	2:40
Home – Good Neighbours	2:37
Ms. Poli Sci – Paul Russell & Khary	2:08
Classic – MKTO	2:55
Trial By Fire – Marc E. Bassy feat. Bibi Bourelly	2:34
Seasons – VEDO	3:20
DFMU – Ella Mai	3:17
Must Be Mine – Kiana Ledé feat. Ant Clemons	2:31
MARS – Mario	3:48
Abracadabra, Pt. 2 – Wes Nelson	2:47
6 months – John K	3:37
Make Me Wanna – VEDO	3:40
Naked – James Arthur	3:53
This City Remix – Sam Fischer feat. Anne-Marie	3:17
Comfortable – H.E.R.	4:15
Love Like This – Natasha Bedingfield feat. Sean Kingston	3:42

Prologue

Isaiah

Three years ago

It's the worst day of the year.

It's the worst day of *every* year.

I typically spend this day traveling with my teammates on a preseason bonding trip. I should be in Cancun or Miami, sipping on a cocktail by a pool, entirely distracted by the party surrounding me.

Only this year, I'm not poolside, drunk, or distracted. I'm hiding in the women's restroom outside of the team's clubhouse because this season starts early, and unfortunately, the first day of baseball isn't enough of a distraction for me.

The women's restroom is immaculate and endlessly cleaner than ours. They've got a velvet couch in here and little perfume bottles on the counter. Pretty folded hand towels and dinner mints in a glass bowl. It smells infinitely better than the men's restroom, and my only hope is that the other boys don't realize how fucking nice it is in here because this is *my* secret hiding spot and has been for the past six years—ever since I got drafted to play shortstop for the Windy City Warriors.

There are no women on the staff here, so no one ever uses this bathroom other than me, when I need a moment to myself.

You could say I'm the wild one on the team. The one who is a little bit reckless and a whole lot cocky. The guy who will make himself the butt of the joke as long as it makes everyone around him smile. So, starting the season off by having a breakdown or potentially crying like a little bitch in front of my teammates wouldn't exactly be on brand for me.

I'm a twenty-eight-year-old man and I'm not ashamed to admit that even after all these years, this day is tough for me. I was only thirteen years old when my brother, two years my senior, had to break the news that our mom's car wrapped around a tree while she was driving home in a storm, and we'd never get to see her again.

So yeah . . . it's the worst fucking day of the year.

With bouncing knees, I sit on the closed toilet lid in one of the stalls, needing to get my shit together. Needing to get back to goofy, everything-rolls-off-his-shoulders Isaiah Rhodes. The one who knows how to make everyone around him happy. The one that everyone here expects to see when I enter the clubhouse.

I like being that guy. Ninety percent of the time, I naturally *am* that guy. I figured out when I was young that I could make my brother laugh even when he was too stressed to smile, and I thrived off that shit. It was as if I had found my purpose in life—to make those around me happy, so I tend to keep the sad, sappy moments private.

I give myself one last moment of sadness before I leave the stall, splash a bit of water on my face at the sink, and exit the women's restroom.

But as soon as I open the door, voices sound just outside. This part of the clubhouse is usually empty, so I pause, recognizing Dr. Fredrick's voice. I keep myself hidden and out of sight, not wanting anyone to know that I just had myself a private cry.

"You lied on your application."

"I didn't lie," I hear a woman say in retort.

2

Dr. Fredrick lowers his voice in an attempt to keep this conversation between only them, but I can hear him perfectly clear. "You misled, and you know it."

"Kenny is a nickname for Kennedy."

At that, I peek around the small partition to see Dr. Fredrick looking down at a woman, annoyance plastered on his face.

I can't see what she looks like since her back is to me, but standing at full height, she barely makes it to Dr. Fredrick's chin, and he's not considered a tall man. Her hair is tied up in a thick ponytail, falling mid-back. I can't make out the color, though I can tell it's a different shade than an ordinary blonde or brunette. I'm just not sure what you'd classify it as.

Dr. Fredrick's eyes flick over his surroundings, ensuring they're alone, so I quickly duck behind the partition to listen once again.

"This is not the place for you. I suggest you decline the job offer and find a position somewhere more suitable for . . . someone like you."

"Someone like me, meaning a woman?"

What the hell?

Dr. Fredrick has never been my favorite. He's the head of our Health and Wellness Department and the lead doctor for the team. All other doctors, nutritionists, and athletic trainers report to him, and any respect I may have had for the guy flies right out the window at his insinuation.

A moment of silence lingers, as if he's calculating the right thing to say without getting himself into trouble.

"The job I was originally hiring for is no longer needing to be filled. From what human resources tells me, I cannot rescind the offer, but I can change it. At this point, I'm only looking to hire an athletic trainer."

"What?" she asks behind a shocked laugh. "But I'm an M.D. You're expecting me to come on board as an athletic trainer?"

"I'm not expecting you to come on board at all."

"Dr. Fredrick, I just moved to Chicago for this job. You've seen my references. You've seen the externships I've done. It's why you hired me in the first place."

"I had a different idea of who I was hiring at the time."

"Because you thought I was a man."

"I'm not going to discuss this with you any further. If you want to work for the Windy City Warriors, you may do so as an entry-level athletic trainer. That's the position I'm hiring for."

She hesitates and I can almost picture her shoulders straightening with the way she confidently asks, "When do you need my answer?"

"By the end of the day."

"Fine. I'll let you know my decision soon."

There's a moment of silence, leading me to believe that the conversation is over, but then I hear Dr. Fredrick cut in and say, "Ms. Kay, if you do decide to come on board, this will be the one and only warning I give you. If there's even a hint of some kind of nonsense between you and one of the players, your position will be terminated. There's a reason I don't hire women to work for me. You'll be in locker rooms, on airplanes, and in hotels with them. I expect you'll make sure you're not a distraction."

There's a reason I don't hire women. Fucking asshole.

"With all due respect, Dr. Fredrick, I just spent the last two years as one of only three doctors for the entirety of the University of Connecticut's athletic program. There's nothing in my history that would have you questioning my professionalism."

"Those were children. These are men," he says in response. "I think you know exactly what I'm getting at here."

She clears her throat, and there's something to be said about her professionalism he's questioning, because if this were me, I'd probably be delivering a right hook to his jaw.

I'm a little impulsive that way.

"You'll have my answer by noon," she says to finish.

Footsteps putter in the distance, and they grow louder with each step, heading in my direction. There's no route for me to leave without getting caught eavesdropping, and though I have every intention to bring this information to Monty, our field manager, I don't plan on clueing in Dr. Fredrick beforehand.

So, to be safe, I duck back into the women's restroom until I know the coast is clear of him.

I already wasn't a fan of our lead doctor. He's a bit of a kiss-ass if you ask me, always wanting to be buddy-buddy with the guys on the team, but the way he just spoke to this woman, as if he were better than her, has me eager to tell every person in the Warriors' organization what a sexist piece of shit he is.

"Sexist piece of shit."

I hear my own internal dialogue spoken back to me in a terrifying tone just on the other side of the bathroom door.

The woman from the hallway pushes into the never-used restroom just as I hide myself behind a stall. I don't sit. I stand like an absolute creep because I have no idea how I got myself into this situation.

Watching through the crack in the stall door, I find her reflection in the mirror. Hands bracketed on the sink counter, and head hung low, still hiding her face I've yet to see.

She laughs to herself. "What the actual fuck just happened?"

Then, she takes a deep breath and finally stands up straight, looking right at herself in the mirror and giving me the same view . . . only for any gut-wrenching grief I was feeling about this day to be put on hold, because now I'm thoroughly distracted.

This tiny woman, with hair color I can't categorize and a tone in her voice that would make any man's balls shrivel up in fear, is fucking *stunning*.

Freckles dot every inch of flushed, creamy skin. Eyes that I could make an educated guess and call them brown, seeing as they look a lot like mine. And lips . . . lips tucked under teeth to keep herself from crying because she's clearly willing herself to be angry instead of sad.

Call it instincts, but I'd imagine her smile could light me up if it wasn't currently turned down in a frown.

Those eyes begin to gloss over as she watches herself.

"No," she pleads. "Not here. Get your shit together, Kennedy."

Kennedy.

Inhaling a deep breath, she shakes her head. "And stop fucking talking to yourself, you weirdo."

And just like that, on the worst day of the year, I feel my lips tilt up in amusement.

I watch with rapt attention as she pulls out her phone and calls someone, placing it on speaker while she paces the restroom.

I should probably announce my presence. This feels like an invasion of privacy, but I have no idea how to explain my current situation.

Hey, I just like hanging out in the women's restroom. Don't worry about me. I'm going to wash my hands real quick. Can you move over?

I eavesdropped on your conversation with the Head of our Health and Wellness Department. I can go to HR with you if you'd like. Also, you're like really pretty.

"Hey, what's up?" a man's voice says on the other end of the phone.

I immediately hate him.

"Do you have time to talk?" she asks. "I kind of need to talk."

"I have team photos right now, and I'm up next. Are you okay?"

She closes her eyes for a moment, composing herself. "Yeah, of course. I just wanted to say hi to my stepbrother."

Stepbrother. Noted.

"Well, hi. I miss you. Is your first day going well?"

She stares right at herself in the mirror and lies. "It's going great."

"Good. Hey, I've gotta go. I'm up for pictures but call me later and we'll catch up."

She plasters on a smile that even I, a complete stranger, know is fake. "Will do." Kennedy hangs up the phone, then drops her head with a quiet "*fuck.*"

I know nothing about this girl, but I do know she needs someone to make her smile, and that's my specialty. I'm also a bit of a believer in fate, and though this day is my least favorite date on the calendar, I tend to find meaning in things on this day.

Maybe I was supposed to overhear that conversation.

Maybe I found myself stuck in the women's restroom because she needs someone to talk to.

Maybe my mom sent me on her path today.

That last belief has me closing my eyes and opening my mouth before I've fully thought it through. "If you need someone to talk to about that job offer, I can help."

God, how fucking creepy was that?

I reopen my eyes to watch hers shoot to the mirror before they find my feet in the reflection.

"What are you doing in the women's restroom?"

"Did the size thirteens give me away?"

"Are you spying on me?"

"Well, technically, I was here first. Remember?"

Her eyes narrow as they trail up the stall, finding mine through the narrow crack. "Are you going to answer any of my questions or just keep responding with your own?"

A bark of a laugh escapes me. I like this one.

"I'm hiding in the women's restroom because I'm having a shit day, and from what I overheard, so are you."

Her shoulders, which were up by her ears, settle back into place. "Oh."

Unlocking the door, I swing it inward until she comes into full view.

Black leggings hug every inch of her toned legs. A dark gray quarter-zip bunches around her elbows, finishing with perfectly clean white sneakers on her feet. Her freckles continue down her forearms and ankles, making me believe her pale skin is painted in them.

Polished for wearing athletic gear. And pretty. So, so pretty.

Her tone is less intimidating when she asks, "How much of my shitty day did you overhear?"

Meeting her at the sink, I rest my hip on the counter and face her. "I heard your conversation in the hallway with Dr. Fredrick. I came back in here so he wouldn't see me."

"Oh." She nods, eyes pulled away from me. "So, all of it."

"We should talk to HR, or I can talk to the field manager, Monty. He can take it to the team owner—"

"No. No, I don't want to say anything. This isn't the first time I've dealt with a sexist boss. I'm a woman working in sports, after all."

I pause. "Boss? So you're taking the job?"

"I don't—" She freezes, eyes examining my entire body. I tower over her with my 6'4" build, but wearing my normal clothes, I don't uniquely stand out. "Who are you?"

It's then I realize she has no idea that I'm the starting shortstop for the team she may potentially work for, and I have every intention to use my unknown identity to my advantage.

"Right now, I'm simply someone to talk to. You said you needed to talk."

There's this untrusting question in her eye as she attempts to assess me, but the need to work through her predicament outweighs any suspicion she has towards me.

"I can't get a job anywhere in professional sports." Her admission hangs in the air for a moment. "It doesn't matter that I graduated at the top of my class at Columbia. It doesn't matter that the doctors I did my residency under sing my praises when called for my references. It doesn't matter that I was the youngest person to become Lead Doctor at a division one school with national championship winning athletic programs. No, none of that matters because I have two tits and a vagina."

My eyes go wide at her candor.

"Oh my God." She grimaces before covering her face with her right hand. "I can't believe I just told a complete stranger that I have two tits."

"I would've been a lot more impressed if you said you had three."

She peeks through her fingers, and I plaster on my most mischievous smirk. Those glossed-over eyes are nowhere to be found when her hand slips off her face, revealing a sheepish smile.

Sheepish, yes. But a smile, nonetheless.

I hold out my hand to shake hers. "Isaiah."

She returns the gesture. "Kennedy."

"Well, Kennedy, now that I'm no longer a stranger, tell me more about these two tits of yours."

She tries to bite back her smile, but this time it's big and genuine, attempting to break through. "I'm going to carry that one with me for a while, aren't I?"

"Absolutely." I cock my head to the side. "I thought I heard your name was Kenny?"

She chuckles, this beautiful but somewhat self-conscious sound. "No one has ever called me Kenny. I just adopted that name after I received six different denial letters when I used the name Kennedy."

"Well, Kenny—"

"No—"

"Talk me through the job offer."

She huffs an exhausted breath. "I've been trying to get into professional sports since I finished my residency. My goal is to be a lead team doctor one day, but I haven't been able to get my foot in the door anywhere. Guys that I went to school with, that barely graduated and have much poorer references than me, are getting jobs that I'm applying for. So, when I got offered the position to be the second doctor here, I jumped on it. I packed my things and moved into a building in downtown Chicago this past weekend. Dr. Fredrick and I have only spoken via email because he was taking time off during the off-season. My references must not have alluded to the fact I'm a woman, I'm not sure. But this morning, when I introduced myself to him, he immediately rescinded the job offer."

So, she's pretty *and* insanely smart. Got it.

"When he told the head of human resources there had been a mistake and the job wasn't available, Dr. Fredrick was informed that, legally, he had to hire me in some capacity. I don't think HR knows that his sudden decision of not hiring a second doctor on staff had anything to do with him accidentally hiring one who was a woman."

The words roll out of her, and she can't seem to stop.

"And now I'm being offered the job of an entry-level athletic trainer, which, don't get me wrong, is a great job, but I didn't spend my entire adult life becoming a sports medicine doctor to have to go to someone else to create treatment plans, you know?" She looks me over from head to toe. "And why the hell am I telling you all of this?"

I chuckle. She's flustered. It's endearing.

"Because I'm a good listener."

That shy smile lifts again. "So, what do you think I should do?"

She's asking *me*? Clearly, she knows nothing about me because I'm typically the last person someone comes to when they need advice. I'm the guy they come to when they need a laugh or someone to show them a good time.

My brother is the serious one, and if Kai were here and not off playing baseball for the Seattle Saints, I'd ask *him* what advice I should give this girl. He's my sounding board and I miss the hell out of him.

But he's not here, so this advice is on me.

I personally think she should walk up to Dr. Fredrick and knee him in the balls, but I also really like the idea of her working here. I like the idea of that freckled face showing up at every one of my games.

She's easy to talk to, and on the worst day of the year, she's made it bearable. Good, even.

"What do you want to do?" I ask instead of giving her my opinion.

"You really do love to answer a question with a question, huh?"

I smirk at that.

"I want to work in professional sports," she states plainly. "Jobs rarely become available because this is a lifelong career for most people."

"You want to work in professional sports," I echo for her to hear.

She nods at the realization. "I should take the job. At least I'll be getting my foot in the door. But God, Dr.

Fredrick is the worst and if he treats women that way, I can't even begin to imagine how horrible the players on the team are."

Fucking *ouch*.

Granted, we're a bunch of idiots, but none of the guys are disrespectful.

"I'll um . . ." I clear my throat. "I'll make sure none of the other guys on the team give you a hard time."

Her eyes narrow in confusion, but still she's got that pretty smile plastered on her lips and it's doing all sorts of things to my insides.

"Who are you?"

"Two tits and a short-term memory, huh, Kenny? I already told you my name."

"Do you work in the front office or for—"

"I should get out there." I gesture to the bathroom door. "Can I walk you out?"

Her eyes latch onto me suspiciously, and all I can do is smile like a fucking dork just from having this smart girl's attention on me.

I'm not naïve. I know she's going to learn I'm one of the players, and if Dr. Fredrick's warning was any indication, once she knows the truth, she'll never give me the time of day again. So, for now, I'll take advantage of what little time I have left.

I open the bathroom door for her, and without having to duck, she walks right under my arm and into the hallway.

"You can't tell anyone," she quickly says.

"About what?"

"If I take the job. You can't tell anyone about what Dr. Fredrick said or about my qualifications."

"You might be the first doctor I've ever met who doesn't want everyone to know she's a doctor."

"Isaiah, please."

Those two little words stop me in my tracks.

My name. She sounds good saying my name.

She sounds good begging too.

I search her face, desperation plastered on it. "I won't say anything."

"And about what you overheard?"

"You mean the part where I learned that Dr. Dick is a woman hater?"

"Yes, that part."

"No, I'm saying something about that. Right now, in fact."

She grabs my forearm to stop me with her pale and freckled hand, starkly contrasting my suntanned skin from all my time playing baseball outside.

But before I can memorize the differences, she pulls away in an instant. "If I'm going to work for him, it's going to be difficult enough. I can't start off this working relationship with a complaint to the field manager or team owner. I can handle this on my own."

Independence and determination radiate off her, and though she's got to be sitting somewhere around 5'3", her shoulders are squared and pushed back, giving her as much height as possible. Making her as *big* as possible.

Good. She's going to need that resolve working for that piece of shit.

"*When*," I correct. "*When* you work for him."

Her knowing smile matches mine, like there's a secret only she and I know.

"Will I see you around?" she asks.

"Oh, I'm fairly certain you'll be seeing plenty of me."

"Rhodes!" Cody, our first baseman, calls out when he turns the corner and finds me standing in front of the women's restroom. He's in full uniform, ready for our team photos today. "There you are. Hurry up! Pictures are starting in five and your uniform is hanging in your locker stall. Monty sent me to come find you."

Cody turns with that and jogs back into the clubhouse.

I slowly face Kennedy, my most innocent smile plastered on my lips.

Her already pale skin is even more drained. "You're a player?"

"Shortstop." I wink.

Any sign of a previous smile is long gone, and her demeanor instantly shifts. I can physically feel the ice in the air around her. She's shocked. Confused. A little bit pissed.

"This conversation never happened." She doesn't hesitate, bolting away from me, Dr. Fredrick's warning blaring in her mind, I'm sure.

"Hey, Kenny!" I call out and she stops, reluctantly facing me. "I promised I'd make sure the other guys don't give you a hard time, but I never said anything about me." Her lips slightly part and I shoot her with another wink. "See you around, Doc."

"Where have you been?" Travis, our rookie catcher, asks as I pull my T-shirt over my head and drop my jeans at my stall, needing to get into my new uniform like the rest of my teammates.

His locker is to the left of mine while Cody's is on my right.

"I was busy."

A picture of me, my mom, and my brother is taped to the top of my stall, hidden from anyone else's view, and my thumb dusts over it when I set my watch down on one of the shelves.

"Yeah," Cody laughs, pointing across the clubhouse. "Busy with that one."

In only my boxer briefs, I turn to find Kennedy speaking

with Dr. Fredrick. I watch as he clenches his jaw and flares his nostrils, and I note the exact moment she tells him she's taking the job.

Travis lets out a low whistle. "Pretty."

"Smart too," I add, but I don't fill them in on what I know because Kennedy asked me not to, and I like knowing something about the new athletic trainer that no one else does. "Hey, what color would you say her hair is?"

"Red," Travis answers simply.

"C'mon, Trav. I've told you. You've got to be more descriptive than that for him." Cody studies her for a moment. "I'd call it auburn. It's a mix of warm red and earthy brown, but she's also got some copper in there."

"Like a penny?"

"Exactly."

This is why I ask Cody these things. The guy gets that I need the details.

Keeping my eyes locked on her from across the room, I watch her find me at the same time Dr. Fredrick is preaching something at her. Her attention starts at my feet and works up my bare legs, only to linger over my boxer briefs and take their time tracing my shirtless chest. But when she drifts up to my face, I smile as arrogantly as possible, making sure she knows I caught her.

She looks away instantly, and I can't help but grin.

Travis nudges my shoulder. "So, who is she?"

On this day, where everything feels like a sign, I don't hesitate when I say, "My future wife."

The boys both burst out in laughter, but I keep my eyes on the only woman in the entire building.

Kennedy tucks a rogue strand of auburn hair behind her ear, and that's when I see it—an impossible-to-miss diamond ring overtaking her left ring finger. Though somehow, I didn't notice it before this moment.

"Sorry, man." Cody laughs again, palm connecting with my shoulder. "Looks like someone already beat you to it."

And just like that, it's the worst day of the year again.

I

Isaiah

Present

"There's my guys." I swing an arm over both Cody and Travis's shoulders when I find them on the casino level of our hotel. "Where are we headed?"

"About time, Rhodes." Travis, our catcher, shrugs out from under me. "You take longer to get ready than anyone I know, and your socks still don't fucking match."

I look down at my feet, where my pants hit right at my ankles. "They match to me."

"We have a table waiting with bottle service at the club in Caesars Palace." Cody gestures down the strip. "Let's go."

Our first baseman takes off with excited strides, the rest of the team following closely behind, with me bringing up the rear of the group.

We've been in Vegas for a few days now, and this is our final night here. Every year, before the season starts, the boys and I take a preseason trip as an excuse for some team bonding. It's typically somewhere hot or tropical as a reward for surviving the Chicago winter, and though Las Vegas isn't too hot this time of the year, the stuffy clubs and overpriced alcohol are keeping us all plenty warm.

Not that we've had to worry about the price of alcohol or pay for much of anything. As a professional baseball team, we've been gifted tables at clubs and endless booze each night we've been here.

Two years ago, my older brother Kai got picked up by the Windy City Warriors, finally putting us on the same team. He's not with us in Vegas, opting to stay in Chicago with his son and soon-to-be fiancée, but I have the rest of my guys here and other than spending time with my family, there's not much I enjoy more than hanging with my friends and throwing back a few drinks.

"Is tonight the night?" Travis slows his strides to walk in the back of the group with me.

"Is tonight the night for what?"

"Is tonight the night you talk to someone other than your teammates in the club?"

"Don't really see the point in that. I'm on a team-bonding trip. I'm bonding with the team."

"Yeah, we're all on a team-bonding trip, yet you're the only one of us who has gone home alone both nights here."

"Not interested," I say with a casual shrug. "And that's not true. Lautner, the rookie from Oregon, hasn't gone home with anyone either. Kid has got zero game."

"Who the hell are you, and what have you done with Isaiah Rhodes? When have you ever *not* been interested? And since when did you stop being the life of the party? Last year in Miami, we had to promise a cop two tickets behind home plate just to keep him from arresting you. You started stripping naked right on Ocean Drive."

"We were in Florida. It was hot. And I'm still the life of the party. I just don't continue the party once we leave the bar anymore."

Travis shoots me a pointed glance out of the corner of his eye, telling me he knows exactly why.

In fact, the entire team knows why.

There's been only one woman who has held my interest and now that she's no longer wearing another man's engagement ring, spending my time with anyone else holds zero appeal.

My teammates have also encouraged me to let go of that pipe dream because in their minds, it's never going to happen. They believe that the one and only woman on our team staff would never try something with one of us, least of all me. Sure, I've given Kennedy Kay more shit than anyone else on the team, but that's only because I made a promise to her that I would.

And I always keep my promises.

When we get to the next hotel over, the line to enter the club seems endless, wrapping and looping, bodies squeezed together in an attempt to get inside quicker, but thankfully Cody gets a phone call telling us to use the backdoor entrance, allowing us to skip the line altogether.

As we pass the waiting patrons, walking in the opposite direction, a hand reaches out to grab my bicep.

"Hey, I know you," a feminine voice says. "You play baseball for Chicago. Number nineteen."

I follow her hold on me to find a woman with light hair and glittery makeup.

"That's me."

Her hand trails down my arm. "Rhodes, right?"

"There are two Rhodeses playing for Chicago now, but yeah, I'm Isaiah." I hold out my hand for hers to shake, being sure to use the one that would force her to stop touching me.

"Bridget. So, what brings you to Vegas?"

"Team-bonding trip." I gesture to the guys halted around me.

Her eyes sparkle before motioning to the handful of other girls around her. "We're here for my birthday."

"Well then, happy birthday to you." I wink at her because old habits die hard and I'm a fucking idiot and now she thinks I'm interested, judging by the smirk tilting on her mouth.

"Do you guys have a table? We'd love to join you."

"We do have a table." I attempt my best disappointed tone, hoping not to hurt her feelings. "But it's guys' night."

"It's most definitely *not* guys' night," I hear Cody pipe up from somewhere behind me.

"You understand, right?" I continue as if no one heard him.

"Sure thing." Bridget's eyes flicker and I think it's with embarrassment more so than disappointment.

"But hey," I interrupt her thought process. "Find us inside and I'll make sure the bartender puts all your drinks on my tab, yeah? Can't have the birthday girl paying for all her own drinks, can we?"

Her shoulders straighten, a bit of confidence returning to her face. "No, we absolutely cannot."

"Have fun, ladies, and happy birthday, Bridget."

Her body sways in a flirty way. "Thanks, Isaiah. See you inside."

Hands in my pockets, I continue to the back door as if nothing out of the ordinary happened. Because nothing out of the ordinary *did* happen.

"First of all," Cody says, continuing to walk with me. "How the hell can you turn someone down and manage to have her still drooling over you afterward? I need some of that Isaiah Rhodes charm."

I scoff. "You pick up more people than I ever have."

"She was beautiful, by the way."

"You should go for it."

"I just might."

"And second off," Travis cuts in. "You're an idiot. Please for the love of God, let this go. Cody, if you don't use your dick, does it fall off? Is Isaiah going to die a born-again virgin?"

"I couldn't tell you. I use my dick plenty." Cody stops in his tracks. "Wait, born-again virgin? Still? That was because of Kennedy back there?"

"You two can both fuck off."

Travis laughs to himself.

"Isaiah, you have got to let that go. It's been three years."

"It hasn't been three years."

"You've been into that girl since the day she walked into the clubhouse for the first time."

"Yeah, but I only realized she was single eight months ago, so *technically* I'm only eight months in on this whole thing."

"Wow." Cody nods. "Trav is right. You are an idiot."

I smack him on the back of his head. "Remember last night when we were a few drinks in and I told you two that you guys were my best friends?"

"Yeah?"

"I take it back. You both fucking suck."

The back door to the club opens and the bouncer nods in Cody's direction, allowing the team to start trickling their way in with the three of us bringing up the rear.

"We're just looking out for you." Cody swings his arm over my shoulders. "You've been shooting your shot for years and look how well that's worked out."

I wasn't shooting my shot. Sure, maybe I've shamelessly flirted with the girl for the past three years, but none of it was serious. She had a fiancé. But now . . . now she doesn't. Now I'm dead serious about my intentions, but she thinks I'm still joking around.

Call me ridiculous. Call me superstitious, but that day I met her three years ago felt like fate. What I typically consider the worst day of the year had a bright light for once.

That same date on the calendar is only minutes away, and still, in the eighteen years since I lost my mom, there was only one time I genuinely smiled on that date, and it was the morning that Kennedy Kay came barging into the women's bathroom and subsequently my life.

I shuffle forward, following my teammates into the club, having to project my voice over the pounding base. "Don't you guys believe in fate?"

"For fuck's sake, Rhodes." Travis shakes his head at me. "Did you really just scream 'don't you guys believe in fate' in the middle of a goddamn nightclub? Please for the love of God, go get laid."

Cody can't help but laugh as the bouncer closes the back door behind us. "I'll start believing in fate the moment Kennedy decides to voluntarily spend time with you outside of work."

Travis chimes in. "Forget spending time with him. At this point, I'd consider it fate if Kennedy so much as said a single word to him outside of work."

Walking backward, I face my buddies as I continue to follow our group to the private table of the busy club. "You have no faith. One day, you'll see." I throw my hands wide. "It's meant to be!"

Without looking, I barrel into someone behind me, stepping right on their foot. I stumble but catch my balance and even over the music, I can hear their low hiss in pain.

"Oh shit." I turn just in time to grab their upper arms, keeping them from toppling over. "I'm sorry! I'm so sorry. I wasn't looking."

"Clearly."

The woman's hair curtains her face as she babies her injured foot by hobbling on one single high heel in agony.

That hair.

Even in the darkness of the club, I know that hair. The shade is one I've memorized. *Auburn* as Cody first taught me.

Kennedy Kay Auburn as I refer to it now.

"Kenny?"

I watch her body instantly stiffen before her brown eyes cautiously lift to look at me. "Isaiah?"

22

"Hi."

Her shocked expression does nothing to stop my eyes from wandering the length of her.

God, she's stunning. I've never seen her outside of athletic clothes, namely the staff uniform of a Warriors' polo and black leggings. But tonight, that hair is down and perfectly styled, her freckled arms and legs fully exposed thanks to the crisp white mini dress and matching white heels.

She looks so fucking good. Her outfit seems expensive and polished, tailored to fit her body.

"Isaiah."

"Yeah?"

"I asked what you were doing here."

My attention immediately darts to the foot I just stepped on. Kennedy is still keeping her weight off of it, clearly in pain. I bend down before stopping myself and realizing that checking out someone's foot in a club is fucking weird, no matter how much I might be crushing on the person it's attached to.

"Is your foot okay? I'll get some ice from the bartender."

"It's fine. Surprisingly, my foot is more sore from wearing high heels than it is from being stepped on by two hundred pounds of muscle."

A smirk lifts on my lips. "Keeping up on my body stats, huh, Ken? I knew you were obsessed with me."

"Don't flatter yourself, Rhodes. It's my literal job to know your body stats. What are you doing here?"

"It's our preseason bonding trip. Well, pre-regular season and post-spring training." I gesture to my teammates, who are being ushered to a roped-off corner of the club. Cody and Travis wave to her from across the room.

It's hard to tell with the low lighting, but Trav is shaking his head in disbelief at the same time Cody mouths, *you've got to be kidding me.*

"Oh," Kennedy says in realization. "Everyone from the team is here."

"Everyone but Kai. He's at home with Max and Miller." Motioning towards our table, I add, "You should come hang out with us."

"It looks like it's guys' night."

I scoff. "It most definitely isn't guys' night."

Kennedy looks back at our table, a bit of longing shining in her eyes as if she actually wants to hang out with us. It's a stark contrast from the immediate "no" I get whenever I invite her to do something outside of work.

"I can't." She throws a thumb over her shoulder to a group of girls, all decked in white minus one wearing a blindingly shiny silver dress. "I'm here for a bachelorette party."

Silver Sparkles is wearing a phony veil with a sash across her chest that reads "Future Mrs. Danforth," posing for a photo with every one of her friends wearing white around her.

Posing with everyone but Kennedy.

"I was just heading to the bar to grab them another bottle of champagne," she continues.

The flashes of strobe light make the dark room bright enough to see the endless line surrounding the bar, waiting to order drinks.

"Don't you girls have a table server? That line at the bar is going to take an hour."

"That's what I was hoping for."

My eyes narrow in confusion. "Come to our table. I can order for you there."

"Isaiah," she sighs. "You know I can't do that. I work for the team."

"And you're the only person on the staff who feels like you can't hang out with us. There are no rules against us being friends."

"It's different for me, and you know it."

As much as I don't want to agree with her, I know in a way it *is* different. No, none of the boys on the team would ever think differently of her if she threw back a few drinks with us. We'd still all agree she's the best athletic trainer on staff, and I'd still be the only person who knew that is because she's grossly overqualified.

She wouldn't get in trouble for it, but she works under a lead doctor who wants nothing more than to find a reason to fire her. Even if that reason is some made-up story derived from pictures that landed on the internet of her spending time with us in Sin City.

Kennedy, unlike any of the male staffers, has to go the extra mile to make sure the professional line is clearly drawn.

People swarm around us, pushing and edging their way to the dance floor, and all it does is cause Kennedy to lean into my space for reprieve from the crowd, seeking a bit of shelter from the bodies packing in around her. Eyes glancing back to the group of women she's with, she takes a step closer to me.

It's the strangest thing she's ever done.

The fact that I'm, for once, not the last person in the room she wants to be around is surprising and concerning all at once.

"Kenny, are you okay?"

"Yeah, it's just kind of hot in here, I guess."

"And that's why you're trying to snuggle up to me in a night club right now? We can go back to my room if you'd like." Leaning down, I whisper, "I'm a big fan of snuggling afterward."

"Please shut up." Her voice holds no edge, and she doesn't even attempt to move away from me.

"Ken, who are you here with?"

She doesn't look back to the table, but blindly gestures to the tall one with the sparkly dress on. "My stepsister. It's her bachelorette party."

"And you two don't get along?"

"It's complicated." Her throat works its way through a swallow. "Could you stay here with me for a minute or two? I just need a break before I go back."

This is what others don't see. This is why I haven't given up on my little crush. Kennedy is comfortable around me. Sure, she might act like she fucking hates me. I might purposefully drive her mad, but there are moments like this one where I'm the person she goes to. Ever since that run-in in the bathroom, there's been a quiet understanding between us. Maybe it's because I know a secret of hers and I've kept it to myself, I'm not sure. But deep down, Kennedy trusts me.

Glancing back at our table, Cody gestures for me to join the group, but when I look down at my favorite athletic trainer tucked close to me while people push and shove around us, that confident woman I'm used to seeing at work is nowhere to be found. She's uncomfortable and I hate it.

I lean down close to her ear, shooting my shot for what feels like the thousandth time I've done so in the past eight months. "Do you want to get out of here?"

Her big brown eyes flit to mine. "Please."

I'm fairly certain my heart skips a beat because the last thing I ever expected when this night began was for Kennedy Kay to agree to hang out with me.

But it's after midnight and officially the worst day of the year, so I count this as a sign.

Her stepsister and all the other women in white are now surrounded by a train of bottle girls carrying endless amounts of champagne lit with sparklers, dancing and cheering as they celebrate the soon-to-be bride.

"Let's go," I say, hand on her lower back, ushering her to the door.

She slightly flinches when we first make contact, but settles into my palm, letting me guide her out.

Once we're outside, I pull up the group text with my two best friends, finding messages already waiting for me.

Cody: *Holy shit.*
Travis: *I cannot believe our Kennedy is here.*
Me: *MY Kennedy is here. And we're leaving.*
Travis: *How long will you be?*
Me: *I'm not coming back.*
Cody: *Shut the fuck up.*
Me: *See you boys at the airport tomorrow.*
Cody: *I feel like I'm living in an alternate reality. This can't be real.*
Travis: *Isaiah motherfucking Rhodes. What happened to the guys' night you were so adamant about?*
Me: *Fate happened.*

2

Kennedy

If you would have told me a year ago that Isaiah Rhodes, of all people, would be walking down the Vegas strip by my side, I would've assumed you were out of your mind.

And if you would've told me the reason I'm in Vegas to begin with is that I'm attending my stepsister's bachelorette party, I would've laughed in your face.

And if you would've told me that the man she's marrying is my ex-fiancé, I would've looked into having you committed.

Because for my entire adult life, Connor Danforth and I knew we were marrying each other.

And my stepsister and I have never been close enough to invite the other to our personal events.

And I can't stand Isaiah Rhodes most of the time.

But here I am, all three of those things being my current reality.

Isaiah closes the back door to the club as we step outside, the pounding music dulling to a low vibration and easing the panic I was experiencing in there.

What the hell was I doing agreeing to leave with him? I was desperate to get out of there, that's what. And though I'll never admit it aloud, there's an understanding between Isaiah and me that no one else knows about.

But the man is carefree, cocky, even downright childish at times and it drives me insane. I'm far too type A for him and when the brisk Nevada air hits me in the face, it clears my brain fog and reminds me of just that.

"I'm staying two hotels over. I'm going to call it a night." I raise my hand to hail the closest cab, but just as quickly, Isaiah pulls it down.

"One drink, Ken."

"No."

He tosses his head from side to side. "Let's try that answer again. I liked it a whole lot better when you gave me those doe eyes inside and whispered 'please.'"

"Fine. *Please* stop talking. You're annoying."

A grin tilts. "Stop flirting with me, Kenny."

"I'm going back to my hotel." I start in that direction, but between the heels and my much shorter legs, Isaiah catches up to me, strutting backward so I have to face him as I walk.

As much as I hate to admit it, Isaiah Rhodes is kind of hot. I noticed it on the first day I started working for the Windy City Warriors, back when I thought he was a charming stranger willing to talk me through my employment problems and not one of the players on the team.

He's in all black tonight, all the way down to his shoes. It's strange. I'm used to seeing him in all different colors, and they typically don't coordinate.

Tonight, his light brown hair seems perfectly styled, but I'm certain he simply ran his fingers through it and got it to stay that way. The guy's got good hair.

Pretty face and stunning body too, and boy, does he know it.

"So, what's up with you and your stepsister?" he asks.

"I'm far too sober to talk about that right now."

He smirks, that little birthmark under his right eye drawing my attention to the mischief sparkling in them. "That can be fixed."

I stop walking, right there on the Vegas strip. "Isaiah, I'm cold and my feet hurt. This weekend sucked. All I want to do is crawl into bed and fly home to Chicago tomorrow."

"One drink, Kennedy. I've got you outside of work for the first time ever. One drink and I promise I'll get you back to your hotel."

I've never had a drink with one of the players. Never even been outside of work with one of them besides the innocent sleepover I had at Isaiah's brother's house last year because I drank too much with Kai's girlfriend and couldn't drive home.

Isaiah has asked me to join countless times and I've always turned him down. But tonight . . . tonight I'm feeling desperate and uneasy. Tonight, I'm feeling reckless for the first time in my life.

I shouldn't even be in this city, shouldn't have had to attend the bachelorette party of the woman who is marrying my ex-fiancé, so fuck it. One drink won't hurt anything.

"You're buying."

That devilish smile is back. "With pleasure. But first . . ." He scans the area. "Come with me."

Isaiah extends his elbow out for me to grab, but instead, I cross my arms over my chest to keep the warmth in. He huffs a laugh, tucks his hands in his pockets, and gestures for me to follow him.

"Did you forget about that whole part about my feet hurting? I'm wearing four-inch heels, Rhodes."

"I know. You're almost eye to eye with my chest now."

"Funny," I deadpan, speed walking to try to match his single stride with two of mine as we cross the street. "And my hotel is that way. Don't you think we should at least start in that direction? Grab one quick drink on the way?"

Isaiah stops in the middle of the street and I almost smack into the back of him before he turns to face me, uncaring that the light just turned green and cars are waiting for us to move.

"Kenny, I'm going to need you to go with the flow, here. I just left my teammates, and don't get me wrong, I'm stoked to be in this position right now, but we're going to do things my way tonight. And I never said anything about this one drink being quick."

A car honks at us, but still Isaiah doesn't budge.

"We need to move."

"I'm not moving."

I exhale, a strand of hair billowing around my face. "I don't know how to go with the flow."

"I know. Give me one night and let me see if I can teach you. Trust me, my way is a lot of fun."

The car honks again, this time laying on the horn.

"I only agreed to one drink."

"You never indicated how fast I have to drink it. Could take me all night, really."

"Can we get out of the road? Jesus, we're going to get run over."

"Only if you agree to do things my way tonight."

"Isaiah . . ."

"Kenny . . ."

The car honks again before the driver swerves around us, flipping us his middle finger.

"Fine," I agree. "Can we please get out of the middle of the road?"

Isaiah finally moves, continuing to the other side of the street. "What size shoes do you wear?"

"What?"

"Shoe size."

"Six and a half." The statement comes out sounding more like a question. "Why?"

He takes a sharp left, holding the door open for me to a shopping mall attached to one of the hotels. Even after midnight, stores are open and busy.

Isaiah doesn't slow down, walking right into the Vans store and finding the women's section.

He grabs a pair off the wall. "You like red, right? You're always wearing the red team gear."

"Those aren't red. Those are hot pink."

"Really?" He cocks his head, looking at the shoes in his hand before setting them back on the wall. "Do you like checkered? Max has checkered Vans."

Max—his two-year-old nephew that he's in love with.

"I don't really—"

"Nah, checkered isn't you." He scans the wall again before zeroing in on a pair of black high tops with a single white stripe and a platform base. "These ones. Do you like these ones?"

I won't lie, they are cute. I don't wear much other than neutrals, unless I'm in the team colors of red and royal blue. And the platform will give me some height. Being 5'3" isn't the worst thing in the world, but it's a little difficult when you work with a bunch of giant men and already feel like your boss is looking down on you.

Metaphorically that is, but still.

"I like those."

Isaiah holds them up to the cashier. "Can we get these in a six and a half?"

"What are you doing?"

"Buying you shoes. Your feet hurt."

I pull my credit card out of my clutch, but Isaiah snags it, slipping it into his back pocket without looking at it or me. He simply continues to peruse the aisle, pulling a pair of socks off the rack by the register before unhooking the hanger of a denim jacket and holding it up for my approval.

"I can pay for my own shoes."

"And I said I was buying you a drink."

"This isn't a drink."

"This is part of the drink. This is my one shot, and if you're uncomfortable the whole time you're never going to want to have a drink with me again and I can't blow my one shot because it's cold and your feet hurt."

"Isaiah, this isn't your shot. It's just a drink."

He completely ignores me as the cashier comes back to the register with the shoebox in his hand.

Isaiah hands him over his credit card, keeping mine slipped into his back pocket as he pays for my socks, shoes, and new denim jacket before handing them off to me. "Get rid of those heels, Kenny, and let's go have a drink."

The light bounces off the crystal chandelier in the center of the room, sparkling with pinks and purples thanks to the curtains draping the walls. I guess the entire room *is* the chandelier, hence the name of the luxe bar located in the center of the Cosmopolitan.

Weaving through the crowd, I follow closely behind as Isaiah cuts a path for us to the bar. He holds his hand behind him slightly in case I need to grab it to keep us from getting separated, but I don't. Regardless of all the bodies I have to plow through to keep up with him, I've never been one for casual touching.

When we make it to the bar and find the only two unoccupied stools, Isaiah pulls one out for me with his free hand. The other is busy carrying my white Louboutin heels I exchanged for sneakers.

"One drink," I remind him as I climb up on the seat.

"So you've mentioned."

Settling into my chair, my feet dangle, unable to reach the resting bar, and Isaiah's eyes fall south before letting out a low chuckle.

"Have I told you lately how much I dislike you?"

"Mmm," he hums. "I should warn you, Ken, I like it when you're mean. It does something to me."

"So that's why you haven't left me alone all these years? I should've been nice to you all this time, I guess."

"I probably would've proposed a handful of times by now if you were. Nice. Mean. I'll take you any way I can get you."

As he takes the seat next to me, Isaiah's attention drifts to my left hand, where a very bare ring finger rests against the bar top.

Even though I haven't worn my old engagement ring in over a year, my finger still feels too light. Too empty. I guess that's what happens after wearing a gaudy eight-carat diamond ring around every day for four years.

The guy sitting in the stool on the other side of me drops back in drunken laughter, falling and resting on my shoulder. It isn't until I shrug out from under him that he realizes.

"Oops, sorry," he apologizes, and I don't miss the way his gaze lingers on my bare legs as he does.

I close my new denim jacket around me and catch the warning glare Isaiah shoots at him, causing the guy to shift his attention back to his own friends.

"He needs to keep his eyes to himself," Isaiah mutters as he reaches down between us, using the leg of the chair to pull me as close to him as possible.

I can't help but laugh. "Kind of like how you are right now?"

Isaiah blatantly checks me out, and in contrast, I don't feel the need to hide every inch of my body this time. It must be this weird trust thing I've got going with him.

His smile is cheeky. "I don't know what you're talking about."

I grab the cocktail list from the counter. "What are we drinking?"

"*We*? Jesus, Kenny, this is a first date. I didn't realize we were a 'we' already."

"At what point in the night do you become less obnoxious?"

He shrugs, eyes on the drink list. "I've been told it's about three or four drinks in. So, what are we having?"

"I'm not sure. I'm not much of a drinker."

"Never? Not even in college?"

"Not exactly. I was a little too busy studying for my MCATs to be throwing up keg stands."

I was also a bit too busy trying to be perfect, but that's a story for a different day.

His eyes crinkle at the corners, a little smile gracing his lips. "Do you want me to order a drink for you?"

"Are you going to order the most annoyingly oversized drink that will take me hours to get through since I'm only having one with you?"

"Nope. I'm going to order you a normal drink that I think you'll like and by the end of it, if you still want to go back to your hotel, we'll call it a night."

I lift a brow in surprise. "Giving in already, Rhodes?"

"I've got faith that you'll want to hang out with me a little longer than one."

"How very cocky of you."

"Self-assured," he corrects.

Isaiah Rhodes *is* self-assured, but in this goofy, annoyingly charismatic manner that doesn't feel too suffocating. He's laid-back and easygoing in a way I can't relate to.

But the years of being around him remind me that he's also reckless and sometimes too carefree. He's been the life of the party for as long as I've known him. He doesn't think too far into the future or wonder about the conse-quences to his actions. He's got this freedom about him, this ease and approachability that probably comes with being the younger brother of someone who always took on the responsibilities.

I can be honest and say I don't know much more than that about him, but I would imagine that Isaiah Rhodes makes smart girls do stupid things. Which is why I've never given into or even thought about the constant flirting and the years of pickup lines he's spewed my way.

He simply wants something he can't have, and if I were to ever change my mind and give in, his thrill of the chase would be over.

"How do you feel about tequila?" he asks.

"I feel like it causes me to make poor decisions."

"Perfect." That signature smile is back before he turns towards the bartender and orders two of the same drink.

Isaiah keeps my high heels in his lap, his long legs open around my chair as he faces me. "When are you going to tell Dr. Fredrick to promote you?"

I exhale a startled laugh. "How long have you been waiting to ask me that?"

He looks at the watch on his wrist, his jaw ticking for some reason when he reads the time is a bit after midnight. "Three years as of today."

"Three years?"

"We met on this day, three years ago, and I've wanted you to tell Dr. Fredrick to promote you every day since. You're overqualified, Kenny, and I'm the only one who knows. You're taping ankles and wrapping ice packs when you're a literal fucking doctor."

"You remember the exact date we met?" Because what the hell? I knew Isaiah had a superficial crush on me, but I've always kind of assumed it was simply an ongoing joke between him and his teammates.

The only woman on the staff? Oh, I for sure want to bang her. You know, that kind of thing.

"Kennedy, focus. The season is starting next week, and I think it's time you say something. Hell, *I* want to say something. Fredrick has been giving you the worst shifts and the least amount of responsibility. Aren't you over it?"

He remembers the day we met? Why? There was nothing significant about that day other than I got a new job. A job that I have come to love in a way, regardless that I don't feel like I'm living up to my full potential. Yes, my boss is the worst, but I love the stakes of professional sports. The travel. The fans. The postseason high.

"I'm not going to say anything, and neither are you."

"Ken—"

"I'm up for a promotion."

He rears back slightly. "You are?"

"Not with the Warriors, but yes."

Isaiah's brown eyes roll as the bartender puts our drinks in front of us. "Let me guess. Atlanta wants to hire you."

My stepbrother plays second baseman for Atlanta and while he's one of my closest friends, Isaiah and Dean grew up in the same town and have a long-standing rivalry. Dean and I became family at the end of high school and didn't become close until college, so I never knew about their history until my stepbrother showed up at Family Day in Chicago last season, only for the two of them to connect the dots.

"No, not Atlanta. San Francisco."

Isaiah pauses with his drink partway to his lips. "California? But that's . . . on the other side of the country."

"Yes. But the weather is wonderful, and their team doctor is retiring after this season. Their second doctor doesn't want the promotion so they're looking for a replacement and my mentor, who I did a fellowship under, recommended me for the job."

I can feel the excitement in my voice with every word. It's my dream job, the job I spent my entire twenties preparing for, and I'm one of three final candidates for the position. I simply have to finish on a strong note with the Warriors this year, interview well when the time comes, and it could be mine.

"California," Isaiah repeats, eyes searching my face.

I take a long swig of my drink, nodding enthusiastically at both the prospect of what next year could look like and how good this drink is. You can't even taste the tequila.

"I'd be the first female lead doctor in the MLB."

Isaiah's lips curve at that. "As you should be. That's amazing, Kenny. You deserve all the good things."

I'm still trying to convince myself of that.

"But just so we're clear," he continues. "We're *not* telling Dr. Fredrick he's a misogynist piece of shit or that his view on women in sports is probably why his wife left him last year?"

A laugh bubbles out of me, the way it wants to most of the time I'm around Isaiah, though I typically don't let it. "Not until I sign my new contract and I'm two thousand miles away."

Isaiah sighs in resignation, sinking back into his seat. "California, huh? Did you know that's my least favorite place?"

"And when did you decide that?"

"About two minutes ago."

He finishes his drink in a few swigs, setting the glass back on the bar top. "I'll walk you back to your hotel whenever you're ready to go."

Huh?

"That's it? You buy me comfortable shoes and a warm jacket just for one drink that took more time to be prepared than it did for you to consume it?"

"You said one drink."

"Maybe I changed my mind."

Isaiah's brows lift in surprise, his posture straightening from the defeated slump. "Are you saying you want to stay and have another drink with me, Kenny?"

I've never been one to be impulsive like him. Never been one to blur the line between work and fun, but there's a comfortableness with Isaiah. A comfortableness I don't let anyone else know about when I'm at work. Maybe it's because he's the only person in Chicago who knows about my secret and now, he's the only one I can share this exciting news with.

Maybe it's because the finish line is so close. I'm one season away from my dream job. So yeah, maybe I want to have a little fun. Maybe I want to turn off the perfectionist in me and be a little reckless after this weekend of hell.

"Yes." I swallow down the rest of my cocktail. "I want to have another drink with you."

3

Isaiah

I have no fucking clue how I got here, having God knows how many drinks with Kennedy Kay. Somewhere along the way we left the Cosmo and made our way through three more bars. Or was it four now?

Fuck if I know.

Kennedy tossed her heels in a trash can on the strip, and I noted the red bottoms on those while I was carrying them, so I made sure to pull them right back out from the bin. Sober her would be pissed she threw away such expensive shoes.

She won a hundred bucks on the penny slots. We found ourselves in a karaoke bar without a single other person under the age of forty. I sang a rendition of Mariah Carey's "Touch My Body" and we left as soon as the older women started taking the lyrics literally.

I took Kennedy to her first strip club where she promptly distributed all the ones in my wallet, and now we're both utterly wasted, standing in front of the fountains outside of the Bellagio.

I think.

Fuck if I know where we are, but there's music and lights and a slight breeze cooling my burning skin. Seriously, I'm on fire. Am I allergic to tequila, or have I just been blushing like a fucking idiot any time Kennedy slightly sways into me or grabs my forearm for support?

Tonight is the best night of my life.

"What?" Kennedy asks at my side.

Did I say that out loud?

Fuck it.

"I said, tonight is the best night of my life."

She rolls those pretty eyes, but it's more dramatic than usual because Kennedy is just as drunk as I am. "You're just saying that."

"I'm not." Leaning my forearms down on the gate in front of me, I make myself eye level with her. "Kennedy, I have feelings for you."

"They'll pass."

Her glazed eyes stay fixated on the water ahead of her.

"I'm serious, Ken. I've got a major crush."

"A crush is just a lack of information."

"Yeah, but I'm getting the information, and it's only making me like you more. Let me get to know you. I've been trying to for three years now."

Her attention finally snaps to me, her gaze perusing my face. "Why?"

"Because I like you."

"You like everyone."

Ouch.

She's not wrong. At least, from what she knows about me. What she doesn't know is that I haven't even looked at another woman since the day I realized she stopped wearing her engagement ring.

So no, I don't like everyone.

I like *her.*

She must note how that hit landed because she turns her body slightly, facing me. "Fine." It's a bit slurred. "What do you want to know?"

"Why did being at your stepsister's bachelorette party make you so uncomfortable?"

She rolls her eyes again, and I can't help but smile.

41

"My mother, she's married to Mallory and Dean's dad. Mallory, she's my stepsister and you know Dean. You *hate* Dean. But Dean is my friend."

Yep, she's drunk.

"My mother, she insisted I be here. You know, because of how it looks for the family."

"The family? You sound like you're in the mafia."

She ignores me. "And Mallory, she was quick to pick the last weekend I was free before baseball season started so I would have to attend."

"You really didn't want to be here."

"She's marrying my ex-fiancé, and I'm fairly certain the only reason she wanted me here this weekend was to rub it in my face."

I must be far more wasted than I assumed because I know I didn't hear that right. "What did you say?"

"She's marrying my ex-fiancé." Her tone holds no inflection. "The guy she only met because I was supposed to marry him, and he always came with me to social obligations. You know, that guy."

Kennedy throws back the double shot of tequila we each took with us from the last bar.

"And you're okay with this happening?"

She holds up her now-empty cup. "Does it look like I'm okay with this?"

"But . . . but what about your parents? They can't be on board with this."

"Oh, they love Connor." She waves me off. "They agree he'll be the perfect candidate to take over the family business, and since I couldn't pull the trigger in all the years we were engaged, everyone is perfectly happy with my stepsister stepping in and doing so. Well, except Dean. You know Dean. You hate Dean."

I do hate Dean.

"He's the only person that's vocalized how fucked up this whole thing is."

Okay, well, maybe I hate Dean a fraction less than I did thirty seconds ago, but Kennedy's stepbrother is still one of my least favorite people, and I'm forced to see the guy a few times a year when we play against Atlanta.

My blurry and tequila-fogged brain has no idea what to say to this fucked-up situation, so the only thing I come up with is, "You should just get married before them."

She startles with a laugh. "What?"

"Get married before them. You know, really stick it to them by going first. I bet they'd hate that. Especially when you made whatever-his-name-is wait for so long."

"I don't even have a boyfriend."

"I've offered."

"Yeah," she chuckles. "Except now, apparently, what I need is a husband."

I keep my attention locked on hers.

She pauses for a minute, rolling something over in her mind before her tone turns serious. "Are you still offering?"

"You're drunk."

"So are you."

"You're out of your mind."

"I think you are too."

I'm completely out of my mind because with the way she's looking at me, little smirk on those lips, brown eyes shining with mischief the way mine usually do, I know in this moment, I'd do just about anything she asked me to.

4

Kennedy

I don't know why he's looking at me like that.

But then again, I think he always looks at me like that.

My skin feels funny. Like it's on fire, but I'm also cold.

I think I like when Isaiah looks at me.

These shoes are comfy.

"You know I can't say no to you," he says.

"That's what I'm hoping for." The words feel silly. I don't think my tongue is connected to my mouth.

What is he even talking about?

Oh, a wedding.

I need to pick a wedding date. That's what my mother always told me.

My mother. She's not very nice.

Connor always said I need to pick a wedding date too.

I didn't like him enough to do that though.

But I think I can pick a wedding date now.

Tonight.

Isaiah is nice.

He's handsome too.

Why did I always ignore him?

Because I knew he'd get me in trouble.

I've never been in trouble.

I follow the rules.

I was the perfect daughter.

Where did that get me?

Maybe if I would've gotten in trouble, my parents would have noticed me.

I want to get in trouble.

I want to date.

I can't wait to date.

For the first time in my life, I get to date without thinking about marriage.

Marriage.

Isaiah shakes his head.

Wait, why did he start spinning?

"You'll hate me in the morning."

"I don't see how that's much different than how I feel about you now."

I don't hate him.

Not even a little bit.

Isaiah bites his bottom lip to hide a smile.

I think.

To be honest, he's mostly a blurry figure who's keeping me standing upright at the moment.

I take the cup from his hand and drink it back.

It's water.

I think.

The water from the fountains is pretty.

Isaiah is pretty.

It's just an arrangement.

Connor came from a wealthy family and so did I.

That was a business arrangement.

This is a revenge arrangement.

They're practically the same thing.

That's all marriage has ever been—an arrangement.

I can feel myself speaking.

I know Isaiah is responding.

He smirks down at me, and that little birthmark by his right eye gets lost between his smile lines.

I want to lick it.

But my tongue isn't connected to my mouth right now so instead I reach up and touch it.

"Fuck," I hear him exhale, and the surrender in his tone is the only thing that's clear right now.

I take his hand.

His hand is big.

I've worked on his hands, but I've never touched him outside of work before.

I never touch anyone unless I'm working.

No one has really ever touched me.

I like Isaiah's hand.

I like his smile too.

I'll never tell him that.

"Are you sure?" Isaiah's voice rings out somewhere around me.

Of course I'm sure I'll never tell him I like his smile.

The air blowing against my legs changes.

It's warmer now.

My arms are already warm.

Isaiah bought me a jacket.

That was so nice of him.

How did I never realize he was so nice?

And cute.

I wasn't allowed to realize.

He's so different from me. From how I grew up.

He's warm.

I'm cold.

This jacket is warm.

The pen in my hand is heavy.

I sign my name on a line. Three lines, and they're all moving.

"Kenny, are you positive you want to do this?"

I like when he calls me Kenny.

I'll never tell him that.

"What song do you want to walk to?" It's a different voice. Not Isaiah's.

Walk to? Walk out to?

Isaiah walks out to a song when he's up to bat.

He looks really good in his uniform.

I'll never tell him that.

Mariah Carey.

Isaiah sang a Mariah Carey song tonight. He was pretty good.

"Obsessed."

I think I might be obsessed. Why do I keep thinking about him?

Isaiah laughs.

I laugh because he laughed.

My new shoes are so cute. I watch my feet as I take one step then another step on a red carpet runner.

Isaiah looks happy.

I feel happy.

"I do." I do feel happy.

My head feels heavy, so I rest it against Isaiah's chest.

His arm feels heavy around my waist.

It's cold outside again.

I bury my face into him.

The sun is bright.

Isaiah is bright.

Yellow.

I bet his favorite color is yellow.

Yellow is such a weird word.

The flash from a camera is yellow.

"I married the girl I've been obsessed with for years."

Obsessed is a weird word too.

I'm obsessed with how soft this pillow is.
My new shoes are so cute.
Isaiah is so cute too.
I'll never tell him that.

5

Isaiah

The ringing coming from the other side of the room goes straight from my ears to my pounding head. It's the loudest thing I've ever heard.

I think it's a phone. I don't know whose it is, but they better fucking shut it off so I can sleep.

No one shuts it off. It continues to ring and ring until it finally pushes through to voicemail, only for another call to come through and the ringing starts again.

Someone at my side grumbles, voicing the annoyance I feel.

My eyes shoot open. Someone is at my side . . . in my bed.

I slowly turn in that direction to find a woman lying on her stomach.

What the fuck?

No, no, no. Regret churns in my gut.

Eight months of waiting for—

Kennedy.

Holy fuck. I recognize that hair curtaining the woman next to me.

Kennedy Kay Auburn.

Kennedy is in my bed.

She growls when the phone rings again, covering her ears with her palms only to showcase her left hand . . . and her left ring finger.

Flashes of last night seep through my foggy memory.

Her pulling me into a chapel.

Me asking her countless times if she was sure about this.

Her being positive this is what she wanted.

Me only hearing the words that Kennedy wanted to marry me.

My last memory was that on the worst day of the year, I had the time of my life.

I suck a sharp inhale in realization because I vaguely remember slipping that ring on her finger, but I could've sworn that everything from last night was a fucking dream.

"What?" she asks on a gasp, sitting up.

It takes a moment, her sleepy eyes roaming over me, for her to put the pieces together of where she is.

"Isaiah?" She pushes the hair out of her face, her mascara smudged under her eyes and her lipstick smeared over her cheek.

I've never seen perfectly polished Kennedy so unkempt. She looks exactly how I feel.

"Why are you in my room?"

"My room," I correct.

Kennedy's eyes move over the hotel room, only for her to realize it's not hers. Then her attention falls to her clothes she's still in from last night, Vans and all.

"Oh my God." She jolts off the bed as if it were on fire. "Oh my God. Did we? Please tell me we didn't."

"Did we what?"

"Did we . . ." She gestures between us frantically, her other hand on her forehead. "Did we, you know . . ."

"Kenny," I draw out her name. "We're both adults here. You can say the word *sex*."

"Please tell me we didn't do that!"

Those brown eyes are pleading for me to say no, which is a bit of a hit to the ego, if I'm being honest.

"Judging by the fact we're both still wearing all our clothes and I was far too wasted to get anything going on my end, I'd bet good money that no, we did not have sex."

She exhales, her eyes closing in relief.

Another blow to the ego.

Still sitting on the bed, I hold up my left hand. "We did, however, get married."

Her eyes shoot open. "What the hell is that?"

"Same thing that's on your hand."

Her right hand covers her mouth the same time she holds out her left for examination. "No, we didn't."

"We did."

"We didn't!"

"Volume. Jesus." I grimace, fingertips circling my temples. "If I'm remembering correctly, there's a piece of paper in here somewhere for proof. But I also don't remember much of anything after the fountains in front of the Bellagio."

She simply stands there in that denim jacket and white dress, shaking her head. Ironic that the dress she wore to her stepsister's bachelorette is now her wedding dress.

I chuckle to myself. *What the fuck did we do?*

Kennedy scans my hotel room, frantically looking for said paper before finding it facedown and discarded on the floor as if it were one of those takeout menus they slide under your hotel room door and not a document that legally binds us together.

"Oh my God," she breathes as she looks over our marriage license. "What the hell did you do?"

Wait. What?

"Me?"

"Yes, you! How could you do this, Isaiah?"

Is she fucking with me?

I'm instantly off the bed. "This was *your* idea. You were the one who was adamant about doing this. I asked you countless times if you were sure."

She shakes her head, not believing me. "I wouldn't . . . I *couldn't* do something this reckless. This has you written all over it."

At that moment, it's as if the rose-colored glasses get removed.

I've never once been mad at Kennedy. Never disliked something she said. Never disagreed with her. But this . . . her blaming me for last night . . .

For the first time since I've known the girl, I'm fucking pissed at her.

"Do not put this on me, Kennedy. You asked me to do this."

"No," she laughs incredulously. "There's not a chance in hell that I, of all people, asked *you* to marry me."

"You *begged* me to!"

Her eyes are wild. "Then you should've told me no!"

"When have I ever been able to say no to you?!"

Her jaw hardens, both our chests heaving in anger. "Take it off."

"What?"

"The ring." She gestures to the ring on my left hand, the same one the officiant at the chapel gave us. It's so cheap, it looks like it's from a vending machine. "Take that ring off your finger."

"You take yours off."

"I told you to first."

"Well, I'm not going to." I've literally never stood my ground against this girl, but as I said, I'm pissed.

"Fine, I'll take mine off." She slips off the cheap plastic band and tucks it into the pocket of the oversized denim jacket I bought her last night. "It doesn't mean anything anyway."

"You're right. It doesn't. All it was for you was the perfect revenge for what happened with your ex. Well, you're welcome, Ken. I hope it feels good when you tell him."

Too much time passes, a thick tension suffocating us until Kennedy's eyes soften with regret. "Aren't they supposed to turn away drunk people at Vegas chapels?"

I don't like other people being upset. Every fiber of my being is mad at her, but my instincts are screaming to make her feel better. I'd much rather see her smile than the hopeless, lost look she's wearing now.

I find my wallet on the nightstand, empty of all the cash I had on me last night. "I'm fairly certain that I slipped the officiant a couple hundred not to."

"I cannot believe we got married."

"Cute story we'll be able to tell the grandkids, huh?"

She grabs a discarded pillow and chucks it at my face, but I catch it before it can make contact. "There's nothing cute about this. This was a drunken mistake."

"I prefer the term 'happy accident.'"

She shoots me daggers. "This isn't how it's supposed to be. I finally have some freedom, and . . ." Her entire body slumps, her eyes closing with a defeated sigh. "We're getting this annulled as soon as we get back to Chicago."

The word *Chicago* has those brown eyes going wide with worry, dainty hands once again covering her mouth. "Oh my God. I'm going to lose my job." Her tone is frantic. "I'm going to lose my job. San Francisco is never going to hire me with a termination on my record. What the hell did we do?"

A sheen begins to coat her eyes, so I swallow the distance to console her, but as soon as I open my arms to hug her, she flinches.

Shit.

I keep my hands to myself instead. "You're not going to lose your job, Kenny. We'll get the annulment papers drawn up as soon as we get home, and no one has to know about this."

"As if you're not going to go running to Cody, Travis, or Kai and tell them about this."

"Oh, I'm for sure telling those three."

"Isaiah Rhodes."

"Kennedy Rhodes," I mimic.

She closes her eyes in frustration, hands finding her forehead. "Monday. We'll meet at my lawyer's office."

"You have a lawyer?"

"Oh my God." Head falling back, she exposes that pretty throat and lets out a whine that goes straight to my cock.

No. No it doesn't because I'm mad at her right now.

"We don't even have a prenup."

"Ken, c'mon. I know you're not going to try to go after my money."

"Yeah, *your* money is not what I'm referring to."

Before I can ask her what in the world that means, that blaring phone starts its ringing again.

She runs towards it, grabbing it off the ground. "Hello? Yeah." She scans the room as if she were still in utter disbelief of what happened. "Shit. I'm on my way. Give me twenty minutes." Hanging up, she folds our marriage certificate and hides it in her pocket. "I'm going to miss my flight back home if I don't leave now. We'll deal with this on Monday."

Frantically, she scans the room again, looking for her belongings, but anything she came with, she's wearing. Other than those white heels I carried with us all night. She grabs them off the dresser before looking back down at the sneakers on her feet that I bought her.

Her voice is small. "Thank you for keeping these."

"You're welcome."

Hand on the door, she's halfway into the hallway before she turns back to look at me with pleading eyes. "Isaiah, I can't lose this job."

A job where she's treated poorly. A job she's overqualified for. But a job that will lead her to her dream one.

"We'll take care of it."

She nods, turning to leave again.

"Hey, Kenny?"

"Yeah?"

"I'm pissed at you right now, but I had fun with you last night."

She attempts to hold back a small smile. "Yeah, from what I remember, I didn't totally hate hanging out with you."

"Geez. Cool it, Ken. I get it. You're into me."

Those brown eyes roll before she closes the door on me, but still I project my voice for her to hear in the hallway.

"Does this mean the honeymoon phase is over already?"

"I hate you!"

"See you at home, wifey!"

6

Kennedy

Miller: *We missed you at Max's birthday party. I hope you're feeling better. Also, I have something to tell you. When can I see you?*

Me: *Still not feeling great. Maybe this coming weekend?*

Miller: *I can't wait that long!*

Me: *Baseball season starts next week. Don't you want to spend as much time with Kai as possible before we go on the road?*

Miller: *Do I want to have as much sex with Kai as possible before you go on the road? Yes, you're right. See you this weekend.*

I set my phone on the kitchen counter next to the cheap plastic ring I've stared at since I got back to Chicago.

I feel bad lying to Miller, but I know what her exciting news is. I know she got engaged to Isaiah's brother, Kai, this weekend. I also know I couldn't show up to Max's birthday party and act like I'm not legally bound to his uncle. I couldn't take away Miller's spotlight on her big day. I couldn't look at her and lie about the fact that technically, she's my soon-to-be sister-in-law. And I can't stand to see her now, with this uneasy pit in my stomach, until I meet with my lawyer and get the reassurance I need that this sham of a marriage will be over as quickly as it began.

I met Miller last season when she started nannying for our Ace pitcher, Kai Rhodes. Miller's dad, Monty, is also the field manager of the Windy City Warriors, and for the first time in my career, I got to have another woman around the club-house. It was refreshing and I'd consider her my first real friend I've made since moving to Chicago three years ago.

Before last year, any free time I had was spent flying back home to New York to see Connor, always having some kind of charity event or social gathering he needed me on his arm for. But Miller wiggled her way past my sometimes-cold exterior, and I couldn't be more thankful to her for that.

The penthouse apartment I live in is one of the many investment properties owned by my family. It's extravagant and over the top and a bit lonely when I allow myself to think about it. But it's also a free place to live and who am I to complain when my current salary isn't enough to afford me much in the city.

It's another goal of mine, to be able to afford my own place, hell, my own *life* without the Kay family name attached to it. With a promotion and a new title, I'll be able to.

Heading into the second bedroom, I rifle through the closet I never use. Business attire, designer gowns, and high heels worth more than some people's rent. There's a gap on my shoe rack where my patent-leather white Louboutins typically sit, but the memory of Isaiah carrying them around Vegas has me hesitant to put them back in this closet. At this point, I want to forget what few memories I have of that night.

I slip on a black pair instead, cramming my feet into the narrow channel before throwing on a camel-colored blazer and black cigarette pants.

I raided this closet for Mallory's bachelorette party, but other than that, I can't remember the last time I dressed in my "old" clothes. They're reserved for mandatory social gatherings, whether that be an excessive dinner at my child-hood home, or charity balls my mother likes to host to convince her wealthy friends she cares about someone other than herself, when we all know she only hosts them as a tax write-off.

But my lawyer works for my family, and showing up in my daily uniform of athletic gear would get back to my mother. She's already going to lose her mind when she hears about what I did this weekend, but I'd rather have a solution before she even learns about the problem.

I'm not sure why their opinion of me matters to me so much. But it always has. I got the best education I could. Became a doctor instead of stopping early and taking a different path in sports medicine. Agreed to marry a man I didn't want to, simply because my parents told me to.

I barely know my mother. I grew up going to boarding schools and while I was home in the summer, I was raised by nannies. My presence was required for public events, but other than that, we lived completely separate lives.

The same goes for my relationship with my father, and when he died, I didn't even cry at his funeral. It would've felt like crying at a stranger's funeral.

That's probably why Connor always called me cold.

My mother married Dean's father after that. He was my father's business partner, so it made sense, from a monetary standpoint, that they marry.

My engagement to Connor was for the sake of business as well. Dean wasn't going to take over the family business, so it was my responsibility to marry someone who would.

It's all business moves.

However, my marriage to Isaiah Rhodes is most definitely *not* a business move.

And there's a part of me, even though I know it was a mistake, that loves that small act of rebellion.

While yes, Connor and I were set up by our parents, it was still eight years of my life, and it hurt my pride when he ended things.

He was vocal that the split was my fault. I wasn't around. I lived in Chicago when he and my parents were based in New York. I traveled for my job. I'd barely touch him when we were in the same city. The list of my issues is much longer than that, but that's the gist of what he mentioned during our breakup.

But now that I've had some time to process, the realization has finally sunk in that I'm no longer bound by some kind of familial duty. I get to marry whomever I want. I get to date. I get to be a normal woman in her thirties.

I just have to get this pesky little annulment out of the way first.

My phone vibrates on the counter, this time with an unknown Chicago phone number. The family lawyer is flying in from New York, so I assume this is him using a local office.

"Paul?" I ask as soon as I answer.

"Umm . . ." The woman on the other end hesitates. "No, this is Denise. Mr. Remington's assistant."

Mr. Remington. Archer Remington. The owner of the Windy City Warriors.

"He's requesting a meeting with you."

Fuck.

I want to tell myself that maybe it's not a bad thing. Maybe he's meeting with his entire staff before the season starts. Maybe it has nothing to do with the fact that I broke company policy by not only fraternizing with one of the players, but *marrying* his shortstop.

But in my gut, I know that I'm entirely fucked.

I swallow. "Okay. I can do that. Would tomorrow work for him?"

"He needs to see you immediately."

"Today?"

"In one hour. He'll be meeting with both you and Mr. Rhodes at the same time."

And there it is.

I'm fired. I'm done.

But how the hell did he find out?

None of the guys from the team seem to be the type to tattle even if Isaiah did decide to open his big mouth and spill the beans.

"Okay. I'll be there."

"See you soon, Ms. Ka—" Denise clears her throat. "Mrs. Rhodes."

The only two things I'm thinking as I hang up the phone are that I'm about to be unemployed and that I never want to hear someone call me "Mrs. Rhodes" ever again.

The halls of the Warriors' front offices are empty. The click of my heels against the marble floor is the only thing I can hear in my ringing ears as I walk to my fate. I cannot believe that after three years of putting up with Dr. Fredrick's sexist bullshit, after grinding and waiting for a position to open somewhere else in the league, I'm going to be fired when I'm only months away from final interviews for my dream job.

I was so incredibly irresponsible this weekend. I'm never rash or reckless.

But the man who fits those adjectives perfectly is standing at the end of the hall, waiting for me.

"Damn," Isaiah exhales when I meet him outside of Denise's office. "You look . . ." He whistles.

He, on the other hand . . .

"Really, Rhodes? Your socks don't even match. You couldn't have tried to at least look presentable to watch me get fired?"

Looking down, he studies his socks in confusion before returning his attention to me.

"You're not allowed to be a brat right now. I'm still pissed at you about the other morning. And you're not going to get fired, Kenny."

"Don't." I hold my hand up to stop him. "Don't try to make me feel better about this. We both know what's about to happen in there. We both know one of us is going to lose their job and seeing as you have the team's best batting average, I'd make an educated guess and say it's not going to be you."

An annoying smirk tilts on his lips. "Keeping an eye on my stats, huh?"

"This isn't funny, Isaiah. Everything I've worked for is about to get ripped away from me, so for once in your life, can you grow up and realize there are consequences to your actions?"

"Oh, here we go." He scoffs a laugh. "*My* actions? I don't remember forcing you to walk down the aisle or say, 'I do.' If I recall, you seemed pretty fucking excited about the prospect of telling your stepsister and your ex that you tied the knot before them. So don't you dare put this all on me, Kennedy."

I knew that'd piss him off. Maybe that's why I said it. He's never been mad at me. I don't think I've seen him get mad at anyone. It's nice to know that he's got a bite to him.

"*Our* actions," I correct. "And I moved our meeting back with my lawyer to eleven. We can go straight from here."

"Great." His voice is even, frustrated.

"Isaiah, I didn't mean that you were the reason—"

"It's fine, Kennedy. We'll go get the annulment papers drafted as soon as this is over, and you can go back to pretending I don't exist." His jaw flexes. "How the hell did Remington find out anyway?"

"I thought maybe someone from the team told him."

"Only Trav and Cody know, but they're not going to snitch. And Kai, but he didn't even want to tell Miller."

How the hell am I ever going to look at those three again? Travis and Cody I can handle, but Kai . . . God, what is he going to think of me?

I've always respected Kai. He took care of Isaiah when they were kids. He took care of his son when Max was left at his doorstep. He'll probably hate me for this. Isaiah is not only his little brother, but also his best friend.

Before I can think deeper into it, the door to Denise's office opens. "Mr. Remington will see you now."

We silently enter and I don't breathe as Isaiah pulls the chair out for me to sit across from the team's owner, and the oxygen still doesn't come when he takes the seat next to mine.

The clock on the wall ticks, making it the only sound in the otherwise silent office, which only adds to the overwhelming tension filling the room.

Mr. Remington sits in silence, fingers steepled under his chin and watching us.

The clock ticks its timely beat, grating on my fragile nerves.

His desk is large and overwhelming even in his giant office, which includes a wall of windows with a million-dollar view above one of the most iconic parks in the league. His other wall is full of banners from the years the Warriors have won it all. There's a single framed photo of him and his late wife, his son and daughter-in-law, and his only granddaughter, who is rumored to be taking over the family legacy as team owner soon, seeing as Arthur Remington is in his seventies and would be retired already if his son had any desire to work with the team.

"I heard you two had a great time in Las Vegas this weekend," are the first words uttered out of his mouth.

Shit.

Isaiah and I both stay frozen in our seats.

The tick of the clock only gets louder.

"I have an old friend who owns the *Chicago Tribune*. He and I have an agreement that if there's any news related to my team or my organization, he will give me a warning before it goes to print." Mr. Remington turns the computer screen on his desk to face us. "This is going to be the cover of tomorrow's sports section."

Right there, blown up on the screen, is a full-color photo of Isaiah and me outside of the little chapel where we drunkenly said some vows. I'm in my white dress, denim jacket, and Vans. He's in black slacks and a black button-up. He's got me tucked under one arm, holding me close to him, the other fisted in the air in victory, dangling my white high heels above his head.

I don't remember much of this moment, other than a random stranger on the street snapping our photo, but regardless of how blurry my memory is, it's clear by the way I'm looking up at Isaiah that I'm just as happy as he is to be there.

Both my arms are around his waist, my cheek is resting on his chest. I've even got a single foot popped like the main character in some kind of rom-com, for goodness' sake.

It's evident, right there on the computer screen, that none of this is his fault. I wanted it too. There was no coercion. No pressure. I was a fully complying participant—a stoked one, by the looks of it.

In big block letters across the top, the article reads "CHICAGO SHORTSTOP MARRIES LONG-TIME LOVE IN LAS VEGAS."

I choke on my own saliva.

If I could find my voice through the shock of this moment, I'd ask what the hell that meant, but I can't even find the oxygen to breathe. All I can do is stare at the computer screen with my fate displayed in full color.

Through the silence, I continue to read a direct quote from the man at my side.

The subhead reads, "I'M FINALLY MARRYING THE GIRL I'VE BEEN OBSESSED WITH FOR YEARS."

I vaguely remember him saying that, but that's not what he meant. He hasn't *loved* me all this time. He simply had a superficial crush on someone he doesn't even know, and now all of Chicago is going to think that their starting shortstop and I had some kind of long-term secret relationship.

A foot nudges mine and I look up to find Isaiah watching me.

You okay? he mouths.

I simply shake my head in response, and instantly watch the spark of fire ignite in his eyes.

He clears his throat, sits up straighter, and looks right at Mr. Remington when he says, "I don't see what the problem is here."

I can feel my eyes widening in disbelief because though I know Isaiah is typically the team clown, he's not stupid.

"The problem here, Mr. Rhodes, is that you and Miss Kay clearly broke the organization's code of conduct. Casual relationships between players and staff are not only against the rules, but cause for termination."

And there it is.

Everything I've worked for is about to be thrown out the window because of one drunken mistake.

"I have no choice here," he continues. "You both signed agreements that you'd follow our code of conduct. Kennedy, I'm sorry, but I'm going to have to—"

"You said casual relationships are cause for termination," Isaiah interrupts him. "Look at the headline. You see what was quoted. I've been in love with her for years. There's nothing casual about this."

What the hell is he doing?

Isaiah reaches for my hand, and holds it tight enough to disguise my reflexive flinch.

"I'm sorry we didn't come to you or HR sooner, but Kennedy and I have been involved with each other for quite a while now. We planned a Vegas elopement. There's nothing casual about our marriage, and there's nothing against team policy that says a husband and wife can't work together." He laces his fingers through mine, really selling the whole thing. "In fact, you remember Oscar Henderson, our old catcher? His wife was the team photographer. There's nothing different about our situation than theirs. Kennedy is the best trainer we have on staff, and you can't let her go just because she finally put me out of my misery and let me marry her."

I'm no longer the only one sitting in this office stunned silent. Arthur Remington is too.

His white eyebrows cinch in confusion. "You eloped without your brother there? I can't believe that."

Isaiah pops his shoulder as if he's had the answer to this rehearsed for days. "Kennedy is an only child. It would have been strange if I were the only one to have someone with me."

"And your rings?" Mr. Remington zeroes in on our bare left hands. I hadn't realized Isaiah took his ring off too. "Where are your rings from the photo?"

"Getting resized," Isaiah says without missing a beat.

I exhale a laugh and quickly cover it with a cough, hoping to God that Mr. Remington's eyesight is too poor to realize we're both wearing plastic wedding bands in the picture on his computer screen.

Isaiah squeezes my hand and for the first time since that night in Vegas, I feel like we're in this together.

"You'd be making a mistake, Mr. Remington. Kennedy is not only great at her job, but the entire team loves having her on staff. Nothing has changed. The only difference between today and last season is that now I get to call her my wife."

How is he so good at this? Thinking on his feet with an answer for everything. He's so convincing that even *I* almost believe him.

"Miss Kay, is this true?"

Is this true? Hell no, this isn't true. For years, this man at my side has driven me nuts with how impulsively he lives his life, doing whatever sounds fun to him that day. It's vastly different from the way I've been allowed to spend my last thirty years.

Only now, his impulsiveness is what's saving my job.

As the owner of the team waits for my answer, the only thing I can think of is the position waiting for me at the end of the season. How badly I want to prove to Dr. Fredrick that he made a mistake all those years ago by not allowing me to work at my full potential simply because of my gender. I want to prove to myself that I can do it. I want to prove to all the other girls out there that want to work in sports that there's room for us too.

It's what has me looking up from my lap, making eye contact with the man who holds my future in his hands and correcting him. "Mrs. Rhodes, actually." The words taste like acid. "Yes, it's true. This thing between Isaiah and me has been going on for years."

Not a complete lie. *This thing* could mean a lot of different things.

For example, we have *this thing* where he blatantly hits on me, and I ignore him.

Mr. Remington's face is frozen in shock.

Would we be liable if our lie caused a seventy-six-year-old man to go into cardiac arrest? I should ask the family lawyer today when we meet with him.

"Okay," Mr. Remington relents. "Okay. Well, I think it's safe to say that I did not imagine this outcome when this article came across my desk this morning."

Isaiah's thumb runs along the skin of mine and while Mr. Remington isn't paying attention, I pull my hand away and tuck them both between my legs.

"There will be some rules, however. You must stay professional while at work. You two are an athlete and a member of the medical staff while here at the field. On the road, I understand that's a lot of time together. I don't expect you to keep your hands to yourselves for ten to fourteen days at a time." He chuckles heartily. "That'd be a long time, especially while in the honeymoon phase. So, we'll make the same rule for you two as we did for the Hendersons when they worked for us. During baseball hours, you are trainer and athlete, and during your off hours, you're free to be husband and wife."

There will be no difference in the way Isaiah and I interact during baseball and non-baseball hours on the road, and at Mr. Remington's age, he can no longer physically keep up with the team's travel schedule, so he'll never know the difference.

"If," he continues, "heaven forbid, something happens and you two no longer find yourselves in a relationship, I don't see how it'd work to keep you both employed here. Not to put pressure on you two, but I don't see any outcome, other than having to let one of you go."

"We understand, sir." Isaiah speaks for us while I'm still mulling over those words.

If this doesn't work, someone is getting fired.

I'm getting fired.

But do I even want this to work? I can hardly think straight right now. Too much is happening too quickly.

"All right, you two. Well, thanks for coming in. I'll see you both around the clubhouse. Exciting week, huh? Baseball is back." He finishes with a playful fist hitting his desk.

With that, we both offer him placating smiles, do the same to Denise on our way out, before closing the door and leaving ourselves alone in the hallway.

"What the hell just happened?" is all I can manage to say.

Isaiah puts his hand on my back, at a completely respectful height to usher me away, but still, I jerk away at the unexpected contact.

"Sorry." He quickly takes his hand away. "But I think we should talk about this away from the offices."

He moves, giving me space to walk by him, and follows behind until we're far enough away.

"I can't do this," I admit to both him and myself. "I can't pretend that what we did this weekend wasn't just one big, drunken mistake."

"Yes, you can, Kenny. It's one season. Seven months if we make it to the postseason."

"Then what? We get a divorce and one of us gets fired? And by one of us, I mean me."

"You get the job in California. The distance doesn't work for us. We divorce amicably. No one in the front offices will even give a shit once you're working for a different team."

"And if I don't get the job? If I'm still here next year?"

He rolls his eyes. "You're getting the job, Ken."

Isaiah's voice is so even, so sure. The rarely serious Isaiah tends to be very serious when it comes to his confidence in me.

"Why would you go along with this?" I ask.

"Why would I go along pretending that the wedding I had with this girl I've had a crush on for years is legitimate? Why would I force myself to spend time with her for an entire season to make sure she lands her dream job at the end of it? Hmm, I'm not sure, Kenny. Let's think about that."

"Isaiah," I sigh in resignation, because there's no reason he should have a crush on me. After all these years, I haven't done anything to make him like me. "You don't even know me."

"Everybody begins as strangers."

"And it doesn't bother you that I can't really stand you most of the time?"

There's a playful glint in his brown eyes. "I think that's what I like most about you."

"You like what you can't have," I correct.

"Nah. I just like annoying you. You get that flat line across your lips and that death glare. Very hot, Ken."

My eyes roll.

"Mmm," he moans. "The eye roll too."

"Please try to be serious for once in your life. If we do this, I'm basically using you."

"Sounds terrible. Please, Kennedy, use me all you want."

"I can't . . ." I gesture between us. "I won't be able to fake this."

I couldn't even pretend for a legitimate relationship, let alone a fake one.

He shrugs his shoulders. "You heard Remington. We have to be professional while here at the field, and it's not like he travels with us anymore. He'll never see us during our time off."

He's really thought this all through. And he's doing all of this for me. Isaiah gets nothing out of this arrangement.

Arrangement. This is yet another arrangement. I'm accustomed to arrangements.

It makes the idea a bit easier to swallow.

"You just did that all for me, but I thought you were mad at me?"

"I am." He runs a hand through his hair, causing the veins in his forearm to flex. "Doesn't mean I want you to lose your job."

"You'd be married to someone as a business arrangement, you know? One day, you're going to have to tell other women that technically, you're a divorcé."

He holds eye contact. "I'm not worried about other women. Haven't been for a long time."

That's not true in the slightest.

Isaiah Rhodes has had plenty of women to worry about in the years I've known him.

I stand straighter, arms crossed over my chest. Part of me wants to hug him for doing this for me, and part of me wants to talk both of us out of this madness.

But we don't have to pretend to be in love. We don't have to put on a show. We have to remain professional. Maybe we'll need to arrive in the same car to keep up appearances, but other than that, we shouldn't have to fake much of anything.

Maybe this could work.

"Kennedy," Isaiah says, pulling my attention to him. "I'm going to need you to loosen up and look at the bright side here. We just kept your job. Nothing has to change except wearing a ring on that finger." He points to my left hand. "You still got yours?"

I chew my lip. "Maybe."

"Sorry, I couldn't hear you."

I glare at him. "Yes. I still have the ring."

Isaiah smirks at that.

"I haven't gotten around to tossing it yet."

"Sure."

"They look like they're out of a vending machine."

He huffs a laugh. "I'm pretty sure they are. I'll work on getting you something different."

"Hold up." I lift my hand to stop him. "I haven't agreed to this yet. We need to think this through. *You* need to think this through."

"I've thought it through. I'm good with it."

"Isaiah, I'm serious. If we do this, you understand what this is, right? We're not in any kind of a relationship here. This is a business arrangement that will end in six or seven months."

"A business arrangement," he parrots. "Whoever said romance was dead?"

"I need some time to think this over."

"Well, while you're making your decision, I'll work on getting you a ring."

"Isaiah—"

"Don't worry. You'll like what I get you."

I raise a brow. "How very cocky of you."

"That's not me being cocky. That's me telling you how it's going to be. I'll let you be a brat about a lot of things, but you're not allowed to be a brat about this."

He holds his hands up, index fingers outstretched as they reach for my face, bringing them to my lips. Each one tugs at the corners of my mouth, pulling up my frown and flipping it into a smile.

"Smile, Kenny. We just saved your job."

He's forcing me to smile, and he couldn't be more pleased about how stupid we look, judging by the mirroring grin on his own lips.

He's strikingly handsome when he smiles, but then again, Isaiah Rhodes is always smiling, even when he doesn't want to.

With that, he rounds my body to head towards the exit, but before he goes, he turns, putting his chest to my back. I can sense his domineering height. Can feel his overwhelming body heat.

Isaiah's breath tickles the back of my neck, and every nerve in my body comes to life, including the ones between my legs that I wasn't sure worked.

"Just think of this as one big game." His tone is low and deep when he leans down to my ear and whispers, "C'mon wife. Play along."

7

Isaiah

"What the hell did you do, Isaiah?" Miller scolds from the kitchen of her and my brother's house. My future sister-in-law is like me in a lot of ways, so when Kai told me I had to be the one to break the news to her, I didn't exactly expect this reaction.

Was hoping for a *nice work*, or *thanks for marrying my friend so we get to be related*.

Aiming too high on that, I suppose.

"How could you do this to Kennedy? She just got out of a relationship. She needed time. Alone."

"What's up with everyone blaming me? Maybe Kennedy was the one begging *me* to marry her."

There's a beat of silence before Kai and Miller burst into laughter.

"Fuck you guys."

"Language," my brother corrects through his laughter.

My eyes dart to the kitchen where my two-year-old nephew, Max, sits on the counter and smiles at me, holding a half-licked whisk that his mom was using.

"Sorry, Maxie. Don't say that word. That's not a nice word."

"Zaya!" He waves his whisk wildly, a bit of chocolate cake mix flying around the kitchen.

Evan Zanders, a defenseman for the Raptors, Chicago's NHL team, sits on the couch next to my brother, holding his daughter in his lap. Now that he's a dad too, he and his wife have been spending more time at my brother's place, letting Max and Taylor entertain each other.

"Kennedy?" he asks. "The girl you've talked about at every family dinner you've ever come to?"

"The one and only," Kai says for me.

"Good for you, man."

"Don't encourage him, Zee."

"Why not? Stevie met her last summer and she thought she was great."

"She is great," Miller and I say at the same time.

She shoots me a look. "That doesn't mean they should pretend as if their relationship is real."

Zanders shrugs. "Worked out for Ryan and Indy."

"All right, Bug." Miller picks Max up off the counter. "I think it's time you and your dad go knock some sense into your uncle."

"Miller, don't be mad at me," I plead. "I'm only going along with this so she can keep her job. Aren't I such a great guy for doing that?"

She laughs. "BS. You're obsessed with the girl. This is as much for you as it is for her."

A flash of our wedding song pops into my head. I still remember how fucking funny I realized Kennedy was as I watched her walk down the aisle with full confidence to Mariah Carey's "Obsessed."

"Stop smiling to yourself." Miller swats me in the arm with her son on her hip. "You're walking around on cloud nine, meanwhile my friend is probably alone and freaking out. I should go over to her apartment."

"She's not alone, and she's not at home. She's meeting with her lawyer to get a prenup drafted. Or a post-nup. Whatever the hell it's called after you tie the knot."

"Shouldn't you be there?" my brother asks from the couch in the living room. "It's to protect *your* assets."

"Apparently, it's to protect hers."

Kai's bright eyes squint in confusion.

"She's related to Dean Cartwright," I remind Kai of Kennedy's stepbrother. "Their family always had money when we were growing up."

Just another reason why I couldn't stand the prick. While we were scraping by, trying to figure out a way to graduate high school without anyone realizing that Kai and I were on our own, I remember Dean showing up to the field every time we played against him, driving a new car, and decked out in the latest and most expensive baseball equipment.

Add that to the fact he's a complete and utter nuisance and slept with every single girlfriend I ever had, it's no wonder I've considered Kennedy's stepbrother my longtime rival.

"Can we go chat outside?" I ask my brother.

All three of their attentions snap to my rarely serious tone, but Max just smiles over at me.

"Do you want to come outside too, Bug?" I take him from my soon-to-be sister-in-law.

"Yeah. Owside."

The little man just turned two this weekend, and his vocabulary is slowly but surely getting there.

"Have you talked to my dad yet? He's going to want to hear about this from you first."

Miller's question gives me pause.

Emmett Montgomery, Miller's dad, is not only the field manager, which is essentially our head coach, but he's also the closest thing I have to a father figure outside of Kai. He gives me shit and I give it right back. That's how we communicate. You might not realize it if you were an outsider looking in, but Monty and I have a lot of love for each other.

"I'll call him tomorrow," I promise her.

With Max on my hip, I follow my older brother outside before putting my nephew down on the grass to play. We join him, sitting with our legs sprawled, when Kai hands over a beer I didn't see him grab from the fridge.

"I have a feeling we're both going to need this." He clinks his bottle with mine.

"Do you think I fucked up?"

"In what context? Getting married or staying married?"

"Offering to keep this going for Kennedy's job?"

Kai takes a swig. "I think things have a way of working out for you. They always have. It's the happy-go-lucky thing and that goddamn smirk that gets you anything you want."

My sometimes-grumpy brother hides his half smile behind the bottle, taking another sip.

He's got a point. When we were younger and it was just the two of us trying to get through high school, college, and eventually, to the big leagues, I saw the toll it took on Kai. Life came at him a lot quicker than it should've for any fifteen-year-old and the responsibility of taking care not only of himself but also me was an obvious burden.

So, when he needed a pick-me-up, I learned how to be the one to make him laugh.

When we only had enough money to order one meal, I charmed the waitress into throwing in some extra fries for free.

When we couldn't afford to take the bus, I made friends with the driver on our route, and he constantly snuck us on board.

I may not be the responsible brother, but I know how to use my strengths to my advantage. People like me. I know how to make others smile. So yeah, sometimes I joke around, but I keep a positive attitude towards life, and things have always found their way of working out.

"I um . . ." I clear my throat. "I was hoping I could get Mom's ring from you."

"Isaiah."

"What? You're not using it for Miller."

"No, but . . ." He keeps his attention on his son, who's running around the grass in front of us. "Look, you know I've been saving Mom's wedding ring for you, but I had hoped you'd give it to someone you see yourself spending your life with. Not . . . whatever you and Kennedy are doing."

"Just trust me on this, okay?"

"Isaiah," he exhales. "Come on, brother. You treating Kennedy like she's your real wife isn't going to make her magically fall for you."

"There are things about Kennedy that you don't know. All you guys see is me looking like a fucking idiot, pining after this girl, but it's different when she and I are alone. I don't know how to explain it, but in my gut, I know it's different."

Kai's eyes soften. "I just don't want you to get hurt. It's happened to you a lot, and I don't see this ending any differently. I don't think Kennedy sees this playing out the way you do. I'm your brother. I want to protect you from that."

In theory, I understand his concern. Kennedy might have an expiration date on this marriage, but all I've heard is that I got six long months to get my wife to fall for me.

Kai laughs to himself, breaking the tension. "I cannot fucking believe you got Kennedy to marry you on Saturday night. This is what I'm talking about. Everything works in your favor. The girl you've been pining after for years randomly shows up in Vegas and marries you." He shakes his head. "What the hell kind of Vegas luck is that?"

I smile with him. "Well, technically it was Sunday morning."

He stops laughing. "Sunday?"

"We got married on Sunday."

"Oh."

Kai takes another swig from the bottle as we continue to watch Max pulling out dandelions from the ground before trying to blow them, much in the way he tried to blow out the candles on his birthday cake. He gives up and wobbles his way to me, stem outstretched for me to help him.

Pulling him into my lap, I hold my nephew and blow at the same time as him, letting him believe he's the reason all the white, feathery tufts are now floating around us.

"I know I don't have to remind you of Sunday's date," Kai says.

"Max's birthday."

"Well, that too."

"No." I clear my throat. "You don't have to remind me." Kissing the top of my nephew's head, I hold him in my lap. "Pretty amazing that Max was born on the same date that we lost Mom, huh? It's almost as if she sent him here for us."

"Yeah," Kai breathes. "That's how I've always thought about it too."

"I met Kennedy on that same date three years ago. I don't know if I've ever told you that."

"You didn't."

"I just so happened to marry her on the exact same date."

His smile is small but understanding. In the same way Max was sent for us, I've had the same belief about my new wife.

"Fine," he relents. "I'll get you Mom's ring."

All the lights are out in my apartment, but it's still plenty bright thanks to the flashes of lightning filtering in through the windows.

I'm a grown man and at thirty-one years old, I still hate storms.

I try to put the TV on as a distraction, but it's no use. My anxiety is too high, my nerves are too fragile.

Another flash of lightning illuminates the night sky and instantly I'm on my feet, pacing my living room and texting my brother.

Me: *You good? Are you home?*
Kai: *All good here. I'm home. You good?*
Me: *I'll be all right. Are both Miller and Max home with you?*
Kai: *They're here.*
Me: *Good. Don't drive anywhere.*
Kai: *You know I won't. Love you.*

I shoot a quick text to Travis and Cody, checking in, though they have no idea why. Cody asks me if I want to come over for dinner and to watch the Chicago Devils game on TV, but he lives far enough away that I'd have to take a car, and that certainly isn't happening.

Then, I shoot Monty a text.

Me: *You home?*
Monty: *Who's asking?*
Me: *I am.*
Monty: *If I say yes, are you going to show up uninvited and remind me that I'm about to be related to you because your brother and my daughter are getting married?*
Me: *By relation, I'm basically your son-in-law now. How exciting for you.*
Monty: *That's not at all how it works. And besides I heard you're someone's else's son-in-law now.*
Me: *You heard about that already?*
Monty: *The whole organization has heard about it.*
Me: *I was going to tell you.*
Monty: *We need to talk about that soon, kid.*
Me: *I know. We will. But on a serious note, are you home?*
Monty: *I'm home.*
Me: *Good. I'll see you at the field.*

It might not be the healthiest of things, but when I can't calm my own intrusive thoughts, I do so by checking in on everyone I care about.

Since I've known her, I've wanted to check in on Kennedy when I'm feeling this anxiousness, but I've talked myself out of it, remembering that outside of work, she isn't obligated to deal with me.

Now though . . . now she's legally obligated.

I might still be upset about how she tried to pin this whole thing on me, but that hasn't changed my feelings for her.

Me: *Hey, Kenny. Are you home?*

I pace while I wait for her reply, but minutes pass and nothing comes. Not even a flash of gray dots dance on my screen.

Though, another boom of thunder shakes my building, fraying my nerves.

Me: *Ken, I need you to text back.*

She doesn't.

Me: *I'm calling you Mrs. Rhodes in front of the whole team if you don't text me back.*

The reply is instant.

Kenny: *Don't you fucking dare.*
Me: *There's my bride.*
Kenny: *Gross.*
Me: *You home?*

Again, she doesn't respond, so I call her instead.

"What?"

"Are you home?"

"Why?"

"Just answer the damn question, Kennedy. Are you home?"

"Yes, I'm home."

"And you're not going anywhere tonight?"

"No."

"Okay, good."

"Why are you asking?"

"Just needed to know."

She exhales like she's already so tired of me and she's only been married to me for less than forty-eight hours.

"You're exhausting, Rhodes."

I have to bite my lip to hold back my smile. "There are other ways I know how to be exhausting. You just let me know when you need a good night of sleep and we can consummate this marriage, Ken."

She lets out this burst of a laugh and it's so free and easy I let my lip go and fully smile while listening to her on the other side of the receiver.

"Have you made up your mind?" I ask.

Technically, I get nothing from this arrangement. We're doing this all for her, but I still find myself desperate for her to say yes.

At the minimum I get to spend time with her if she agrees, and that's all I really want anyway.

There's a heavy pause on her end of the line. "This is the last thing I wanted."

Damn. Straight to the point.

"I mean," she corrects. "I meant to say that I wanted to have a choice. My last engagement, that wasn't exactly my choice."

Huh?

"I've never had the chance to date for fun, and I was looking forward to that, but now I'm . . ."

"Married," I finish for her.

"Yeah. I'm married."

"I'm sorry."

I'm still annoyed that she blamed this on me, and now I'm over here apologizing for it.

"It's my fault," she admits. "I got us into this mess, and you're trying to get us out. I just ... Isaiah, you and I will never be more than this arrangement."

"How can you be so sure of that?"

Because I'm sure as hell not.

"We're too different, and I don't want to agree to this if you're hoping for anything in our future other than an end date. It's only for six months. When this season is over, I'm going to get back to the life I was looking forward to finally having."

Maybe if I wasn't such a goddamn hopeless romantic, her insistence would hurt a bit more, but all I keep hearing are the words *six months*.

I have six months to change her mind about me.

"What kind of life are you looking forward to having?" I ask, and how is it any different than the one she had before our night in Las Vegas?

She laughs, but it's kind of sad. "A normal one."

"What's normal to you, Kenny?"

"You're going to think I'm weird."

"At this point, it might be best if I find one or two negative qualities. My obsession hasn't been able to come up with any yet."

She laughs again and it's then I realize I don't hear that sound often.

I'll have to work on that.

"A normal life to me is one where I date whomever I want. Where I maybe get hit on at a bar and go to dinner with a guy that's not also some extravagant black-tie affair. Where I don't drunkenly marry someone for revenge, but where I'm also not engaged to someone as a business arrangement either."

Huh?

"I'm going to need you to expand on that last one for me."

"Maybe another time." She sighs. "I want to do this. Selfishly, I want to do this."

"Well, that's good because I got you a ring already."

"Oh. That was quick. I should probably get a ring for you too, huh?"

"It's only fair."

"Do you have any preferences?"

"Do men wear diamonds?"

"You want diamonds?"

"I want this to be extravagant as hell. You wanted subtle so we're going to blow the budget on me."

She chuckles into the line again, which is weird. She never laughs this freely. She's never so upfront and honest either.

"Kennedy Kay, are you drunk right now?"

"A little."

I keep the phone held up to my ear as I lie back on my bed, one hand tucked under my head, the previous anxiousness no longer sitting on my chest.

"I thought you weren't much of a drinker."

"I'm not."

"I'm driving you to drink already?"

"Oh, you have no idea."

"What are you drinking?"

The question sounds a whole lot like "what are you wearing," which is also something I'd love to know.

"Tequila."

My grin takes over my entire face. "Dangerous. I've heard people make drunken mistakes on tequila."

"I've also heard them referred to as happy accidents."

Eyes on the ceiling, I'm sure she can hear my smile through the line.

"Isaiah?"

"Hmm."

"Are you still mad at me?"

Hesitating, I think it over. "Kind of hard to be mad at you when you just agreed to be my wife."

"It's okay to be mad at me if you need to. You don't always have to keep that smile plastered on your face."

I pause, feeling this conversation hitting far too close to home, but attempt to playfully push off the vulnerability. "You've been noticing my smile, Kenny?"

"Mm-hmm. I notice that you smile even when you don't want to. Like with me. I hurt your feelings today, and instead of leaving me to deal with everything on my own, you saved my job and made sure I was smiling before you left."

I didn't realize she noticed that. I didn't think anyone noticed that.

"But you're allowed to be mad at me," she continues. "It won't change how I feel about you."

You're allowed to be mad at me. It won't change how I feel about you.

I clear my throat. "So, you'll still hate me?"

"Exactly." I hear her swallow. "Isaiah?"

"Yeah."

"Why didn't you try anything with me that night in Vegas?"

Jesus.

"You're drunk, Kenny."

"Doesn't mean I don't want you to answer."

Every ounce of blood in my body shoots south at the sound of Kennedy Kay asking why I didn't try something with her.

"By *try something*, you mean other than marrying you?"

"Yeah. Other than marrying me."

"Did you want me to try something?"

"I don't know. I'm just wondering why you didn't."

"Well," I exhale. "I was just as wasted as you, so there's that. Plus, I think my mama would come back from the grave and take me with her if I ever touched a woman while they were drunk. But at the end of the day, even though I've spent all this time trying to get your attention, I won't try anything with you unless I know you want my attention too."

There's a heavy beat of silence.

"Did you want my attention that night, Kenny?"

She chuckles into the phone. "Good night, Isaiah."

Kennedy hangs up the phone just as another flash of lightning illuminates the sky.

It's only then I realize that I kind of forgot about the storm for a bit.

8

Kennedy

Isaiah: *Meet me in the women's bathroom by the clubhouse.*
Me: *Why are we meeting there of all places?*
Isaiah: *It's where we first met. I'm being romantic.*
Me: *You should really stop using my bathroom.*
Isaiah: *But it's so much cleaner than ours.*

I shouldn't be surprised when I walk into the women's restroom and find Isaiah leaning a hip on the sink counter and popping dinner mints into his mouth. I've caught him in here a handful of times over the years, after all.

He's too busy exploring all the privileges of the women's bathroom to notice my presence, but maybe for the first time while at work, I notice him.

His baseball cap is turned backward, but his too-perfect hair is still making its appearance around the edges.

He's tall. Ungodly tall.

Then there's his clothes. Khaki pants that hug his thick thighs perfectly and an olive-green bomber jacket laid over a crisp white T-shirt, showing off the muscles in his chest. His sneakers are a fresh white, with socks too low to tell if they match today or not.

"Hey."

Mouth full of mints, he finds me standing by the door and that signature smile blooms. "Hi, wifey."

"I'm regretting this arrangement already."

He ignores me. "The stadium is filling up and the game doesn't even start for a couple more hours."

Makes sense. It's Opening Day against Minnesota and fans have been itching for baseball to return.

Isaiah eyes my yoga pants, running shoes, and Warriors' polo. My hair is up in a ponytail and my cheeks are warm from lifting boxes of medical tape and other supplies for the past three hours.

In fact, I haven't looked any less exhausted all week. There hasn't been a day I haven't arrived to the field after seven in the morning, or left before the sun has gone down. And I have a strong suspicion why Dr. Fredrick decided to throw the entire medical staff's to-do list on my shoulders this week.

"How long have you been here?" Isaiah asks, his eyes crinkling and not from his smile, but instead, concern.

"All morning. Dr. Fredrick decided that Opening Day was the perfect day for me to reorganize the medical supply cabinet. I got here at six."

"Don't you guys have interns for that kind of stuff?"

"We do."

Understanding dawns on him and the typically happy-go-lucky guy seems pissed. "Have you eaten?"

"I'll be okay."

"Have you eaten, Kennedy?"

"I'll grab something in the dining hall after this."

He eyes me as if he doesn't quite believe me and steps into my space.

I'm not sure why, but I don't move, flinch, or hesitate. I find myself okay that he might be invading my space to touch me.

Weird.

But he doesn't. He simply reaches past me and turns the lock on the main bathroom door, keeping everyone else out.

"I have something for you." He reaches into his pocket. "It's not as flashy as the last one you had."

"I hated the last one I had."

A mischievous smile lifts at his lips. "So did I."

Isaiah holds the delicate ring out between his index finger and thumb.

"Oh, wow," I hear myself say. "That's . . . beautiful."

Taking it from him, I let the light shine off the center stone. It's a stunning purple. Amethyst, I'd assume. Small diamonds create a halo around it, and the band is a patinated gold.

It's clear there's a history to this ring, a story behind it that new jewelry doesn't have. This ring seems worn and cherished and loved.

"Fingers crossed that it fits," Isaiah cuts in. "My mom had small hands too, so I'm hopeful."

Wait. What?

My eyes shoot to his, only to find him watching me. "Your mom?"

The typically cocky man in front of me blushes at my question. "That was her wedding ring."

I can physically feel the blood drain from my face as I hold his mother's ring between my fingers.

I can't wear this, not when our marriage is simply a transaction.

While I may never understand holding sentimental value for something from my parents, the Rhodes boys adored their mom.

From the little I know, Isaiah was only thirteen and Kai fifteen when their mother tragically passed. Miller has mentioned that Kai sings her praises when he speaks of her, so much so that when Miller was featured in *Food & Wine Magazine* last fall, she named a dessert after the woman she never got to meet.

Isaiah doesn't talk much about her, but then again, he doesn't talk about anything too serious, though I know he must miss her the way his brother does.

"I can't wear this."

"You don't think it'll fit?"

"This is your mom's ring, Isaiah. This should be saved for someone else. Someone you care about."

"I care about *you*."

"You know what I mean."

He holds eye contact, not backing down, but neither do I.

"Please," I continue, holding it out for him to take back. "I don't want to dishonor her memory by wearing her ring when I'm only married to her son as part of a business arrangement. I'll wear something else."

Too many silent moments pass, until finally, he takes the ring from me.

"When my mom died, this is the only thing I asked for," he says, looking at it between his fingers. "I'm not sure why. I probably wasn't thinking straight at the time. I should've asked for some of her clothes or her favorite books, but I just wanted this ring because I remember how pretty the color looked on her skin. I've always planned on giving it to the girl I marry, and whether this marriage is simply for convenience, you *are* the girl I married, Kennedy."

He takes my hand in his and I don't even flinch as he runs the pad of his thumb over my currently bare ring finger.

"So please, for me, just wear it, okay?"

His tone is pleading for me to agree, and he doesn't wait for my answer before he slips it over my knuckle.

It fits perfectly.

He circles his thumb over it. "I will, however, divorce your ass if you lose this."

I can't help it, I burst a laugh.

After trying for years not to laugh around this man, it's kind of nice to give into the urge.

I relent, my voice soft. "I'll take care of it for you."

"I know."

"And I'll get it back to you as soon as all of this is over."

He doesn't respond to that.

"These are for you," I say, reaching into my pocket and holding my palm open with both the black metal band and its silicone counterpart. "I know it's not diamonds, but—"

"Shouldn't you be getting on one knee or something?"

I shoot him a look. "Take the goddamn rings before I change my mind."

His smile grows. "Did you get me both a metal and a rubber ring so I could wear something during my games?"

Okay, my cheeks are definitely pink. Why the hell did I do that?

I guess because Isaiah seems like the kind of partner who would wear a silicone ring during his games since he couldn't wear the metal version. And as his supposed wife, I would know that.

"You don't have to wear it while you play if it's uncomfortable, I just thought it might sell the whole thing, especially since Remington is here at the home games."

He slips the silicone band onto his left ring finger. "I was just going to get your name tattooed there since I couldn't wear a ring while I was playing, but this will do." He unlocks the door, holds it open, and says, "You better get back to work, Doc."

As I'm walking out, I laugh to myself about the tattoo thing before realizing, I'm not entirely sure he was joking.

With Kai's hand in mine, I work his muscles, giving extra attention to his adductor pollicis, which tends to tighten up in the early innings if he doesn't get it worked out before his starts on the mound.

I use my thumb to dig in and pull out the tension.

I work on relaxing the lumbrical muscles between his fingers then flip his hand, palm up, and open the abductor muscle by his thumb.

My fingers glide over his tendons and smooth over his skin.

His hands are big and his muscles are overdeveloped, grown from years of needing to control the path of a baseball.

They feel like Isaiah's.

A flash of a memory from our night in Vegas zips through my consciousness. I remember freely holding his hand, the tequila keeping me from overthinking.

I wish I could be that natural about physical touch all the time.

But everything about *that* physical contact was completely different than the kind here, when I'm in the training room.

I started working in sports medicine back in undergrad. Dean was on our university's baseball team, and I remember finding him in the training room after one of his games.

The team doctors and trainers were working on the athletes' bodies, running them through different types of post-game therapy and helping them cool down with stretches. I remember how nonchalant it was for the medical staff to touch the athletes they were working on.

At the time, touch was such a foreign concept to me that it was both shocking and intriguing to see an entire profession dedicated to using your own body to fix someone else's.

I had never really been touched. I couldn't tell you a single time I was hugged as a child. Never had someone hold my hand or cuddle next to me. At the time, I didn't know that was abnormal, but once I got to college, I realized there was something wrong with me when my entire body would tense up because my new university friends would try to hug me in greeting.

The next semester, I started interning for Dean's baseball team and changed my major to premed. I fell in love with the science of it all. How the human body was able to break down and recover. How you could build strength to avoid injury.

I learned that there's something so amazing about using your own two hands to help heal someone else. Sure, physical contact outside of the confines of medicine is still unnatural for me, but I'm working on it.

"Are you going to make eye contact with me at some point, or . . ."

I continue to work on Kai's hand as he sits on a training table. "Not if I can help it."

He chuckles.

"Do you hate me?"

"Damn, Kennedy. I've never known you to be so dramatic."

I drop his hand, finally looking up. Yes, *up* because even though he's sitting and I'm standing, the Rhodes boys are ridiculously tall. "Do you think differently of me now?"

"Of course not."

"I'm basically using your brother."

"He doesn't seem to mind. I'm fairly certain he'd volunteer for the job if given the opportunity."

I'll never understand Isaiah's so-called crush on me. If he knew anything about me, his feelings would evaporate. Connor was offered the keys to my family's company. All he had to do was be with me, and even he couldn't.

Kai's voice is low, for only us to hear. "This will, however, be a very different conversation if he gets hurt."

"He can't get hurt. It's not personal. It's a business arrangement. One that ends in six months."

He taps his mom's ring on my finger. "I'm not so sure he sees it that way."

That's my concern too. This ring feels far too real for what we're doing.

A paper plate with a homemade sandwich drops onto the training table next to Kai. "Eat," Isaiah says, directed at me.

I look up at the other overly tall Rhodes.

"I told you I'm fine—"

"Eat the damn sandwich, Kenny. You look like you're going to pass out." He turns to his brother. "She's been here all day and won't stop working. Don't let her work on you any more until she eats."

Kai bursts a laugh as his brother walks away and leaves me with a homemade sandwich and very strict orders.

There's a dining hall here, and I'd imagine that's where he put this together. As part of the staff, I'm allowed to eat the food provided there too, I just haven't had a chance yet. When my colleagues get breaks, I don't let myself stop.

Dr. Fredrick may not want to promote me, but when called for a reference, he won't be able to say I'm not the hardest worker on his staff.

I take Kai's hand again to finish our pregame stretch, but he pulls it out of my reach, pushing the paper plate towards me. "You heard him. I'm not going to be the reason my sister-in-law passes out."

"You did not just call me that."

His mischievous grin looks a whole lot like his brother's.

"Can I get everyone's attention?" Monty announces to the entire training room. "Our team owner, Mr. Remington, has something he'd like to say."

With the entire team and staff in here, I immediately find Isaiah across the room. He's looking at me too, sharing a silent conversation that something doesn't feel right.

"I won't keep you long," Arthur Remington says, holding up his hand. "I want to wish you all luck today. I'm looking forward to yet another successful season for us here in Chicago. This is my forty-second season as the owner of the Windy City Warriors, and I couldn't be prouder of the group in this room. But before this year officially begins, I wanted to make an announcement that this season will be my last."

Isaiah and I find each other for a brief moment again.

"Next year, my granddaughter, Reese, will be taking over as team owner for our family." He holds his hand out, gesturing to a woman who I assume to be his granddaughter.

She's beautiful. Mid-thirties if I had to guess. Short blonde hair, full body, and dressed to the nines. Bombshell in every sense of the word.

But more importantly, she's a *woman*.

A woman is about to run this entire organization.

Another woman in a male-dominated field.

Part of me wishes I were going to be around next year to see it.

"I'll miss seeing you all every day and being here at the field, but I'm looking forward to passing our family legacy down to my granddaughter."

The room collectively gives a polite clap and Reese simply holds her hand up in greeting.

"You'll be seeing her a lot more than me this season. In preparation for taking over, she's going to be stepping in where I haven't been able to be as present. That includes both home and away games. She'll be traveling with you all this year and reporting back to me, so when you see her around, just treat her as you'd treat me."

Hold up.

Traveling with us?

I find Isaiah again, expecting to catch a look of horror on his face to match mine, but he's just standing there, hands in his pockets and a shit-eating grin on his face.

He knows as well as I do that simply saying we're married isn't going to be enough. Now, with constant eyes on us, we're going to have to fake this entire thing.

9

Isaiah

Watching Kennedy scarf down the sandwich I made her gave me an instant hard-on.

So did the little moan that came from her throat mid-bite when she didn't think anyone was watching her eat in the corner of the training room.

Kennedy has always worked hard—it's one of the things I admire most about her—but this week she's been moving at a different pace. Maybe it's because she's excited to be back to work, but in my gut, I just know that Kennedy's increased hours are due to Dr. Fredrick making her job harder than usual.

Of course I don't want her to leave, but I could see her work life being a whole lot easier if and when she lands that job in San Francisco. She'd be her own boss, with staffers reporting to *her*.

The sun beats down on me as soon as I'm out of the club-house, and I can't describe how incredible it feels to be back in this uniform and on this field. Springtime screams baseball to me and I'm lucky enough to spend my life playing a game I love. Even better, I get to do it on the same field as my brother and my two best friends. How could someone in my position *not* be absolutely stoked to go to work?

It doesn't hurt that I get to see the stunning redhead I married while I'm here either.

I'm in the dugout, checking on my box for my batting gloves and helmet, when I hear her name.

"Kennedy, you're on hydration today."

My attention snaps to Dr. Fredrick because there's no way in hell he just told Kennedy, a woman who's as educated as him and in the running for his exact position with a different team, that she's essentially the water girl for today's game.

Not to mention we have an eighteen-year-old intern here for that exact purpose. He'd probably piss himself at the opportunity to fill our water bottles.

"Got it," Kennedy says without showing her disappointment.

"Sanderson—"He turns to our other athletic trainer. Our *male* athletic trainer. "You and I will be working on the bench and Will"—the second doctor he hired the season after he didn't give Kennedy the job—"you'll work both the club-house and bullpen."

"Why?" The question comes out of my mouth before I can stop it.

Fredrick turns in my direction, confused. "What?"

"Why is Kennedy on hydration?"

"Isaiah," she quietly scolds.

I don't listen to her. "You have Will working two sections that are on completely opposite sides of the field and you have Kennedy filling up water bottles. Why?"

"Isaiah, stop." Kennedy's voice is pleading.

Fredrick crosses his arms over his chest. "Because that's where I assigned her. Do you have an issue with the work your *wife* has to do today?"

He says the word *wife* in the most demeaning way, as if she's my property and not a human being.

I take a step towards him. "Yeah, I do. Or would you like me to enlighten everyone here why I think it's ludicrous that you have her, of all people, filling our fucking water bottles."

"Isaiah, stop. Please."

Realization dawns on the Head of Health and Wellness. He knows that I know Kennedy is overqualified for the position he's kept her in.

"Actually, I'd love to know why." Reese Remington joins the conversation. I hadn't realized she was even in the dugout. "If you have four positions needing coverage and four medical staffers, why aren't they evenly distributed?"

Kennedy is fuming, I guess because I'm drawing attention from the soon-to-be owner of the team, but it's hard to remain professional at work after watching her being treated differently for years. And it's clear this season is going to be worse for her than it's ever been before.

All because she married me—a player. Dr. Fredrick is punishing her for it. I know it.

"That's a great point, Mrs . . ."

"Reese," she corrects.

"Reese," he repeats, and I can't explain the satisfaction I have in knowing that starting next year, Fredrick's boss is going to be a woman. "So, Kennedy, you'll cover the bullpen and, Will, you take the clubhouse. I'll get that new intern on hydration."

"Well, that sounds evenly balanced now, doesn't it?" Reese's smile is forced.

"It was a great idea, Mrs . . . Reese."

Good to know that Dr. Fredrick's ass-kissing extends to not only the players, but upper management too.

Reese takes a long look at me, then Kennedy, before leaving the dugout—to the owner's suite if I had to guess.

Fredrick's jaw hardens once she's out of earshot. He's pissed, but he wouldn't dare chew out a player, especially right before a game. No, instead he focuses his attention once again on Kennedy.

"We'll discuss keeping your personal life at home, later."

Fuck that. She didn't do or say anything wrong. *I* was the one who called him out on his bullshit.

The group disperses at that.

Kennedy stays next to me but refuses to make eye contact. "Don't ever do that again."

"Ken—"

"It's bad enough that I'm the only woman he's ever hired, and, in his mind, I hooked up with one of the players. I'm not some pathetic girl that needs my husband to fight my battles. Just . . . let me do my job, Isaiah."

She leaves the dugout, heading to cover the bullpen where I won't see her for the rest of the day.

I hear her, I do, but she's been busting her ass all day, all week in fact, and I couldn't help myself from stepping in like a fucking caveman.

I also heard her call me her husband.

"Nineteen," Monty calls my number.

I assume he's silently telling me to get out there for warmups, so I grab my glove, passing by him on the steps up to the field, but he puts his hand around my arm to stop me.

"I'm going to let you in on something." He looks around, keeping his voice low. "Fredrick is a prick, we all know this, and he's pissed that Remington kept Kennedy on staff after you two fucked around in Vegas. He wanted her fired."

"Well, that explains why he's been making her put in extra hours this week."

"I know it might not seem like it to you, but you two getting hitched just made her life a whole lot harder. She's trying to make a name for herself, but instead of being one of the athletic trainers, now her peers are only going to view her as one of the player's wives. It's not fair, but that's reality. The best thing you can do for her is to let her handle her own business while here at the field. You trying to save her is only going to make things worse for her."

Goddammit. Monty's right. I hate that he's right.

"She's a big girl. She can handle it, but if it ever gets to a point where someone needs to step in, you come to me, okay? I don't need one of my guys starting a fight with the team doctor."

Nodding, I agree. "She's pissed at me now. I thought I was helping her."

A small smile plays on his lips. "Married life is fun, isn't it?" He cups the back of my head.

"Now get out there and score some runs and maybe she'll forgive you."

"She doesn't give a shit about that."

"Well, score some runs and maybe *I'll* forgive you for getting so fucked up you got married. I swear to God that you, Kai, and Miller better be housing me in my old age for all the stress you three have put me through over the years."

"Aw, Monty," I coo, throwing an arm over his shoulders. "You want to grow old with me?"

"Get your ass on the field, Rhodes."

10

Kennedy

Dean: *Apparently our parents are in town for business and we're doing dinner tomorrow night after the game.*

Me: *Sounds terrible. Have fun with that.*

Dean: *By "we" I mean you and me. You're in Atlanta. You're not leaving me alone with them.*

Me: *No one told me about it, so I'm going to keep pretending I know nothing.*

Dean: *I'll be sure to remind your mother to call you, then.*

Me: *Don't you dare.*

Dean: *Then I'll see you there. Besides, I need you to drop the bomb that you got married so maybe for once, my father won't focus on what a disappointment I am that I decided to play a game for a living instead of taking over the family business.*

Me: *Oh, yes. Such a disappointment that his son is playing in the majors. Is Mallory going to be at this family dinner?*

Dean: *I don't see why she'd be here. My father is in town closing some investment deal.*

Me: *I'll think about it.*

Dean: *See you at the field tomorrow. And don't think we're not going to have a very serious conversation about your terrible taste in men.*

Me: *Shut up.*

Dean: *First Connor and now Isaiah Rhodes? I swear to God, Kennedy, I almost jumped on a plane to kick his ass when you told me the two of you got drunkenly married.*

Me: *You know Connor wasn't my choice.*
Dean: *But Isaiah was?*

Staying towards the back of the line, I wait for the players and coaches to grab their room keys from the table by the front desk.

Hotel check-ins would be a nightmare with how many people we travel with if it weren't for the team coordinators who have everyone's hotel keys ready and waiting for us as soon as the buses pull up outside.

The crowd ahead of me disperses until it's my turn.

Searching the table lined with key cards, I look for the paper sleeve with my last name. There's only a handful of rooms left, and none of them are mine.

I look around, trying to find one of the team travel coordinators to inform them they forgot a room, only to find Isaiah leaning on a pillar in the lobby, too knowing of a smile on his lips.

He's the only player still down here. Everyone else has gone up to their rooms.

It's been a week since Opening Day and things have been better between us around the clubhouse. He hasn't gone off on my boss again. In fact, he's swung in the opposite direction. Now, he's bordering on *too* professional. He hasn't once publicly hit on me the way he had for the past three years.

I kind of miss it.

I wheel my luggage towards him. "My key is miss—"

Isaiah holds up a single room key with "*I. Rhodes & K. Rhodes*" clearly printed on the sleeve.

"K. Rhodes better be referring to your brother, because there's no way in hell I'm sharing a room with you."

"Guess again."

"No," I hear myself say.

Isaiah chuckles. "I'm a cuddler, Ken. Are you a snorer? I

hope not, but then again, I'll probably snuggle you so hard you won't be able to breathe anyway."

My eyes narrow. "Was that supposed to be romantic? Telling me you're going to suffocate me?"

"But in a loving way. I'm going to suffocate you in a loving way."

I shake my head in disbelief. I married this guy. Drunkenly, yes, but still.

"We're not sharing a room. No one else shares a room."

"No one else is married either."

Frantically, I look around the lobby, finding Glen, our main travel coordinator, speaking with Reese.

I take my luggage with me to sort this out.

"I book our hotels as soon as the schedule comes out," he explains to her. "They typically fill up, and we were lucky this year . . ." He spots me waiting to speak to him. "Oh, hey, Kennedy, I was just telling Reese how lucky we got that you and Isaiah are sharing a room this season, so I was able to give your hotel room to her."

Shit.

"Oh." My tone is too high, too forced. "That's . . . perfect. I just wanted to check in with you and make sure it was okay for Isaiah and me to share a room?" *Please say no.* "I wasn't sure with the team rules . . ."

"My grandfather gave the approval," Reese cuts in.

Fucking fantastic.

"Well, isn't that . . . *thoughtful* of him."

Glen chuckles. "You two are newlyweds. Even if I booked you two separate rooms, you'd just end up in one anyway. Man, with how long you guys were sneaking around, you two could have saved us a lot of money by just rooming together the whole time."

Reese and Glen share a laugh.

Glad someone finds this funny.

My cheeks hurt from the fake smile. "That's probably true. Well, I'm so happy this worked out for everyone."

"Me too." Glen gestures to the front desk. "There weren't any more rooms available once I found out Reese was going to be traveling this year."

Of course there weren't.

Isaiah's grin is knowing and annoying as I cross the lobby to meet him once again. He holds up the key card, twirling it between his fingers before I snatch it from him.

"You're not cute when you're gloating."

"Only cute the rest of the time. Got it."

He happily takes my suitcase from me, wheeling both of ours and leading the way to the elevator. And he doesn't even glance back to me when he says, "Nice shoes, by the way. Great taste, whoever picked them out."

My cheeks warm when I look down at my platform Vans, more commonly referred to as my wedding shoes—the ones he picked out.

"Gloating."

His head falls back with a laugh, his Adam's apple distracting and prominent along with his contagious joy.

How very inconvenient that my temporary husband has to be so attractive.

There's only one bed.

Of course there's only one bed.

There's usually only one person to a room, so there's no need for a second bed.

There's no couch in here, only an uncomfortable-looking chair nestled in the corner.

I can't share a bed.

Sharing a bed seems intimate. It never was with Connor, but it seems like under normal circumstances, it would be.

There's a big part of me that wants to protest. To throw

out some snarky remark to make Isaiah think I can't stand him instead of revealing that this makes me feel vulnerable, possibly even uncomfortable.

But we're in this situation because of me, so I suck it up.

"Which side do you prefer?"

When I look over my shoulder for his answer, I find him already watching me intently. "I'll take the floor."

"Isaiah—"

"I don't mind."

"You have a game tomorrow. You can't sleep on the floor. It's my literal job to make sure your body is ready to play."

That timely smirk is back. "Oh, baby, trust me. My body is ready to play."

"Isaiah." My voice tries to come out stern, but there's a smile attempting to break through. "Shut up."

He smiles at my smile, as if he knew I was in my head while looking at that bed and needed to lighten up.

"I'll take the floor," I decide.

"I'm not letting you sleep on the floor. I'm good, Kenny." Stealing a pillow off the bed, he drops it on the three feet of floor space between the mattress and the wall.

"We could call for a cot."

"You think we should get a rollaway bed delivered to our room while the entire team is staying on this floor? And risk the staff or Reese seeing it and believing we're having marital problems? No thanks, I'm good."

"Who cares if they think we're having marital problems? Maybe that will help sell it in a handful of months when we separate."

His smile dims slightly. "We've got plenty of time before we need to start selling that storyline."

Isaiah's phone dings in his pocket. Pulling it out, he reads it before saying, "Trav and Cody want me to go grab a beer with them."

"Okay. Have fun."

"I'm not sure if I'm going to go."

"Why wouldn't you go? It's better than being stuck in this tiny hotel room."

"I guess so," he says. "I don't have any other plans, right?"

He's looking at me as if asking me to tell him to stay here or give him plans for the night.

I don't.

With that decision made, he uses a single hand to reach over his back, and in one swift movement, removes his shirt. He drops his hat on the nightstand and removes his shoes.

"What are you doing?" I ask in disbelief.

"I'm changing. If I'm going out, I'm not going to wear my airplane clothes."

"There's a bathroom right there."

He looks at it, then me, holding eye contact as he undoes his belt. "So there is."

"Isaiah."

"Yes?"

His pants hit the ground, and I don't have anything left to say.

Yes, I've seen his body, but from a medical standpoint. I've never looked or touched for any reason other than science.

But I'm looking now, and it most definitely isn't for science.

Isaiah crouches, rifling through his suitcase while only wearing a pair of boxer briefs.

He's strong and sculpted. I know this, but I've never *noticed* this.

His back is long and defined, muscles moving in a mesmerizing pattern as he rummages through his things. His suitcase is pure chaos, but I'm not paying much notice, especially when he runs a hand through his unruly hair to get it out of his face and the veins in his forearm decide to make their presence known.

"Nothing you haven't seen before, Doc." Isaiah doesn't even have to look back at me to know I'm staring.

I glance away anyway.

Well, I try to look away but then he stands, and I get to watch the way his powerful legs flex to get him up from crouching. Thick thighs from all the years of playing short-stop in that squatting position.

And boxer briefs tight enough to make it clear why this man is so popular.

That birthmark by his eye disappears behind a smile line when my attention finds his handsome face again. He wears a knowing grin while pulling on a different pair of pants, and I finally find the strength to look away and occupy myself by unpacking my things.

My planner first, because I need to finish filling out this month's schedule. Then my laptop, knowing there's a research article about muscle regeneration after injury that I've been dying to read. I also set my daily crossword from the *Times* on the nightstand to ensure I finish. Since discovering that hobby, I've yet to miss a day, but I didn't quite finish today's puzzle on the flight over. Those few things that will keep me plenty busy while Isaiah goes out with his friends.

Then I open my suitcase.

"Kenny," Isaiah laughs from behind me, looking down into my luggage. "Are you a perfectionist and I had no idea?"

Perfectionist.

Type A.

Cold.

Just a few things I've been described as.

"*You're so cold, Kennedy*," Connor had said. "*You're the least affectionate woman I've ever been with. No man is ever going to want to be with someone who flinches every time they come near you.*"

"Of course you're a perfectionist." Isaiah rests his chin on my shoulder. "Because you're freaking perfect!"

"You're annoying." I shrug him off, taking my toiletries bag to the bathroom.

"I'm calling down for more blankets," Isaiah calls out.

Emptying my toiletry case, I line each of my products on the counter in the order in which I'll use them. It's then I notice my missing toothbrush.

I peek my head out of the bathroom to find Isaiah on the phone. "Can you ask if they have an extra toothbrush? I forgot mine."

"Okay, great," he says into the receiver. "And do you have an extra toothbrush down there? My better half, she forgot hers."

He shoots me a wink over the words *better half*.

"Oh. Okay, well do you have any for sale?" He nods. "You're out. There's a drugstore around the corner. Perfect. Will do. Thank you so much, Polly, and I hope you have a great night too. Don't work too hard."

Flirt.

He hangs up the phone. "They're out of the free ones and their market doesn't sell any. There's a drugstore close by and I got directions."

"From Polly?"

His lip twitches in a smirk. "Jealous." Finding a nearby shirt, he slips it on, followed by his hat.

Backward, of course, because my body needed another reminder that it's willing and able and very much not disgusted by my drunken choice of husband.

"Ready?" Isaiah slips the room key into his back pocket.

"Ready for what?"

"To go to the store."

Confusion is written all over my face. "You're going out with Travis and Cody."

"I was only going with them because I didn't have any other plans. But now I have plans, so let's go."

"A run to the drugstore doesn't qualify as plans."

"It does to me." He holds the door open for me. "C'mon, Kenny, let's go be domestic."

Standing side by side, Isaiah and I stare at the wall of toothbrushes.

I don't know why I'm not just grabbing one so we can go, but I'm kind of lost, utterly thrown off by the giant baseball player standing by my side who I've only known to be a ladies' man. Who, instead of spending his night off with his friends, is shopping for dental hygiene products with me.

Finally, Isaiah reaches out to grab one.

"Here," he says, passing it over to me. "Red. You like red, right?"

"This is orange."

"Oh." His cheeks tinge pink. "My bad."

Taking it back, he hooks the toothbrush on the wall, before immediately tucking his hands into his pockets as if he were embarrassed.

He did this in Vegas, grabbing a pair of shoes he thought were red, but weren't.

I don't ask for an explanation, but still, he decides to give one.

"That color kind of looks like your hair and Trav once told me your hair was red. I know it's not just red. It's auburn. Kennedy Kay Auburn, in fact."

Travis had to tell him my hair was red?

The mismatched clothes. Choosing the wrong colors. Having to ask what color my hair is.

"Isaiah, are you colorblind?"

His smile is sheepish as he rocks back on his heels. "Yeah."

How did I not know or catch on to this before? Did I pass by this on his medical chart?

But it makes so much sense. His mis-paired socks. His uncoordinated outfits. A pang of guilt rattles through me for the shit I gave him for dressing like he didn't care, when in reality, he just didn't know when things didn't go together.

"It's not like everything is black and white," he continues. "It's called protanopia. I have trouble with reds. They're all just green to me. At least, that's what I'm told."

Of course I know what protanopia color blindness is. It means his long-wavelength cones are missing or defective, essentially making him unable to see shades of red.

Oranges and warm browns would also appear to be shades of green or blue to him.

"You memorized my hair color?"

"Yeah," he laughs to himself. It's a self-conscious sound I've never heard come from the cocky shortstop. "That day we met in the bathroom, I couldn't classify it. For the most part, I've gotten blonde and brunette figured out, so I asked Cody what color your hair was and he told me it was auburn. Kennedy Kay Auburn." His eyes follow my hair falling past my shoulder until he gently twirls a piece around his finger. "Nothing else has ever been Kennedy Kay Auburn."

That's not true in the slightest, but I'd be lying if my supposedly cold heart didn't warm a bit at that.

Looking up, I watch him, this man who smiles too much and memorizes the color of my hair.

He's not at all what I was expecting.

His hand moves from the end of my hair to cup around my elbow.

I involuntarily flinch, but only because he's warm and it was unexpected, not because I disliked it, but still, he instantly pulls his hand away.

"Sorry."

Great.

He'll quickly realize, just as Connor did, that there's something very, very wrong with me.

Cheeks flaming, I return my attention to the wall of toothbrushes, hoping I can hide them.

"Kenny, can I ask you something?"

No.

"I like soft bristles. Do you see the soft bristled ones?"

"Kennedy."

Cautiously, my eyes find his. So much concern on his typically smiling face.

He's going to figure out eventually that I'm in my thirties and physical touch is still sometimes foreign and uncomfortable for me. That crush he thinks he has on me should disappear soon. It's for the best. He'll get over the idea of who he thinks he married once he learns how screwed up I actually am.

"Can I ask you something?" he repeats.

"Fine."

His voice is soft. "Did someone touch you in a way you didn't like?"

Oh.

"No," I quickly reassure him. "No, that's not it."

"I just don't want to make you uncomfortable and sometimes I think I make you uncomfortable."

May as well lay it all on the line. As I said, it's for the best that he moves on from the feelings he thinks he has for me.

My attention quickly flicks to his, hoping to memorize the stars in his eyes before they disappear for good. "It's not that I've been touched in a way I didn't like, it's that I've never really been touched at all."

Are my cheeks red? They feel warm.

"I don't understand."

"I um . . ." I clear my throat. "I think the first time someone gave me a hug was in college."

His brown eyes widen. Here we go. This should dispel those supposed feelings he has real quick.

"My upbringing, it's probably not what you're used to. My childhood was kind of lonely and isolated. I was raised by nannies and sent to boarding school once I was old enough. Privileged sob story, I know." I release an uncomfortable chuckle. "I only saw my parents at holidays and social gatherings. I didn't realize until I was older that hugging and touching is a common part of life. I know it's weird and I'm weird, but I'm working on it. It's just that sometimes it surprises me, I guess, when you touch me."

Here, standing in the dental hygiene aisle of a drugstore in downtown Atlanta, I have a front-row seat to watch Isaiah Rhodes fall out of like with me.

He doesn't say anything, simply searches my face until finally he asks, "Do you want to be touched?"

I blink. That's what he has to say? Not, "Now it makes so much sense why you're such a frigid bitch to me."

Do I want to be touched? I've never been asked that before.

My answer comes out in a whisper. "Yes."

"By me?"

"Yes."

His smile is small but genuine. "Okay."

Isaiah immediately turns back to the wall of toothbrushes, as if I didn't just tell him I'm an absolute freak.

"The soft bristled ones are up there." He points to the top right corner of the wall.

That's it? That was the whole conversation?

"What's your favorite color?"

Yep, that was the conversation apparently.

"I like neutrals. Black. White. Beige."

"I'm not buying you a beige toothbrush. You can see every single color on the spectrum, and you pick beige? C'mon, Kenny."

I examine the wall in front of me, a small smile lifting. "Maybe purple?" Reaching up on my toes, I try for the purple toothbrush on the row second from the top.

Even in my platform Vans, I can't reach it, so Isaiah leans over me to grab it.

I notice he's careful not to let any part of him touch any part of me.

I think I hate that.

"Is it this one?" he asks, pointing to the one I was going for.

"Yes."

He pulls it off the wall for me.

"Are purples hard for you to see too?"

"Yeah, I thought this was blue."

His attention lands on my left hand, but he doesn't touch it.

"That," he says, referring to his mom's ring. "That's purple though, right? I always thought it was purple."

"Yes." I examine the amethyst stone. "It's the prettiest shade of purple I've ever seen."

He smiles at that, nodding towards the cash register. "Come on. Let's go pay for this."

Isaiah walks side by side with me as we leave the aisle.

"So do you have a favorite color?" I ask.

The backs of his fingers graze mine.

The movement earns my attention, but I don't flinch or pull away. The touch is gentle, tentative, but very much purposeful.

"Besides my favorite shade of auburn, no, I don't have a favorite color."

Our hands continue to rub against each other as we walk.

"Why not?"

He shrugs, keeping close enough that our hands never lose contact. "I was always nervous that I was going to get it wrong. Like what if I picked a dumb color but thought it was cool, you know?"

I chuckle. "There are no dumb colors."

We get in line at the cash register just as his fingertips fall in the spaces between mine. He asked me if I wanted him to touch me, and he's doing just that at a pace I feel comfortable with.

It makes me want to cry.

"Will you pick a favorite color for me?"

I huff a laugh under my breath. I vaguely remember thinking about this answer before. "Yellow."

"Yellow." He appraises my answer. "Why yellow?"

"It's like you. Bright. Happy."

Reminds me of the sun.

"Yellow," he repeats. "Good color. My favorite color, in fact."

His smile is warm as he looks down at me, and maybe that's exactly what my coldness needs.

11

Isaiah

"Kenny," I whine in my typical way. "Come on. Please."

"No. I'm busy."

Trav peeks over his shoulder and smirks at me as he lays on the training table while my wife loosens up his hamstring.

"Ask Sanderson if he's free." She nods in his direction.

I find Sanderson on the other side of the visitors' training room, wrapping an ankle for one of our outfielders. He's almost done, but I'm not going to tell Kennedy that.

"He's busy. Really busy."

She shoots me a look because, as always, she knows when I'm full of shit. Ignoring me, she continues to work on our catcher, so I step closer so only the two of them can hear.

"My shoulder is fucked up because of you, wifey."

"Don't call me that."

"You made me sleep on the floor. The least you can do is rub it out."

"Can you please not say 'rub it out' as if you're trying to proposition me for more than a shoulder massage?"

I don't hold back my knowing smirk. That's exactly what I was trying to do.

Travis laughs into the table. "Kennedy, you made him sleep on the floor? You two are getting pretty damn good at acting like a real married couple."

"I didn't make him sleep on the floor." She looks around, lowering her voice. "I offered to sleep on the floor so he could have the bed, and he's the one who refused."

"Trav, she was so comfortable. Out like a light. Snoring like you wouldn't believe. All the while I was just trying to get a couple of hours of sleep on the cold, hard floor."

"Travis," she says, ignoring me. "How exactly did you make the very poor decision to become his friend?"

"Probably the same way you decided to become his wife."

"Too much tequila?"

"Exactly."

"Well, as fun as it is to hear you two discuss how grateful you are to be in my life, Kenny, I really do need my shoulder worked on."

She must notice the serious tone in my voice.

"All right. Travis, is that feeling looser?"

He works his leg around before hopping off the table and crouching into his catcher's stance. "Much better. Thanks, Ken."

Kennedy pats her now free table. "Take your shirt off."

"Damn. No foreplay?"

"Don't flatter yourself. I've said the same thing to about twelve different guys today."

I bite back my smile. I like when she's feeling up to sparring with me. There's also no part of me that's jealous her hands were all over my teammates. This is her job and she's really fucking good at it.

It's why I always ask her to work on me, even though I was tempted to refrain today. Her words played on a loop as I laid on the ground, trying to catch some sleep. Physical touch is foreign to her. I didn't want to force her to have to touch me, but when I thought about it, I've never once noticed Kennedy being uncomfortable at her job.

And I notice everything about the girl.

This isn't the physical contact she's referring to, and I don't want to treat her any differently after what she told me.

So instead, I bugged her until she agreed to work on me. Just as I typically do.

"It's the right one," I instruct her, taking off my shirt. "Under the shoulder blade. It feels like I pinched a nerve."

She brackets her left hand on my other shoulder, the metal of her ring cool against my skin.

"Right here?" She rubs her palm over my shoulder, warming up my skin.

"Yeah. Towards the top."

She runs a hand down my arm, confidently situating my upper body where she needs it. With the back of my palm placed against my lower back, my shoulder blade opens, giving her room to dig into the tender muscle.

"Oh, yeah, I can feel it." Her fingers press into my skin. "This got knotted up from sleeping on the floor last night, didn't it?"

"No. I was playing with Max the other day, tossing him around. I must have tweaked it and not noticed until today."

Complete and utter lie. Of course I fucked up my shoulder from sleeping on the rock-hard floor last night, but I'm not going to let her know that. She'd offer to share the bed with me, even though it's the last thing she wants to do.

Kennedy manipulates my muscles, adding pressure where she needs to break up the tension. Her movements are so practiced, so confident, that I'd have no idea that she was uncomfortable with physical touch if she hadn't told me.

She was never hugged as a kid.

Who the hell doesn't hug their kid?

I wanted to hug her right there in the toothbrush aisle of the store when she told me that, but I also didn't want to overwhelm her.

It made me realize that even though I've had a crush on Kennedy for years, there's so much I don't know about her, but all her admission did was make me want to know more.

"My family is in town," she says quietly.

"To watch Dean play?"

"No." She scoffs. "For some business deal. I'm having dinner with them tonight."

She continues to rub my sore shoulder as I think about how I wouldn't mind meeting the woman who never hugged her daughter. Wouldn't mind saying a few things to her that are on my mind either.

"I just thought you should know. In case someone asks where I am, I mean. It'd be strange if you told them that you didn't know where your wife was."

"My wife, huh?"

"Technically speaking."

"Say it again. I liked it."

She breathes a laugh as she moves to the front of me. With my legs spread, Kennedy stands between them, continuing to work on my rotator cuff.

I watch her.

So focused on her job that she doesn't notice me noticing how long her lashes are, or when I start counting the freckles dusted on the bridge of her nose. She doesn't see me visually trace the slope of her jaw or locate the indent from the dimples she tries to hide with all her scowling at me.

She's so pretty and sometimes a little mean. It's a lethal combination for me.

Speaking of, there's another person I'd like to have a few choice words with. Someone who never viewed her the way I do. It's what has me asking, "Will your ex be there?"

She continues to work. "No."

"Okay."

"Okay." She gives my shoulder a reassuring squeeze, yet to look and realize I'm only inches away from her and wanting her attention. "Can I ask a favor?"

"I already married you once, Kennedy. What else do you want from me?"

Her lip twitches in a grin. Her, more than anyone else, I like making smile when I can. Especially after what she told me last night. No one ever hugged her? Well, I'd bet that no one made her laugh much either.

"Can you try not to get in a fight with Dean today?"

"No promises on that."

"I'm just saying, if you hurt each other, I'd have to pick sides and Reese might find it odd when I run over to my brother instead of you."

She finally meets my eye, and her sharp inhale only confirms that she had no idea how close we're standing right now.

Kennedy's hands stop moving, but they don't drop from my shoulder. She also doesn't move from between my legs.

With my palm resting on my knee, I ever so slyly reach out to dust my fingertips against the back of her thigh before curling them in. My silent way of telling her I like exactly where she's standing.

She doesn't move. Doesn't flinch.

Freckled skin. Pouty lips. My eyes immediately drop to them, and I find myself licking my own.

I want to know what those lips taste like, what her mouth would feel like against mine. I've wondered for years. And the idea that I may have already kissed this girl, but was too drunk to remember, kills me.

"Kenny," I whisper.

Her gaze drops to my mouth, and she doesn't move or shy away. That little victory feels like I won the lottery.

"Yeah?" It's soft, kept only between us.

"It's kind of fucked up that you'd pick your brother over your husband."

"What can I say? We've got history."

"Yeah, well we've got history too, Kennedy. You just haven't been paying attention."

I take a practice swing in the on-deck circle just before Cody earns his fourth ball, getting him to first on a walk.

It's why he's our lead-off hitter. He knows how to get himself on base, whether that be through a walk or a hit.

Then comes me, second in the lineup. Last year, I finished with the most home runs on the team, but the second most RBIs. That's because Travis is our power hitter. He cleans up in the fourth spot. If I'm at bat and don't bring myself home, I make sure I'm out there on a bag so he can.

I miss the cheers from the home crowd when we're on the road. I miss my walk-out song. I miss the comfort of being in our own clubhouse, but I fucking love to score on someone else's field.

I catch Kai in the bullpen, elbows on his knees as he watches me intently. Lucky bastard only has to work once every five games and gets to sit on his ass for the other four. The guy has always been my biggest fan though, and half the reason I'm the hitter I am today.

Your swing develops real quick when you spend your entire childhood practicing against Kai Rhodes. He is still, to this day, the best pitcher I've gone up against.

I'm booed on my way up to bat and it only makes me smile. Flattering if you ask me, that I've scored so much in this stadium that Atlanta's fanbase remembers me.

My cleats dig into the dirt, my center swaying in rhythm as Atlanta's pitcher shakes off his catcher's call. He accepts the second one, standing straight with his hand on the ball in his glove. He quickly checks on Cody at first before sending a fastball a little high and inside the plate.

That's a ball, I think to myself as I let it sail past me.

"Ball," the umpire calls.

We do the whole thing again. This time, Cody tests the pitcher, taking a bit more freedom and space away from first base.

It must distract Atlanta's pitcher enough because when he throws, it's a curveball I can spot from a mile away. From the film I watched this week, I know he likes to use it on a second pitch. I've also gone up against Kai Rhodes' curveball for the last thirty-one years, so I decide to take this one.

I swing, stepping into it before it fully crosses the plate. The contact is strong, sending the ball sailing deep into right field.

I explode, rounding first and sliding into second just before the ball lands in the glove of Atlanta's second baseman. While lying on the ground, with my hand on the base, I spot Cody safely at third.

The ump calls me safe and I look over my shoulder from the ground to wink at Atlanta's second baseman.

Dean motherfucking Cartwright.

Kennedy's words ring in my mind as I stand and wipe the dirt off my pants, making sure to keep one cleat on the bag.

I know she doesn't want me to get into it with her stepbrother, but it's not my fault he's got such a punchable face.

"Hi, honey," I say as Dean throws the ball back to his pitcher.

"Fuck you."

"That's not very nice, Deanie. We're family now. That's no way to talk to your brother-in-law."

I take my batting glove off and Dean's eyes blaze into the silicone ring on my finger. "She did good, huh?"

His jaw hardens as he takes a single calculated step in my direction.

"Keep it clean," the second base umpire says.

"Why'd you do it?" Dean asks, invading my space. "Why her of all people?"

My attention flicks over to third where Cody is watching me carefully, then to the dugout where most of my team-mates are on their feet and ready if needed.

"Was it because of me? Is that why you married her? You took our rivalry a little far with that one, Rhodes."

"What the hell are going on about, Cartwright?" My tone is equal parts exhausted and uninterested.

His chest bumps my shoulder, but I keep my foot on the bag.

"Watch it," the ump warns, his tone serious.

"Or did you marry her for her money? Is this some fucked-up childhood trauma? You spent your entire life poor, so you go after someone with more money to their name than you'd ever see in your lifetime?"

Fuck him.

Sure, you could say I was shocked when I saw the prenup, outlining Kennedy's family assets, but truthfully, I couldn't give two fucks about the amount of money she has to her name.

"Pretty fucked up to know that's what you think of your stepsister, Dean. That someone would only want to be with her because of her bank account."

He ignores me. "Or was it because you don't have your own family so you had to get Kennedy blackout drunk so you could try to take mine?"

These were always his favorite things to bring up. That we didn't have money to own anything that weren't hand-me-downs, and that we didn't have any family left who wanted us.

Today, he sounds more pathetic than usual. I don't feel him under my skin. I don't care what he has to say.

My attention drifts to the dugout again, finding that auburn hair. Even from here, I can sense how tense Kennedy is as she watches us. Her shoulders are tight. Her eyes are pleading for me not to do anything.

I couldn't begin to count how many times Dean and I have swung at each other over the years, and I know he's goading me to do it again, but today I feel like I've already won. And I really don't want to find out if Kennedy was telling the truth about who she'd check on if we got into it.

I simply smile at my wife across the field as I tuck my batting glove into my back pocket.

"Some things never change, Deanie boy. You're still the selfish prick you've always been. All you've talked about is yourself. Marrying her to fuck with *you*. Marrying her to steal *your* family. From what I've heard, I don't want anything to do with your fucking family." I find Kennedy once again, working her lower lip between her teeth. "Look at her. She's worried. I don't like when my wife is worried, Dean. She asked me not to fight with you so stop saying shit that makes me want to punch you in the face, okay?"

Before he can respond, the crack of a bat echoes through the stadium and I take off, rounding third and heading straight for home, putting us up by two runs already.

Cody and I both make it back to the dugout, connecting fists on the way with Travis, who's headed up to bat. My teammates smack my helmet, my ass, my shoulder as I make it to my box, discarding my gear until my next at-bat.

"Nice job, nineteen."

With my hands gripped to the edge of my box, I look down to find Kennedy, wearing our team polo and those shoes I bought and married her in. "Nice shoes."

"Thanks for that, by the way," she says.

"That's it? You're not going to tell me what a good boy I am for not getting in a fist fight with your brother?"

"You want me to call you a good boy?"

"Mmm, yes, please. Preferably while we're naked and you're on top of me, but now would do too."

That smile I'm quickly becoming addicted to blooms. "I'll keep that in mind."

*   *   *

"Married?" Ryan asks. "You got fucking married?"

I hold my hand up to show him the ring.

"And you're wearing a wedding ring. You're not getting this annulled?"

"Can't," I tell him happily as I kick my feet up on the bed in my brother's hotel room. "A picture of us in Vegas got leaked and Kennedy was going to lose her job over it. We've been pretending it was planned all along."

Ryan nods his head because if anyone could understand faking a relationship to get them further in their career it's him. It's how he met his wife, after all.

Ryan Shay is the captain of the Devils, Chicago's NBA team. They flew in a few hours ago for their game against Atlanta tomorrow.

Kai and I were planning to grab a drink down at the hotel bar, seeing as Kai is struggling over being on the road without Max. It's the first time he's left his son home from a road trip, and even though Max is with Miller, it's obvious how much Kai misses having them both on the road with him the way he did last year.

But with Ryan Shay in tow, we can't go anywhere in public, hence the three of us hanging out in my brother's hotel room.

"Miller said the girls were going over to our place tonight," Kai says.

"Yeah." Ryan sits himself on top of the desk in the corner of the room. "Indy has been begging Miller for baking lessons, so she and Stevie went over there for the night."

My brother grabs his phone. "We should call them and say hi, don't you think?"

"Absolutely not." I snatch his phone from him, holding it out of reach. "You've called your fiancée like six times tonight already. Leave her alone."

As if I haven't been staring at my phone, wondering if Kennedy might call or text to tell me her dinner is over, but it's not the same thing. I just want to make sure she's okay. Kai is calling Miller nonstop to make *himself* feel okay for being on the road and leaving them back at home.

"Isaiah?"

My head snaps to attention when I hear Miller say my name.

"No, it's me, Mills," my brother says, holding my phone out until eventually Miller's face overtakes the screen.

That sneaky motherfucker took my phone and video-called his fiancée.

Miller laughs on the screen while wearing her signature overalls. "Kai, we're fine. Max ate. He's in bed. The girls are here and the house hasn't burned down."

"Hi, Kai!" Indy pops onto the screen, her blonde hair cascading around her face. Kai turns the camera so Ryan is in view. "Oh damn. That one is hella fine."

"How are you feeling?" Ryan asks his pregnant wife.

Ryan's sister, Stevie, pops onto the screen. "She ate Cheerios for dinner. Nothing else."

"Blue," Ryan scolds.

"What? It's what the baby wanted. Don't blame me. Blame them."

"It's also what I wanted." It's a voice in the background. Male. Boston accent.

"Is that Rio?" I ask, taking my phone back from my brother.

Suddenly, Rio's dark hair and goofy grin take over my phone.

"I thought this was girls' night?"

His eyes narrow in confusion. "It is."

"Where's Zee?"

Zanders, or Zee as we call him, is not only Rio's teammate on the Raptors, but he's also Stevie's husband and therefore Ryan's brother-in-law.

It's one big clusterfuck, I know.

Rio's confusion only deepens. "I just said it was girls' night."

Miller snatches her phone back from him, but in the background, I hear him call out, "If you can hear me, Ryan Shay, I love you!"

Ryan laughs to himself because his wife's best guy friend might be more in love with him than she is.

Miller pops back onto the screen. "Why is Kai calling from your phone?"

"Because I stole his in an attempt to keep him from harassing you again."

"Good effort. Thanks for trying, but the guy is so in love with me he can't help it."

Kai lays back on the bed, fixes his glasses, and shrugs because there's no use in denying it.

"I'd probably describe him as clingy and needy if you're asking me. A bit pathetic too."

"Glad no one asked you," my brother pipes up.

I don't fully register his words because a text from Kennedy drops onto the screen, stealing my focus.

The Mrs: *Can you call me?*

"Miller, I gotta go. Kennedy needs me to call her."

She barks a laugh. "And you call your brother pathetic."

The video call ends, and I immediately dial Kennedy.

"Everything okay?" are the first words I say after she picks up.

"Are you busy, or could you come to this dinner?"

"To your family dinner?"

"Yes. I'm sorry for asking, but I need you."

I need you.

I'm off the bed and shoving my feet into my shoes. "Send me the address. I'm on my way."

"Isaiah?"

Her tone causes me to pause. "Yeah?"

"Everyone is here."

Everyone is here. Her words are begging me to put the pieces together and it doesn't take long for me to register what that means.

Her ex is there. Maybe her stepsister too.

"I didn't tell them the truth," she continues.

She didn't tell them why we're still married. Probably didn't tell them why we got married in the first place.

I like that far too much.

"Don't worry, Kenny. I got this."

12

Isaiah

The car drops me off outside of a restaurant in downtown Atlanta and as soon as I step inside the dim lobby, lit only with candlelight, I'm instantly aware of how severely under-dressed I am.

It's all the more evident when Kennedy rounds the corner. She's in a little black dress that falls just past her knees, strappy black heels on her feet to match. She's old-Holly-wood glam with her red hair curled and pinned to one side, showing off an exposed shoulder and more of her freckles than I've ever had the chance to see before.

She's stunning, classically beautiful, walking right towards me, and I'm wearing fucking jeans.

One foot crossing over the other like she's walking a runway, Kennedy holds a small black clutch in one hand, the other smoothing over her dress like she needs it to lay more perfectly than it already is. Formal and polished and perfected.

It's strange to see this side of her when the majority of time we've spent together is at work, but as I said, I'm quickly real-izing I don't know much about the girl I've had an infatua-tion with for the past few years.

"I'm underdressed," I say before she gets the chance to.

She shakes her head. It's a frantic disagreement, like she's nervous. "It's fine. You look great."

"Great, huh?"

"Sorry, I meant decent. Average at best. I forgot I need to keep your ego in check at all times."

"Well, I can't say the same about you. Average, I mean. The way you look in that dress . . ." I shake my head in disbelief. "You look like you're going to say something a little bit evil, break my heart, and I'll end up thanking you for it."

"Don't tempt me, Rhodes." A tick of a smile lifts, but it drops just as quickly when she throws a thumb over her shoulder and says, "I was going to tell them the truth, you know. But then Connor showed up with my stepfather, and then Mallory walked in, and I just couldn't give them the satisfaction of knowing we got married because I was feeling petty over them."

It's odd, seeing her this way. She's so confident when she's at work, like she knows she belongs, but here, with her family just inside, she seems entirely lost.

"Look, I need to warn you. My family, they're not nice people. Money is the most important thing to them. Comparatively, you'll think I'm an angel after meeting them."

"I already think you're an angel."

She shoots me a deadpan look.

I nod towards where she came from. "Do you think you could try to pretend to like me for a couple of hours?"

"I don't know. I'll do my best, I guess."

"Still keeping my ego in check, I see." I hold my hand out for hers.

She eyes my outstretched hand for a moment before cautiously slipping her own into my palm.

It's clear how unnatural it is for her by the stiff way she barely curls hers around mine. I shake it out, hoping to rid the nerves for her before going ahead and lacing our fingers together.

She looks down and watches, as if she's studying the way it appears for her pale, freckled fingers to rest between mine. Or studying the way it looks to hold someone's hand in general, I'm not sure.

"C'mon, wife." I lead her back into the dining room. "Time to play along."

Kennedy points in the direction of the private dining room and when I reach out to open the door for her, a server steps up and does it for us instead.

He's in a three-piece suit and I don't miss the way his eyes quickly scan my clothes on my way into the dim room. My bad for thinking a nice button-up and clean jeans qualified for dinner attire.

As soon as I step inside behind Kennedy, I realize the look he gave me maybe wasn't judgment at all, but instead a warning that I should turn around and run in the other direction as quickly as possible.

A long wooden table stretches the center of the room. Six people sit on one end, one of whom I assume is Dean's dad, seeing as his son is the spitting image of him minus thirty years or so.

But now that I think about it, I don't remember ever seeing him at one of Dean's games growing up.

I catalog the woman to his left as Kennedy's mom. Call it intuition, but when I look at her, there's a burning desire to light her ass up with my words, which would only make sense if she were Kennedy's mother.

She looks like one of those women who would send her kids off to boarding schools because they're a nuisance to her. Add that to the fact she's prim and proper and has a dirty scowl on her face when she finds my hand connected to her daughter's.

Kennedy must spot it because she drops my hand immediately, clasping her own in front of her body.

Yep, not a fan of her mother at all.

An older couple sits on one side of the table, and across from them, another couple who couldn't be anyone other than Kennedy's ex-fiancé and stepsister.

The guy—Cameron, Conrad, *something*—smirks this little smirk that doesn't work for him at all. That kind of smirk only works when you're not radiating douchebag energy behind it, but he just looks creepy doing it.

His attention drifts down to both Kennedy and me as if he were calculating our body language, and when he spots the twelve inches of space between us, that smirk turns evil and knowing.

It's then he slides his palm over the woman's knee who is next to him. Mallory, I think was her name. I vaguely recognize her from the quick moment I saw her the night of her bachelorette party.

She's tall. Brown hair, tan skin. She looks a lot like Dean and somehow, I think I might like her even less than her brother.

Mallory takes the cue and leans into her fiancé before rubbing her hand over his chest. Her left hand, mind you. Where a diamond ring is on full display for both of us to see.

Yeah, I don't like these people at all.

There's so much money and entitlement suffocating this room. Not a single warm smile. No welcome to their family dinner.

The family dinners we have back in Chicago are filled with laughter and friendship. I used to bail on them if I had other plans, but over the last eight months, I've looked forward to those family dinners. For Kai and me, coming from a family of two, it's nice to have our friend community around who has become our new family.

As discreetly as possible, I glance down at my wife, but her attention is locked on the man she was planning to marry and the woman at his side. I give one of her heels a small nudge with my foot, trying to remind her that we're standing in a silent room with her family who is waiting for her to introduce me.

She doesn't notice, so I clear my throat. "Sorry I'm late." Fuck this is awkward, and even more so when I lift my hand and wave like a fucking dork. "I'm Isaiah. Kennedy's . . ." My words drift off, unsure.

"Husband," she finishes for me.

Calvin rolls his eyes.

She takes a step into me, her hip resting against my thigh as he watches.

Atta girl. There it is.

I take her hand in mine again.

"Isaiah, this is my mother, Jennifer. Dean's father, Henry. My stepsister, Mallory, and her . . ." she hesitates. "Her fiancé, Connor."

Now Mallory is wearing that stupid fucking smirk too.

"Mr. and Mrs. Smith are business associates of Henry's, and lastly—" She turns to the other end of the table. "You know Dean."

Yes, I know Dean. The idiot who's sitting by himself and throwing back a shot of amber-colored liquid. Top buttons of his shirt undone. Legs sprawled like he couldn't care less about being here.

No one stands. No one says hello. It's simple nods of acknowledgment before returning to their previous conversations. Tonight, Kennedy dropped the bomb that she's married and no one seems to give a fuck.

Well, no one but Connor, who I spot watching us out of the corner of his eye as we take our seats. So I make sure to drop a chaste kiss to the back of Kennedy's freckled hand before I let it go.

His jaw works.

I fucking love it.

This is going to be fun.

The conversation continues at the other end of the table. Something about hotels, expansions, and franchising. It doesn't take long for me to figure out that Kennedy's family owns a hotel chain. A big one that most everyone has heard of and one I've stayed at on multiple occasions.

All those zeros listed on our post-nuptial agreement make a whole lot of sense now.

Henry constantly pulls Connor into the conversation. They tag team kissing the Smiths' asses. Apparently, they're trying to buy an inn that the Smiths own in Midtown and convert it to a high-rise.

Mr. Smith doesn't seem ready to make any decisions, so Connor orders a bottle of red wine for the table.

A two thousand-dollar bottle of red.

Dean orders another Macallan single malt neat and shoots it back as if it were Jack or Jim and not a seventeen-hundred-dollar bottle of Scotch.

"What?" he asks when he spots me watching him. "Want one or something?"

"That's like a two-hundred-dollar shot."

"Three hundred, but Daddy's paying so go ahead and order one."

Henry shoots Dean a dirty look from the other end of the table. It doesn't take a rocket scientist to figure out those two don't get along.

He's always harped on my lack of family but I'd take Kai any day over whatever the fuck you'd call the group in this room.

"Go ahead, Rhodes. It'll impress his clients. Show them how much money he has to throw around."

"Dean," Jennifer scolds from the other end of the table. She then sends that same dirty glare in Kennedy's direction for no reason, as if silently reminding the two of them that they're the family's biggest disappointments.

One is a fucking doctor and the other is a professional baseball player, which only speaks volumes to the priorities this family has. If you're not in the family business, or contributing to the family business through marriage, you're not important.

"I'm good," I say quietly to Dean before checking in on the redhead at my side, who is very much not doing well.

No one else has spoken to her or her stepbrother.

Dean, I understand because he fucking sucks, but Kennedy . . . I can't imagine not having all my attention on her.

She sits primly at my side. Listening intently to the conversation in case she's needed. The perfect daughter. She nods and smiles, but no one has noticed her.

Mallory has, I guess. Connor too. Why else would they suddenly be all handsy with each other, as if they're giving her a show to tell her what she's missing out on.

The smallest entrée I've ever seen is served on the plate in front of me, and I catch Kennedy watching them throughout the course. Each bite is accompanied by a subtle glance to her stepsister, tracing the way her fingers toy with the ends of Connor's hair. The way Connor turns and whispers into Mallory's ear, earning an overacted laugh. The way he runs his palm up and down her leg.

Kennedy's stare is full of . . . *longing*.

Is she jealous?

Does she miss him?

I can't imagine when she was blackout drunk and asking me to marry her that she thought about this current reality—her sitting with me and having to watch them together.

Kennedy bends over to take a bite of her food, and I watch Connor glance down her dress from across the table. Mallory doesn't notice her fiancé checking out his ex, but I sure as fuck do.

My blood instantly heats.

He doesn't get to sit here and put on some public show with his new fiancée while still checking out his old.

Especially when his old fiancée is my new wife.

"Kenny," I whisper.

She sits up, looking in my direction. Out of the corner of my eye, I catch the tick of Connor's jaw before I use a single finger to push the auburn hair away from her ear.

I lean down and whisper, so only she can hear. "Can I touch you?"

Goose bumps erupt along the skin of her neck, and I can't help but smile at that.

"What do you mean?" Her words are too loud, and not at all intimate.

"Nope," I whisper. "Curl into me, put your cheek against mine while you're talking to me right now."

She hesitates, so I slide my palm over her throat and up along her jaw, fingers intertwining her hair as I pull her in to speak with me quietly.

"Why?" she whispers.

"Because he's watching and I want him to know that you're mine."

"He's watching?"

I hate that her tone holds hope.

"Yeah," I swallow. "So, tell me, Ken. Can I touch you?"

She squirms in her seat before nodding against me. "Okay."

"A little more enthusiasm would be appreciated here."

She chuckles. "Yes, Isaiah. You can touch me."

Fuck me if I don't get half hard just from those words alone.

"Just kick me under the table or something if it's too much or you don't like it."

"I have no problem doing that."

"Brat."

She hums against me, and I'm fairly certain that was involuntary. "What are you going to do?"

"What do you want me to do?"

"Whatever you want, I guess. Whatever would sell this."

"Mmm." This time it's me purring at her words. "Such an agreeable wife."

Her laugh is louder, but it's genuine, no part of it for show. I fucking love it.

She pulls away, a suppressed grin attempting to fight through when she returns her attention to her plate. I fix her hair, back to the way it was before I swept it behind her ear.

Eyes are on us right now, I can feel them, and I'll let Kennedy believe this is all for show, but in truth, I've been dying for her to let me touch her for years. Been dying to have her attention. Been dying to simply sit and eat dinner next to the girl.

Wouldn't mind if she caught up on that same need, but I'll let her believe faking it is enough for now.

Henry and Jennifer are busy speaking with the Smiths so Mallory turns her attention to us. "I was wondering where you went off to the night of my bachelorette party." Her eyes zero in on the ring on Kennedy's finger—my mom's ring. "I guess now we know."

Kennedy is stiff in her seat next to me so I gently drape my arm on the back of her chair, fingertips toying with the strap of her dress.

She doesn't flinch.

Mallory continues, still staring at Kennedy's left hand. "Quite a downgrade if you ask me."

"I didn't ask you," my wife shoots back.

Her body is tense, and not from my touch, so I try to distract her by brushing my fingertips along the top of her shoulder, dusting the back of her neck.

Connor tracks the whole thing.

"I'm just saying," Mallory continues. "Compared to your last ring, this one is—"

"Something I actually like." Kennedy reaches over the table to clasp my other hand. "If you're so obsessed with my previous engagement ring, Mallory, why don't you ask for it from the man who gave it to me."

Mallory's lips thin. "I don't want it. I love mine." Her fingers wiggle to show off the diamond that is much smaller and more subtle than the one Kennedy used to wear.

To be frank, it looks much more like Kennedy's style than her previous ring.

I lean in close, running a soothing palm down her arm. "You good still?"

She nods, a small but proud smile on her face. Maybe for putting her stepsister in place. Maybe for not recoiling at my touch.

I decide to test the theory by moving my palm to her upper leg, under the table, fingers curling on the inside of her thigh.

Her hand that's holding mine on the table grips tighter.

I lean down to whisper, "Tell me to stop."

She shakes her head no.

With a knowing grin on my lips, I inch my hand higher.

Words are spoken, but I'm not paying attention.

I'm only watching Kennedy, noting the quickening of her pulse as I run my hand over her thigh.

She bites her lip and it reads as if she were nervous.

I give her leg a squeeze. "Kick my foot under the table."

"No," she breathes.

Fuck.

Instead, Kennedy slightly widens her knees, giving me another couple of inches I could travel north, and I swear to God, I'm on the brink of losing it thanks to her permission.

"Connor will be taking over the company when I retire," Henry tells his guests. "My son, Dean, over there wanted no part of the family business. He wanted to play a game as his career, so we're lucky that my soon-to-be son-in-law has the business sense that he does."

"Jesus, fuck," Dean mutters under his breath.

I trace my fingertips on the inside of Kennedy's thigh, thankful for the black material of her dress acting as a barrier to stop me because I'm fairly certain I'd die a quick death if she ever let me touch her properly.

"How long have you two been engaged?" Mr. Smith asks Connor as Mallory runs her hand over his suit jacket. She's practically on top of him already, but still she tries to get closer.

"What is it, babe?" Mallory asks Connor. "Eight months already?"

Her stepsister shows off her engagement ring again, but I don't think Kennedy is even paying attention this time. Her eyes are on my traveling hand, her knuckles are white as they grip mine, and she still won't kick me under the table.

In theory, it's innocent. A man resting his hand on his wife's leg, fingertips drawing lazy circles on the inside of her thigh. But Kennedy has never been touched, so nothing about this feels fucking innocent.

"Best eight months of my life." Connor turns and places a kiss on Mallory's lips.

"More like the best three years of your life," she corrects.

I freeze my movements.

Kennedy goes still.

The room goes silent, all but Henry's business guests understanding why.

Kennedy and Connor split just over a year ago.

"Fucking asshole," Dean says from next to me and maybe for the first time in my life, I agree with the guy.

"Oops," Mallory laughs, left hand going over her mouth

to hide her smile, ring on full fucking display. She looks right at my wife when she says, "Cat's out of the bag, I guess."

Kennedy's foot nudges mine. It's not exactly a kick and I'm not sure if it was done on purpose, but I remove my hand from her thigh regardless.

"Why don't we go have a nightcap on the terrace," Henry suggests to the Smiths. "I'm told the view is amazing and we can talk more about how incredible it would be to work together."

It's evident by the way he ushers the Smiths out of the room and doesn't make eye contact with his kids that no one other than his wife is welcome to join.

Jennifer is the last to leave the room. But before she goes, she stops next to Kennedy and leans down to hiss, "You don't get to throw a fit over this. You wouldn't pick a wedding date. You wouldn't touch the man in public. You can't blame him for finding that elsewhere so don't you dare pout in front of Henry's business guests."

Pout? She's sitting here entirely emotionless.

"Excuse me?" I stand from my seat. "Watch your fucking words when you're speaking to my wife."

She blanches. "What did you just say to me?"

"I don't think you need me to repeat myself."

She scoffs, trying to cover it with a disbelieving laugh. "Kennedy Elizabeth Kay, I suggest you either tame the wild animal you brought with you to dinner or leave him at home next time. This behavior is unacceptable. Know your place."

Jennifer leaves the room at the same time Kennedy pulls me back down to my seat.

I face her, legs spread as she turns and tucks her knees between mine.

"I'm sorry," I whisper, remembering the last time I tried to stand up for Kennedy.

She shrugs, no smile in sight. "It's nothing new."

Unexpressive, her face taking on a cold, almost vacant look. Like everything has been turned off.

"I don't know why you're being so dramatic, Kennedy." Connor sits forward, arms crossed over the table.

I hold my hand up to stop him. "There's really no need for us to hear your opinion right now."

There's literally not a single part of her that's being dramatic. From the looks of it, she's barely feeling the hurt she should feel, and even that's not good enough for them. It's as if these people won't allow her to be anything other than exactly what they want her to be.

I feel that way sometimes too. Set by my own precedent, but still.

Connor continues. "You did the same thing. I saw the newspaper article. You two have been together for years, right?" He drapes an arm over Mallory's. "Well, so have we. We're even now."

We're even now.

Fuck. Him.

Kennedy was never unfaithful. We haven't been together for years. We're not even together *now*.

And she can't even correct him.

I squint in confusion. "Why are you still talking?"

Dean chuckles under his breath. "Because the guy is obsessed with the sound of his own voice."

"It's okay, you know." He's still fucking talking to her. "We're not what each other needed. You needed whatever the hell you found in this guy who can hardly dress himself properly, and I needed someone who could kiss me in public without having a mental breakdown over it."

"Shut the fuck up—"

"Shut the fuck up, Connor. You pretentious, entitled asshole." That's Dean, jinxing my words and ironically calling his brother-in-law a name I've used on *him* once or twice.

"It's okay." Kennedy quickly stands, her body still sandwiched between my open legs. "He's right."

She's looking right at me, eyes pleading for permission. Permission for what though, I'm not entirely sure.

"He did need someone who would kiss him in public and we all know that was never going to be me."

Her small hand reaches up to cradle my cheek, her index finger grazing over the small birthmark by my right eye before she leans down and does the most shocking thing she's ever done.

She presses her lips to mine.

Soft. Cautious, but warm. Measured and practiced, like she needed to become the perfect kisser before ever trying it for the first time.

Once I catch on, I inhale her scent, her presence, the moment.

Her lower lip nestles into the dip between mine and I'm beyond tempted to suck it into my mouth and see what kind of noises I could pull from her throat.

She's kissing me.

Kennedy is kissing *me*.

Her other hand comes to bracket my jaw before her fingers move to the back of my head, cupping my skull and pulling me close. Her body sags into mine, perfectly nestled between my hips as her lips take their time exploring my own.

She works to find a pace that feels right for her, and I let her lead. I want her to have the moment of taking control when she hasn't been allowed any.

My palm curves around the back of her thigh, rubbing along her soft skin, and apparently the movement acts as a reality check because she instantly pulls away.

Hands still around my face, her eyes go big and a little bit wild, shocked that she kissed me.

I'm shocked that she kissed me.

"Well, *goddamn*," Dean chuckles, throwing back another shot. "Looks like Kennedy found someone she actually wants to kiss in public."

Utter disbelief is plastered on her face, lips I finally touched now trembling slightly.

She doesn't take her eyes off me, but she's drowning. She was brave, trying to prove a point, and now she's drowning.

I dust the pad of my thumb over her lower lip, forcing my signature smirk to appear as I say, "I think that's our cue to get out of here, huh?"

She nods against my thumb.

Taking the initiative, I slip my hand into hers and lead her towards the door without giving anyone time to say something shitty to her that'll just end up pissing me off.

I don't want to be pissed right after I had the best kiss of my life.

"I'm sorry," she bursts out as soon as the private dining room door closes. Her hands fly to her mouth. "I cannot believe I just did that. I'm so sorry."

"You don't have to apologize. You can kiss me anytime you want, Kenny. *Please* kiss me anytime you want."

"Isaiah." Her eyes close. "That wasn't what it—"

"I know what that was. I know you kissed me to prove a point about the shit he was saying. I fucking loved it. You want to use me to shut him up? I'm happy to volunteer."

She opens her eyes, with a smile that screams "I can't believe I actually did that" trying to break through.

God, she's fucking cute when she's proud of herself.

She dusts a finger over her mouth as if to remember what it felt like when we kissed only moments ago, and I'm over here knowing I'll never be able to forget.

"What he said though," she begins, her tone frantic. "He wasn't wrong. I . . . I don't know how to be affectionate. The way they were with each other tonight, I want to be like that, but I don't know how to. I don't know how to be the kind of woman that a man would want."

"You're out of your mind if you think you're not exactly the kind of woman a man would want. Just because you're not comfortable with showing physical affection doesn't make you any less of a woman, Ken."

"But I want to be. Comfortable, I mean. With affection."

"Okay," I say softly, soothingly. "You'll get there."

She chews on her lower lip, eyes nervously finding mine, with a voice so quiet I'm certain I mishear her when she says, "Will you teach me?"

13

Kennedy

"So you were in an arranged marriage."

They're the first words Isaiah has spoken to me since leaving the restaurant. After I asked him to teach me, he stood in shocked silence, mouth slightly agape. I swear minutes passed where he simply stared at me in disbelief before saying, "I need you to start from the beginning." Then ushered me out to my waiting car, where we're currently sitting in the back seat.

"We never got to the marriage part, but yeah. You could call it that, I guess."

He rests his head back against the seat. "All these years, I thought you were engaged to someone you were in love with. I would've tried a little harder if I knew."

"You tried plenty hard. Trust me."

His lips tilt in a knowing smile. "I'm just saying. I would have pursued you a little more seriously, been a little more focused, than just blatantly hitting on you like an idiot because I knew I didn't really have a chance anyway."

It wouldn't have mattered.

Partly because Isaiah isn't someone I'd go for, but mostly because my eyes have never been open in that way. I knew from a young enough age that I'd be marrying for financial or business gain. There was no part of me that romanticized the notion of dating, falling in love, and marrying a person of my choosing.

That freedom was never on the table for me until now.

"So will you?" I ask Isaiah again, turning in the back seat to face him. "Teach me?"

"Fuck, Kenny," he exhales, palm running down his face. "I'm too malnourished to have this conversation right now. Who in their right mind thinks it's okay to charge those prices for two bites of food? Does anyone actually get full from eating at that fancy of a restaurant?"

"If they say they do, they're lying."

He checks on me out of the corner of his eye. "You hungry?"

"Starved."

He grins to himself. "I have this place in mind. Real nice. Might be hard to get a table on a Friday night, but let's try."

"Chili's." My voice holds no inflection as I slide into the booth across from Isaiah. "The real nice place you had in mind is Chili's."

"Look around, Ken. This place is packed. Had to call in a few favors just to get us a table."

"Well, lucky me, I guess."

"I thought maybe my rich wife never had the privilege of eating at Chili's."

"I haven't." I raise a single brow, opening the menu in front of me. "Is this the part where you tell me to order anything I want and it's on you?"

He scoffs. "Absolutely not. What do you think? That I'm made of money? You can order off the two-for-twenty menu, and if you're a good girl and eat all your dinner, maybe I'll splurge and get you a molten chocolate cake for dessert."

I can't contain the absolute cackle of a laugh that bursts out of me. The skin around Isaiah's eyes crinkle with his smile, hiding his birthmark.

It's dangerous. That smile. That face.

Isaiah makes an ungodly amount of money from his contract with the Warriors, but I decide to go along with it, flipping my menu to the back to select from the discounted selection.

I could not be more out of place in my Chanel dress and Louboutin heels, but I've also never felt more comfortable than I do sitting in a booth that's covered in cracked vinyl, sharing a laugh with my technical husband.

Isaiah is good like that. Always knowing how to soothe the tension or ease an uncomfortable situation with a smile and a joke. Sometimes even at his own expense.

Our food is ordered and our drinks are delivered, when Isaiah finally asks, "So what *exactly* are you wanting me to teach you?"

His cheeks tinge pink at the question. It's got to be illegal for cocky Isaiah Rhodes to be this cute when he's shy.

I shrug. "Everything."

He immediately chokes on the club soda he's attempting to swallow.

"Fuck me," he says, dipping his head. "For my sanity, I need to know if we have different definitions of 'everything.'"

Swallowing, I cross my legs and straighten in the booth. This conversation would be embarrassing if I were having it with anyone else, but with all the weird things Isaiah and I are already faking, what's adding one more aspect to our business agreement?

"I want to be normal."

"You are normal."

"I mean, I want to be good." I circle my hand for him to finish my sentence, but he waits for me to elaborate. "At it."

"*Fuck my life.*" Head falling back, he eyes the ceiling, Adam's apple prominent against his throat. I have this insane urge to press my lips to it, maybe lick or bite it, which only solidifies the fact that Isaiah is the right person for this job. I'm undeniably attracted to the man.

That's good. Even if he's somehow lousy in bed, at least he'll look good doing it.

His eyes are heated when they meet mine. "Good at what?"

Sitting forward, I bring my elbows to the tabletop, linking my hands together, as if this were a real-life business proposition. "For the first time in my entire life, I get to date whomever I want. Well, after this . . ." I motion between us, clarifying. "I want to be good at it. I've never gotten to date or flirt with a stranger or whatever else people learn in their twenties. I'm about to be thrust into the dating pool with absolutely no experience."

He circles his temples with his fingers. "Please don't say 'thrust' right now, Kenny."

"I just want to feel like a natural at holding someone's hand or that thing they do in movies when they play footsies under a table. I don't want someone to ever be able to say the things Connor said tonight."

"Fuck Connor."

Yes, fuck Connor, but he wasn't entirely off base.

"Isaiah," I exhale, needing him to understand. "I've spent my whole life believing I was never going to have this opportunity, and I don't want to blow it simply because I'm lacking life experience. If a man who was going to inherit an entire hotel franchise, simply by being with me, couldn't even handle my intimacy issues, then I can't expect a new, random guy with nothing to gain would be able to either."

His jaw hardens, the tendons in his neck flexing. "If you stop worrying about unworthy men, maybe you'll begin to realize that you're not the problem."

"It's not really about anyone else," I tell him. "I want to do this for me."

I assume it's the perfectionist in me that feels the need to excel before I'm put to the test, but I refuse to start an entirely new life in San Francisco, working my dream job but floundering in my personal life.

"Let me get this straight." He links his fingers on the table-top, mirroring me. "You want to practice on *me* in order to be better at dating *other* people."

"Exactly!"

His eyes widen.

"Shit. That sounds bad."

"Not exactly my favorite thing to hear." He exhales a defeated sigh. "But you didn't ask to be in another unwanted marriage. Well . . ." He bobs his head from side to side. "You definitely did ask. Multiple times. Begged me, really."

I stifle a laugh. "Shut up."

His lips lift in a smirk at the sound. Like he's proud of himself for making me laugh.

Isaiah leans back in the booth, his button-up shirt pulled taut over his biceps, perfect hair finger-combed without any need for product. You'd have to be blind not to find my husband attractive, but more importantly, he's *experienced*.

Very experienced.

Experienced in a way that I know his little crush on me isn't anything serious. I've simply told him no too many times and that intrigues him. He wants something he can't have. He'll eventually get bored of waiting for me to view him differently or he'll spend so much time with me that his fantasy of sleeping with the only female on staff will fade. He'll move on soon enough.

That's all perfectly fine, but what I really need is his experience.

Isaiah is confident in ways that I'm not. He has no problem with physical affection. He doesn't overthink his words before they come out of his mouth. That's what I need. I need him to lay it all on me, so that when I start dating someone else, someone with an average level of self-confidence and swagger, it'll be a breeze to navigate in comparison to my current husband.

I'm a scientist. This is research. Trial and error.

"So what do you want me to do, Kennedy?"

My eyes flick over our surroundings, making sure no other patrons are sitting in the listening range of our conversation, but still I keep my volume to a whisper. "I want you to touch me."

Isaiah's gaze heats.

"But also," I continue, "I want to touch you."

"You want to touch me?"

"If that's okay with you."

"Yeah," he deadpans. "I think I could live with that." Propping an elbow on the table, he runs his thumb and forefinger over his closed eyes. "But in what context are you wanting to touch me? Publicly or privately?"

That's a great question.

Chips and salsa get delivered to our table, so I snag a chip and chew, giving me time to mull it over.

After seeing Connor with Mallory and the way their hands easily found each other tonight, it hit me like a freight train that I may never be so comfortable in public. Hence the idea was born that Isaiah, the man I'm married to, might be able to help me get there.

There's a huge part of me that longs for the romantic parts of life. To be grabbed and kissed. For my hand to be held like someone's lifeline. To be flaunted because someone loves me for me, and not for the monetary gain that comes with me.

But privately, I'm no different.

I'm not entirely shocked Connor cheated on me. It's not out of the ordinary for relationships in our world to be strictly for appearances as most unions are based on business arrangements. But I tried. I really did try to hold his attention.

Isaiah doesn't touch the chips, just sits and waits for my answer.

I swallow a sip of my iced tea, unable to look at him when I say, "Both."

"Jesus," he exhales, falling back into the booth once again.

"I mean that in private, maybe we could be the same as we are in public. I'm doing this for myself so I can learn. We're already trying to convince others of our fake marriage, so I don't see why it would need to stop behind closed doors."

I don't really know what I'm asking of him. I don't know where the line should be drawn. Kissing. Cuddling. Exploring. I'll let him create his own conclusions and boundaries on that.

And then he does. "Are you asking me to fuck you, Kenny?"

Oh.

"Because I don't know if I can handle that. Fucking you so you're better prepared to fuck someone else."

Isaiah's brows are furrowed as if he hurt his feelings simply from his own conclusion. Sure, there was a part of me that thought the cocky playboy would jump at the chance if I asked him to fuck me. One and done, out of his system so he could move on from his little crush, but he seems almost hurt by the idea.

"I'm . . . I don't know how to answer that. I haven't thought that far, I guess."

He runs a hand over his face. "Is this all because of Connor? I saw the way you were looking at him tonight."

"This has nothing to do with Connor. Sure, there's a part of me that's hurt over the whole thing. He left me for someone who was physically what he wanted and who could touch him without overthinking it, but there's a

148

bigger part of me that's thankful he ended things. He gave me the freedom to have the life that *I* want. And I wasn't watching *him*. I was watching *them*. Together. I want to be comfortable and confident like that. I've never experienced intimacy. Communication. Exploring someone's body and them exploring mine. Touching someone that I *want* to touch."

Isaiah's eyes soften with sympathy, a soft exhale leaving his lips. "Kenny, have you ever thought that maybe you're not the problem? That maybe the issue is no one has ever let you feel safe and that's why you're not affectionate?"

Oh.

"I . . . I don't know. I haven't had the chance to test that theory."

He swallows hard. "Why, of all people, do you want to test that theory on me?"

There's a heavy pause between us in the crowded restaurant. "Because I trust you. I think I always have."

A soft grin lifts on his lips as his eyes appraise me from across the booth. "I've always trusted you too. You did catch me crying in the women's restroom on day one and haven't mentioned it since."

I chuckle. "You ever going to tell me what that was about?"

His leg brushes mine under the table. It's light, but intentional, and I don't move away.

"Maybe someday."

He wraps his foot around my high heel, his calf rubbing the skin of my exposed leg. I lean into the touch, playing footsies with my husband under the table at the local Chili's.

"I'll do this if it's really what you want, Ken."

The server drops off our food, both of us ordering burgers. His with fries, but mine with a side of loaded mashed potatoes because they sounded good, and I've never been to a restaurant where you could order loaded mashed potatoes with your burger.

Isaiah doesn't untangle his leg from mine as we begin eating.

"It's what I want."

"Okay." He takes a massive bite and smiles over at me with a mouth full of his burger.

I do the same, and mumble with my mouth full, "Okay."

Reaching across the table, I steal a handful of his fries.

"Excuse me."

"What?" I ask. "We're married. What's yours is mine."

He playfully scoffs. "I want to share my life with you, Kenny, not my food." With that, he reaches over and steals a forkful of my mashed potatoes.

I strategically arrange my fries under the bun as he watches with horror on his face.

"What? It gives it some crunch. Leave me alone."

"Remind me again why I married you."

I take another bite and while wearing a twenty-seven-hundred-dollar cocktail dress, I speak with my mouth full of a greasy burger. "Because you're obsessed with me. Remember?"

I know our wedding song is playing on a loop in his mind the way it is in mine. That becomes evident thanks to the knowing smile he wears as he watches me scarf down my food.

"You've never been hotter than you are right now, just so you know."

"Thank you." My tongue darts out to lick off the drop of ketchup lingering on my lips.

He tracks the whole thing. "*Fuck*."

The rest of the night continues like that. His legs wrapped around mine as we inhale our food. Dinner is greasy and filling and delicious, and the conversation is teasing and light with no more mentions about my intimacy issues I'm hoping to correct.

Thankfully, the material of my dress is stretchy because Isaiah orders a molten chocolate cake for dessert that disappears at an embarrassingly quick rate, but it's the ending to the best dinner I've had in a long time.

The food, sure, but mostly the company.

14

Kennedy

"Why exactly are we doing this?" I ask Miller as we both position ourselves in downward dog in my hotel room in St. Louis.

"Yoga is supposed to be good for stress."

Hanging upside down, I glance over to her. "You're stressed?"

"No. But you must be. You are married to my brother-in-law, after all."

A laugh instantly bubbles out of me, and it only grows louder when Max, Isaiah's nephew, mirrors our position, hands and feet on the ground, booty in the air.

"Good job, Bug!" Miller encourages. "You're better than both me and Auntie Ken!"

Miller and Kai have referred to me as Auntie Ken for a while now. It just feels a little differently now that, legally, I am.

Facing the window, opposite the door, I lean into the stretch. We've been on the road for over a week, and my body is feeling the stiffness of the constant flights and sleeping in a bed that's not mine.

I can't imagine how Isaiah's feeling. Well, actually I can. I've had to work on his back, shoulders, and hips before each game because he insists on sleeping on the floor. I've offered him the bed to himself. I've offered to share. And still he takes the floor each night.

It's been over a week since I asked him to touch me, to teach me how to touch him, and he has yet to try anything.

Miller is right. I am stressed being married to her brother-in-law because I've been on my toes, eager and nervous, all week, waiting for him to try something. Anything.

I don't know what he's waiting for, or maybe he changed his mind.

There's a nagging part of my brain that's berating myself for asking him to help me in the first place. I should've done the work myself. Gone to therapy. Dealt with my issues alone without involving someone else. I should've fixed myself in silence.

"Okay, yeah. Screw this." Miller drops to her knees, sitting on her heels, but I continue to stretch, extending through my heels and elongating my calves and hamstrings.

The door opens behind me while I'm in my pose and I look through my legs to find Isaiah leaning against the door-frame of our hotel room, arms crossed over his chest, cheeky smirk on his lips, and eyes on my ass.

The blood rushes to my cheeks and not just because I'm upside down.

But still I don't break my pose. Instead, I stretch further, ass on display as much as I can make it, because for the first time since I've known him, I want to tempt my husband.

Isaiah chuckles under his breath, muttering, "Fuck my life," quietly enough his nephew can't hear him.

"There's my boy." Kai charges right at his son, playfully tackling him, wrestling with him on the ground and covering his cheek with kisses. He reaches over, hooking an arm over Miller's shoulders and pulling her into their pile. "And my girl."

Max's giggles fill the room.

I drop onto my yoga mat and can't help but smile as I watch them. Max completely changed Kai's life, and Miller turned both those boys' worlds upside down last summer. But in the same way, those boys changed her too, and I couldn't be happier that my friend found everything she was missing.

I look back to Isaiah, expecting to find him watching his family, but instead his eyes are glued on me.

"What?" I ask.

He shakes his head.

Miller sits up. "Kennedy, what are you wearing tonight?"

I motion to the leggings and sweatshirt on my body, confused. "This."

"You're not coming out for Cody's birthday?" Kai asks.

"No."

"Wait. Why not?" That's Isaiah piping up from his spot at the door.

"Because I never go out with the team."

"Yeah, but I flew out for this," Miller says.

I laugh. "You flew out because Kai was trying to fly home on our day off to see you, but Monty wouldn't let him."

Miller shrugs. "Well, yeah, that too."

"Ken," Isaiah says. "No one is going to give you a hard time for going out with us. We're technically married. It'd be weirder if you *didn't* go out with us."

"Yeah, you should go." Kai lays on the floor, holding Max's hands as he walks across his stomach. "Even I'm going." He tickles his son. "Maxie boy is hanging out with his grandpa Monty tonight, huh?"

Max giggles again, folding over his dad's hands in laughter.

I had a whole night planned. I was going to finish my crossword, use a new face mask, and be in bed by 9:30 since I have an early showtime at the field tomorrow.

But I'm also trying new things. That's what the next few months are about and being spontaneous by doing something that's not penciled in my planner for the day would be very new for me.

"Okay," I say. "I guess I'll go."

"That's my girl!" Miller hops up from the ground with excitement. "See you in a few. I have beers stocked in the mini fridge in Kai's room so come grab one when you're ready!"

"Of course she fucking does." Kai pats his brother's shoulder as the three of them make their way out of our room.

Isaiah keeps his eyes on me. "So, you're going out with me tonight. *Willingly*, might I add."

"It's Cody's birthday."

"Cody, *my* best friend." He takes a step closer, into the room, and I don't move from my spot.

"And Miller is in town."

"*My* sister-in-law." Another step in my direction.

"You really need to make this about yourself, huh?"

"Of course I do." That timely smirk makes its appearance. "Put me out of my misery, Kenny, and tell me you're coming for me."

That phrase could be taken in an entirely different way, and as much as I try not to imagine the alternate meaning, I still feel my cheeks warm.

"I'm trying new things, remember?" I raise a brow. "Or have you forgotten? Because it seems like you may have forgotten."

His head falls in laughter. "Trust me, Ken. There's not a second that's gone by in the last week that I've forgotten about the new things you want to try."

"That's weird. Because I've been waiting for you to remember."

"I know you have."

"So, when are you going to do something about that?"

"When you least expect it."

But I'm always expecting it now. Every time we're in the same room, I'm expecting it. No, *expecting* isn't the right word. I'm *hoping* that he tries something.

I crane my neck to look up at him. He's invading my space, my chest almost to his stomach. Isaiah softly moves my hair behind my ears, cupping my jaw, his thumbs slowly stroking over my cheekbones. His sparkling brown eyes bounce over my entire face, taking me in. The pads of his fingers grip the back of my neck. His breath dusts over my skin.

My pulse is thundering, beating wildly with anticipation, and it only pounds faster when he licks his lips and leans down.

Eyes closing, I suck a breath, expecting, waiting, but instead, he drags his lips across my jaw until his mouth meets my ear. "Lesson number one, Kennedy. You can't pencil affection into your little planner, so stop overthinking it."

He finishes that with a chaste kiss on the pounding pulse point under my ear, and I'm left panting for this man.

The tilt on his lips screams that he knows the tables have turned. We're both aware that for the first time since we've known each other, *I'm* waiting on him instead of the other way around.

And he fucking loves it.

I don't know if I can handle the spontaneity. If it were up to me, I'd schedule out an hour a day when I knew he would be touching me.

Isaiah rounds my body, right to his open suitcase, pulling out his clothes for tonight, laying a pair of khaki-colored pants on the bed, followed by a bright red tee and his olive-green jacket. He proceeds to dig out a clean pair of boxer briefs and two socks. One navy-blue, the other black.

Maybe I should let him go out in that outfit.

Maybe other women will stay away from the guy dressed like it's Christmas in April.

But is that what I want?

Surprisingly, I think I do want other women to stay away from him. Which is unfortunate for me because I know no matter what the guy is wearing, women have never been able to stay away from Isaiah Rhodes.

He's got this knowing smile on his lips when he says, "So now that I've held your hand and you've laid one on me, should we just skip ahead to the showering together lesson or do you want to go first?"

He motions towards the bathroom with a naughty twinkle in his eye, and all I can think about is whether or not that's really a lesson he has planned.

I don't think I'll mind learning a thing or two from my husband.

I clear my throat. "You go ahead first."

Standing there in front of me, not moving a centimeter, he reaches over his head and takes his shirt off. Isaiah doesn't even bother to act like he doesn't want me to see every single inch of him, and I don't try to hide my staring.

"Eyes are up here, wifey."

"I'm a doctor, Rhodes. Aced anatomy, in fact. I know where your eyes are located. I just don't care right now."

I keep my attention on the lines in his stomach, the way they coil and move with his laughter. I want to touch them. My fingers are itching to make contact, to test the warmth of his skin, to splay out against the tan and toned planes of his stomach.

But I don't do anything because I'm a coward.

Isaiah reaches out for me, his hands gently gripping my wrists. Looking up, I visually check in with him to find him carefully watching me.

He brings my hands to his body, pressing my palms to his stomach, and as soon as we make contact, he sucks in a sharp inhale.

"Sorry, cold hands." I attempt to pull away, but he keeps me connected to him.

"Perfect hands."

Oh.

His skin is warm, his stomach is taut. He's big, towering over me, and my hands seem comically small in comparison to his body. These are things I don't notice at work because why would I? I've never noticed the way his breath hitches when I spread my fingers over him or how pleasingly his tan skin contrasts against my fair complexion.

I slowly run my palms over his abs, curving over his obliques.

His breaths grow ragged as he steps into me.

Slipping my hands around to his back, Isaiah wraps his arms over my shoulders in a hug.

"That feels good," he says quietly, his cheek curved into mine.

"Yeah?" I slowly move my palms up and down the length of his spine, rubbing his back.

"Mm-hmm. You don't have to wait for me, Kenny. You can touch me whenever you want, okay? Don't overthink it."

I nod against him.

His hold on me doesn't loosen to let go. Instead, he closes me tighter in a hug.

I don't remember the last time someone hugged me. Maybe last season when Miller threw her arms around me in the training room. That was nice. Unexpected, but nice.

This is different from that hug. That felt like I was someone's friend. This feels like I'm someone's everything.

Keeping his arms folded over my shoulders, he moves his lips by my ear. "I'm glad you're coming out with us tonight."

"You might change your mind about that when you realize having your wife around is probably going to be a total cockblock for you."

He doesn't laugh at my joke. "That's perfectly fine by me. I'd rather be hanging out with you all night, anyway." Isaiah presses his lips to the top of my head. "But now I need to go take a very long and very cold shower after having your hands all over me, so thanks for that."

With that, he releases me from his hug and heads into the bathroom.

I don't know how true that statement really is that he'd rather be hanging out with me, but I like the possibility that it could be. Because, admittedly and shockingly, Isaiah Rhodes is far from my least favorite person to be around.

I wait until I hear the water running before I take the navy-blue sock from the pile of clothes on the bed and search for its partner in Isaiah's suitcase, folding them together. Then I grab the rogue black one and place it on the bed for him to wear tonight.

15

Isaiah

The blues club in the Delmar Loop hosts a contemporary R&B night once a week. It just so happens to fall on Cody's birthday, and of course the birthday boy knew all about it when planning his own night.

Travis and I attempted to take over coordinating, but Cody insisted, not trusting either of us with the job. I don't blame him. He is our team planner after all, always having something fun for the boys to do on our days off.

The dark and moody club is packed, but thankfully there's a roped-off corner for us to have our own space.

That's where I've been all night. Sitting back on a velvet couch with a perfect sightline to watch my wife in the crowd, swaying those pretty hips, a smile plastered on that perfect mouth. She's dancing with Miller and thanks to my friends and teammates surrounding the two of them, no one has tried to invade her space.

Her safe little bubble to have fun in.

This past week has been torture since Kennedy asked me to touch her. What alternate reality am I living in that my fake wife, who I very much have feelings for, asks *me* to touch *her*?

I've been tempted to every second of every day for the past week, but she's been so on guard, so on edge, that nothing about it would feel natural if I did. If she knew I was going to kiss her, she would have done her typical Kennedy thing of overpreparing and overthinking.

She wants to learn so she can be better prepared to date other people.

Fuck that.

She may think I'm okay with that plan. She may believe I'm happy to help her, but she doesn't need to learn to be comfortable with another man touching her.

The way I see it, no other man ever will.

And to top it all off, when I got out of the shower, she explained the colors of the clothes I picked to wear tonight and pulled out other options for me in case I wanted to choose something else. She's not even trying to keep me from falling for her.

"Hey, man." Kai takes the seat next to me, handing me a beer. This is my second and last of the night, seeing as we play tomorrow. "You look happy."

"I'm always happy."

"No, you're not. You may always *look* happy, but you're not always happy. Tonight though, you are."

I find my favorite redhead in the crowd with plenty of space around her. She seems like she's out of her head for once tonight, and that alone brings a smile to my face.

"I think you're right about that."

Cody slides onto the couch on my other side. "I just made out with the bartender."

"Okay, birthday boy!"

"He used way too much tongue, but now I'm getting free drinks for the rest of the night." He pops his shoulders in a shrug as if it's the most common thing in the world for him.

People love Cody, and Cody equally loves them, but the guy will never settle down with one single person. Says he's got too much love in him not to share it.

We've been the two on the team who have never had a problem with getting attention, but the difference between him and me is that I always knew I'd want to have something serious and lasting one day. I want what my brother has, but the only person I ever had any interest in was engaged to someone else.

Until she wasn't.

"Hey," a woman says from the other side of the rope, facing me. "I'm Lacey."

The music is soft, so I don't have to scream to be heard the way I typically do when Cody drags us to a nightclub. "Nice to meet you, Lacey."

I can feel both Kai and Cody watching me out of my periphery, stupid knowing smiles on their faces because we're all aware this is the first time I've gotten hit on since I've been married.

"You've been on this couch all night. I've been waiting for you to come out on the dance floor."

"What can I say? This couch is exceptionally comfortable."

She giggles. "Would you please come dance with me?"

My brows shoot up. I don't know why, but I didn't expect her to be so direct. I've perfected the art of indirect letdowns over the past nine months, and now she's not giving me the chance to do this subtly.

That's all right though. I've got a black metal band on my finger that's anything but subtle.

I hold my left hand up to show her. "I've already got a dance partner. Sorry, Lacey."

I'm not sorry about it one bit.

Glancing over her shoulder, back into the crowd, I find Kennedy staring at me and my displayed hand from the dance floor.

I shoot my wife a wink, but she quickly averts her attention back to Miller.

Lacey turns to Kai, and he holds both hands up in surrender, refusing to make eye contact. "I may as well be wearing one of those things." He nods towards my ring. "And you should probably stop looking at me. My fiancée is kind of scary when she gets jealous."

She then tries her luck again, turning towards Cody. "Fuck it," he says, standing from the couch. "Third time's a charm, huh, Lacey?"

With that, he follows her out to the dance floor.

"You're fucked," Kai mutters next to me.

"Shut up. So are you."

"Yeah, well the difference is that Miller is equally as fucked. Kennedy, on the other hand, is out there planning a move to San Francisco and thinking about all the dudes she's going to date after she divorces you."

"She's not going to be dating anybody. I just need the next few months to inform her of that."

"You hopeless little shit." Kai throws his arm over my shoulder. "I love you."

"Love you too."

"Hey, I need to tell you something, but I can't really talk about it too much or I'm going to start crying, and I'm not trying to cry in the club tonight."

I turn to face him, noting the serious tone in his voice and the soft smile on his lips.

"Miller and I are talking about trying for a second."

"Yeah?" The excitement is evident in my tone.

"Yeah, but um . . ." He clears his throat, the emotion evident. "She's uh . . . she's worried about how that'll make Max feel to have another, and for that one to be biologically hers. She doesn't want him to grow up feeling like he wasn't enough or that she needed her own when Max is hers too, you know?"

I could understand that. Max will one day learn that Miller is not his birth mom. But he'll also learn that though his biological mom didn't want to be a mother, Miller couldn't live her life without him.

"Before we start trying, Miller wants to become his mom. Legally, I mean. I just wanted to let you know that Ashley gave up all parental rights and we're going through the paperwork for Miller to adopt Max."

My eyes immediately burn. Fuck, I love that kid. I also love that he has the two best parents in the world that want nothing more than to make sure he knows how cherished and chosen he is.

"He's lucky, you know. To have you two, but yeah, you're right." I clear my throat, sounding equally as choked up as him. "We can't keep talking about this here."

Kai swallows down a swig of his beer and I concentrate on fixing my shirt that doesn't need fixing.

Thankfully, Travis interrupts the moment. "This guy just tried to dance with Miller, and she told him that if he touches her again, she's going to knee him in the balls."

A smile spreads on Kai's face. "That's my girl."

Standing from the couch, he makes his way out to the dark dance floor, but thanks to his height, I'm able to follow him with my eyes. I watch as he finds Miller and snakes a possessive arm around her. I also watch as Cody hands Kennedy a shot and begs her to take it with him. There's a lime on the rim so I can only assume it's the same liquor that convinced her it was a good idea to marry me.

She grimaces as it goes down her throat, so I guess the good news is at least she's not at the point where she thinks it's water.

The vocals of the lead singer are slow and sensual. The music is smooth and romantic. I could sit here all night, watching Kennedy slowly sway to the rhythm while wearing those tight leather pants and a sweater that's short and cropped. Her arms and legs are fully covered, including the heeled boots she's got on, but that sliver of freckled skin peeking out above her belly button every time she moves has been tempting me all fucking night.

And just as I'm staring at her waist, watching the way it moves to the music, a hand that's not hers or mine slides against her pale stomach, fingers splaying wide over her entire midsection.

My vision goes blurry as I discard my beer, flying off the couch to jump the barrier rope, dodging the crowd and finding my way to her.

When I finally make it to the front where our group is, the guy is gone. My brother is also missing, so I can only assume he took care of that issue for me.

But Kennedy is still here, back to me and auburn hair falling in loose waves. She's not dancing anymore, her eyes darting around the area frantically, and I allow myself to believe she's looking for me.

From behind, I wrap my hand around her waist, exactly where someone else's just was.

She instantly jerks to get away.

"It's me, Kenny." I pull her back into my chest, curling down to speak quietly into her ear.

Her body stops fighting me and instead melts back into my touch.

"Are you okay?"

She nods.

"Do you want to leave?"

She shakes her head, her hand reaching up to grip onto my forearm, as if silently telling me to keep my arm right there wrapped around her.

I breathe her in as the music continues, this girl I've had to keep my distance from most of the night. There's a part of me that's afraid of going too fast, of pushing her too quickly because of how long I've wanted this. Whatever we do, she's going to have to set the pace.

Cody shows up in front of us with a sneaky smile on his lips and another shot in his hand for Kennedy.

"Absolutely not," I tell him. "Stop trying to get my wife drunk. She's known to make very poor decisions while drinking tequila."

"Someone's got to have fun tonight and we all play tomorrow."

"She works tomorrow too. What happened to that chick you were dancing with?"

"Lacey? Turns out the third time was definitely not the charm." Cody throws back the shot of clear liquid. "Don't tell Monty."

"Lacey, huh?" Kennedy asks when it's just the two of us on the crowded dance floor again.

"What about her?"

"Was she the brunette who was hitting on you while you were on the couch?"

A knowing smile sneaks across my lips, but she can't see it, both of us facing the stage. "I couldn't tell you what color her hair was, and I caught you over here watching me, wifey."

"I happened to look over there at that exact moment, is all. She was cute."

"She's not you."

I can feel Kennedy roll her eyes, but still she drops her head back to my chest.

The club is dark. The music is impossible not to move to. Ever so slightly, I rock my hips and Kennedy sways with me, her head on my chest and her hand on my forearm.

I drop my lips to her hair as the music takes over, her body melting into mine.

When she's prepping and planning, she can't get out of her own head, overthinking every little contact. But right now, with her guard down, she's a natural at this.

We continue to sway as my fingers splay wide over her belly, pinky toying with the waistband on her leather pants and thumb dusting the lace fabric of the underside of her bra.

She shudders against me.

"Tell me to stop."

She shakes her head, her body fully falling into the cradle of my arms.

I run my hand over her stomach, wrapping and curving over her waist and holding her to me.

She stays there, one arm dangling at her side, the other gripping my forearm as if she has no idea what to do from here.

"Do what feels good," I whisper into the dark space.

Kennedy runs her hand across my forearm that's holding her, her palm finding the back of my hand before dipping her fingers in the space between mine, lacing our hands as I hold her to me.

"Mmm, I fucking love that."

"Yeah?" she asks over her shoulder.

I slip my other arm over her waist as well, lips ghosting the shell of her ear as I dance with her. With a bit more confidence, Kennedy lifts her dangling hand from her side, mentally cataloging what she wants to do with it, but instead drops it right back to her thigh, stiff and uncomfortable.

"I'm in my head," she admits.

I quickly glance around the room. I can't see too much thanks to the crowd and the darkness, but I find an empty corner in the back.

"Come with me." I keep our hands intertwined as I bring her to the dark corner.

There's a barstool waiting, so I take a seat, pulling her to stand between my spread legs.

We're almost eye to eye at this height, and I stare right at her when I tell her, "Touch me however you want to."

Her brows cinch, her eyes almost taking on a glossy sheen, and I don't know if it's because she's embarrassed or what.

No one is watching, everyone's backs are turned to us as they listen to the live band play in front of them.

Kennedy studies me, researching and trying to figure out the best way to start.

"Don't overthink, Ken."

She lifts her hands, but instantly drops them to my knees with a smack.

My chest rumbles.

"Don't laugh at me."

"I'm not laughing at you, baby." Moving her hair away from her face, I tuck it behind her ears. "I just find it funny that you're so in your head right now, while I'm over here desperate for you to touch me and knowing there's nothing you could do that I'm not going to like."

Her brown eyes peek up at me through her lashes. "Really?"

"Promise. Think of this as part of our game." Going first, I let my hands find her outer thighs, fingers working to pull her closer. "Play along."

Kennedy steps into me, her palms dragging up my legs, thumbs gliding along the inside seam of my pants.

I'd like to say I've got this under control. That I've been touched by enough women to handle the fact that my wife's thumbs are languidly tracing a path straight to my cock, but I'd be lying if I said I were anywhere near calm or collected right now.

"This okay?" she asks, her hands working their way to my upper thighs.

My voice is strained. "More than okay."

She's watching her hands as they move over my thighs and I swear to God I know she can see, even through the darkness, that I'm half hard and needy as fuck.

This. This is why I haven't slept in the bed with her, because she's innocently touching me and I'm over here getting a hard-on because of it.

As her hands move up my legs, my fingers dig into her hips, gripping onto her for dear life, and when she's only two inches away from where my body needs her attention the most, she takes her hands away.

My lungs find a bit of oxygen again when she moves to my forearms, working the same path upward. She stops at the bend in my elbow. "Can you take this off?" she asks, referring to my jacket.

"You can take it off for me."

She attempts to hide her smile by slipping her bottom lip between her teeth, and fuck if I don't want to get it out of there and slip it between my own.

I've been aching for another kiss, a somewhat real one.

Kennedy's hands press against my shirt, her palms gliding up my chest until her fingers dip under my jacket, pushing it over my shoulders. Her body falls into me as she reaches, but I help her out by slipping my arms out and letting my jacket fall onto the stool.

She doesn't move, her hips settled into the cradle of mine, our equally pounding chests only inches from each other.

Again, I wait for her. She watches, her eyes roaming over every inch of my body.

The darkness is helping her. The hidden corner and the melodic music too.

Kennedy's hands find my chest, gliding over my shoulders and the back of my neck, until she falls into me with a hug, her cheek pressed to mine.

Bending, I kiss the top of her shoulder then the soft skin of her neck as my hands wrap around her, fingers tempting and toying with the material of her pants just above her ass.

"You still doing okay?" I whisper.

She nods against me. "I like touching you."

"Yeah?" I let my hands drop a bit further south.

"And I'd like it if you touched me too, Isaiah."

Fuck. Me.

My lips are toying with the shell of her ear when I drop my hands and let them glide over her ass, squeezing and kneading.

She hums in my ear, her arms tightening around me.

"You like that, Ken." I grab her again.

Her breaths are ragged, her body writhing against me. "Yes."

We could blame the music for the way our bodies are rocking against one another, but we both know it could be dead silent in here and we'd be doing the same damn thing.

This time, when I grab her, I let my fingers dip down to the fold where her ass meets her thighs, and I trace the line with the pads of my fingertips.

Kennedy's hips roll over me, this delicious friction between the apex of her thighs and my cock.

There's nothing half hard about me anymore. I'm aching, painfully aching by having this woman on top of me.

With my face hidden in her neck and curtained by her hair, I breathe her in, gripping the underside of one of her legs, situating her bent knee to rest on my thigh. I leave her standing on one foot, but half on top of me.

"Isaiah."

My lips meet her throat. "You still okay?"

She rolls her hips. "God, that feels good."

I note the moment her clit gains friction because she's a shuttering mess against me. I'm two seconds away from grabbing her other thigh to make her straddle me. I'd be able to work her hips and in no time, I'd have her coming, still fully clothed in my lap.

And again, this is why I'm sleeping on the goddamn floor. I can't help myself with her.

I slow things down a bit, hand curling around her waist to grip her hip and keep her from grinding on me. She pulls back to look at me, confusion plastered on her face, and I can't fucking help myself any longer.

Other hand cupping her cheek, I pull her in until my mouth collides with hers.

She moans into me, and unlike last time, *I* set the pace.

It's frantic and needy.

God, her mouth is soft. Eager too, like she's been waiting her whole life to kiss someone the way she's kissing me.

While my fingers tangle into that auburn hair, Kennedy's tongue ever so slightly licks my bottom lip, and the needy groan that leaves my throat might be the most desperate sound I've ever made.

She smiles into me, my wife who has no idea how fucking badly I've wanted this. *Wished* for this. *Dreamed* of this.

Lips parting, her tongue—her *perfect* fucking tongue—slides against my own and this time it's Kennedy moaning into my mouth.

God I'm going to lose it. I'm going to fucking come from a kiss and a leg slung over my lap. But the way her mouth moves, the way her tongue glides, she doesn't need to be taught anything about kissing, that's for goddamn sure.

It feels far too sexual for this to simply be a kiss. It feels like we're fucking each other with our mouths and when Kennedy's nails scrape against the nape of my neck, when she tugs at the ends of my hair, I have to pull away.

"Fuck, Kenny," I breathe, forehead falling to hers.

"Was that okay?"

I can't help but laugh in disbelief. "Shut up." Pulling her hips into me, I make sure she feels just how hard I am. "You know that was more than fucking okay. It was goddamn perfect."

"I like kissing you."

"Mmm, how did those words feel coming off your tongue?"

She smiles against my lips. "Like acid."

I'm so fucked.

In what world does she think she's going to start seeing anyone else after this? After me?

Not a chance in hell.

To make sure of it, I lean in, taking her mouth once again. It's softer this time as my palm runs the column of her spine, up and over her shoulder to glide along her left arm. I stop when I find her hand holding onto the back of my neck.

I cover hers with mine, toying with the ring on her left hand as we kiss in the back corner of the dark nightclub.

She wants intimacy? This feels intimate as fuck.

Someone clears their throat next to us, loud enough for us to stop, but Kennedy is still half on top of me, leg still slung over my hip. I've got one arm wrapped around her waist, my other hand still bent back to hold hers.

Her forehead is pressed to mine when we look over to find Kai, Miller, Cody, and Travis watching us with a range of expressions. Kai and Travis have wide, disbelieving eyes. Miller is laughing and the birthday boy is shooting us two thumbs up from the back of the group.

Kennedy straightens, fixing her cropped sweater and readjusting her leather pants.

"Cars are here to take us back to the hotel," is all Kai says.

Kennedy clears her throat. "Okay."

My brother looks to me for a response.

"I'll uh . . . yeah, just give me a couple minutes."

"Jesus, fuck," he mutters with a laugh before slinging an arm over Miller and heading towards the exit.

Travis and Cody follow behind, but not before Cody turns back to us with his hand over his heart. "Love this for you guys."

Kennedy takes a step to follow them, but I hook a hand over her hip to stop her.

"Hey." I pull her back between my legs, placing another kiss on my wife's mouth, making sure she knows this doesn't have to end right now, in this club, confined to a dark corner.

Without thinking about it, she wraps her arms around my shoulders again, eyes bouncing between mine. "Thanks for my first lesson."

I huff a laugh until she shuts me up with another quick kiss.

I didn't teach her shit tonight. That was all her. I, on the other hand, have quickly learned that I'm going to be entirely fucked if she's serious about this thing between us having an expiration date.

16

Kennedy

It wasn't supposed to be like that.

I didn't know it *could* be like that. I wasn't aware my brain could quiet itself, or that my body knew exactly what to do when the moment presented itself.

Kissing Isaiah wasn't supposed to be like *that*.

He was supposed to teach me how to be comfortable dating other people, not ruin my every waking thought because all I can do is replay that moment. How good his hands felt in my hair. How eager I was to have my leg slung over his lap.

This was supposed to be an innocent experiment. Get the awkwardness out of the way with someone I don't see a future with. We're technically married so what's the harm in adding a little physical contact into the equation? A little kissing. A little hand holding.

Well, I'll tell you what the problem is. The problem is I want more, and that can't happen. It shouldn't. After all these years of him blatantly hitting on me, I can't crumble because of one freaking kiss.

It's been days. *Days* since we've been back in Chicago, and I can't get him out of my head. That night in St. Louis, for the first time, I didn't invite Isaiah to sleep in the bed. He's refused every night prior, most likely realizing my offer is made purely out of guilt. But after that kiss, I didn't even give him the option.

I needed space to organize my thoughts.

Rationally thinking, he's just the first. Not my first kiss, by any means. Just the first time a kiss felt intimate. That's all it is. He's the first guy I've allowed myself to be open with, and I'm sure it'll feel just as good when I open myself up to other people.

So, yeah, things are fine. I'm fine, and this experiment is working exactly how I need it to. Sure, I've completely avoided him since we've been home, but yeah, things are going just fine.

The training room has been busy all morning thanks to our afternoon game today. My thumbs throb in pain from rubbing sore muscles and ripping athletic tape to secure uneasy joints. I haven't had a spare moment for food or even a sip of water, but I couldn't care less.

I love this.

I love game days and I love my job.

I love working on athletes and the one benefit of being an athletic trainer over a team doctor is that I get to work on them every single day.

Will, our second doctor, does a good amount of therapy too, but I couldn't tell you the last time Dr. Fredrick was hands-on in the training room. As Head of the Health and Wellness Department, he's too busy working on schedules, overseeing the nutritionists and strength training coaches, and being the department's face.

The only time he has any real involvement is when one of the players has a serious injury or surgery and we have to run our rehabilitation plans through him.

That's it. That's the only thing he does that we can't.

It's something I'll have to look into if I get the position with San Francisco. I don't want to be stuck at a desk doing paper-work. I want to do exactly what I'm doing now, but with the title of Lead Doctor.

And judging by that call I got a few days ago, I might be having that conversation sooner rather than later.

"You're all set, Cody." I toss his specific tape aside as our first baseman flexes his hand, making sure his mobility is still there, regardless of his taped fingers.

"Thanks, Ken. Where are you working today?"

"Clubhouse."

"Again?" Cody's brows furrow in confusion.

I've been stuck covering the clubhouse for the past five games. The medical staffer who is left to cover the clubhouse is essentially a floater. We're there to help out if extra hands are needed in either the visitor or home training rooms. We watch the game on one of the four giant televisions hung in the center of the room, but most of the time, we simply sit and wait for the game to be over.

But it's not hydration, so I'm not complaining. Dr. Fredrick hasn't made that mistake again after Reese put him in his place for assigning me as the water girl on Opening Day.

"I don't mind," I assure him.

"What the hell did you do to piss off Dr. Fredrick so badly?"

"I married your best friend."

Cody's eyes twinkle. "A fact you seemed perfectly okay with while we were in St. Louis."

I wave him off. "I had too much to drink, thanks to you."

"You had one drink thanks to me."

"Well, then we can call it a fleeting moment of weakness."

"You call it whatever you want if it'll make you feel better, but you don't need to justify it to me. I get it."

"You get it, huh?" My lips tilt in amusement. "You got a thing for my husband, Cody?"

"Isaiah?" He barks a laugh. "Fuck no. Isaiah is too pretty for my tastes. I like them a little more rugged. I meant that I understand if your opinion of him has changed now that you're getting to know him. He's my best friend for a reason. On the surface, he comes off like this arrogant little shit, but deep down, he has a heart of gold and maybe you're starting to see that."

I have seen it. The protectiveness while we were at dinner with my family. The lack of judgment when I explained my inexperience in the dating world.

I ignore the rest of Cody's statement. "He is pretty, isn't he?"

"Who's pretty?"

My attention snaps up to find Isaiah standing behind Cody, only wearing a backwards hat and a pair of shorts, holding a paper cup in his hand.

I try to keep my eyes on that pretty face instead of that pretty chest, those pretty abs, or those stupidly pretty arms.

Cody covers for me. "This guy I went out with last night. I was just showing Kennedy a picture." He hops off the training table. "See you guys later. Thanks for the tape job, Kenny!"

"Excuse me?" Isaiah whirls in his direction. "What did you just call her?"

There's absolutely no confusion on Cody's smirking face as he walks backwards towards the exit. "What? I called her Kenny. Isn't that what you call her?"

"And in what fucking world does that mean you get to call her that?"

Cody's head falls back in laughter, muttering "Lovesick motherfucker" as he leaves the training room.

"Shithead." Isaiah's scowl turns into a smile as he turns back to face me. "There's the Mrs."

"Do you lay awake at night thinking of names you know will annoy the shit out of me or what?"

He sits on the now vacant training table, making us almost eye to eye.

"No." He takes a sip of whatever is in his cup. "I lay awake at night thinking about those noises you made while I was kissing you and wondering how much louder you'd be if instead of your mouth, my tongue was on your—"

"Isaiah Rhodes!"

He gasps. "Kennedy Rhodes!" His smile is all mischief as he hooks a foot around my calf, pulling me to stand between his legs. "Hi."

I shoot him a glare. "Hi."

"You've been avoiding me."

"I don't see how that's physically possible when you've already come to see me four times today, trying to feed me."

Without thought, my hands land on his thighs in front of me.

Isaiah looks down and I catch the suppressed smile on his lips.

"Well, you need to eat."

"I don't have time."

He rolls his eyes and takes another sip of his drink, but now that he's closer to my height, I can tell it's a smoothie of some kind. Berry, if I had to guess.

"Go ahead and admit that you've been avoiding me since we got home because you can't stop thinking about that kiss and in turn, you can't stop thinking about *me*."

I scoff a laugh. "That couldn't be further from the truth."

"Welcome to the club, Ken. It's distracting when all I can think about is you. Now you get it."

I place the back of my hand on his forehead. "Are you feeling okay? You seem to have a bad case of delusion, and I would know. I'm a doctor, after all."

"Mm-hmm," he hums, nodding towards my feet where I'm wearing the shoes we got married in. "Nice shoes."

I motion to his bare chest. "Nice shirt."

"Nice ass."

I don't have a retort for him, and Isaiah's sneaky smile

screams how proud of himself he is for taking the win. "Where are you working today?"

"I'm covering the clubhouse."

Isaiah whips his head around, glaring through the glass windows of Dr. Fredrick's office, but he doesn't notice.

"It's fine." I step away from him, taking the opportunity of a rarely quiet training room to reorganize my equipment.

"It's not fine, Ken. The guy treats you like you're incapable of doing your job when the entire team agrees you're the best member on the medical staff. You should be on the bench with us."

"Isaiah, it's fine. I might not be here much longer anyway."

The words are out of my mouth before I can take them back.

I was going to tell Isaiah, but for some reason, it felt like a conversation that should've been planned in private, not a public declaration.

He knows this is the plan. It's always been the plan, but still, he should hear it first and maybe not in the middle of the training room right before he's about to play a game.

I can feel his gaze boring into the side of my face, but I continue to clean, trying to ignore his attention.

"Kennedy . . ."

My eyes cautiously move to his direction.

"What does that mean, 'not much longer'?"

Looking around, I keep my voice quiet as I step back into his space. My smile nervously blooms. "I got called for a final interview in San Francisco."

Isaiah's brows shoot up in surprise.

"They called me a couple of days ago. I'm flying out there next month. If I get the job, they want me to finish the season shadowing their current lead doctor."

"But . . ." Isaiah shakes his head. "You're in a contract until the end of the year."

I can't quite figure out if he's referring to my actual contract with the Warriors or the metaphorical one we have between us. Either way, he seems entirely not okay with the prospect of my contract getting cut from six months to three.

"I think we both know that Fredrick would have no problem letting me out of it early."

"But . . ."

"Isaiah, this is a good thing! This is everything I want."

"Yeah." He finds a genuine smile at the same time his hand finds the small of my waist, pulling me into him. "You're right. That's great news, Ken. Congratulations."

My cheeks burn. "Thank you."

The door to the training room swings open. Monty holds it for Reese to enter first, but it's fairly obvious that him holding the door open is the only cordial part of their interaction.

Their voices are quiet so no one else can overhear what they have to say, but judging by their facial expressions and body language, they're getting into it about something.

Monty's hands go wide as he argues his case, and Reese does nothing to back down from the giant man covered in tattoos. The blonde bombshell holds her ground, with a single hand resting on her popped hip and an unimpressed expression on her pretty face.

She says something in return, keeping complete composure before Monty's head falls back to gather his frustration. He inhales through his nose, his nostrils flaring, before giving her a single nod in agreement and ending their conversation.

Reese turns in my direction, wearing a body-hugging pencil skirt that shows off every one of her curves. "Kennedy, where are you working today?"

I open my mouth to answer, but Dr. Fredrick bolts out of his office before I have the chance to. "The clubhouse, Miss

Remington." He gestures to me. "Kennedy is covering the clubhouse. I have the intern on hydration as you asked."

Kiss ass.

"Reese," she corrects. "As I've told you before, you can call me Reese. And I want Kennedy working the dugout today."

"But Will and I are covering the dugout."

"As I said, I want Kennedy out there today. You can cover the clubhouse for once, Dr. Fredrick."

His mouth opens to protest, then closes just as quickly, words evading the doctor who typically has too much to say.

"Of course, Reese."

She finds me across the room and shoots me a wink before she turns back to the door, but stops just in front of Monty on the way.

"Emmett," she says, taking her leave.

His tone is clipped. "Reese."

"I like her," Isaiah declares.

My head whips in his direction, far too quickly and far too startled.

But she is a beautiful woman who is only a few years older than us.

"Easy, tiger," he laughs. "No need to get jealous. I meant that I like that she has your back."

"I'm not jealous."

He rolls those glinting brown eyes. "Keep telling yourself that, wifey."

"I cannot stand that woman." Monty keeps his voice low for only Isaiah and me to hear as he stands at the edge of the training table. "Who does she think she is?"

Isaiah hesitates. "The new team owner, perhaps?"

"Exactly! She's going to become the team owner the same year I'm up for a new contract. She's coming in here, wearing those fucking high heels around *my* clubhouse, wanting to change everything." Monty laughs condescendingly. "I don't think so. I've worked under her grandfather for six years and guess what? The guy never once told me how to run my team. There's no way in hell I'm letting some thirty-four-year-old waltz in here and tell me how to do my job."

He sets his fists on the table, leaning his weight on them. Bulging forearms and flaring nostrils. Monty could very easily be mistaken as a scary man if you didn't know what a big teddy bear the guy actually is.

"So, uh . . ." I clear my throat, looking to Isaiah and finding a mirrored, knowing grin. "What do you really think about Reese, Monty?"

"I think she's going to drive me fucking insane before she even officially takes over."

The big man stands to his full height, turning on his heel and throwing the training room door open with more force than necessary as he leaves.

"Well, that was interesting." Isaiah holds his paper cup out for me. "Anyway, you've got to try this smoothie I made in the dining hall. It's the best one I've ever created."

I bring the cup to my lips and Isaiah's attention is zeroed in as my mouth meets the same part of the rim where his just was.

"Mmm. That's good."

"Glad you like it because I made it for you. Drink this before the goddamn game starts, Kennedy."

I huff a laugh. "Cody's right. You really are a little shit."

"Oh, no, baby. That's where you're wrong. There's nothing little about me. Maybe one day you'll learn exactly what kind of size I'm working with."

"I'm sorry. He said *arrogant* little shit."

He stands from the table, big and overbearing in a way I'm getting far too accustomed to. "You left this on the sink in the women's restroom." Reaching behind his back, he pulls out today's *New York Times* crossword I've been working on in my spare time.

"When are you going to stop using my bathroom?"

He ignores me. "Seven down. I believe the word you're looking for is 'Denial.' Six letters. The act of asserting that something alleged is not true."

Looking the paper over, I realize he's right. The "N" and the "L" line up perfectly with my existing answers.

He steps into me, his voice low, close to my ear. "I'm surprised you didn't get that one, Kenny. You know a thing or two about denial, don't you? Like how you're telling yourself you've been avoiding me because you're too busy and not because you can't stop dreaming about our kiss and thinking about how you want more. I thought the answer might be 'Kennedy' but seven letters is too long."

My pulse races because he's not wrong. I do want more.

But I don't let him know that.

"Hmm. You're right. It is 'Denial'. Six letters. The act of asserting that something alleged is not true. I kept trying to use 'Isaiah' and it wasn't working. 'Rhodes' too. Because you're wrong. I haven't thought about that kiss one single time since it happened, and I sure as hell haven't thought about more."

The little birthmark by his right eye disappears behind his smile line. "The most beautiful liar I've ever met."

My body hums with his proximity, with his confidence and assertiveness I once found unattractive. Now I know it's just what I need. The constant permission he gives me to do what feels good.

Isaiah tucks a rogue strand behind my ear, running his palm over my hair until he wraps my ponytail around his fist once. Twice.

He tugs, ensuring I'm looking up and making eye contact with him. "Make sure you keep your eyes on me tonight, wifey. I have a feeling I'm going to have a good night at bat, and I want you to watch."

"You always want me to watch."

"Mmm, and I like to watch too, you know."

My mouth goes dry at his insinuation.

"But yes, I do love your attention."

"Because you're obsessed with me."

He chuckles close to my ear. "I think that's the perfect word to describe how I feel about you, Doc." Isaiah nips my earlobe before soothing it with a soft kiss on my neck.

With that, he takes off towards the exit, shirtless chest, backwards hat, and bare feet. He makes it to the door before turning one-hundred-eighty degrees to jog right back to me.

I have the smoothie in one hand and my crossword puzzle in the other, but Isaiah throws his arms around my shoulders, pulling me into a hug.

It's foreign yet comforting, and my body holds no protest to his hug. He holds me as if I were important to him, *needed* in order for him to get through his day. It feels good, *so* good. *He's* so good.

"What are you doing?" I ask into his chest.

"This is why I came in here in the first place, and I almost forgot. Wanted to give you a hug and tell you how much I missed you this week. Stop avoiding me, Kenny. I don't like it."

He jogs out of the room with that.

"Aw," someone coos from the corner of the training room. "You like your husband!"

Turning, I find Miller holding her hands over her heart, wearing her signature overalls with her fiancé's jersey unbuttoned over the top.

"You little creep," I laugh. "When the hell did you get in here? And *how* did you get in here?"

She throws a thumb over her shoulder, motioning towards the side entrance that's rarely used. "Just long enough to watch you swoon over the man you married."

"Gross. I'm not swooning over anyone. Especially Isaiah Rhodes."

"Mm-hmm."

"So, I assume that you were also here long enough to see your dad lose his shit over Reese."

She waves me off. "He's been bitching about her for weeks. Old news. New news, however, is that you, my beautiful sister-in-law, like your husband." From behind, Miller wraps her arms around me in a hug, just like the day we decided to be friends. "Love that for us."

I laugh. "Don't call me that and don't get your hopes up, Montgomery. If my interview goes well, I'll be leaving town soon, regardless if my tolerance for Isaiah has changed."

She scoffs, hopping up on my training table. "Let's not talk about you moving away please, Ken. I finally land in a permanent spot and my first friend decides to move away?"

"You'll be fine."

"Doubtful, but you know who definitely won't be fine? That smitten kitten back there."

"Isaiah will be more than fine. He gets plenty of attention to keep him occupied."

Miller's forehead creases as if she were confused, but I don't know why. We're all aware of Isaiah's reputation. I don't know what he does with his nights while we're home in Chicago. It was never a stipulation I set, and it would be awfully unfair of me to insist he not see other women while I'm using him to learn how to date other men.

As much as I hate that idea.

"You do realize I saw you two tongue-fucking in St. Louis, right? And just now." She motions towards the door. "He's trying and you like it."

185

"He's . . . *helping* me with something. That's all this is."

She chuckles under her breath. "Well, word of advice, my friend. That boy has chased you for years. If you're enjoying his *help*, may I suggest you stop running and give him some kind of sign of approval."

"And how do you suggest I do that?"

She shrugs. "He doesn't always have to be the first to make a move, you know."

It's a perfect Friday night for Chicago baseball.

The stadium is sold out, the May air is warm enough that I can get away with only wearing a light jacket while in the dugout, and we already got a man on base during our first at-bat.

The entire team leans against the barrier to watch. Well, everyone except Kai, who's our starting pitcher tonight, and even though his brother is about to be up at bat, he stays sitting on the bench, keeping his shoulder warm for the second inning.

The guys cheer on Cody as he jogs to first base, thanks to his walk, and Isaiah takes his final practice swing in the on-deck circle before removing his bat weight and dropping it to the dirt.

Then he finds me over his shoulder, sandwiched between two of the players, attempting to watch him through the fence. He smirks, this mischievous and knowing grin lighting up his face when he should be focusing on the game.

At first, I think he's giving me shit for making sure I've got a good view of him in those goddamn baseball pants, but then his new walk-up song begins to play over the stadium's speakers, and I know exactly what that scheming smile is all about.

Mariah Carey's "Obsessed" is blaring from all angles around me.

Kai barks a laugh from the bench, but other than him, no one questions his brother's song choice. Instead, the entire stadium is bursting, singing along with the lyrics while Isaiah's teammates are joining right in with their own karaoke renditions.

Our wedding song is on full blast as Isaiah makes his way to the plate, but before he gets there, he turns back in my direction. With the entire stadium singing the song I walked down the aisle to, Isaiah extends his bat, points at me, and winks.

He *fucking* winks.

It's the moment reality hits me . . . Miller was right. I think I might have a crush on my husband.

17

Isaiah

Cody: *Come out with us.*

Me: *For the hundredth time, I'm not going out tonight.*

Travis: *We're only two blocks away from your place.*

Me: *Still not going out. I'm tired and my back is sore from carrying you both with my two-run homer today.*

Cody: *Changed my mind. Don't come out.*

Travis: *I'll be running to your apartment to take a piss if this line at the bar doesn't move a little quicker.*

Cody: *And I'll be running to your place and pretending it's mine when I bring someone home with me tonight. Make sure to clean up. I don't want anyone thinking I'm a slob.*

Me: *The door will be locked for both of you.*

Cody: *I made myself a key.*

Me: *Cody, what the hell is wrong with you?*

Travis: *Cody has for sure fucked in your guest room FYI.*

Cody: *Not cool, Trav.*

Kai: *Annnnd this is why I keep the group chat on mute.*

Travis: *Multiple times, might I add.*

Me: *You're changing the sheets next time you're here and no more fucking at my place. And no more pretending it's yours. You have your own apartment.*

Cody: *I have roommates. There's nothing sexy about telling someone they have to be quiet because I have roommates.*

Me: *No more fucking at my place.*

Travis: *Someone should be fucking at your place. It's practically a monastery these days.*

The city bustles with Friday night liveliness just outside my apartment windows. The bars are packed, the streets are rowdy, and my entire team is out there somewhere enjoying the night off with a travel day tomorrow.

Well, everyone but my brother, who is home with his family. And me, who is here alone in this quiet apartment because going to bed early, knowing I'll get to see my wife first thing tomorrow at the airport, sounds far more appealing than drinking with my buddies.

What the fuck am I doing?

It's the question I've asked myself daily since this ring landed on my finger.

I'm in too deep, way too fucking deep, and I don't know which way is up. I don't *want* to know which way is up. I'm enjoying this little game Kennedy and I are playing, with her letting me treat her as if she were mine. Except my mind is starting to confuse the game with real life. Everything feels genuine to me, and I have no idea if that's due to my own delusion, wishing it were, or if she feels it too.

And instead of drowning my worries with my friends, I'm the sad fucking sap who's about to order a midnight pizza before going to bed by myself once again.

At least when I'm back home I get to sleep in a bed. That goddamn floor is going to be the death of me and my thirty-one-year-old back, but I refuse to sleep next to Kennedy until she asks me to in a way that's not offering out of guilt. No more of the "you can sleep here if you want." I need to hear her say *she* wants me to be there next to her.

I need her to give me something. *Anything* that tells me she's enjoying our little game as much as I am because all I'm getting right now is avoidance.

With the TV playing tonight's highlights from around the league, I grab my phone and dial my favorite late-night pizza spot, but when I'm two ringtones in, there's a knock at my door.

Fucking Cody. Or Travis. Either way, I need new friends.

It takes me a moment to get to the door, thanks to the awkward slide I had today, fucking up my groin. "Cody, I swear to God. I'm not lying about whose apartment this—"

Swinging the door open, I expect to come face to face with one of my teammates, only to find Kennedy standing on my doorstep.

"Hi." Her voice is small, nervous, but trying to be brave.

And all I do is blink like a fucking idiot because I'm sure this is a mirage. The prettiest auburn-haired mirage to ever exist. When do you start hallucinating due to abstinence? Because I'm currently around the nine-month mark and starting to see things.

I shake myself out of the daze. "Hi."

"Sorry, were you expecting Cody?"

"No. No, you're *much* better than Cody."

A tense smile lifts on her lips.

This woman is standing at my door, entirely out of her comfort zone, but why? I saw her at the field less than two hours ago.

Kennedy's hair is tucked under a baseball cap. She's still wearing her wedding shoes with a pair of leggings and a long tee, covered with that oversized denim jacket I bought her in Vegas.

She looks so fucking cute, and it's only amplified from those dusted freckles shadowed by the brim of her hat, but best of all, she's looking like that while standing at *my* door.

"What are you doing here, Kenny?"

"I . . . um . . ." Her voice shakes and she avoids eye contact. "I thought you might be going out tonight."

"And you're checking up on me?"

I like the idea of that. That she could be so jealous that I might be out on the town with the boys that she couldn't help herself from coming over and checking for herself.

"Because I'm not," I answer for her. "Never planned to."

"I . . . uh . . ." Her small hands fidget and that's when I see it. My hat. One of my countless team-issued hats in her hand. She holds it up. "You left this in your locker stall, and I thought you might need it . . . if you were going out tonight."

I find the top of the doorway, hooking my hands around the frame, my knowing smile impossible to suppress. She didn't come over here because of my fucking hat that I intentionally left at the stadium. She came over because she wanted to.

I'm equally tempted to give her a hard time as I am tempted to pull her inside and lock the door. Kidnap my wife and never let her leave.

I opt for the former. "You thought I might need my hat at midnight?"

She hesitates, her not-so-smooth cover blown already as her attention roams over my bare chest. "Yes."

"And you didn't think you could wait and give it to me on the airplane in the morning?"

"You were um . . . having a bad hair day. I didn't think you'd want to go out without it."

"I'm never having a bad hair day, baby."

She hands it over, but doesn't leave, her feet still glued to my entryway mat.

Yes, she's nervous and a bit uncomfortable. Maybe this is her first time ever putting herself out there for someone, but after three years of chasing the girl, I'm going to revel in the night she finally came to me.

"How'd you get my address, Ken?"

Her eyes flit away from mine. "I asked Miller for it."

"So you could return my hat."

"So I could return your hat."

"And that's the only reason you're here?"

Her eyes find mine again, feigning confidence. "Yep. Glad I could avert that crisis for you."

"And there's absolutely no other reason you came over? Is there something you're needing *help* with? A certain game you'd like to play tonight?"

She swallows, looking towards the elevator, but doesn't move an inch. "I should go."

"Then why aren't you?"

A retort sticks in her throat, her brown eyes begging for me to make this easy for her. To ask her inside and not question her motives.

But I can't. I want her to work for it. I *need* her to taste just a sample of the years of torture I've endured, wanting a woman I couldn't have.

The difference is she can have me. She can have fucking *all* of me.

She only needs to ask.

After too many seconds pass, neither of us admitting what we really want, Kennedy starts for the elevator.

"Good night." Her steps are quick, frantically carrying her away from me. Any faster and she'd be running. "See you at the airport."

"Kenny," I call out to stop her, stepping into the hallway. "Has anyone ever cooked for you?"

It's an out because I'm a lovesick idiot who can't stand to see her leave. I might talk a big game, but she will always have the upper hand when it comes to us.

Kennedy slows, turning to look at me over her shoulder and shaking her head to tell me no.

"Seems like something you should have on that checklist of firsts, huh? Probably want to experience it once before you find yourself back in the dating pool."

"I guess we could do that. I hadn't really planned on staying. I was just here to drop off your hat."

I huff a laugh. "How someone could be so beautiful and so full of shit at the same time is astounding to me."

Her smile blooms.

I motion towards my open door. "C'mon, Doc."

"At what point are we going to talk about the signs?"

Kennedy sits on my couch—shoes, jacket, and hat discarded. Legs crossed under her body and auburn hair tied up in a knot that looks effortless, yet she tried three times for it to stay that way, so I know it wasn't. Her bowl of spaghetti is already half gone, but I wish she'd eat slower. I'd like to obsess over the image of her cozy on my couch a little longer.

"I was planning to pretend as if they don't exist, so eat your pasta like a good girl and stop scanning my apartment."

Kennedy bursts a laugh. "How do you ignore the *Live, Laugh, Love* sign on your bedroom door or the fact there's a *Bless this Mess* entryway mat just outside." Her head falls back in contagious joy, that slender throat protruding against her fair skin. "You have a canvas painted with a glass of red wine hanging in your kitchen that says, 'You had me at merlot.'"

I wasn't impressed when the boys picked out my home décor, but now I'm thankful they chose the shittiest signs possible because I rarely get to see this woman laugh like this.

"Isaiah," she giggles. "I didn't peg you as an art collector. Is that what you're doing with the millions you make every year?"

I can't hold back my smile as I sit across the couch from her, bowl of spaghetti in one hand, fork in the other. "I lost our fantasy football league this year, and the boys each got to pick out a piece of décor that I have to keep displayed in my apartment for the year."

"God, that's genius. And just how many women have run for the hills since the makeover?"

Huh? "None."

She playfully rolls her eyes. "Of course not."

The only woman who's been in this apartment since last summer is currently sitting on the couch right now.

"How's the spaghetti?" I ask.

"So good." She takes another bite, talking with her mouth full in the most un-Kennedy-like way. "I think I might want a second bowl."

"I'm a fairly shit cook, but I have about three solid recipes in my arsenal and that's one of them."

"Are you going to make me the other two someday?"

"I'm sure you could talk me into that. But the spaghetti is my favorite. My mom taught me how to make the sauce when I was a kid."

Kennedy takes her time chewing as she watches me. "She did a good job."

"She was a great teacher."

"She did a good job with you too."

Fuck me.

I've got my handle on snarky Kennedy, shy Kennedy, and even drunk Kennedy, but sweet and honest Kennedy? I'm a goner already.

As I sit facing her, my legs extended in the space between us but bent so as to not take up too much of her space, Kennedy uncrosses hers, slipping her feet between mine. The couch isn't long enough for my tall frame, but I couldn't be happier about having to share it now, the two of us using the armrests as back support to face each other as we eat our midnight dinner.

Her voice is gentle when she says, "If you ever want to tell me about her, you can."

A simple request, that if I *want* to, I can. No expectation. No demand to know more.

I swallow down any unwanted emotions that could be sitting at the back of my throat. "I don't really like talking about her."

Because there's not a world in which I could pretend I'm not still that heartbroken thirteen-year-old boy waiting for his mom to get home, and I don't know how to keep my lighthearted, easy mask on when she's the topic of discussion.

Kennedy's bare foot grazes mine, a smile on those lips I want to kiss again. "Okay."

"Okay."

"The woman knew how to make one hell of a bowl of spaghetti though." Kennedy gestures to her nearly empty dish.

Huffing a laugh, I smile. A rare smile when I'm speaking of my mom.

"It's not that I don't want to tell you about her, Ken, it's just that I miss her. A lot. I've lived more of my life without her than with, and still I haven't stopped missing her."

She drops the bowl to her lap, a grin gracing her lips. It's not a pitying smile, it's a genuine one. "How lucky is she to have two boys who love her as much as you and your brother do. And how lucky are you," Kennedy continues, her knee nudging mine, "to have a mom you love so much you still miss her all these years later."

I've never thought of it that way. I've never looked at the thirteen years I had with her with gratitude. It's always been with anger, that I didn't have enough time.

But I had thirteen years of being loved by a mother when Kennedy has had none.

"Grief seems like a privilege, in a way," she says. "To have loved someone so much that you can't imagine life without them. I've never felt that."

"Not even when you lost your dad?"

She shakes her head, occupying herself by twirling her fork around her remaining noodles. "But I hope one day I'm capable of loving someone that much." Her smile is optimistic as she looks up at me. "Maybe one day, even *I'll* be missed."

My heart sinks at her hopefulness.

Who the fuck has to hope that one day someone will care about them enough that their presence will be missed?

My wife, I guess.

Kennedy's set on leaving Chicago, and I know that when she goes, there won't be a day I won't be missing her. There won't be a day I won't think about her dimples that hide when she scowls at me or her crossword puzzles or the way she bites her bottom lip when she's concentrating at work. But it's not her fault she doesn't understand this yet. She was raised by fucked-up people who didn't teach their daughter how important she is. How special and loved she is.

She wants me to teach her things? Well, that's one lesson I'll be sure to drill into that pretty head of hers.

"Another bowl?" I ask, grabbing hers and standing too quickly.

A sharp pain shoots through my groin and it happens so fast that I can't hide the grimace on my face.

"What's wrong?"

"Nothing." My limp is impossible to mask as I hobble my way to the kitchen.

"Isaiah Rhodes." Kennedy sits up. "What happened?"

Hands bracketed on the counter, I slowly open my hip flexor, stretching out the pained ligaments.

Kennedy stands from the couch when I don't answer, carefully examining my movements. "Did you get hurt in the game tonight?"

Fuck.

She's one of four people I was hoping wouldn't find out.

"When I slid into third base during the fifth inning, I tweaked something in my hip flexor."

"Why didn't you come in for post-game treatment?"

I huff an exasperated laugh. "And have you rub out my groin in public? Wasn't exactly trying to let the boys see just how hard I get for my wife."

"Well, let me check it now."

"No."

"Isaiah, you can't be playing injured. Dr. Fredrick is going to lose his mind that he wasn't informed immediately. You have to tell the medical staff when you're hurt. It's in your contract."

"Well, good news. I just did, but you're not telling anyone else, Ken. It's not a big deal and they're going to make it something, keep me out of games I don't need to miss. It's just a little sore. I'll be fine."

"You could have a tear."

"I don't."

She stands straighter, arms crossed over her chest. "I'll be the judge of that. I need to examine you. Go lay on the couch."

"I don't fit on the couch."

"Well then . . ." Her eyes roam my apartment. "Your bed."

My brows shoot up. "Are you sure about that, Doc?"

She rolls her eyes. "Live, laugh, love, Isaiah. Get your ass on the bed so I can check your injury."

Chuckling, I hobble to my door and open it for her to enter first. I watch the way her eyes scan my bedroom, the same way they did when she first entered my apartment. I track her movements, noting the smile that ticks on her lips when she finds the framed picture of Max on my dresser and the silent laugh she heaves when she lands on the painted canvas of a hot pink unicorn hanging over my bed. The words *I'm Magical* are even spelled out in sparkly silver and the chosen location was thanks to Travis.

"I'm magical? That may as well say 'I'm good at sex,' hanging over your bed like that."

I shrug. "You said it, not me."

Laying on my bed, I keep myself close to the edge where she stands, stretching out my long legs, hands folded behind my head. I'm fully undressed minus the pair of cotton sweatpants that hang low on my hips.

Even though this is work, nothing about this moment feels all that professional. We're in my bedroom, I'm nearly naked, and I've been dying for this woman's hands to be on me in a non-medical way.

"This hip right here?" she asks, referring to my right one, closest to her.

"Yeah. I don't know if it happened when I exploded into a sprint or when I slid into the bag."

Her hands find me, pads of her fingers exploring, smoothing over my entire hip flexor, warming the area and looking for injury.

"Has the pain gotten worse since the game ended or remained about the same?"

"It's stayed about the same."

"Hmm," she hums, that bottom lip tucking between her teeth with her concentration.

Then her fingers dip into the crevice where my leg and abdomen connect, and my body is begging to concave in on itself. Partly from the shock of her hand on me in an area I've always wanted it to be, and partly because of the amount of blood that's rushing to my cock right now is a bit alarming.

"That hurt?"

I shake my head to tell her no and her eyes narrow in suspicion.

Gently, she takes my knee in one hand, other fingers still pressed into my groin, literal inches from my dick. "Tell me when it hurts."

Oh, it hurts all right. It fucking *aches*.

Sure, I've given Kennedy shit for years while I'm on her training table, but I've never actually gotten hard from the woman touching me at work. She's a medical professional and I'm an athlete, but I'm having a real hard time seeing that boundary while I'm sprawled out on my bed, and she's fingers deep into my hip.

She stretches my leg out to the side, fitting herself between it and the mattress before pressing into my groin, examining and circling her fingers over my sweatpants.

This is torture. Fucking torture.

It's like her hands are where I want them, but they're not doing what I need them to do. Similar to the way I'm married to her, but not in the way I wish I could be.

I lift my eyes to the wall above my head, attempting to focus on the fucking unicorn and not on the only woman I think of when I fuck my hand in the shower.

I exhale deep from my lungs.

"Still okay?" Kennedy asks.

"Yep." The word is strained, thrown out through gritted teeth.

My eyes find her again, completely focused on the task at hand as she rotates my joint and presses into my ligaments. "Is the area hot?" she asks.

Is the area hot? *Fucking please*. My entire body is on fire right now.

"Not sure."

"Can I check?" She doesn't look up at me, thank God, her focus remaining on the way my joint reacts when she moves my hip.

"Mm-hmm."

Her small hand slips under the elastic waistband of my sweatpants, fingers sliding along my ligaments.

"Yeah, it's warm."

No shit. All my blood is headed straight in that direction.

Brows furrowed, she gently presses into my flesh. "I think it's just a sprain. Doesn't feel like a tear to me, so that's good. But you need to be on a regular icing regimen to keep the swelling down."

"Yep. Good."

Her hand smooths over the joint, the same time her pinky dusts along my pubic bone, and it's as if that alone causes her to jolt back into reality where her hand is down my pants and I'm practically dying over it.

Her eyes shoot to me in horror. "Oh my God, I'm so sorry! I didn't mean to."

She pulls her hand out from under the fabric, but I snatch her wrist before she can get too far.

My breaths are labored, my eyes boring into hers.

"I wasn't—"

"But you could," I finish for her.

"Isaiah."

"You've diagnosed me. I've got a sprain in my hip flexor. Work is officially over. You were professional and all that shit I don't care about." Gently pulling her by the wrist, I bring her palm to my lower abdomen. "But you don't have to be professional now, if you don't want to be." I cover her hand with mine. "*I* don't want you to be."

18

Kennedy

"What do you want me to do?"

My voice is almost a whisper when Isaiah's fingers lace between mine.

"I want you to do what feels good to you."

If this were any other man, I'd be crippled with embarrassment, but it's Isaiah and for some reason this cocky shortstop with terrible home décor has quickly become the person I trust most.

Do what feels good.

My body is screaming to touch him, to ask him to touch me, but the room is bright, and I'm on full display standing over him like this.

This position right here doesn't feel good.

Pulling my hand away, I watch the instant disappointment take over his face but he quickly catches it and offers me an understanding smile instead.

"How about that second bowl of spaghetti?" he asks, following me to his bedroom door, but when I get there, I don't leave.

I close it with us inside.

This . . . this feels good. Safe. Controlled.

Isaiah stops in his tracks, his mouth parting, his erection straining against his thin sweatpants as he cautiously approaches.

"Kenny?"

I don't answer, flipping the lights off and instantly flooding the room in darkness minus the glowing rubber ducky night-light plugged in next to his bed.

I huff a quiet yet nervous laugh. "Who picked that one out?"

My eyes have adjusted enough to watch him stalk towards me, closing the final steps between us. With my back flush to the door, he presses his palms to it, caging me in on either side.

"Would you believe me if I said it was me?"

"Not a chance."

"Good." He cranes his neck, bending to place a soft kiss on my lips. "Because Zanders put that there."

I smile against his mouth.

"What do you want, Kennedy?"

It's simple, really. I want to feel confident and prepared. I don't want these nerves to be rattling through me the next time I'm in a man's bedroom. But I also have no idea what the steps are to get there other than experience.

Slipping under his arm, I back away towards the other side of the bed, holding eye contact with him while I dip under the covers.

"I want this," I say once fully hidden by both the darkness and the sheets. Then I pull my T-shirt up and over my head, tossing it to the floor.

"*Jesus*," Isaiah exhales from across the room, running a palm over his disbelieving face. "I've always imagined what you might look like right there."

I watch the careful steps he takes to his side of the bed. They're calculated and slow, done in a way that makes me think he's attempting to catalog every moment of this.

He gets under the covers with me, keeping his body to his side, careful not to touch me, with his eyes locked on mine, and not allowing them to drift anywhere else.

It's sweet in a way I never expected Isaiah to be. In the years I've known him, I've categorized him as the impulsive team clown, always doing or saying something ridiculous to earn a laugh from his teammates.

But here, with me, he's . . . patient.

And shirtless.

Why is he always shirtless?

"Kennedy," he whispers, facing me. "I need you to use your words and tell me exactly what you want. Or what you don't want."

"I don't know what I don't want."

"Okay. How about we have a safe word then? Something you can say when you're feeling uncomfortable."

"I don't want a safe word with you. I know I might be uncomfortable, but that's the point of all of this. To get the awkward firsts out of the way."

"Well, I'd feel better if we had one. I don't want to accidentally cross a line you don't want me to cross."

If I'm being honest, at this point, there's not a single thing he could do that I wouldn't want him to. But still he doesn't back down.

"Fine." I lift my chin. "If I have to have a safe word, I guess it'll be 'Mrs. Rhodes.'"

He barks a laugh. "You picked the one thing you'll never say?"

"Yep."

"You're such a fucking brat."

I smile back at him, my head resting on his spare pillow.

"Here's the thing, Ken." Reaching out, he cradles the back of my head, thumb dusting over my jaw. "You're going to have to set the pace because I have craved you here, in my bed, since the day we met, and that need has only gotten worse now that I know you. Regardless of whatever bullshit I said while under the spell that was Chili's, the truth is, I'd fuck you right now if you asked me to. I'd go slow if that's what you wanted. Or I'd make it rough. But I also can't read your mind, so again, I'm going to need you to use your words and set the pace."

Words? He thinks I have words to say after that?

I try to find some. "I want to take it slow."

He nods in agreement. "Then we'll take it slow."

It's not like I'm a virgin. I've had sex, but it hasn't exactly been the kind of sex you read about in books or see romanticized in movies. It's always been straight to the main event and over as soon as he was done.

As a scientist, I tried to justify it to myself—if he finished, at least it was enjoyable enough for him to do so.

But as a woman, I want more.

I just don't know how to say the words without sounding entirely inexperienced, so instead, I take Isaiah's hand that's cupping my jaw and guide him down, his calloused fingers grazing the skin of my throat until I leave him lingering against my sternum.

Looking up, I find his eyes locked on my face, watching me and not letting his attention dip below the sheets just yet.

"Please look at me," I beg.

I want, no—I *need* to know the way it'd feel for Isaiah to look at me.

He inhales sharply, closing his eyes to gather himself and when they open, his pupils are entirely blown out as they trail down my throat and land on my chest, looking at me as if I were the greatest thing he's ever seen.

I've never, not once, been looked at the way my husband looks at me. Wanted. Important. Devastating to his life plans.

His thumb dusts over the freckles of my sternum. "I love these," he whispers, before shifting to skim the lace of my bralette. "And this . . . this looks so fucking good on you, Ken. What color is it? White?"

I swallow down the nerves. "Yellow."

A grin hitches on his lips as his eyes come back up to find mine, that birthmark I'm obsessed with hidden behind a smile line. "My favorite color."

Fuck me. Yes, I knew exactly what I was doing when I picked it out. I knew that he'd ask, and I knew I'd tell him, but now that it's clear I wore this for him, I can feel the heat creeping up my chest.

Apparently, so does he when he spreads his hand to cover my entire décolleté.

"Don't be embarrassed with me, Kenny. You know I'm over here losing my shit that you wore that for me."

My hands are living at my side because I'm awkward and uncomfortable—the good uncomfortable, I guess, where you're pushed out of your comfort zone and grow. But uncomfortable, nonetheless.

"Turn it off," he whispers. "Turn off your brain and do what feels good. It's all just a game, right? You and me, it's all a game, so play along."

This doesn't feel like a game. The way he touches me doesn't feel fake, neither does the way he looks at me—with longing and reverence all at once.

But telling myself Isaiah isn't in my future helps the perfectionist in me. If I can see this as practice for someone else I may meet down the road, I can fumble, mess up, and learn without the debilitating need to be flawless the first time I attempt something.

Even if that something is as simple as fully exploring a man's body for the first time.

"It's hard."

"Fucking tell me about it." His tone is dry. "Hard as a motherfucking rock."

I swat him in the chest. "It's *hard* . . . to turn off my brain sometimes. I tend to overthink. Overanalyze. Over plan."

"I know. I see you, Kenny, even if you haven't been looking at me."

There's a heavy pause, a bit of tension clouding the room. Isaiah may have noticed me years ago, but I never allowed myself to really look until now.

"Come here." The request is so quiet, I almost don't hear it.

We meet in the center of the mattress, where I use his bicep as a pillow, my forehead to his. And for some reason that I still haven't been able to pinpoint, calmness washes over me.

This wild boy who has endless friends, chooses to spend his time with me. He makes me feel centered. He makes me feel *normal*.

He makes me feel like our *arrangement* is normal.

With his palm still flush to my chest, I wrap my hand around his wrist, sliding it down his forearm, over his shoulder and around his back, resting it along his lower spine. My nails trail his skin the whole way.

He hums. "That feels good."

I glide that same hand over his oblique and down to his lower abdomen, where his entire stomach contracts with a sharp breath when I trail my fingertips over the line of hair there.

"Still okay?" I ask, both of us looking down and watching.

"Yeah," he breathes out. "Keep going."

I take my time tracing every crevice on his stomach, smoothing his chest and curving around the back of his neck to pull him in for a kiss.

It starts slow, soft, and sweet. Our mouths take their time exploring one another as we hide under the sheets in his bedroom. He tenderly cups my face, holding me to him, but in no time at all, it heats, kisses turning long and deep. I hum in approval when his tongue touches mine, sweeping in and taking control.

His hands are gentle as they touch me, but his mouth . . . his mouth *takes*.

"I have fucking dreamed about this," he pants against my lips. "About kissing you. About touching you. I don't want it to stop."

So I don't let it.

Lifting my leg, I drape it over his hip and as I do, Isaiah pulls the sheets up to cover us completely.

A weird emotion clogs my throat at that. Because this . . . this feels safe to explore, while the lights are off, and we're hidden under the covers. It feels safe to not be perfect, where no one else but him will see.

Hooking a hand around my ass, he tears his mouth away just in time to look down and watch the moment he pulls my hips into his. His erection is impossible to hide behind the cotton material of his sweats and even more apparent when it presses against my core.

A moan slips from my lips, my back arching when he grazes my clit.

"*Fuck*," he draws out as he watches himself do it again.

I have never, not once, felt so comfortable touching someone the way I touch Isaiah. In fact, I never *have* touched someone the way I touch Isaiah.

"Keep going," he encourages, fingers smoothing any flyaway hairs from my face, thumb gently dusting over my cheekbone.

I languidly trace every dip and curve of his chest and stomach as he patiently watches, holding himself back and giving me room to explore.

"Feels so good, Kenny."

It's the confidence I need to keep going, keep touching.

I study the way his eyes shut as my palms cover the expanse of his back. The way his nostrils flare with each exhale as I discover the ropes of his arms. The way his breath hitches as my fingertips trail back down to trace the V that dips into his sweats.

I have this aching need to touch him everywhere, this beautiful boy who used to drive me insane.

Pushing my hips, I roll my body into him and watch his Adam's apple protrude with his deep swallow.

I lean over and press my lips to it.

"Jesus, Kenny, do that again and I'm going to come in my fucking sweatpants like some kind of pent-up teenager."

I smile against his skin.

His entire body shivers against me, his breathing turning shallow as I trace a forefinger along the line of the V that dips down to his cock.

"Touch it," he commands. "Fucking hell, Kennedy, please just touch it."

Wow, this arrogant man sounds fantastic when he begs.

I do as he asks, dipping a hand under the waistband. My fingers trace over his warm skin, over his taut muscles and protruding veins, dusting over the hair there, before sliding down and grazing the soft skin of his erection.

Isaiah grits through his teeth, every muscle in his body firing as his fingers dig into my thigh that's draped around him. "Please," he begs. "Please wrap your hand around it."

"You're very polite when you want something."

His chuckle is dark. "Oh baby, I told you already. I'm a good boy, especially when I want something."

I circle his width with my hand, the pad of my thumb smoothing over his crown to gather a bead of moisture.

"And that . . ." He whimpers against my neck, the desperate sound sending a pulse straight to my clit. "That is what I want most."

I didn't know I could have this effect on someone. On *him*.

The man is experienced, and this is just a little touching, a little exploring.

"Your hand," he grits out. "Goddamn, I've been dreaming of it, Kenny. Of your mouth. Of your fucking pussy. I bet it's as perfect as the rest of you, isn't it?"

Isaiah thrusts into my hand, looking for friction, and it's when he runs his entire length through my fist that I feel exactly what kind of size he's working with.

Jesus.

"Does that feel good?"

"Shut up," he laughs, his voice strained as he desperately pushes into my hand again. "I'm hard as a fucking rock for you and you know it. You can feel it."

My cheeks burn, but I can't seem to stop myself from telling him, "I've never really had the opportunity to ask, so I just want to make sure I'm doing what you like."

He halts his movements, holding his hips steady, but doesn't ask any probing, embarrassing questions. Lifting his head away from my shoulder, he looks at me, those curious brown eyes watching and reading, but not in a way that makes me feel silly or inexperienced.

"I've never really talked this kind of stuff through," I continue. "Never had someone I could communicate with."

"Well, you're fucking perfect on your first go, Kenny." He meets my hand in pace. "Of course you are."

"But tell me what I can do to make it better for you. I want to learn."

He shakes his head, chuckling at me because I can't help but want to be the best. And yes, apparently that means at giving hand jobs too.

"You could grip a little tighter if you want."

I do exactly that. "What else?"

"I like it when you give the head a little attention."

I circle my thumb again, spreading the moisture over the tip before coating my fist in it and running it down his shaft.

"Mmm," he moans. "That's it, baby."

Isaiah's body is tense, his breathing shallow. He sounds like he's close, but it's far too soon. I don't want this to end just yet.

As much as I love touching him, I want *him* to touch *me*.

Reading my mind, he throws his hand over mine to stop me. "I'm going to come too fast, and I really need to make you feel as good as you're making me." His lips softly meet mine. "Can I make you feel good, Kenny?"

My answer is a far too eager head nod matched by his soft eyes and boyish smile as I remove my hand from his sweatpants.

He cups my ass, pulling me flush to him. His fingers toy with the seam of my leggings, achingly close to the spot I need them most, as his lips trail down my throat, my collarbone, my chest, tongue darting out to lick over the fabric of my bralette.

"Oh," I exhale when his tongue flicks over the lace, creating this delicious friction on my stiff nipple. "Okay, I like that."

His silent chuckle rumbles against me as he does it again, this time closing his mouth over the peak.

Fuck.

"These need to go." He snaps the elastic material against my skin before slipping a hand under the waistband, curving over my ass, squeezing me in his palm.

My body freezes with a moment of hesitation.

He rolls me onto my back, licking and kissing a path down my stomach. "Tell me to stop, Ken."

"No."

He grins against me as he pulls my leggings down in a motion so fluid that it impresses even me. Sitting back on his haunches, he clears them from my ankles and tosses them to the floor.

"Same color." His attention immediately snags on my matching thong, stroking a thumb over the elastic band.

Yes. Yes, it is.

And now it's as clear to him as it is to me that I had a plan when I came over.

Did I want to end up here when I knocked on his door tonight? Yes.

Was I perfectly okay if we kept our clothes on and ate spaghetti on his couch if it meant I just got to hang out with him? Also, yes.

Which feels like a problem.

One I can't think about or diagnose because I'm currently distracted by the giant baseball player laying hot kisses along my stomach as he crawls back up my body, his erection thick and hard against the inside of my thigh.

"You still okay?"

It's sweet, it is. It's all so *fucking* sweet, but even though Isaiah is being so good, so patient with me, part of the reason I knew he was the right man for this job was his experience. I don't need him to treat me like a fragile bird who might break. I need him to treat me like a woman he can't get enough of.

I gently run my palm down his face. "We should stop being so fucking polite, don't you think?"

"Well, it's either that or me ruining you for all other men, so it's your choice, wifey."

"Is that so?" I chuckle.

"You're the one who wants to date after this. I'm trying to make that possible for you to do so."

"That sounds like some awfully high expectations you're putting on yourself."

His laugh is a little bit evil when he flips us, leaving me straddling him in only my bralette and thong. He pulls at my hair tie to let my hair drop down my back.

"You wanna play, Kenny? Let's fucking play."

He smooths his hands over my thighs, gripping my hips and gliding me to rock over his erection.

"Mmm," I moan. "Do that again."

"You do it." He crosses his arms behind his head, an arrogant smile on his lips. "Fuck yourself on me, Ken. Show me what you can do."

My skin flushes with heat and prickles with anxiety. *He's* supposed to be the one in control, showing *me*, teaching *me*.

But my body's natural inclination is to roll my hips and find friction, so I do just that, rolling my entire core over the length of his cock, and it feels fucking *incredible*.

I drop my hands to anchor on his chest, slowly writhing on him. His sweatpants are light enough that I know, I *know* he's going to be able to see just how wet I am. He's going to be able to see just how much I *don't* hate him.

But I don't care because everything feels so good with him.

So easy. So comfortable.

"God, look at you. So fucking beautiful, rubbing your pussy all over me. Are you going to come like this, Kenny?"

"I think so," I choke out, rhythmically sliding my clit over the head of his erection.

"Yes, you are. It feels so fucking good. You're making me so fucking hard. Don't stop until you come. I need to see it."

I can see his arm muscles tightening, fighting to stay behind his head. But I don't want them back there. I want them all over me.

"Isaiah?" My fingernails dig into his pecs. "Will you help me finish?"

His swollen cock pulses beneath me, his eyes closing, as if he needs to try to control himself.

"When have I ever been able to say no to you?"

It's the same question he asked the morning after we said some drunken vows. This time with a little less bite and a whole lot more struggle through hard-earned breaths.

His hands find my waist before curling around my back, smoothly running up and down the length of my spine. "I . . ." He shakes his head. "I cannot believe you're here. I feel so fucking lucky." He palms my breasts, thumbs tracing circles over my peaked nipples, under the lace of my bralette. "And these . . . these are fucking perfect."

My boobs? No, they're not. Far from perfect, in fact. Fairly small and uneven, but goddamn do they look perfect in his hands.

Isaiah sits up with me in his lap, bringing his mouth to mine for a quick kiss. Then he whispers in my ear while his hands slide around to my ass, pushing and pulling, guiding me to rock over him.

"I have never ever been more turned on than I am by you, Kennedy Kay. By this little matching set you wore for me. By your fucking hair bouncing down your back every time you writhe on my cock, and I have never, *never* been more turned on than I am right now, knowing you're going to come all over me, and I haven't even had the pleasure of properly touching you yet."

He drags his hands down my outer thighs.

He whispers more encouragement as we both look down to watch me move over him. "That's it. You're doing so good for me, Kenny. God, that feels fucking amazing."

Isaiah lays back down, his back to the bed. With his palms bracketing my thighs, I brace my hands on his forearms.

The pressure in my lower belly builds fast and heady, ready to spill over. It's so close, *I'm* so close. Which has me thinking, why have I never come so easily with someone before? What did I do wrong that I'm doing right this time? Why is it as simple as dry humping this frustratingly charming man?

Why am I in my head right now and why is my impending orgasm leaving me because of it?

A desperate whimper escapes me when the pressure begins to dissolve. I fight to keep it, but my muscles refuse, uncoiling themselves, my breathing evening out as the momentum fades.

"No," Isaiah refuses. "Give me one. I need one from you. I need to see it."

His thumb swipes over my panties, right over my clit.

He rubs softs circles there and my hips follow the pattern, the pressure slowly building its way back again.

"Yes," I hiss through my teeth. "Help me."

Isaiah slips a single index finger into my thong, right where it narrows, his knuckle grazing the skin just above where I need him touching me most. The moment I'm convinced he's going to push the fabric out of the way, give himself easier access, he hooks his finger, looping the material and giving himself something to hold on to. Something to guide me.

He pulls my panties towards him, subsequently pulling me, the lace taut and causing delicious friction over my clit.

"Oh my God." My head falls back from the sensation.

It feels fucking euphoric, having him under me, his finger so close in combination with the rough fabric on my overly sensitive skin.

He moves me, rocks me over his sweatpants, pushing and pulling me by his single finger hooked into my thong.

Like a fucking rein.

And I follow his direction willingly.

"You're doing so good, baby, fucking yourself on me." He can hardly get the words out through his ragged breaths. "Use me."

And I do, I roll and writhe and grind over his length until the pressure boils, spilling over, and my entire body contracts in a blinding orgasm. My eyes are desperate to shut, the release almost unbearable, but I can't close them. I can't help but watch the man below me as he watches me, looking at me like he can't believe he's seeing me come.

He touches me through it, softly running his hands over my thighs, my stomach, my breasts. He's soothing and patient as I come down, slumping my entire spent body on his chest.

He holds me. He fucking holds me post-orgasm.

I've literally never been held once in my life and now, while riding a high, I've got this man's arms around me and holding me as if he couldn't bear to let me leave.

And I have to remind myself it's not the time to get emotional about it.

One day, someone else will see me this way too. I can only hope.

I tuck my face into the crook of his neck as he strokes my hair and wraps a heavy arm around my back, keeping me tight to him.

"You are . . ." He kisses my temple. ". . . the most beautiful woman I have ever seen, and I will die a very happy man after getting to witness that."

"I don't think I've ever come like that."

"Yeah? Just wait until I get to use my fingers or my mouth on you. *Fuck*, I'm going to come just thinking about it."

I chuckle against him, rolling out of his arms and onto my back.

We're both glistening with a bit of sweat, me from exertion and him from holding himself back. But we lie there, catching our breaths next to one another.

He extends his leg, sprawling out, and that's when I see it. The wet spot on his pants I knew I was leaving in my wake, as well as his very hard, very present erection that hasn't been taken care of yet.

His hand slips under his waistband, pumping and tugging, and I'm mesmerized by the way his hand moves, the way his forearm bulges.

"I've got to hit the bathroom real quick. Be right back. Don't you dare leave, or I will find out where you live and drag you back to my bed."

"I feel like you probably already know where I live."

The naughty smirk he shoots me screams that he absolutely does.

"Stalker."

"Miller had to drop something off at your apartment around Christmas and I may have begged to tag along so I could see you. She told me if I came I had to stay in the car though."

I chuckle. "It was winter in Chicago and you still decided to go with her?"

"It was the off-season. I was desperate to see you."

He says it as if it's not the most obvious statement, before sitting up on the edge of the bed to go to the bathroom.

"Wait." I grab his arm. "Finish here. I want to watch."

His brow lifts as he looks at me over his shoulder. "Are you going to help me?"

I'm positive my cheeks are crimson red, but still I nod against the pillow.

Isaiah keeps his attention locked on me as he stands from the bed. Big and tall and proud, he runs a single hand through his hair before using the other to wipe across the spot I left on his pants then dipping his hand into his waistband and using it to coat himself.

Holy shit.

My mouth falls open in shock, while this man stands completely unashamed and unaffected by my reaction.

He pumps himself, his big hand moving along his shaft, but hidden behind the fabric of his pants.

God, I want to see it.

"How are you going to help me with this problem, Ken?"

"I . . . um . . . however you want me to?"

He licks his bottom lip. "Are you going to take me in that smart mouth of yours? Suck me off until I'm coming down that pretty throat?"

Oh.

I hesitate. An obvious hesitation because I'm not sure I'm ready to go there tonight. I'm not prepared. The only blow jobs I've ever given were all to the same man, who told me they weren't very good. I don't ever want to be told that again, and I know Isaiah will walk me through it if I ask him to, I just wasn't expecting to have to ask him tonight.

My voice is small. "I can do that."

He hesitates just as long as I did. "Next time." Pushing his sweats down, he lets them drop to the floor. "Tonight, I want your hand around me."

It's the first time all night that I'm mad at myself for turning off the lights because I want to see him properly. In all his glory. I felt his cock in my hand. I literally dry humped the man. I knew he was big, I could feel it, but I didn't realize he was this . . . *blessed.*

Thick but not in an ungodly way, and long, but proportionate to him. The man is 6'4", big hands, big feet, and a big, pretty dick. Pretty as the rest of him. So pretty, in fact, that I have to remind myself I'm going to have to keep my expectations low after him.

"You like my cock, Ken?"

"I'm not answering that. Your ego is already big enough."

"Mmm," he hums. *"Big* was the first adjective on your mind, huh? Wonder why."

I huff a laugh.

"Eyes are up here, Kennedy."

I keep my attention locked on his stroking hand, on the head that's red and leaking, on the angry veins running down his length.

"I, and I can't begin to express this enough, don't give a fuck where your eyes are at."

"Oh, I get it," he chuckles as he crawls onto the bed. "I'm just your sex doll now. Only here for your pleasure."

"Exactly."

He opens my legs, fitting his naked body to lay on top of me. "That sounds like my dream job, to be honest. If I knew the position was open, I would've applied for it years ago." Placing a soft kiss on my smiling lips, he takes my hand and guides it to wrap around his shaft. "Now be a good little wife and make me come."

He moves, slowly thrusting into my waiting hand just as he did earlier tonight, only this time there's no clothing in the way to keep me from watching.

His body is flush to mine, so not only do I get to feel him throbbing in my hand, but his cock also grazes against my wet panties with every pass.

It feels incredible.

I'm still so sensitive and he's so hard, and holy hell everything just feels so good.

"Fuck," he breathes as I pump him in my fist. "I'm not going to last long."

He laces his fingers through my free hand, pinning mine to the mattress as he circles the pad of his ring finger over my wedding band, the way he tends to do when holding my left.

With his other hand, he desperately grips the bars of his headboard above my head.

I stroke him to the tip, gathering his precum and using it to coat his shaft.

"Yes, Kennedy. You're doing so good. Just like that."

I continue that motion before switching it up and giving more attention to the head, the way he told me he liked it earlier, keeping my fist tight and my pumps short and shallow.

"Yes," he pants. "Yes. Yes. Please. Please don't stop."

I don't. I meet his pace as he rocks into me, using my hand to fuck himself.

He looks like he's fucking *me*, with my legs open around him, his cock thrusting against my core. God, I just know he'll be good at it.

His movements grow sloppy, his hips jerky as he nears his release, and he comes at the exact moment I run my thumb over his slit before dragging it down the protruding vein on the underside of his crown.

"Oh *fuck*," he curses as he finds his release on my stomach, coating me in him.

I don't stop working my hand. I continue to stroke him, up and down, wanting every ounce he has to give me.

God, he's mesmerizing like this. Desperately clinging to me, and I can't believe *I* was able to do that to him.

His face drops into my neck, panting and whimpering against my skin. "So good. You did so good. *You're* so good," he continues on repeat like some kind of post-orgasm praise chant.

It works. My ego is currently through the fucking roof.

"You're okay with that?" he asks.

"I'm perfect."

"I know." He kisses my throat. "I've been trying to tell you."

He keeps his naked body on me for some time, breathing me in, snuggling close. I stroke his back, toy with the ends of his hair and hold him to me because I have *never* felt so comfortable with another person.

The heated moment slows to something soft and sweet as we lay together.

He dots warm kisses up across my jaw as he speaks. "As much as I would love for you to walk around for the rest of your life with my cum dripping all over you, I need to clean you up."

Isaiah lifts his giant body off of me, before grabbing a fresh pair of sweatpants and jogging to the bathroom.

He, of course, still doesn't go for a shirt.

The water runs while he whistles, and I lay on the bed covered in him, stupid goddamn smile on my face and wondering what the hell just happened.

It's what I asked for—a lesson in intimacy, but what the hell was that? Is that what I've been missing out on all these years? That was just *foreplay*.

He might very well be right. He might ruin me for any man after him and I can't allow that to happen because all of this is temporary. All of this is *practice* for what comes after.

Isaiah quickly returns with that boyish smile and a damp towel in his hand.

"I can do it," I tell him, sitting up and reaching for the cloth.

"Good for you." He holds it out of my reach. "Now move your greedy little hands and let me clean you up before I wrap them around my cock and we do this all over again."

"Jesus." I startle with a laugh.

He cleans himself off me, the towel warm to the touch. He takes his time, his fingers soothing over my skin with every pass of the washcloth.

It's sweet and kind and gentle. Three words I now associate with this man when once, I could only think of him as cocky, impulsive, and childish.

"Kennedy." His voice shakes as if he were nervous, keeping his eyes on my stomach as he cleans me up. "Do you think that maybe you would sta—"

The sound of a lock unbolting stops his sentence short. Our eyes shoot to each other, keeping quiet to hear his apartment door open and shut.

Footsteps and keys rattling.

Someone is in his apartment. More footsteps. More people.

"Please ignore the home décor," the male intruder says. "It was my grandmother's, but I miss her so much that I just had to keep it all up for sentimental value."

"That's sweet," another voice says—a female voice.

"Yeah." Followed by a heavy sigh. "She meant the world to me."

Cody. That voice belongs to Cody.

Isaiah's eyes go wide as he stands from the bed. "I'm going to fucking kill him."

He makes it to the door before turning around and jogging back to me to place a quick kiss on my lips.

"Don't." He holds his hands out as if to say he wants everything to stay exactly as is. "Don't leave, okay?"

I can't help but allow my laugh to break free when he storms out of the room, making sure to close his bedroom door behind him, leaving my almost naked self safely inside.

There are voices. Lots of voices. Three, maybe four people. I think one of them is Travis. And the last one has a slight Boston accent.

I take the opportunity to redress, throwing on my T-shirt and slipping on my leggings because I know what Isaiah was going to ask me. He wants me to stay the night, but I need some space. A moment to register what just happened as practice not reality.

There are some passionate words exchanged in the living room. A few "fuck you"s followed by so much drunken laughter.

"Wait, please don't go," Cody pleads. "We can go to my real apartment!"

A door slams, followed by it reopening and Isaiah yelling, "His grandmother is alive and well, by the way! She lives in Jersey!"

I open the bedroom door to find Isaiah's head sticking out in the hallway, those words directed at the girl Cody brought back here and Isaiah ran off.

"Well, that was a bust." Cody tosses his hands up. "Can I crash here at least? Oh my God, you made spaghetti. This is why we're best friends!"

Cody, Travis, and Rio—one of the defensemen for the Chicago Raptors, Chicago's NHL team—gather around the bowl of leftover pasta.

"You can call a rideshare and take that whole bowl with you, but you all need to leave."

Rio's mouth is full when he turns around in confusion. "Why?"

"Where the hell did you come from, Rio?"

"I ran into them at the bar. Saw Cody trying to get some girl to go home with him. Well, to your place, and I had to hear what the fuck he was going to say to excuse these god-awful signs. You still got the one I bought you for the bathroom? Hello, sweet cheeks!" He catches me out of the corner of his eye. "Oh. I meant . . . the sign says. I'm sure your cheeks are sweet too, Kennedy, but I was referring to the sign."

Isaiah shakes his head, listening to his drunk friend spew nonsense. "Shut your fucking mouth. No need for you to be thinking about my wife's cheeks in any capacity."

"Yep." Rio motions as if he were zipping his mouth shut. "Not doing that."

Cody turns away from the spaghetti, knowing grin on his mouth as his gaze ping-pongs between his best friend and me. "*Hello*, Mrs. Rhodes."

I lift a single finger in protest, but my bite feels less sharp than usual. "Watch it."

"Kennedy!" Travis's hands go wide, his mouth full and ringed in red sauce. "This is the best night ever."

"Some girl made out with him on the dance floor," Cody explains.

"Good for you, Trav!"

Isaiah shoots me a deadpanned glare, mouthing, *don't encourage them*, from across the room.

"I'm ... *We're*"—Cody motions to the three of them—"going to leave."

Isaiah opens the door without hesitation. "That would be best."

"Actually," I interrupt, gathering my shoes, hat, and jacket that are scattered around his living room. "I need to go home anyway. Early flight tomorrow."

"But—" Isaiah's brows are cinched in confusion as I slip on my sneakers.

"Good to see you, Rio." I hold my hand up in a wave. "Cody, Trav, good game tonight."

I can feel Isaiah's stare following me to the door. Once in the hallway, I slowly turn to him, unsure of what to say.

Thanks for the lesson? Thanks for the orgasm? Can you teach me how to give a proper blow job next time?

He blocks the doorway, keeping his friends out of the conversation, brown eyes soft and pleading. "I want you to stay."

"I know."

"But you won't? Even if they left?"

Shaking my head, I tell him no.

I expect an argument, him pushing me to do something I'm not ready to do, but instead, he relents. "Can I at least drive you home?"

A smile ticks on my lips. "I've got it from here."

"All right." He exhales a defeated sigh before the typically happy Isaiah comes back. "And what about me?" he asks, crossing his arms and leaning into the doorway. "Did I have a good game tonight?"

The insinuation in his tone screams that he's not referring to baseball.

"I think we had a great game tonight."

He chuckles, leaning down and placing a soft kiss on my lips. "I think we did too."

19

Kennedy

"One of our old travel coordinators, Josh, is working for San Francisco now," Dean says. "I asked him to see if he could get any insight on your upcoming interview and from what he's heard around the clubhouse, you're their top candidate."

I sit up straighter while in my parked car, phone to my ear and my stepbrother on the other end. "Wait. Really?"

"Yeah. Apparently at this stage, there's only three people left being interviewed. Things are looking good. You should be stoked, Kennedy."

"Well, yeah, I want to be excited about it, but after what happened on my first day in Chicago when I had my offer rescinded, I won't believe anything until my name is on the door of my very own office."

An office I'll be sure to use less frequently than our current head doctor does. I'll be continuing to practice sports medicine, not just telling everyone else how to.

"I told Josh to put in a good word for you. You should hit him up when you're out there for your interview. He's cool. Divorced. Mid-thirties. He's got shit fashion taste, but I think you could fix that for him."

"Dean," I huff a laugh. "What are you talking about? I'm married."

Whoa. Why the hell did I say that? Why the hell did I *think* that?

"Yeah ..." he slowly draws out in confusion. "But you won't be once you're living out there. Josh is a good dude. I think you'll like him. You should let him show you around the clubhouse while you're visiting."

I sink back, head relaxing against the seat. "Yeah. Yeah, you're right. I'll give him a call when I'm in town."

Keeping my eyes scanning the players' parking lot at O'Hare International, I watch for Isaiah's car to pull in.

"I'm counting down the days until you get that job and can finally serve that fucking tool divorce papers."

"Dean," I startle. "Don't talk about him that way."

"Kennedy," he laughs incredulously. "How many times have you talked shit about Isaiah Rhodes in the past?"

"Yeah, well, he's my husband. I can talk shit all I want, but it doesn't mean you can."

"Jesus. You're sensitive today."

"I'm not being sensitive. I'm just over your weird hatred of the guy. You don't even know him. What did he ever do to you?"

"He's just . . ." Dean hesitates. "I just don't like the guy. He and his brother are . . ."

"Good to each other?" I finish for him. "Is that your problem? That they only had one another and still have a better family situation than us?"

He exhales on the other end of the line. "Why are we even talking about this? It doesn't fucking matter."

"It matters to me. He's currently in my life and you're my stepbrother. It'd be nice if you two were cordial with one another."

"Key word here being *currently*. Let's *not* have this conversation and once you two legally split, we can just pretend this never happened."

That was my plan when I agreed to this whole thing, only now, I don't know how I'm supposed to forget any of this ever happened.

I sure as hell won't be able to forget about last night.

Speaking of the man I'm married to, Isaiah pulls up, parking his SUV right in front of mine, his boyish smile glowing through the windshield when he catches me waiting for him.

"Speaking of he who shall not be named." I gather my keys and slip on my sunglasses before opening the driver's side door. "He's here. I've got to go."

"Remind him how much I hate him for me, will you?"

"And you think *I'm* being sensitive today? The guy is living rent free in your head. I'll talk to you when you're being less of an asshole."

I hang up the phone and slip out of the car.

My stomach dips when I see Isaiah, an odd fluttering that makes me feel equal parts sick and excited. The memory of the way he moved in my hand, the way he panted my name low in my ear last night as he came, is all I can think about as he rounds the hood of his car and meets me by the door of mine.

"There's the old ball and chain."

"That's a new one."

"We've been married for over a month now. I figured with the short lifespan on this whole marriage thing, it's probably time we move out of the newlywed phase."

He's got this knowing smile on his lips, this goofy sparkle in his eye that screams he's giving me a hard time. But the reminder causes my chest to sting, as if I didn't know there was an end date to this whole thing. As if *I* wasn't the one who set it.

"Sorry I'm late." With an arm over my shoulders, he pulls me in for a hug, pressing his lips to the top of my head in the most casual way. As if we've done this all along. As if we'll do this forever. "I had to swing by the market on the corner of my block. I wasn't sure if you'd have enough time to grab one of these this morning, seeing as you had yourself a late night and all."

He pumps his brows a couple of times like a fucking dork before unfolding the newspaper under his arm and handing me today's issue of *The New York Times*.

"I heard Saturdays are the hardest, so you just let me know if you need some help with that."

I huff a laugh, but it's a choked, watery laugh because this is insanely sweet of him to do, to think of me without begging him to.

"Have you ever even completed a crossword puzzle?" I ask, instead of gushing about how grateful I am.

"Nah. I'm more of a word search guy myself."

Popping my trunk, he pulls my bag out of the back, dragging both of ours behind him as we head through the private airport terminal, past security, and out towards the team plane on the tarmac.

This has been our routine since the season started. We meet in the parking lot and walk on board together. Reese has yet to beat us to the plane, but we haven't wanted to risk showing up separately and opening ourselves up to questions.

"Isaiah," I begin, as he passes our luggage off to one of the line guys to place in the pit of the plane. "Why do you and Dean hate each other so much?"

"I think it's best if you get that answer from Dean himself."

"I tried. He won't tell me what happened."

Isaiah huffs a laugh. "Of course he doesn't want to tell you. Guy's a fucking tool, but as much as I can't stand him, you care about him, so I won't be the one to try to change your opinion of your brother."

At the base of the stairs, I pause, looking up at him. "I wish you would tell me, but okay."

"Okay."

With a soft squeeze to the back of my neck, Isaiah motions up the stairs for me to go first. We're here a bit later than we typically try to arrive at the plane, and when I turn the corner and face the aisle, ninety percent of the seats are already full.

Thankfully, we have somewhat assigned seating, especially for the staff up front, so my empty seat is waiting for me next to Sanderson.

Monty and his staff sit in the first row, followed by team ownership where . . . *Fuck.*

Reese is already on board, sitting in the third row. Tailored pencil skirt, high heels, and blonde hair that's perfectly styled. She smiles at me, but there's a bit of confusion etched between her brows as she looks around, I'd assume for Isaiah—my husband. Who I should've arrived with. Because we live in the same apartment. Because we're happily married.

I freeze in my spot, right there in the front of the plane with eyes on me, when Isaiah barrels around the corner and right into my back.

"Shit, Kennedy." His arm flies around my waist from behind to keep me steady. "I almost took you out. What are you waiting for?"

His thumb strokes over my hip bone where his hand has yet to release me.

Good. This looks good.

I don't move and he must sense my nervousness because he drops his hand immediately.

But I'm not nervous about him touching me. I'm very quickly becoming comfortable with his touch. Quickly *craving* his touch.

So I turn, trying to convey with my eyes that Reese is here, we're being watched, and *that's* what I'm nervous about. So if he could play along right now, that'd be great, but Isaiah doesn't catch on to any of it.

"What's wrong?" he asks loudly enough for the first few rows to hear him. "Are you feeling okay?"

Boys, I tell you. Clueless sometimes.

I take control of the situation, slipping my hand in his, lacing our fingers together right there in front of the entire team and staff.

Isaiah softens, his mouth turning up in a smile as he looks down at me. His thumb dusts over the back of my hand before he brings it to his lips, placing a quick kiss there. "Hi," he says before placing another one.

It's sweet, sure, but this is all for show and I'm not sure he's picking up on that.

I watch as his eyes move from my face to the people around us. Watch the moment he finds Reese tracking us from the third row. Watch as his smile falls at the realization of what this moment actually is.

His eyes bounce around the cabin as he puts the pieces together, and I can visibly see the second it hits him. He looks devastated, as if he thought I was holding his hand because I wanted to and not because others needed to see it.

It's not that I *don't* want to, but that's just not what this is.

Isaiah clears his throat, pulls his eyes away from everyone else and with my hand in his, he leads me to my seat.

I slip into the spot next to Sanderson and in the most un-Isaiah-like way, he doesn't even acknowledge my coworker to my side.

Isaiah always acknowledges the staff, whether it be here on the plane, or at the field, or even at a team party.

But today, he doesn't speak to anyone. He simply places a quick kiss on my cheek, obviously done for onlookers, and leaves me at my seat before taking off for the back of the plane.

I catch Dr. Fredrick roll his eyes in my periphery.

"Is Rhodes okay?" Sanderson quietly asks from beside me.

"I'm not sure, actually."

Slipping my headphones on, I pull out my phone to find out, but it takes a moment to find Isaiah's name.

Because he changed his contact info.

Me: *Did you steal my phone last night and change your contact name?*
World's Best Husband: *I have literally no idea what you're talking about.*
Me: *Is everything okay?*
World's Best Husband: *Yep.*

Lie.

Me: *What's wrong?*
World's Best Husband: *Nothing. Just forgot what we were doing for a minute. All good now. I remember.*
Me: *You seemed upset.*
World's Best Husband: *Everything is all good. It always is.*
Me: *Isaiah.*
World's Best Husband: *Just tired. Late night if you remember correctly ;) Gonna sleep for the flight. See you there.*

A boom of thunder vibrates our hotel room, and if I hadn't already been lying awake, the sound would've jolted me out of sleep.

There's no rain to accompany the summer storm, only loud rumbles and bright flashes of light, but it's kind of beautiful to watch from the safety of inside as the lightning illuminates the Minneapolis skyline.

Isaiah is only feet away, on the floor while I'm in the comfort of this king-sized bed, and still I can't find rest.

I have no clue why he's still down there. After last night, I don't know, I thought sleeping in the same bed was a given. I told him he could sleep up here if he wanted to, but he refused, and I have no idea what I could say that would make him change his mind.

My mind still isn't clear, still hasn't fully categorized last night as practice. Maybe he knows that. Maybe he knows I'm not ready for more because I'm still reeling over the fact that Isaiah made me come by simply grinding me over his body.

What the hell am I doing?

Kicking one leg out from under the covers, I flip onto my back as another flash of lightning explodes outside, brightening the space just enough for me to find Isaiah up on his feet and pacing the room.

That's weird. I could've sworn from how quiet our room is that he's been sleeping through the storm. I never heard him get up.

The thunder crashes again and I watch as his entire body flinches from the sound. His eyes screw shut and his lips tremble with a shaky exhale.

I don't speak. I don't make it known that I'm awake and can see him now that my eyes have adjusted to the darkness.

I simply watch.

His perfectly disheveled hair. His shirtless chest, expanding and contracting at an alarming rate. His bare feet carrying him around the room silently.

Isaiah hovers his thumb over his phone screen before deciding against pressing it. He drops his arm back to his side as he continues to walk, wearing down the carpet by the door, but when another bolt of lightning lands, he doesn't hesitate to lift his phone and make a call.

Isaiah's free hand clenches and releases. He bounces on the balls of his feet, his nervous energy palpable even from the bed where I watch.

"Did I wake you up?" His voice is a whisper, his eyes closing in relief at the sound of whomever is on the other line.

There's an uneasy pit in my stomach, both from seeing this confident man so frazzled and knowing he called someone to calm him down.

That part isn't jealousy, though. Definitely not jealousy.

"Are you in your hotel room?"

Hotel room? This hotel?

A flash of Connor runs through my mind. How many times did he run off to my stepsister when he thought I was asleep? When we were at family functions, did he slip away to Mallory's room in the middle of the night?

Is that what Isaiah is doing? Planning to slip into someone's else's room?

"And you're not going anywhere?" he continues. "Yes, I know it's the middle of the night, Kai, but you're not leaving your room, right?"

Kai.

An embarrassing amount of relief floods me.

"And Max and Miller? I don't know what the weather is like in Chicago right now." He pauses, listening. "Okay, and Monty, he's passed out, right? Not driving anywhere either." Nodding, he stops pacing, listening to his brother talk on the other end. "Yeah, Kennedy is here. She's asleep. I'll be all right. I still need to check in on Travis and Cody. Okay. Can you text me after you talk to them? Yeah. Yeah, I know. Logically, I know that, Kai, but I'm not thinking rationally at the moment." Another pause. "Thanks, man. I love you too. See you in the morning."

He hangs up at the same time he hangs his head, breaths coming a bit more even now.

What the hell is going on?

Isaiah turns in my direction, and I'm quick to close my eyes before he catches me staring. Moments later, the floor creaks and the bed dips. I cautiously peek an eye open to find him sitting on the edge of the mattress, elbows to his knees and back to me.

"What the fuck is wrong with me?" he mutters under his breath.

I watch his back, the way his muscles strain with tension. He runs a palm over his head, pushing his hair away from his face before dropping back down to lean on his elbows. He stays like that for a while. Not moving. Just sitting.

I wish he'd crawl back here, maybe realize I'm awake and tell me what's going on. But there's a bigger part of me that hopes he doesn't, because what am I going to do to help? I've never been someone's comfort. I'm cold, that's what Connor always said. I have no idea how to be what Isaiah needs.

I don't want to be cold with him. I just don't know how to be anything else. He makes me feel vulnerable, like he can see all of me when no one else has even tried to look.

Isaiah's phone dings with a text. He reads it, lets out another sigh of relief, then tosses it to the ground where his makeshift bed is.

Once again, he turns to look back at me, but this time he's not looking for my face. He finds my leg that's untucked from the covers, reaching over and settling his palm over my ankle, gently rubbing his thumb over the bone.

He seems a bit more settled and when another boom of thunder rattles the room, this time, Isaiah doesn't flinch.

Ironic, in a way. I tend to recoil from physical contact, but it's what keeps him from doing the same.

He stays there, holding my leg for a moment before giving it a gentle squeeze and leaving the mattress, dropping himself back to his bed on the floor.

I don't want him to go. I think I want him to stay. I want him to be okay. I want to be the one to make *sure* he's okay. Yeah, that seems like something that someone in a relationship would do. It'd be a good learning lesson if I felt the need to spin it to myself that way.

But the truth is, I don't care about learning how to comfort anyone else. I just want to comfort *him*.

Another boom of thunder rattles the room, and the subsequent sound is the ruffle of blankets—Isaiah adjusting on the floor.

I'm off the bed before I can think twice about it.

I find him with his arms folded tightly over his chest, back flush to the bed frame.

"Kenny," he whispers when he finds me, as if there's someone in this room who is actually sleeping, and he needs to remain quiet. "Why are you awake?"

"Couldn't sleep."

He quickly sits up, as I stand by his feet. "Are you okay?"

"Are you?"

His concern melts away, his voice even softer as his attention drops. "I didn't mean to wake you."

"What's going on?"

He shakes his head before falling back to lay on the single pillow positioned on the floor. "It's late, Kennedy. Get some sleep. Please." Turning his back to the bed frame again, he faces the wall.

I can do this. My instincts are screaming to lay down there next to him.

Do what feels good.

Isaiah's words are echoing in my ears as I crawl into two feet of space between him and the wall, angling my body to face him.

"Fuck, Ken. I don't want you on the floor."

"You're on the floor, so why can't I be?"

"Because you're my wife."

The words come out sharp, like he forgot that though we're technically married right now, soon enough, we won't be.

He lifts his head, urging me to lift mine, only to slip his one and only pillow behind my head, leaving his own to rest on the ground.

Then he takes his blanket off his body and drapes it over me.

"Isaiah, what's going on?"

He shakes his head. "Please forget you saw anything. I don't let people see me this way."

I can attest to that. I've *never* seen him this way. Frazzled. Uncomfortable. Not smiling through a shitty situation.

His bare chest is right there in front of me, and I want to touch him. *Feel* him.

Do what feels good.

Without concern if my hands are too cold or anything else I could overthink, I reach out, placing my palm over his heart before running it up over his skin to gently hook around the back of his neck, keeping us connected.

His eyes close at the contact, nostrils flaring through an exhale.

"I don't let people see my weaknesses either, Isaiah. But still you know all of them."

"There's nothing weak about you, Kenny. You're just a perfectionist who doesn't see how perfect she already is." He places his hand over mine, behind his neck, fingers toying with my wedding ring. "Please go back to bed. This is fucking embarrassing."

"Why? Because someone is seeing you be something other than arrogant or happy? This isn't going to make me like you any less. In fact, knowing that life affects you might make me like you even more."

"I don't know how that's possible. We both know how absolutely obsessed you are with me already."

A tick of a smile raises on the corners of his lips before it immediately falls.

I lift, moving the pillow, and Isaiah accepts it back under his head, but I only give him half, keeping the other half for myself because I'm not going anywhere, and neither is he.

I try to give him back some of the blanket, but it's too small to cover two people.

"There's nothing to be embarrassed about." My voice is a whisper. "Whatever is going on, you care about your brother enough to call him. Cody and Travis too. How is that embarrassing?" I toy with the ends of his hair, overgrown around the nape of his neck. "You don't have to tell me what's wrong, but you also said I should do what feels good and laying down here with you feels good to me. So I'm going to stay."

His brows furrow, more emotion shining in his eyes than I've ever seen, but he doesn't say anything else and neither do I. I simply keep my hand on him and close my eyes, willing the sleep to come.

It almost does. I'm not sure how much time passes, but I'm seconds away from sleep, random thoughts blurring my mind, when Isaiah finally admits, "I've always cared, Kenny. Too much sometimes, but people don't want that guy. Who wants to hang around the guy who has anxiety attacks over the fucking weather?"

The constant smiles, the playful jokes. Isaiah has endless friends. He tends to be the center of attention and maybe that's because he knows how to play the part and be exactly who people want him to be.

"I do."

His eyes search my face, his mouth opening as if he wants to say something, then closing when he changes his mind.

"I want to be around that guy," I repeat.

I don't break away from the eye contact I'm not accustomed to or the physical closeness I tend to avoid. I stay, running the pad of my thumb across his stubble.

Because I want to. Because it feels good to be here.

"My mom died in a storm like this one," he admits.

Shit.

"It was raining so hard she probably couldn't see more than a few feet in front of her. A car hydroplaned on the road, and my mom, she swerved to avoid them and ended up getting her car wrapped around a tree. I was thirteen years old when it happened, and it was still storming outside my windows when Kai came into my room and told me."

"Isaiah—"

"I don't know what's wrong with me, Kenny." His tone is desperate, as if he needs to be fixed and I could be the one to do it. "It's been eighteen years and every time the weather is like this, I can't calm myself down. Every worst-case scenario runs through my mind, and I can't relax until I hear from every single person I care about." His fingers continue to toy with his mom's ring on my finger, his face pained. "My skin gets hot and the way I breathe . . ." He taps his chest. "It's not normal."

"Anxiety *is* normal, Isaiah. You experienced the worst thing imaginable when you were only thirteen years old. If that didn't affect you, then—"

"It was the worst day of my life, but I'm not typically like this, I promise."

His words are pleading for me to not think of him any differently, but this version of Isaiah, vulnerable and honest . . . it *is* different. It's the most attractive he's ever been to me.

Human. Real. A man who cares so much about other people that he has anxiety attacks at the mere thought he could lose someone else.

"Did you ever go see a therapist about this? Or someone else you could talk to?"

He huffs a forced laugh. "You think I could afford therapy after it happened? I could barely afford to eat."

"What about Kai? Could you talk to him?"

"He had it worse than me. He lost her too and he still had to take care of me. I wasn't about to put my shit on him."

My throat tightens. Because he was once just a kid who lost his mom. Who didn't have anyone to talk to about it. Who didn't have food to eat because his dad left him too, and my eyes burn when I think about all the times Isaiah has adamantly fed me.

Miller filled me in. After their mom died, their dad went down a bad path and never came back for his boys even once he cleaned himself up. It was just the two of them, getting each other through life.

From an outsider's point of view, you'd think Kai was the one who had the burden on his shoulders, getting his younger brother through their teenage years. But what about Isaiah? Knowing their dynamic, I would imagine he took on the burden of making his brother laugh, even when Isaiah was heartbroken. Even when he didn't want to smile himself, he probably did so for Kai. Wanted to convince him he was okay. That they'd *both* be okay.

Under the blanket, Isaiah runs his palm down my forearm and over my shoulder until it settles on my waist. "Thinking about that day is the only thing that makes me this way."

"And you're allowed to feel those moments. You don't have to be on 24/7."

I scoot closer to him until his hand wraps around my lower back and his feet touch mine. My sleep shirt has ridden up, and Isaiah uses the opportunity to circle the pads of his fingertips against my skin.

I've never done this. Intimately spoken in the dark, but for some reason, nothing about it feels foreign with him.

"Please, Ken." He squeezes me, his desperation evident. "Don't think any differently of me."

"But what if I want to?"

I'm met with utter confusion.

But the only one of us who should be concerned if my opinion on Isaiah Rhodes has changed is me. Because I think I might like what I see.

I bring my body closer to him until we're chest to chest, his arm fully surrounding me, our legs tangled, and his lips ghosting my forehead.

Why doesn't this freak me out? Why doesn't this feel unnatural?

The scariest thing about this is that it feels so right.

"The day you and I met." His words are soft against my skin as he speaks. "I was hiding in the women's restroom because that was the same date my mom died. I was having a bad day, and I didn't want anyone to see me like that. I'm always having a bad day on that date, but for the first time in a long time, while I was talking to you, I felt this spark of genuine joy that I couldn't ignore. For the first time in a long time, I didn't have to fake it. So, it's your fault, Kenny. You're the reason I've been hooked from day one."

My throat feels small. My nose and eyes prick with heat.

I've been a bargaining piece. A second-choice fiancée and even an unwanted employee, but I've never been someone's joy.

I bury my face in his neck so he can't see me. "Isaiah?"

"Yeah?"

"We got married on that date."

He curls into me, lips dusting the skin of my neck before placing a soft kiss there. "I know."

Isaiah turns onto his back, bringing me with him and draping my body over his. My short legs fall between his long ones, and though he took the pillow for himself, I'm perfectly happy to go without one when the alternative is his chest.

A hand settles on my lower back as I adjust the single blanket to cover us both.

"On the worst day of the year, I had two of the best days of my life."

My eyes screw shut as I hide myself against his bare chest.

Just like I've never been someone's joy, I've also never been someone's best.

I don't know how to process that.

I exhale a shaky breath. "Isaiah?"

"Yeah?"

"Do you ever wear a shirt?"

He huffs a laugh. A genuine, beautiful laugh that he needed.

"Thank you for that, but no, not around you anymore, Doc. I see the way you look at me."

I smile against him.

"Please. Stay here with me tonight, Kenny."

I nod. "I'm not going anywhere."

20

Isaiah

The driveway is packed when I pull up to my brother's house and the endless voices can be heard from outside. I know Cody and Travis are here, and judging by the parked cars, quite a few of our other teammates are too.

Not that I blame them. I'm lucky enough to have a world-renowned pastry chef as a sister-in-law, and wouldn't dare miss one of these nights at my brother's house.

With my hands full, I use my foot to open and close the front door, and as soon as I pass the threshold, Max's laughter is the first thing I consciously hear.

It's the best thing I've heard all day, and the second best follows closely behind.

"Do you think that's funny, Bug?" Kennedy asks my nephew, her tone pitched high for him.

Listening harder, I search for her voice again, not convinced she's actually here right now, with all my friends and family, when she's always been adamant about keeping her work and social life separate.

Max giggles again and I finally follow the sound to find the two of them on the floor in the living room, Kennedy with her back to the wall with my nephew standing between her outstretched legs. He's pressing her cheeks together, trying to see what kind of faces he can make her do, and man, is it fucking cute.

A few of my teammates are on the couch, even more sitting on the floor with their eyes glued to the television screen where another baseball game is playing.

But they're not who I'm looking at. I'm watching Max with my wife.

Whatever I'm feeling for Kennedy is far more serious than the once superficial crush I had on the girl. I didn't know her then, but now that I'm learning exactly who she is, I more than like what I see.

She slept on the goddamn floor with me, listened and understood parts of me that even my closest friends don't see. And don't get me started on that night in my apartment, making her come, seeing her fall apart . . . *Fuck,* I feel ruined. Entirely destroyed for anyone else.

I can't begin to fathom the idea of wanting someone else, so how does she? How the hell does she expect for me to let her go soon? Just sign some divorce papers and call it a day.

In what fucking world?

Sitting on the floor in my brother's packed house, she's got this casual T-shirt on and loose-fitting jeans, cuffed once around the ankle to make them the correct length for her. Her auburn hair is split into two braids, falling over her shoulders with pieces pulled out and framing her pretty face with those freckles on full display. They trail down her bare arms and feet, where her toes are painted—I'm just not entirely sure of the color.

I move into the kitchen, hoping to catch either her or my nephew's attention, but they don't pay me any mind as I set the bags of groceries on the counter where Kai and Miller are busy prepping her baking equipment.

About once a month, since Miller moved to Chicago permanently, she hosts a night of experimenting, testing out new recipes for her patisserie. Monty and I are always here. Sometimes, Cody and Travis will join. Sometimes, even our friends who play for other teams in the city. And tonight, with an evening free from baseball, half the team is here.

I just had no idea that Kennedy would be too.

"Hey, man," Kai says, rounding the island to give me a hug. "Is there more in the car?"

"No, Mr. Three Thousand, this is everything."

"Shut up."

"Yeah, that's not going to happen. I'm going to be annoying as hell about this. My brother just earned his three-thousandth strikeout. You know who does that in their career? Hall of Famers."

Kai slightly shakes his head as if it's not a huge fucking deal and something that only nineteen other pitchers have done in their lifetimes.

"He's right," Miller agrees. "This is huge, Malakai. The Remingtons confirmed the ceremony is going to happen Saturday night after the afternoon game."

"That feels a bit ridiculous. People don't need to take their nights off so I can celebrate that I'm good at throwing a baseball."

"Maybe *we* want to celebrate you," I cut in. "Stop being such a little bitch about it and own it. My brother is one of the best pitchers in the game. I want to celebrate that."

"Think about Max," Miller says. "You're his hero. Don't you want him to see what you've accomplished? I know I do."

Kai's blue eyes soften, cutting to me then back to his fiancée. "Fine," he relents. "But I'm only doing this for you three."

Miller shoots me a knowing look because the two of *us* should win an award for our talents of teaming up against my brother.

"Thanks for going to the store, Isaiah," Miller says as she digs through the groceries I bought her, pulling out fresh bags of sugar and flour. "Any requests?"

"Just send me home with all the leftovers."

"With how many people came tonight, I'm not sure there's going to be any leftovers, but I'll see what I can do."

I glance over my shoulder to the crowded living room, but still Kennedy and Max have yet to notice my presence, which is super fucking annoying because I've always been Max's favorite and I was hoping I was getting close to Kennedy's.

"I didn't know she was going to be here," I whisper to Kai and Miller.

A knowing smile hikes on the corner of Miller's mouth. "I told her you were coming over and she asked if she could tag along too."

"That's interesting."

"I thought so too."

"And she knew that most of the team was going to be here?"

She nods, the excitement evident on her face.

I motion Miller to lean across the kitchen counter, meeting me partway as I keep my voice low. "Do you think she likes me?"

"Jesus," Kai laughs. "You're a thirty-one-year-old man. Get it together. Where the hell is my cocky little brother who would just tell a girl she was going to like him? I still have no idea how that worked so well for you."

"Isaiah," Miller whispers right back. "You're married to the girl. I think that gives you the right to ask your wife if she likes you."

Glancing over my shoulder, through the crowd, I finally catch Kennedy notice me. Those brown eyes slowly make their way to mine, a sweet smile following right behind. But Max won't have it, pulling at her cheeks and begging for her attention again.

He had never really been all that comfortable with women until Miller came along, and though Kennedy has known my nephew longer and babysat when my brother needed help, it wasn't until this season that Max has really grown attached to her.

I don't blame him. I completely understand that sentiment when it comes to her.

Crossing the room, I meet them, squatting down, heels to ass so I can be at their eye level.

"Excuse me, Maxie. Are you not going to say hi to me?"

He shakes his head no, a mischievous smile on his mouth that looks a whole lot like mine.

"What?" I ask in faux shock. "But I'm your favorite uncle."

"Ken," he says.

"Kennedy is your auntie Ken, but that doesn't mean I'm not still your favorite uncle."

"Or your only uncle for that matter," Kennedy mutters under her breath.

"Hey now," Cody argues from the couch.

I shoot her a warning look, but it doesn't hold much weight when I know I'm staring at her like she's the best thing I've ever seen. She's got this playful smile on her mouth and a sparkle in her eye as she teases me.

At that, Max melts forward, leaning into Kennedy, putting his head on her shoulder, and hiding from me.

"Hey, man. That's *my* wife, not yours."

"Mine," he says, finishing with a giggle.

Travis bursts a laugh. "Wonder where the hell he got that from, Rhodes."

Kennedy wraps a hand over his back before leaning her cheek on his head. It's done in such an effortless way, as if any hang-ups she has ever had with the concept of hugging another human being don't exist when it comes to Max.

It's cute. It's really fucking cute.

It had always been just Kai and me until Max came along. It was terrifying when he was left to be raised by my brother, but at the same time it felt like hope. We had always kept a small family circle, as if we were protecting ourselves from losing anyone else, but then Max came along and forced that circle to grow.

Miller bulldozed her way in shortly after, and Monty too. Though I think Monty had wormed his way into our family long before my brother started dating his daughter.

And now there's Kennedy, who views this marriage as temporary and convenient, but I won't lie and say it doesn't feel right having her here in my brother's house with the rest of my team while wearing my mom's ring on her finger.

"Fine," I relent. "It's a good thing I love you so much, Bug, because there's not a chance I would share her attention with anyone else."

"Max," my brother calls out as he crosses the room to us. "Time to get ready for bed."

"No!" Max turns, hiding his face entirely from his dad against Kennedy's shoulder.

"Come on, Bug. Say good night to your aunt and uncle. And to everyone else too."

"Monny."

"Yeah. Grandpa Monty is on his way. We'll let him be the one to read you a story before bed, all right?"

Max lights up at that because he *loves* Monty.

I can barely call him "Grandpa Monty" with a straight face. Monty is in his forties, solid mass of muscle, covered in tattoos, and intimidating as fuck if you don't know him. But his non-biological daughter now has a non-biological son, and though there's no blood relation, Monty is very much Max's grandpa.

I'm sure to remind him of that fact as often as possible. Typically, in front of the team or when I'm feeling especially eager to mess with him.

"Aw, Grandpa is coming over?" Travis asks.

"I can't wait to see Grandpa Monty," I chime in.

"But we've got to get through bath time first," my brother continues. "So we should start now, don't you think?"

Max's bright blue eyes scan Kennedy for her opinion and she gives an excited nod of approval, as if that's the best idea she's ever heard.

That doesn't seem to be the response he was looking for, so instead, he shifts his attention to me.

"Oh, now you want to talk to me, huh? First you steal my girl and now you want my help to get out of bath time?" I laugh incredulously. "I don't think so, little man. You're on my sh . . . *poop* list."

Max's head falls back in a fit of giggles at the word. "Poop," he repeats.

"Amazing." Kai's tone is all sarcasm. "Exactly the word I was hoping you'd add to your vocabulary. Your uncle is about to be on my poop list for that. Say good night to the boys, Bug."

Max walks himself through the entire living room, tapping knuckles with all our teammates before Kai picks him up and slings him on his hip.

Max waves goodbye at me, then to Kennedy before bringing his chubby little hand to his mouth and blowing a sloppy kiss her way.

"Oh, come on!" I protest. "I'm right here, man!"

Kai shakes his head with a suppressed smile and Max's laughter follows them all the way down the hall to his bedroom.

The room settles back into watching the game on TV.

"Jealous of a two-year-old," Kennedy says quietly. "That's a new look for you."

"I've been jealous over you for years, Ken. Couldn't care less how old the guy is."

She bites back her laugh as I adjust, taking a seat on the floor next to her, back to the wall.

"Hi."

"Hi." Her smile is soft, her posture relaxed, vastly different from the type-A doctor I'm accustomed to seeing at work. She's comfortable, which, with the team here, I didn't expect.

The front door opens and Monty walks into the already crowded house, right over to his daughter before swinging an arm over her shoulders and placing a kiss on the top of her head.

"Grandpa is here," Travis announces. "Do you need help getting your walker out of the car?"

Cody glances into the kitchen. "Oh hey, Grandpa Monty. I found a pack of little blue pills in the clubhouse. I'm assuming those are yours."

"Shoot," I begin. "I should've sent you to the grocery store instead of going myself. It's senior discount Wednesday."

With a slow blink, he turns to his daughter. "Is Max around?"

"He's taking a bath."

"Great." He brings his attention back to us. "You three idiots can all shut the fuck up. Travis, when you're done running sprints tomorrow, then we can talk about who needs a walker. Cody, if you need medication to get your dick up, just say that. Nothing to be ashamed of, but you don't need to pretend to have found them when we all know those are on a subscription delivery to your apartment. And Isaiah, I'm going to restrain myself, so I don't embarrass you in front of your wife. We all know you do that plenty on your own." He sighs, looking down at his daughter. "I'm so looking forward to this year's trade deadline."

"Cranky old man," I mutter loud enough for him to hear.

Monty flips me the bird from the kitchen.

"Kennedy," one of our infielders begins. "I heard you're interviewing with San Francisco next week. Married life with Rhodes has been that shitty you're going to take the same job but all the way across the country to get away from him, huh?"

She hesitates at my side. To everyone else's knowledge, this interview is simply a lateral move to a new city. No one else knows her qualifications or that this new position is for a lead doctor role.

No one besides me.

I catch Monty's eye from across the room as he waits for Kennedy's answer.

"It's complicated," is what she settles on, trying not to lie.

Cody and Travis's attention darts to me because even though they know our marriage is bullshit and this will be an easy way to uncomplicate things, they also know how I truly feel about her.

"I was wondering what the hell you two were going to do," another teammate chimes in. "Either you were going to have to go, or Rhodes would have to take a trade."

"We've had a plan from the beginning," Kennedy explains.

"Wow. This makes so much more sense than you two staying fucking married forever to keep your job safe."

"With how Dr. Fredrick treats you, I don't blame you," someone else says. "You could have a fresh start under a lead doctor who isn't a complete asshole."

A fresh start.

I equally hate that and want to cheer her on. Is that what it means to unequivocally care for another person? To want what's best for them even if it's going to hurt like a bitch to sit by and watch?

I want Kennedy to thrive in the position she trained for. I want her to get away from Dr. Fredrick. I want her to be comfortable in her own skin, to understand what it means to feel loved and cared for.

I just wish she could do all those things with me.

"They're hiring mid-season for an athletic trainer?"

Monty asks from across the room, suspicion laced in his tone.

Kennedy hesitates. My little planner didn't have a plan for that question.

"They want to make sure she'll fit in with the rest of the staff," I answer for her.

His brows pinch together. "Sounds like something they'd do for a lead role and not for a member of the support staff."

I shoot him a look, silently telling him to let it go, but he continues to study us from across the room.

Thankfully, the crack of a bat on the television steals everyone's attention, our interrogation now in the past.

Kennedy exhales a sigh before resting her head against the wall to look at me. "Maybe I shouldn't have come."

"Trust me, Kenny. I always want you to come. As your husband, it's my responsibility to make sure you come."

With the back of her hand, she smacks me in the stomach.

I chuckle. "I would've invited you myself, but I got so used to you turning me down all these years. Figured you would've said no."

"You make it seem like you consistently asked me for three solid years. It wasn't that often."

"There hasn't been a single night out on the road that I haven't invited you or forced one of the boys to ask for me, but you, Kennedy Kay, are excellent at keeping my ego in check."

She pauses, watching me, the skin between her brows creasing. "I'm sorry. You were just being nice, and I—"

"Oh, don't go soft on me now, Kenny. I wasn't just being nice. I was hitting on you. Blatantly, might I add."

She doesn't laugh. She doesn't answer, her face telling me everything I need to know.

After the other night in Minneapolis when she witnessed a vulnerable side to me, she's viewing me differently. She's *treating* me differently.

I just don't know if that difference is a good or bad thing.

I nudge her knee with mine. "Well, I'll give you the chance to make up for it. If I invited you to something right now, would you say yes?"

"Depends."

"Depends on what?"

"On the details."

I lean into her space, and she doesn't retract.

"You've got to give me an answer before I give you the details. Be spontaneous, Kenny. Yes or no. Do you want to go?"

"Isaiah, I'm a planner."

"Oh, trust me, I'm aware, but right now, the only thing you need to plan on is that I'll be there."

Her face softens, the hesitation falling away.

"So, tell me. Are you in?"

She leans into me, our heads resting against the wall and our lips only inches from each other. "I'm in."

"That's my girl."

Without backing away, Kennedy bends her legs, letting her left one fall into my lap. It's only there for a split second before she overthinks it all, breaking eye contact and lifting it back to her chest.

I don't allow the moment to get uncomfortable or awkward for her, so I slip my hand between her knees, pulling her leg back down to rest over my lap.

"I know you said you haven't been on a date that wasn't a black-tie affair," I continue, as if nothing happened.

"A date, huh?"

"Call it whatever you need to, Ken, but Kai's award ceremony is on Saturday night, and it might be weird for me to show up without my wife. The Remingtons will be there."

"Is that why you want me to go?"

I run a palm over her denim-covered thigh. "You know that's not the reason I want you to go, but if you need to tell yourself that's the reason *you're* willing to, then you can."

She doesn't hesitate for a moment when she says, "I don't need to tell myself anything."

Her tongue darts out, wetting her bottom lip, and it takes everything in me to keep from closing the two inches of space between us and pressing my mouth to hers. But the room is crowded with people she works for and though she's getting accustomed to physical affection, I'm not sure she's ready for the public display variety.

Kennedy's phone dings in her lap, breaking the moment, and my eyes can't help but land on the name that pops onto her phone.

Connor Danforth.

"Why is he texting you?"

She shrugs. "He hasn't stopped since that dinner in Atlanta."

I sit up straighter against the wall. "What?"

She opens her messages to show me the screen with dates of texts ranging from weeks ago until today. She hasn't responded once.

Connor Danforth: *Whatever the hell you're doing with that guy is a fucking joke. Break it off, Kennedy. It's not a good look for your family.*

Connor Danforth: *If you're not responding because of what Mallory said, you really need to get over it. What did you expect? You wouldn't even touch me. Of course I had to look elsewhere.*

Connor Danforth: *I wanted it to be you. Sometimes I still want it to be you.*

Connor Danforth: *Did you really cheat on me with that guy?*

Connor Danforth: *You're not going to answer me? We were engaged and you can't even give me the courtesy of a response? What the hell happened to make you so fucking cold, Kennedy?*

I snatch the phone from her, my thumbs moving a mile a minute across the screen as the seething anger spills out of me.

"Don't." Kennedy places her hand over mine to stop me. "He's not worth it."

"Fuck that, Ken. He's harassing you."

"I don't care."

Her face is entirely impassive as if she really doesn't care. As if he's truly not affecting her.

I like that far too much.

"Fine," I resign, handing her back her phone. "But if he keeps it up, you let me know and I'll handle it, okay?"

"Okay." She sets it on the floor, screen down.

With my hand still holding her thigh, I gently run the length of it, rubbing my palm absentmindedly against the denim as we both shift our attention to the game that's on the TV.

My teammates shoot the shit around us, the house rowdy as hell, but Kennedy and I sit in complete silence. Me softly rubbing the inside of her thigh and her head awfully close to resting on my shoulder.

We stay that way for an entire inning before Kennedy quietly asks, "Do you think I'm cold?" for only me to hear.

I could fucking kill him.

With the back of my hand, I test her forehead. "You feel pretty warm to me."

"Isaiah, I'm being serious. I think something is wrong with me."

I adjust to face her. "There is absolutely nothing wrong with you and fuck him for making you think there is, Kennedy.

No one has ever been warm to you, including that guy, so how would you know how to be anything different?"

"So you do think I'm cold?"

I let out a slow breath.

"Yeah, maybe I do. But I don't think that's wrong or bad or something that needs to be fixed. It's part of your personality. You're a little reserved. A bit hesitant towards people." I take her hand in mine and she doesn't resist for a moment. "But it also feels like I won the fucking lottery knowing you're no longer hesitant towards me. I like that you're a tough one to crack, because when I say something stupid and get to see you smile, I know it's only for me. And that smile, it's all warmth."

Her brows are furrowed, her lips slightly parted. She's looking at me as if she can't believe I could like her cold exterior. As if I couldn't like that she hasn't made it easy for me. I'm not sure how she doesn't see it. It's been years, and there hasn't been a single thing Kennedy has done or said that hasn't kept me coming back for more.

"Besides," I continue, toying with the ring on her finger. "Winter has always been my favorite season anyway."

She bursts this unpolished, un-Kennedy-like laugh, her smile I was hoping to see coming back to life.

"I can't win with you sometimes," she says before dropping her head to my shoulder and leaving it there.

There's no denying it. I'm an absolute fool when it comes to this girl.

21

Isaiah

"I'm almost ready!"

Leaning back against the sink, I cross my arms over my chest. "Take your time, Kenny. They won't start without us."

I don't want it to start at all.

Under the bathroom stall, I can see her hopping around on a single foot as she hurriedly tries to slip on her other high heel.

Dr. Fredrick tried his hardest to force Kennedy to work in the training room tonight, cleaning, organizing, and reordering medical supplies while he and the other staff attended my brother's ceremony. Reese found out and put a quick stop to that, but still he had Kennedy working until the last possible minute, which had me bringing her dress, shoes, and jewelry to the bathroom for her to quickly change.

"Who does he think he is?" she asks with a huff. "From what he knows, he believes this is my brother-in-law's ceremony. If anyone from the medical staff had to work late, it shouldn't be me."

"This *is* your brother-in-law's ceremony."

"You know what I mean." I can picture her waving me off behind the bathroom stall. "I cannot freaking wait until I no longer work for that guy. He was more than happy for me to take Monday's game off for my interview, but not tonight after I've already worked all day? How did he find so much audacity?"

I want to say something, agree with her, encourage her that things will be better once she's in San Francisco, but there's no part of me that has the energy to act as if life will be better then.

I hope and pray that for her, it is, and then maybe her happiness will be the thing that gets me through missing her the way I know I'm going to.

Tonight is going to fucking suck, and it's even worse knowing she's going too.

"Would you mind zipping me up?"

Her tone is entirely too casual as she opens the stall in the women's restroom, as if she weren't going to completely steal my breath the moment I saw her.

A white, beaded dress has the privilege of molding to every inch of her body before skimming the floor. It cuts in and wraps around her neck where she is holding the fabric together for me to secure. Her hair is curled in big waves and pinned to one side, the way she typically wears it when she's dressing up, and her jewelry is all silver, minus the gold band and purple stone on her left ring finger.

Her focus is on the ground as she holds the back of her dress together, so she doesn't realize that I'm fucking speechless and unmoving, glued with my ass to the counter because this woman is the most stunning person I've ever laid eyes on, and I still don't know how I got so lucky to call her my wife—even if she thinks that part is temporary.

"The zipper is kind of a bitch because of all the beading. It needs a good tug."

I toss my head from side to side. "If I had it my way, it'd stay down."

Finally, she looks up, a smirk lifting at the same time. "I can either go out there with this hanging on my hips or you can zip up my dress, but just a heads-up, Rhodes, I'm not wearing a bra."

Fuck me. That image goes straight to my cock and even though I'm dressed to the nines, topped with a fucking tie, my body has no issue getting hard at the idea of my wife going braless with that backless dress.

"Yeah, not a chance." I round her body, her back to me as we both face the mirror. "The first time I see you fully naked, I sure as hell won't be sharing the view."

I watch her suppress her smile through the mirror before my eyes wander down her spine. Her soft skin is decorated with light freckles creating a visual path to where her hips flare out, holding the dress tightly to her body. I watch as her back rises and falls with a breath. Watch the way her delicate fingers hold the clasp together. I can't help but note where the dress needs to be zipped, splitting open around her lower back and giving me a prime view of the top of her ass. I equally can't keep my eyes away from her sides, that backless dress teasing me with the slight slope of her breasts.

Jesus, she looks incredible.

Outside of work, Kennedy tends to gravitate towards a wardrobe that consists of black, white, and neutrals. My classic girl who I once thought needed all the color in the world, I now realize is perfect in her simple tones. I can typically identify them on my own, and they act as a backdrop for her. Not stealing the show, but simply complementing how beautiful she is.

"I can't get the zipper to budge, and the buttons up here are giving me trouble."

With a single hand, I move her hair, letting it drape over one shoulder before stealing the two pieces of delicate fabric from her. I slip the small satin buttons through their looped counterparts, keeping the dress secure around her neck.

I watch her throat work its way through a swallow when I trail the pads of my fingertips down the soft curve of her spine, taking my time finding her zipper. I slip my fingers into the fabric, letting my knuckles graze against her lower back. I'm sure to keep a connection the entire time I slowly pull the zipper closed, and don't lose contact when both hands smooth over the now closed dress, wrapping around her hips and pulling her back to me.

She relaxes into my chest as we meet each other's eyes in the mirror.

"Beautiful," I whisper while we stand in the same bathroom where we met for the first time.

She breaks eye contact, still leaning back into me. "I've never seen you so dressed up before. We almost look like . . ."

Her in a white dress. Me in a black suit.

"Like we're getting married?" I finish for her.

Her brown eyes slowly drift back up to mine in the reflection.

I could see it. This is what it could look like. What it *should've* looked like, but I wouldn't trade the visual of her in a white mini dress, denim jacket, and platform Vans walking down the aisle to me.

Kennedy's eyes drag over us, watching, assessing. It doesn't feel sexual. It feels curious.

My fingertips dig into her hip. "What are you thinking about?"

"That I couldn't be more thankful I didn't have to marry Connor."

But are you thankful that now you're married to me?

The question is on the tip of my tongue when my phone dings in my pocket, breaking our moment.

Kai: *As much as you don't want this to happen, we've got to start before Max passes out. You two coming?*

I exhale an unsteady breath. "You ready?"

Kennedy folds her clothes and leaves them on the sink for her to grab after. Seeing as she and I are the only ones who use this bathroom, it's safe to assume they'll be safe for the night.

Holding the door open, I let her exit first.

I follow her to the dugout, up the stairs, and out onto the grass. My palm finds her lower back when we pass patches of dirt, silently reminding her to pick up her dress so the edges don't drag. Regardless of her heels, Kennedy still only meets my chest, and it takes everything in me not to just pick her up and carry her to keep her from getting that pretty gown dirty.

Since our game ended earlier this afternoon, a small stage has been constructed just off the third base line with round tables and chairs acting as the audience. The entire team is here. Upper management. Coaching staff. Even a handful of season ticket holders I recognize that I assume the Remingtons invited as a thank you for all the years they've followed the team.

Everyone is dressed to impress. Floor-length gowns, tuxedos, and suits. You'd think this was a wedding for royalty, not my brother's career milestone ceremony.

But the Remingtons wanted this to be an *event*, seeing as Kai is the first ever Warrior to earn 3,000 strikeouts in their career, so here we are. Dinner, dancing, the whole thing.

A hand slips into mine, small and cautious. I look down to watch as Kennedy laces her fingers with mine, her pale skin contrasted against my tan.

I don't let hope spark for a second. Instead, I look around and quickly find Reese and Arthur Remington approaching. My heart doesn't even have to sink with disappointment. I already knew that if Kennedy was holding my hand, it wasn't simply because she wanted to.

"How are the newlyweds?" Arthur asks.

"Well, now that Kennedy isn't being forced to work instead of attending her brother-in-law's ceremony . . ." Reese mutters under her breath.

Arthur's white brows cinch. "What do you mean?"

"We can chat about it later."

The stern look on Reese's face tells me they will, without a doubt, be chatting about Dr. Fredrick later.

Good. That guy needs to be put in his place, and the past three years I've had to sit and watch the way he's treated the only woman on staff tell me Arthur isn't the owner to do something about it. But maybe Reese could be.

"Thank you for saving me," Kennedy says from my side. "I didn't want to miss this, and Reese, you look beautiful."

"As do you, Mrs. Rhodes."

I give Kennedy's hand a teasing squeeze.

"Isaiah, you look beautiful too," Arthur chimes in.

I chuckle. "Thank you both for hosting this for my brother. It means a lot to our family."

Without thought, I look down at my wife as I say those words, but whatever. It helps sell this whole thing, I guess.

"As you know, it's always been just the two of us, so seeing all these people here to celebrate him . . ." I nod. "He deserves it."

This time, it's Kennedy squeezing *my* hand.

"He does," Arthur agrees. "We're proud to have you both playing for this organization. It's always felt like family around here, and lately, a lot of you have become actual family. You two, your brother and Monty's daughter. It's a legacy I'm proud to leave behind." He puts a hand on Reese's shoulder. "Now we just got to get you married off and I can die a happy man."

"Jesus, Granddad." Reese shakes her head. "Morbid."

"You're single?" Kennedy asks.

"*So* freaking single."

"That's only because those boys she brings home are intimidated by her," Arthur chimes in.

"Don't let him fool you," Reese quietly says to Kennedy. "I haven't brought a *boy* home in quite some time. Dating is the last thing on my mind when I'm training to take over an entire MLB franchise. I'm about to be the first female team owner in the league. People are already going to assume there's a man running the show behind the scenes. You know what I mean?"

Kennedy is looking at her, nodding in agreement, as if she can relate to every word she has to say. "I know exactly what you mean."

There's a heavy pit in my gut because I know she's referring to me. When she goes to this interview on Monday, they'll know she's married to me. Will that contribute to her getting the job? No, absolutely not. She'll get it because she's qualified and real fucking good at what she does. But when she does get that offer, is there a part of her that's going to assume it's because of me?

Arthur waves his granddaughter off because he's old school and doesn't understand how difficult it is for either of them to work or thrive in a male-dominated sport.

"You'll be great," he says casually, before someone leans down to say something in his ear. "We should find our seats. Your brother wants to get started."

"Good to see you," Reese adds before following her grandfather to their table.

Kennedy drops my hand, though I tell myself it's because she needs to use her own to pick up her dress. "I like her."

"Yeah, she's cool. She'll be good next year."

"Part of me wishes I was going to be here to see it."

The statement is thrown out so easily, whereas *every* part of me wishes she were going to be around next year to see it.

We find our table closest to the stage. Miller in her dark green dress, sitting on my brother's lap. Kai and Monty in their suits, but the cutest of them all is Max in his bow tie.

He's clearly sleepy as it's getting close to his bedtime, resting against Monty's shoulder.

"Ken, you look good!" Miller whistles.

"Same to you!" Kennedy wraps an arm over Miller's shoulder from behind, squeezing her in a hug before bending down to pop a kiss on the top of Max's head, as if it were the most natural thing for her to hug her friend and kiss my nephew. She then takes her seat, leaving an open chair for me next to her.

Miller stands from my brother's lap and retakes a chair, she and Kennedy leaning over my empty seat to chat among themselves.

"You ready for this?" Kai asks quietly, standing to his full height.

I huff a dry laugh. "Nope."

He studies me. "Tell me the truth, Isaiah. Are you going to be okay with this?"

"Kai, if this is what's going to make you happy, I will learn to be okay with it."

A soft smile ticks up on the corner of his lips as he nods. "Yeah. This is what will make me happy."

"Then do it. That's all I've ever wanted for you."

He cups the back of my head, pulling me into him for a hug. "I love you, kid."

"Yeah. I love you too."

"Thank you for everything."

"Fuck," I exhale. "Don't start that now."

"Kai," someone says, and we separate. "Are you ready to start?"

He nods, running a hand over Max's hair then bending to give Miller a kiss before following the emcee to the stage.

We take our seats, Kennedy to my left and Miller to my right with Monty and Max across the table.

Arthur Remington says a few words, welcoming the crowd and introducing my brother before stepping to the side and giving him the stage.

Kai clears his throat before leaning down to the mic, pulling out his notecards from his suit jacket, then bracketing his hands on either side of the podium. "First off, I want to say thank you to the Remingtons for hosting this night. I've worked under different team ownership before, have had teammates of mine tell me about their experiences, and it's no question that here in Chicago, we're lucky to have such generous team owners. So, thank you."

My brother pauses, clapping for the crowd to join him, and once it dies down, he begins again.

"I want to say thank you to everyone who took the time to come here tonight. My teammates who weren't too stoked to dress up." The crowd laughs. "The team staff who we couldn't play this game without, and my family who are the center of my world." His attention goes right to Miller.

"Three thousand strikeouts is a milestone I never dreamed of reaching. There are some legends who came before me that did the same, and I wouldn't dare imagine putting myself in the same category as them. They paved the way for me to be here tonight, so I want to say a huge thank you to the nineteen guys who did this before me." He flips to his next notecard. "Some of you are players that I grew up idolizing, and I know for certain that I wouldn't be here today if it weren't for you sparking a dream in me to play this game as well."

Kai exhales a deep breath, clearing his throat. "To my son." His attention swings to Max with a smile. "Who is about to pass out on Monty's shoulder because it's past his bedtime. You are by far the best thing that has ever happened to me. I once thought that my life goal was to play this game, maybe break some records, and hope that my body would allow me to do it long enough that I got my fill, but I couldn't have been more wrong. You are everything I didn't know I needed, and you bring this contagious joy and meaning to my life every single day."

I catch Miller wipe her cheek out of my periphery.

"I couldn't think of a better group to raise my son around." Kai nods, looking over our teammates. "There are not enough words I could say to thank my teammates for getting me through his first year. When I didn't know what the hell I was doing, you all were there, offering babysitting or bringing me groceries. Cody even learned how to change a diaper for me, and I'm not sure he's ever fully forgiven me for that one."

The crowd laughs again.

"But the biggest person who helped me with him that first year was this guy right here." He points to Monty. "Before I was picked up by Chicago, I had only ever played for field managers or coaches who were just that—coaches. Outside of baseball, they didn't necessarily worry about you or care about you. But this guy." Kai clears his throat and I just know he's trying to choke back his emotion. "This guy is not only my coach, but he's also my sounding board, he's a father figure to me and my brother, and most importantly, he's my friend. They don't make them much better than Emmett Montgomery, and I'll be forever grateful that Chicago drafted my brother because that's the whole reason I'm here in a place where I got to meet him and his daughter. And lucky for Monty, he's stuck with me forever because he's not only my coach, he's also about to become my father-in-law."

Monty nods, tongue in cheek as he rocks Max to sleep, but it's obvious to anyone who can see him that his eyes are glossed over.

"Which brings me to Miller." Kai's got a smile on his face when he turns his attention to her. "Goddamn, I love this crazy woman." A small laugh settles over the crowd. "You are the second greatest thing to ever happen to me and I know you understand what I mean when I say that because you feel the same way." Miller quickly nods in agreement, looking up at him. "Who would have thought that a single elevator ride would bring us to where we are today?" He chuckles at the memory. "Thank you for loving me. For loving Max. Thank you for coming home when you were ready. Thank you for making me laugh when I forget to and thank you for supporting my dreams all while chasing your own. You are the absolute light of my life, and I cannot believe I get to spend the rest of my days with you."

Miller wipes at her cheeks, as does her dad. As does half the crowd as my brother speaks, but I keep it in. Knees bouncing, throat clogged with emotion. I don't want my team to see me like that. They've never seen me like that. I'm the fun one. The goofy one. The one that never lets anything get to him, but I don't know how the fuck to hold it back when I know exactly what's coming next.

"With that being said," Kai continues, "Miller and I have some new dreams we are looking forward to chasing. I've thrown out the retirement conversation a few times over the years, but most of that was due to feeling like I needed to clear time so I could take care of my responsibilities. Feeling bogged down and unable to juggle everything at once."

Kai pauses, looking right at me. We talked earlier this week. I know this announcement is coming, but that doesn't mean it hurts any less.

"I'm officially announcing my retirement from professional baseball." A murmur begins over the crowd, but he continues. "But I want you all to know that it has nothing to do with feeling bogged down or trying to find enough time to take care of everyone else. It's with absolute joy that I get to leave this career I love so much to do something I love even more, and that's to be there for my family. I'm looking forward to supporting my future wife in her career and getting to work on giving Max some siblings."

Kai chuckles, though a bit choked, and it breaks the tension in the crowd when they begin to laugh too.

"I feel honored that I'm stepping away from this game to be a present husband and father. It's truly my favorite job I've ever had."

The crowd claps for him, but I can't. I'm happy for him. Happy for Max and Miller too. But I have played baseball with my brother for almost thirty years, and I don't know how I'm supposed to keep playing without him.

He holds his hand up to settle the group. "There is one last person I still need to address." His attention finds me, but he instantly breaks eye contact, taking a moment to gather himself as he holds the podium with both hands, stretching back, head down. When he looks up again, it's clear a few tears have already fallen behind his glasses.

"There's one single reason I have loved this game for my entire life. It's not the winning, the strikeouts, the fans, or the glory. I have loved baseball because of my brother. Isaiah was four years old and I was six when we first joined the same t-ball team. He wasn't technically old enough yet, but I told our mom I wasn't going to play unless he was out there with me. And it's been that way for us ever since. He and I together."

Lip tucked under my teeth, I nod in agreement, the burn sharp in my nose, the sting evident behind my eyes. I want to hold it in front of these people. I want to hide in the restroom so I could cry the way I want to.

But when Kennedy slips her hand between mine and my thigh, lacing our fingers together and squeezing my palm in encouragement, I can't hold back any longer.

I quickly assess the area around me. There are no team owners watching us, only her looking at me. *Being* there for me.

I hold her hand tighter as the first tear falls.

I hate you for this, I mouth to my brother on the stage.

He laughs, tears still falling down his cheeks because he's never been afraid of admitting when things are sad or hard or hurtful.

"As much as I love this game, what I'll miss most is sharing the field with you. Traveling with you. Spending every single day with you. How lucky am I that I got a best friend and a brother all at once? There are things no one else will understand besides us. Things we experienced, people we lost, and the entire time, our goal was to be here, in this league together. Well, we did it, little brother. You and me, and you were right. It feels good when you end it like this."

A choked sob shakes my chest, but I hold back the noise. It does nothing, though, to keep the tears from streaking my cheeks. I don't even want to know what my teammates are going to think after seeing me this way.

But that worry quickly disappears when, out of my periphery, I see Kennedy pat her face with the back of one hand while still holding mine with the other.

My even-tempered girl never cries. She almost did once, on the first day I met her, but never since. And now she's crying for me.

"You okay?" I whisper to her.

Kennedy shoots me a look that screams she's not upset for herself. She's upset for me.

She pulls my hand to her mouth, placing a kiss on the back of it before resting it on her lap, covering it with her other hand as well.

I'm glad she didn't ask if I was okay, because the only answer I have is no. I'm not okay in the slightest.

My brother is leaving the team next season and so is she.

"So, I wanted to tell you all now," Kai continues. "Before I publicly announce it tomorrow. This will be my last season, and I'm going to enjoy every minute of it I've got left. Thank you."

22

Kennedy

Cocktail in hand, I watch Isaiah and Miller on the dance floor. Kai has been so busy since his speech, talking to team-mates and staff, so Isaiah took it upon himself to take Miller for a twirl.

Their friendship is easy. I suppose because they're similar in a way. Free-spirited, relatively easygoing, know how to be the life of the party if needed. It's evident how much they care for each other, and I think their mutual apprecia-tion is due to knowing how much the other cares about Kai.

The man of the hour says his thank you to a season ticket holder before turning to the dance floor, finding his brother and fiancée together. He smiles at that, then turns his atten-tion to me.

"You look great, Ken," he says once he crosses the dance floor, clinking his glass bottle with my drink.

"Retirement, huh?"

"It's time. I'm thirty-four next year. I don't want to be one of those guys who tries to play long past their arm will allow them. I want to be able to pick up my kids, and honestly, whenever I'm at the field, I'm thinking about being at home these days. It feels right."

"You don't have to explain it to me. I think you're lucky to have people you care about so much that you want to be with them. I think that's every woman's hope, to be thought of the way you think of Miller. It's mine, at least."

I feel him watching me out of the corner of his eye. "You don't really have to hope for that, Kennedy."

I let the insinuation hang in the air, but don't agree. Verbally or internally.

"What did you mean?" I ask, turning his way. "In your speech when you were talking to Isaiah. What did you mean when you said he was right? That it felt good ending it this way."

Kai softly chuckles to himself. "Years ago, we used to talk about what retirement would look like for us one day. I was fucking terrified of the idea because this is all I'd ever known. All I'd ever wanted and worked for. But Isaiah said he looked forward to it. 'Imagine that when this all ends,' he would say, 'that you've met your person, they're at home waiting for you to be done, and now you get to have this entire life with them. Think of how good that's going to feel.'" Kai smiles to himself, watching Miller on the dance floor. "He was right. It feels really fucking good."

My eyes narrow in confusion, pointing towards said dance floor. "You didn't always know you wanted that life?"

"Absolutely not. That was the last thing on my mind, back in those days. After getting Isaiah into the league all I wanted to do was have fun and not worry about any kind of responsibilities. I was trying to make up for the years I felt like I had missed out on being a normal kid. I didn't see a future beyond that, but Isaiah did. That's all he's ever wanted."

My head jerks back. "What exactly did he want?"

"A family. To settle down with one person. You know, all the domesticated shit I'm about to do."

"Isaiah Rhodes?" I laugh in disbelief. "He once wanted that?"

"Still does." He says the words as if they're so obvious, so apparent to everyone around him.

But Isaiah is a playboy. Sure, I've seen a more serious and vulnerable side to him, but that doesn't negate the fact that this man has never slowed down for one single woman. Yes, he's been patient and understanding with me, but what?

It feels as if my entire belief system is in question at the idea that Isaiah Rhodes really, truly wants to settle down.

Kai turns to me. "You might not be aware of this, but Isaiah used to be a relationship type of guy. He always had serious girlfriends. Committed. Faithful. I didn't once ever catch him looking elsewhere when he was in a relationship. It's the same attributes that make him such a good friend, but yeah, the guy loved the stability of being in a relationship. Well, until he didn't."

My attention drifts from Kai to his brother on the dance floor. Isaiah's head is thrown back in laughter thanks to whatever Miller said, birthmark next to his eye disappearing with his smile.

I have looked at Isaiah plenty of times before, but if what Kai is saying is true, I have never truly *seen* him. Sure, Kai could lie for his brother if he wanted to, but I know in my gut he's not. Which only has me questioning . . .

"Why did he stop? Being a relationship type of guy, I mean."

Kai's head falls back with a groan, sneaking a quick glance at his brother. "He'd kill me if I told you."

"Tell me anyway."

"Damn, Ken. For being in the medical field, you're not at all concerned about my well-being."

"Let me be selfish here, Ace."

Kai exhales a resigned sign. "Dean, your stepbrother, is what happened. Well, kind of. It's not entirely his fault, but it partially is."

"What exactly happened? Because Isaiah won't tell me."

"That's nice of him." His tone is all sarcasm. "Doesn't want you to know how much your stepbrother sucks, but I'll be happy to fill you in. Dean went to a rival high school, but he had always had it out for Isaiah. I was older, so he didn't try anything directly with me, but he would constantly go after my brother. It started when we were kids, the shit he would say . . ." Kai shakes his head. "Our first game back after our mom died, I remember him mentioning something shitty about her while Isaiah was running the bases. A huge fight broke out. It never stopped from there. Any time our teams met, there'd be a fight. Then when Isaiah got a little older and started dating girls, it was a new way for Dean to fuck with him. Isaiah was this sweet, loyal kid, but I couldn't name one single girl that my brother dated who didn't fuck around behind his back with your stepbrother. Which yes, those girls are also at fault for doing that, but fuck Dean too because he went after them intentionally. After being cheated on who knows how many times, Isaiah hasn't attempted a relationship since."

"That was well over ten years ago," is the only thing I can manage to say, because my heart hurts at the mere idea of a kind, naïve Isaiah finding out his girlfriends were secretly seeing the person he disliked most.

"You've got to understand, Ken, he was thirteen when our mom died. Then immediately after that, at the age he's learn-ing about relationships, every girl he ever had feelings for left him too. He's a little fucked up because of it, and I don't blame him. All the guy ever wanted was for someone to stay and love him back, but he never got that. He's allowed to be jaded, and I'm allowed to hate Dean because of it."

I think I'm allowed to hate Dean because of it too. I don't care that he was just a teenager at the time, he and I will be having some words for how he's treated my now husband.

"You're the first person he's been with in over a decade, and—"

"But we're not together. Not like that, at least."

Kai nods to his mother's ring on my finger. "You sure he knows that?"

"Of course he does." The words come out with a slight stutter because I'm not sure even *I* believe them.

Yes, we're faking it. Playing a game. But the way he looks at me, the way he takes care of me . . . Those things feel very fucking real.

Kai continues. "It's nice to see him like this again, with you, and the last thing I want is for him to feel so burned after it all ends that he goes back to being the guy he was for the last ten years. I'm not saying you have to want him back, but protect him for me, will you?"

But what if I do? Want him back. What if he could want more than just one night, the way I've always believed? What if this isn't a one and done for him?

My eyes track him on the dance floor, moving slowly with Miller, hand resting on her mid back, the other holding hers out to the side. He catches me watching him from across the way and a slow, sleepy smile spreads across his lips. It's quickly becoming my favorite thing to see, but in the same breath, I find him just as handsome when he's not smiling. When he's vulnerable and real.

"Kai, do you think he's going to be okay next year? Without you."

He exhales a deep breath. "I don't know. I want him to be, but it'll be a big change. Even when we weren't on the same team, we still had the same life. Still had the same job. He's losing both me and you next season, and even though you think you're temporary in his life, you're not."

He's not temporary in my life either. At the very least, Isaiah Rhodes is quickly becoming my closest friend. And for maybe the first time, I can admit that when I move, I will miss him too.

"Kai Rhodes," someone interrupts us, hand slapping the back of his shoulder. "Huge fan. We've been season ticket holders since—"

I don't listen to the rest of the fan's sentence, instead slipping away to let them drool over our Ace pitcher.

I wander, saying hi to a few coworkers and team players. I avoid Dr. Fredrick like the plague as he wears the cheesiest fucking smile on his face while kissing as much ass as possible, mostly notably to Arthur Remington. But if I were him, I'd turn my focus to Reese. She's going to be his boss next year, after all.

But then again, the idea of Dr. Fredrick kissing ass to any woman, even one who is his direct superior, seems like an impossible task.

With an empty glass, I find my way to the bar, climbing onto a stool and taking a seat. "Vodka soda, please."

I pass the bartender a tip before slipping my hands between my crossed thighs and waiting for my cocktail.

"Drinks are on me." Someone steps up to the bar beside me, not sitting on the stool, but instead standing between the next one over and mine.

A man. Thirties. Objectively attractive.

"It's an open bar," I remind him.

A slow smile spreads on his mouth. "Well, then it looks like I'll have to take you out after this and buy you a real one."

I huff a laugh. "That was smooth."

"Vincent." He holds his hand out and I shake it in greeting.

"Kennedy."

"Are you a baseball fan, Kennedy?"

"Something like that."

He scoots a little closer to me. Too close, if I'm being honest, but this is what I'm working on, being okay with physical contact. If I were out in the real world getting hit on at a real bar, it'd be crowded. They'd stand close. This is fine.

I'm fine.

"So what do you do for work, Miss Kennedy?"

Mrs, my brain screams, but I shut it off.

"I'm a . . . doctor."

Vincent's eyes go wide. "Impressive. What kind?"

"Sports medicine."

"Athletes, huh? Bet they love you. I've been an athlete my whole life, you know. Still play occasionally."

"Oh yeah? Who do you play for?"

"I play pickup at the gym."

I burst a laugh, but quickly cover it with my hand. "Sorry."

"It gets heated out there. It's intense. Some of those guys played in college and really had a chance at going pro if they didn't injure themselves. That's what happened to me. I blew out my knee freshman year." He shakes his head in disbelief as if his high school highlight reel was playing on repeat in his mind. "So, what kind of athletes do you work with?"

"The professional kind. I work here, for the Warriors."

"Oh shit. Well, I sound like a fucking idiot, trying to impress you when you're over here working with professional athletes."

I'm married to one too. It's the first thing that crosses my mind, but I don't say it. Because soon enough, I won't be.

"It's fine. You don't need to try to impress me."

His sly smile grows as he steps even closer.

My skin instantly feels hot, not in a good way, but in an uncomfortable way. His hip grazes my thigh. He leaves it resting there, full, intentional contact, and I hate it. I try to turn away, but there's a couple on my other side so there's no room.

This wasn't supposed to happen. I've been practicing. I should be getting better at physical contact and casual touching. This is innocent, but I can't breathe because of how much I despise this simple graze of my thigh. I don't want him touching me.

And that scares the hell out of me because will I ever want anyone other than Isaiah to touch me? Will he always be the only man I'm comfortable with? And if so, what the hell are we doing with these lessons then? What's the point of it all if it's only him?

Holy fuck. Is it only him? Has it always been him?

"I'll be at the game on Monday," he says, dropping his palm to my thigh.

I flinch and don't even try to hide my body's visceral reaction to his touch.

He doesn't seem to notice or care, leaving his hand to rest there when he says, "My dad is a season ticket holder. So, after the game, maybe I can take you out for that drink?"

"I'm sorry, but can you please take your hand off me?"

He huffs an uncomfortable laugh. "What?"

I turn my body away from him, into the couple of inches of space I have. "Your hand. Can you please take it off me?"

"Okay . . ." The word is drawn out as if my question made me an absolute freak. Maybe I am.

He lifts his hands, both of them, holding them up in surrender as if what I said to him was threatening, and not a simple request.

I wish Isaiah were here.

Vincent attempts to save the moment. "So, what do you do for fun?"

"I uh . . . I work a lot. Or study. I'm kind of always trying to keep up on the newest research in my field, and I enjoy my alone time. I've gotten pretty good at entertaining myself over the years."

The face he makes . . . Oh God.

"So you've clearly been single a while, huh?"

How am I so bad at this?

"What do you do in your free time?" I ask.

"I spend a lot of my time at the gym. Play golf. I work for my dad, so I kind of make my own schedule."

He's literally every boy I ever grew up with.

I miss Isaiah.

His conversation. The way he looks at me. How he knows my cues, when to speed up. When to slow down.

He's simply across the field and I miss him.

"Do you have a last name, Kennedy?" Vincent asks as he once again steps into my space and places his hand on my shoulder, completely disregarding that I asked him not to.

I flinch, but it's only there for less than a second before his hand is forcibly removed.

Isaiah shoves him back a step.

"Rhodes," he says. "Her last name is Rhodes. Now get your fucking hands off my wife."

"Whoa, man," Vincent says with an awkward laugh. "It's cool. I'm a big fan of yours."

"I don't give a fuck who you are." Isaiah puts his body between us. "She asked you not to touch her."

"She didn't tell me she was married."

"She doesn't have to tell you shit. You clearly don't listen anyway." Isaiah grabs my left hand that's sandwiched between my legs and places it on the bar top. "But there's your fucking evidence."

"Everything okay, here?" a security guard steps up and asks.

"No. He needs to go."

"I didn't even do anything."

"Get him out of here."

"Isaiah," I say, attempting to reason with him.

"Please," Isaiah says only to the security guard, eyes begging. "Get him out of here before I do something stupid."

"You heard the man." The security guard holds his arm out to gesture the way to the exit.

"I didn't do anything wrong," Vincent argues.

"Well, it's his brother's award ceremony and I work for them, so you're out of here."

The security guard escorts Vincent to the exit.

There's an awkward tension hanging in the air, other people at the bar looking at us.

And Isaiah is *pissed*.

"Isaiah, that—"

"I'm not having this conversation right now."

His voice is hushed for only us to hear before he rebuttons his suit jacket as if nothing happened and uses those long legs of his to put as much distance between us as possible. He's across the field and down the dugout in no time at all.

I'm stuck in a state of disbelief before I put it in gear and chase after him.

"Isaiah!" I call out once I'm past the dugout to where it's only us.

He doesn't stop, continuing into the hallway that leads into the clubhouse.

"What's wrong with you? What the hell are you so pissed off about?"

Those words finally stop him, turning him back to face me, anger and hurt written all over his face.

"What's wrong with *me*?" He exhales out a dry laugh. "Oh, I don't know. Maybe that my brother just announced his retirement and I'm a fucking mess right now, Kennedy. And yeah, I get it. You're leaving too, but if you want to do that shit while we're still married—" He motions towards the field and bar where we just came from. "You can go ahead and give me divorce papers right now."

That halts me where I am, feet glued to the floor. "What?"

"You heard me." He loosens the tie around his neck. "I get what this is to you. I know you're going to see other people after me, but it's sure as shit not going to happen while you're still married to me."

"I didn't do anything!" My voice betrays me, frustration compounding because the entire time another man was hitting on me, I was thinking about *him*. Wanted it to be *him*.

That realization is too uncomfortable to admit, so I don't. I put it back on him.

"I didn't want him near me. I didn't want him touching me. But you can't stand there and say you haven't touched another girl since we were in Vegas."

His head visibly jerks back. "Are you fucking kidding me right now?"

"And we had no agreement in place that said you couldn't. I'm just saying, you can't tell me not to innocently talk to someone when you're—"

"When I'm what, Kennedy?" His voice is loud and angry. "When I'm constantly thinking about you? When I'm trying my best just to get you to *notice* me? Or when I'm too busy *not* touching other women. Because I haven't laid a finger on anyone other than you. Not once. And not just since we got married. I haven't even looked at another woman since the day I found out you ended your engagement. I would've waited for you since the day I met you had I known you weren't in love with your fiancé. For years, I thought you were happy with someone else. But I only found out ten months ago, Ken. For the last ten months, I thought I might have a real shot, so I've tried my fucking best. I've waited for you to see me, and I'd wait the rest of my life if I thought I ever had a real chance with you, but I don't. Do I? Never have."

I'm stunned silent, right there in the hallway with the field behind me and him in front.

"God." His exhale is full of agony. "Why can't you see it? Why can't you see me?"

I . . . I don't know what to say, what to do. Everything I thought I knew about this man has been flipped entirely on its head tonight. Though I guess it's been changing for weeks now.

I remember the day Isaiah found out about my failed engagement. I hadn't been wearing that gaudy ring for months at that point, but he didn't realize until one Sunday afternoon in the training room.

He startled me while I was working on his body, grabbing my left hand to inspect the bare finger. He quickly asked if I was okay, and once I told him I was, this guy's face lit up like a goddamn Christmas tree.

I didn't know then what I know now, that he completely changed his ways—or reverted to the old Isaiah, according to what his brother told me tonight.

Because of me.

Because he wants me.

Because he wants me to want him.

I've never been so comfortable. Never been so drawn to someone the way I am to him. I've never wanted to touch someone the way I touch him. Never wanted someone to touch *me* the way he so naturally does. Never wanted to be around someone the way I feel pulled into his orbit.

What the fuck am I doing?

It's as if all this time together, I've been practicing to be good enough for someone to want me, and he's been here all along, waiting.

My eyes may have been closed for a long time, but they're not anymore.

I *see* him.

Lifting his bowed head, he exhales a hard-earned breath. "I need a minute. Don't follow me," he says before turning down a side corridor, but I know exactly where he's going.

23

Kennedy

When I push open the door to the women's restroom where we first met, I find Isaiah with his hands braced on the sink counter, tie loosened, the top buttons of his shirt undone.

He's looking at his reflection as if he can't recognize the person looking back. Then his attention swings to me.

"I'm pissed off right now, Kenny, and I don't want to talk to you."

I try to ignore the sting of his words. He's upset. He's having a bad day and doesn't believe he's allowed to have them.

"Good." I lock the door behind me. "Be mad at me. I'm not going anywhere. You being pissed off doesn't scare me."

His brown eyes flash with confusion.

I slide into the space between him and the sink, reaching up to slip his tie over his head, tossing it to the side before my fingers find the still clasped buttons on his dress shirt.

"That's fine if you don't want to talk," I continue, undoing his shirt until it falls open. "I don't need to use words to show you that I want you."

He stills in confusion, as if he doesn't believe the words I said. And that's my fault. I confused him. I never let him believe there was a chance with us.

Because I never let myself realize he was there.

So, I do something I didn't know I would ever do in front of him—I begin to drop to my knees.

He sucks in an audible breath at the sight, but I keep my

eyes locked on his, waiting for permission, hands on my knees as I lower myself.

I'm waiting for his resolve to wash away. For his anger to fade, but it doesn't.

"Stop," he says harshly, taking a step back and forcing me to stay on my feet.

My stomach sinks with embarrassment at his command.

As much as I was trying to fake it, I'm in no way *comfortable* doing this. But I wanted to, for him. This is my worst fear, after all, letting myself want someone only for them to realize they're good without me. It's why I never have.

"I'm sorry," I apologize, arms crossed over my middle.

"Don't fucking apologize." He watches me with rapt attention as he peels off his suit jacket and drapes it on the bathroom floor between us. "*Now* you can get on your knees in front of me."

Oh.

There's absolutely no playfulness in his tone. It's commanding and harsh in a way I never thought I'd hear him be with me. But at the same time, I love it. He feels secure enough to be whoever he needs to be when I'm around. He's not the goofy and lighthearted Isaiah right now, and I have the privilege to see this other side of him.

With feigned confidence, I drop onto his suit jacket, propping myself up on my knees in front of him, palms braced on his quads. My hands look comically small in comparison to his legs, the ring on my finger shining like a goddamn beacon.

"Look at you," he says, running his thumb over my mouth. "Plump lips parted and ready for me. Brown eyes big and so fucking innocent."

"Can you teach me what to do?"

His erection is evident against his zipper as his jaw visibly tics.

"You've never sucked a cock before?"

"I have." My words are quiet as I start undoing his belt. "But I was told I wasn't very good at it, and I want to be. So, I need you to teach me how to do it."

He runs a palm over my hair, his nostrils flaring as if he were trying to stay in control. "I'll teach you how to be good, baby, but I'm sure as fuck not going to teach you for anyone else. I'm going to teach you how to be good for *me*."

Fuck.

I swivel my hips in a slow circle, looking for friction, but there's none with my knees spread the way they are. So instead, I focus on unbuttoning his pants and dropping his zipper.

He uses his forefinger to lift both my chin and my attention to him.

Jesus, he's downright feral.

"I don't want to be nice to you right now, Kenny. I'm pissed off, and I don't feel like faking it."

I run my tongue over my lower lip, and he tracks the entire thing, looking like some kind of predator.

"I don't want you to fake anything with me."

The words hang heavy in the air because I'm no longer referring to him faking his demeanor.

We don't break eye contact, me on my knees and him standing over me.

His jaw tics. "Take it out."

I do what he says, dropping his pants to his ankles and tugging his boxer briefs down with them. His cock springs free, right in front of me, pulling this desperate sound from deep in his throat as he watches me. He traces every inch of my face as if he plans to paint it soon.

His cock is only inches from my face, and I can't look away. Angry veins and leaking tip. Fuck, I want it. I want him.

He runs a palm over my head again, my hair slipping between his fingers, cupping the back of my skull to keep me held in my exact position.

"Get it wet."

My eyes shoot to his.

"Spit on it. Lick it. I don't give a fuck, but get it wet for me, Kenny."

Jesus. I'm a squirming mess as I use the tip of my tongue to lick a path over the slit, cleaning up the bead of precum.

His eyes instantly roll back.

"Mmm," he hums, his entire body vibrating. "Just like that."

His words spur me on as I grip his shaft with one hand and lick a path from root to tip.

"Yes," he hisses between his teeth. "I've wanted this for so fucking long."

I attempt to make it worth his wait as I look up at him, flutter my lashes over my heavy eyes, and round my lips to suck him in. Head bobbing, I stroke my tongue in tandem with my lips, but he hits the back of my throat far too soon because he's much bigger than I've ever been with. I keep him there, swallowing around the tip until my eyes are forced closed with tears gathering at the corners, my throat constricting with a choke.

"Jesus, fuck." He falls forward, bracing himself on the sink with one hand, using the other to tug my hair, forcing me to pull back and take a breath. "Who told you that you weren't good at this?"

I don't answer because he already knows. I simply suck in some hard-earned oxygen.

His jaw flexes as he's bent over, face hovering just inches above mine, cock glistening with my saliva. "He's a goddamn liar. I don't need to teach you shit."

Isaiah runs his thumb by the corner of my eye, gathering the moisture that pooled there.

"I'm going to ruin your makeup." There's no warning in his tone. It's simply a statement. "Then I'm going to ruin you for anyone else. You got it?"

I eagerly nod in agreement.

"Use your words."

"Yes," I exhale.

"Now keep doing what you're doing."

So I do. With my fist, I stroke him, turning my hand to create friction. Then I add my mouth, sucking him deep before coming off him with a lewd pop.

"So fucking good, Kenny. Don't listen to anyone else. Listen to me. You know exactly what you're doing."

I don't know what I'm doing, but I follow his cues. His entire abdomen contracts when I use my lips to stroke him, so I keep doing that. His breathing picks up when I flick my tongue over the underside of his head, and then completely stops when I reach up and cup his balls while pushing him into the back of my throat again.

"Fuck." His curse is sharp as he pulls out of me. "I'm going to come. It's been way too long and I'm going to come already."

I nod eagerly, in my fancy gown on the floor of the bathroom with mascara running down my cheeks and spit gathering around the corner of my lips.

Like the classy lady I was raised to be.

He bends over me, gripping my chin. "You going to let me come in your mouth?"

"Yes." My breaths are short and choppy. "Please."

"Are you going to be a good little wife and swallow it all for me?"

I nod far too enthusiastically.

"Good." He licks across my lips and finishes it with a kiss. "Now, take a deep breath because it's the last one you're going to get for a while."

He runs a gentle thumb over my cheekbone, starkly contrasting the warning that he didn't want to be nice to me, but that's the only tender moment he gives before guiding my head forward.

As soon as my lips are around him, he sets the pace, fucking my face in a steady rhythm. Palms covering my ears, it's as if everything else drowns out around me. It's only him and his body reacting to me.

God, the way he's looking down at me, his anger mixed with so much need. It's the hottest thing I've ever witnessed, and I have never felt more powerful than I do now, knowing I'm capable of unraveling him.

I use his legs for support, fingernails digging into his flesh to hold on.

"Hmm," he hums.

Isaiah watches the way my hands move over him, softly exploring his thighs until they curve around and squeeze his ass. He holds my head and pushes his cock to the back of my throat when I do.

He's big, towering over me like this. It's a vulnerable position to be in, at the mercy of someone his size, but I've never trusted someone the way I do Isaiah. He pushes into me, but never too far. He keeps pace, but always makes sure I can breathe, visually checking in with me that I'm okay.

"God, you're so fucking good, Kenny, and that pisses me off that you'd be this good for anyone else."

Eyes locked on his, I shake my head.

"What's that?" he asks in this menacing tone, knowing I'm not able to respond with words. "You're not going to be good for anyone else?"

I shake my head as he continues to fuck my mouth.

"You're only going to be good for me?"

His thrusts are equally as frantic as his words, and I love it. I nod, my eyes begging for him to believe me.

"Only me, Kenny?"

I moan around his length, my hips rhythmically searching for friction.

"Goddamn, baby. Are you turned on from sucking me off?"

He pulls out of me, giving me a moment to breathe properly. Giving me a chance to *think* properly. "Yes."

"Slip your fingers under that dress of yours and show me."

Heat prickles my skin. I feel a little shy, a little exposed. A bit contradictory seeing as he's the one almost entirely naked, cock out in the bathroom at our place of work.

He uses a single shaking hand to run through his perfect hair. "Show me."

I tentatively reach under my dress and gather my arousal on two fingers, holding the evidence up for him to see.

"Fuck," he growls, his eyes going dark as they lock on my fingers. "You'd do anything I told you to do right now, wouldn't you?"

"Anything."

Isaiah bends over, grabbing my hand, and slipping my fingers into his warm, wet mouth before flicking his tongue over the tips in a way he might do to a very different part of my body.

He nods towards his cock, covered in my saliva, hard and ready to come. "Finish the job, Ken."

I can't hold back my smirk, seeing him a little bit unhinged, a little bit wild with me.

"You think this is funny? I'm out of my goddamn mind right now. I don't ever want to see another man touch you again."

In response, I hold eye contact, gripping his shaft, and bringing my mouth back to cover him.

"Yes," he moans, head falling back. "Never again."

"Never."

I work his length with one hand, wrapping my lips around the head. It doesn't take long until his hips jerk in short, sloppy movements. His breathing is labored, his sounds mesmerizing.

"Kenny," he cries out, followed by a whimper of desperation.

Contrary to his words, Isaiah tenderly holds my other hand—my left hand, rubbing his thumb over my ring—and then he's coming in my mouth.

I watch the whole thing. The way he folds over and braces himself on one arm, using the sink behind me. The way he tries to keep his eyes locked on mine until the sensation forces them to close. The way every muscle coils up when hot pulses hit the back of my throat. The way he holds my hand the entire time, as if he needed some part of him to be sweet with me the way he typically is.

Reopening his eyes, every ounce of anger washes away.

He gently brushes my hair out of my face. "So pretty like this," he says. "Mouth full of my cum." The pad of his thumb traces down the line of my throat. "Now swallow it."

I don't even hesitate and do as I'm told.

In one swift movement, he pulls his pants up and drops onto his haunches to be eye level with me. "Did I hurt you?"

His question is frantic, his tone concerned.

"No."

"Tell me the truth, Kennedy." He quickly tries to wipe away my smeared mascara streaks, his thumbs frantically attempting to clean any evidence of what just happened. "I shouldn't have talked to you like that."

"I am telling you the truth."

He pauses, as if he can't believe me, those concerned brown eyes meeting mine.

My thoughtful husband is back.

"I liked it," I reassure him.

His grin is lopsided and lazy before he pulls me in for a searing kiss. It's desperate and apologetic all at the same time.

He stands, pulling me to stand with him, keeping me pinned to the sink as he reaches behind me and wets a towel. He takes his time, gently cleaning up my face, under my eyes, my lips.

"I'm okay, Isaiah."

"You're better than okay, Kenny. You're perfect."

"Are you still mad at me?"

Hooking his hands under my thighs, he lifts me, wrapping my legs around his waist as he carries me to the couch on the far side of the bathroom. I don't know that anyone has ever sat on it, seeing as I'm one of two people who ever come in here, unless Isaiah is spending his free time relaxing on the couch in the women's restroom.

He sits and positions me to straddle his lap, my gown bunching up around my hips.

His voice is low, kept quiet in the small space between us. "You followed me when I told you not to."

"Sometimes I don't like to listen to you."

His eyes sparkle with mischief. "And sometimes you listen and obey real fucking well." I huff a laugh as he pushes my hair back, big hands bracketing my jaw. "Why though?" he asks.

"Because I'm not afraid that you're human. You having a bad day or a bad moment is not going to make me want to be around you any less. I have lots of bad moments and still you come back for more."

"I'll always come back for more when it comes to you."

"Then why can't you believe that I'd do the same for you?" I ask.

Lips parting, Isaiah's eyes bounce between mine, but he has no retort. Instead, he pulls me in and kisses me.

Softly at first, but it quickly turns hard, rough, and desperate.

A moan escapes me when he wraps an arm around my waist, using his other hand to push my hips into his. He's getting hard again.

"Already?" I ask against his lips, continuing to rock myself on his lap.

"I walk around with a constant hard-on thanks to you, wifey." In a swift movement, I'm on my back and Isaiah is on top of me, his long body between my legs. "But I'm more concerned with this right now."

Palm covering my belly, his thumb traces a slow line over my clit.

"How wet are you from blowing me in the bathroom at our place of work?"

"I'm soaked."

He groans.

"Dripping," I continue. "I felt it run down my thighs when you held me in place and used my mouth."

"You liked that?"

A smirk lifts on my lips. "I loved it."

His smile matches mine when he leans down and presses his mouth to mine. His tongue sweeps in and the way it moves has me imagining how it'd glide over a different part of my body.

"What do you need?" he whispers.

"I need you to fuck me."

Isaiah stills above me.

"What?"

"I. Need. You. To. Fuck. Me." They're words I never thought I'd say.

"Tonight?"

"Right now."

"Ken." His forehead falls to my chest. "I have been dreaming about the day you might say that to me, but I can't. Not like this. I'm having a shit night. You leave tomorrow. There's a lot of emotions going on and I don't want you to regret it in the morning."

"I won't," I quickly disagree. "I know I won't regret it."

He doesn't believe me, and I don't blame him. I've resisted this for years. From his point of view, it *does* seem like I suddenly changed my mind. And shit, maybe I did. Maybe everything I learned about him tonight is what I was wishing for from him all along. Maybe now I know his feelings towards me aren't spurred on by wanting something he can't have.

"Fine," I relent. "Then I'll take your mouth."

His lips tilt, that devilish, knowing smile he's mastered over the years. "Where?"

A heat creeps up my cheeks, but it quickly cools when I remember who I'm with. "On my pussy."

"Fuck," he growls. "My prim and proper wife did not just say 'pussy' to me. You keep talking like that and I'm going to come again."

I chuckle below him. "I would really love it if we stopped talking altogether and you got to work. Show me what you've got, Rhodes."

He laughs. "You know I like it when you're a little bit mean to me, Kenny. Makes me want to work harder for you."

Hand wrapping around his nape, I thread my fingers through his hair, running my nails up his scalp until I get to his crown and push down, leading him down my body.

He chuckles to himself as he scoots back on his knees, finding a comfortable spot between my open legs.

He slowly lifts my dress, pushing it up my thighs. "What color panties am I going to find under here?"

My dress gathers over my middle, the back still pinned under my ass, and I watch as Isaiah's eyes instantly heat, his nostrils flaring when his attention snags on the apex of my thighs.

"You're not going to find any at all."

Sitting back, heels to ass, he doesn't take his attention off me. He scrubs a big palm over his mouth as he traces every inch of my core with his eyes.

"You weren't wearing panties this whole time?"

I shake my head no. "It caused lines with my dress."

"I have no fucking clue what that means, and I don't care." He runs the pad of his thumb up my inner thigh, cleaning up my arousal. "Fuck me. You really were dripping, weren't you?"

"Everywhere."

"We've got to clean you up, baby. You can't be walking around like this. God, this must fucking ache."

"So much. I need you to help me."

"I will."

Isaiah slides down the couch, hooking his forearms under my legs and using his fingers to separate me. The pads of his thumbs sweep up my center, and our matching moans echo off the bathroom walls.

"I should've known," he says, licking a path down my inner thigh, cleaning up my previous mess, "that your pussy would be as perfect as the rest of you."

"Did you ever think about it before tonight?"

"Are you fucking kidding me?" His hooded eyes bounce up to mine as he licks another path on the opposite leg. "Countless times, Kenny. I thought about how you'd taste." His tongue darts out to clean up his lower lip. "Fucking heavenly, by the way. I thought about the way you'd squirm under me. I thought about the way you'd grip my fingers and one day, maybe my cock. I thought about it all. But my imagination wasn't nearly as good as the real thing."

He licks a line up the center of my pussy, eyes locked on mine when my back bows off the couch. He hums against my core, sending a wicked vibration up my entire body.

"I want to be so good for you."

I nod quickly. "You always are."

"Has anyone ever done this to you?"

"Yes. A few times."

His eyes flash with annoyance. "Did you come?"

"No. You're the only person who's ever made me come besides myself."

He places a soft kiss on my clit. "Do you touch yourself, Kenny?"

"Sometimes."

"Good." He licks me in one long, languid stroke. "Show me."

"What?"

"You want to learn, but so do I. Teach me how you like to be touched."

Isaiah gently takes my hand in his, guiding it down my body, over my bunched dress and between my legs.

"Teach me."

His breaths are labored, his exposed chest expanding and contracting at a quickening pace, but his breathing entirely stops when I glide my fingers down, running the pad of my middle one over my clit.

"*Fuck.*" It's silent, as if he forgot to use his voice.

"I start like this." My hips follow my fingers. "Then I do small circles."

"Like this?" he asks when he takes my fingers away and bends, his tongue mirroring my movements, circling over my clit in a rhythmic pattern.

"Oh," I moan. "Yeah, just like that."

"What else?" He replaces my fingers as he pulls back to watch, his lips glistening with my arousal, and that image alone almost sends me over the edge.

"This." Up and down, up and down in short fluid motions.

He holds my hand out of the way, using his tongue to match my fingers.

But it feels infinitely better. He takes his time, licking me with pressure, and I can't help but chase his mouth with my hips as they lift from the couch, looking for more.

He moans. He *fucking* moans from tasting me.

Nothing about this is hurried. For the first time in my life this doesn't feel like a simple checkmark on the way to sex, done quickly and inattentively, ready to move on to the next thing.

Isaiah is tasting me as if there's nowhere else he'd rather be.

He's sprawled on the couch, one leg bent, the other extended, laying like a goddamn sniper as he eats me out. He's never been more handsome than he is right now between my legs, hair tousled, lips shining.

"What about fingers? You ever finger yourself?"

"Sometimes."

"Show me."

There's not a single moment of hesitation. I feel drunk on him, mindless and loose as I slip my fingers between my legs and push the middle one inside.

"Goddamn," Isaiah exhales. "That is the hottest fucking thing I've ever seen."

I pull it out and push it back in again.

"You're fucking soaked, Ken."

"I really want to come." My voice is a whine, my finger moving frantically, as if I could make it happen myself.

"I know, baby. You're close, aren't you?"

I nod, desperate, begging eyes connected with his.

"Can I show you something I think you're going to like?"

"Please."

He pulls my finger out, slipping it into his mouth to clean off before latching his lips around my clit again. In the same breath, my single finger is replaced with his two. They curl upward, stroking a spot I've never had touched before, and I'm done. I'm a mess. I'm entirely at his mercy.

My whole body is almost off the couch, writhing with the sensation. His mouth never leaves me, moving in tandem with his fingers, both our bodies rocking together as if he were really fucking me and not with only his mouth and hand.

"Holy fuck, Ken. You're so goddamn tight. I can feel you pulsing around me."

As his hair falls over his eyes, I slide my fingers through it, pushing it back, holding it to his head to give me a clearer view of what he's doing.

He wickedly smiles up at me, his tongue moving in long, languid strokes.

Isaiah adds his thumb against my clit, rubbing small circles over the bud, his tongue flicking it in tandem, and I'm out of my goddamn mind.

The pressure is too much. It sits right on the edge until it spills over and I'm falling.

"Isaiah," is all I can plead before I'm coming.

Wave after wave rip through me. I keep my attention on him until I can't any longer, my eyes screwing shut with the force of my orgasm. It doesn't stop. It feels like it lasts for minutes on end, and Isaiah keeps his mouth on me the entire time, licking up the evidence.

I can feel his eyes on me before I hear him chant my name like a desperate, pleading prayer, and it only extends my release.

When I finally come down, my muscles uncoiling, I slump back onto the couch. My breaths are labored and earned, and I can only imagine how untethered I look.

Auburn hair sprawled beneath me. Ruined makeup and a wrinkled gown.

Unpolished and imperfect.

It's the most relaxed I've ever felt.

"Shit," Isaiah exhales when he climbs onto his knees, eyes focused on the crotch of his pants.

"Did you . . ."

"Come?" he finishes the sentence for me. "Yeah."

"From . . ."

This confident man holds no apology in his gaze when he looks up at me, devilish smirk tilted on his lips.

"From eating you out. Watching you come. Hearing my name as you did. I couldn't help it. You turn me on, Kenny. It shouldn't come as much of a surprise that I came in my fucking pants like some inexperienced dork seeing as you know exactly how obsessed I am with you."

He might not blush, but I do.

He crawls over my body, draping himself over me on the couch, and with a heavy, exhausted sigh, he melts into my shoulder.

"We should get you home and into bed," I whisper.

"I know. I should get going. It's not like I can go back out there like this anyway."

I hold him there, my arms wrapped around him. There's a moment of hesitation before I ask, "Can I stay with you tonight?"

"Yes." He lifts to look at me, quickly agreeing as if I were going to change my mind. "Of course you can."

He bends to kiss me before resting his head on my shoulder once again, too exhausted from everything that happened tonight.

My fingers twirl the ends of his hair. "I don't think I'll ever be able to be comfortable with someone the way I am with you."

Fuck, that didn't come out right.

A heavy pause lingers between us.

"I'm sure you'll get there," he eventually says. "I know that's what you want."

It's supposed to be said in an encouraging way, but his voice is full of defeat.

But what if I don't? The question is on the tip of my tongue because that's what I meant.

I don't think there's any part of me that *wants* to be this comfortable with someone else.

24

Isaiah

The ride to my apartment is silent.

I offered to swing by her place tonight, let her change and grab her suitcase for tomorrow, but she assured me she would have time before her flight and would rather we just get home.

Yes, *home*. As if it were both of ours and not just mine. As if she doesn't have her own penthouse apartment eight blocks away. Ridiculous fantasies were playing on a loop after she threw that word out, and I had to quickly shut them down.

I'm driving with my left hand on the wheel, my right one resting on her thigh, stroking a repeated pattern with my thumb. Back and forth. Back and forth.

Like a silent apology she says she doesn't need.

I hated every word that came out of my mouth in that hallway, regardless that they were true. I never wanted to admit to her that I knew she wasn't interested, simply because I wasn't ready for her to agree.

If it were any other day, maybe I could've laughed it off, let her explain to me how some guy hit on her while I held in my bitterness towards our fucked-up situation. Maybe I wouldn't have shown how much it hurts to not only know she's going to move on after me but have to physically see it happen before my eyes.

She barely entertained him, simply spoke to him enough to not be rude. But he looked like he could've been another rich asshole her parents would've forced her to marry, and I snapped.

Today I'm fucking wrecked, emotionally wrung out from the realization that next season, I will once again be alone. Kennedy flies out for her interview tomorrow, and sure, Kai will still be living in Chicago, but it's different knowing that he won't be on the field with me ever again. I didn't expect his retirement to come so soon.

And I took it out on her.

Because she's leaving me too. We all know she's getting that job, and I'm tired of people I care about not sticking around. I play it safe, hoping if I'm enough of a laugh, if they have a good enough time around me, they'll stay. It never works. Kennedy's leaving anyway, so I guess I thought she may as well see all the facets of me I'm too scared to show everyone else before she goes.

Jaded, and bitter, and really fucking tired.

God, I'm so fucking tired.

When I park in my spot outside of my apartment, I kill the engine and sit. Too exhausted to move and too ashamed of how I was with her to say anything.

We sit in silence for a couple of minutes until Kennedy gets out of the car and rounds the hood to open my door.

"Come on," she says, standing there in that pretty white dress.

"I was going to open the door for you. You didn't give me a chance."

A knowing smile lifts on her lips. "You were going to fall asleep if you sat there any longer."

She holds her hand out for mine and leads me into my apartment building, as if she's been here countless times before and knows her way around.

I like it far too much.

She chuckles to herself when she sees the *Bless this Mess* doormat, and when she goes inside, she doesn't hesitate to kick her heels off by the couch and turn her back to me, holding her hair up with both hands.

Crossing the room, I take my time undoing the top buttons of her dress, fully expecting her to use a hand on her chest to hold the fabric up.

She doesn't.

She continues to hold her hair, letting the dress fold over her waist.

And when I slowly unzip the part that connects just above her ass, I practically choke when she lets the entire thing fall and pool at her feet.

My wife stands there, butt-ass naked in the middle of my living room. The only thing on her body is her jewelry.

Hands dropping, her auburn hair falls over her back as she walks right to my room, moving slowly and allowing me to watch, done in a way that her heart-shaped ass sways with each step.

Fucking mesmerizing, seeing Kennedy Kay walk her naked self into my bedroom.

"I thought you wanted me to go to bed," I call out.

"You are. But I thought I'd give you a little reminder that you told me you wouldn't have sex with me tonight."

"You're not a nice woman. I'm not sure if anyone has told you that."

She shoots me a devastating smile over her shoulder, and when she reaches the door to my bedroom, she taps her fingers on the "live, laugh, love" sign. That grin instantly turns cute and teasing before she slips into my room.

I want to follow her, toss her on the bed, and change my mind about not fucking her tonight. Maybe see if the lesson she wants to learn next is how to ride my cock.

But I'm not wrong here. It was an emotional night and I don't think I could survive if Kennedy woke up tomorrow and looked at me with regret.

Not to mention, the reminder of what she said back at the field sits heavy on my mind. That she doesn't know if she'll be able to be so comfortable with someone else. It doesn't change the fact that she wants to be. That's what we're doing here, after all.

Staying married so she can get a job on the other side of the country. Playing a game I wish was real. Teaching her things that she doesn't need to learn, because she's a fucking natural at them when she's doing them because she *wants* to.

And I'm in so fucking deep there's no way up.

This disappointment I've avoided my entire adult life is compounding into one person that I let myself truly fall for. That I let myself truly believe I could have a shot with. It doesn't matter that our marriage is fake. The heartbreak is going to be so fucking real.

The door to my bedroom opens, and my groan is involuntary. "You're joking."

She stands there in the threshold, wearing one of my tees that may as well be a dress on her, and then she slightly lifts the hem, revealing the pair of my boxer briefs she's planning to sleep in.

"What's yours is mine," she teases. "Isn't that how this whole marriage thing works?"

"You can have literally whatever you want as long as you're wearing that when you ask."

"So, you'll have sex with me then?"

"Ken—"

"Kidding." She nudges her head towards my bedroom. "C'mon. I started the shower for you."

My dragging feet carry me to my room, where Kennedy ushers me to sit on the edge of the bed. Standing between my spread legs, she removes my tie and unbuttons my shirt.

"I can do it." My statement is hardly a protest and I make no move to stop her.

"So can I."

"Kenny—"

"Let me take care of you for once. You're always doing things for me. It's time I return the favor."

God, and it feels good to let her. My head lolls as she slips her hands beneath the fabric of my shirt, pushing it over my shoulders, and once it's off me and draped on the bed, I drop my forehead to her stomach.

"I'm sorry for taking it out on you tonight, everything I was feeling. None of it was your fault."

She slides her fingers into my hair, holding me to her. "You don't need to apologize to me."

"But I do." I glide my fingertips to the back of her thigh, gently tracing the soft skin there. "I just . . . It's been a rough day, and I'm not used to showing people my rough days. So, thank you for coming back to find me."

"Always."

My head lifts at that. I want to believe that she truly means *always*, but the fact of the matter is, tomorrow, she's leaving for an interview she's waited for her entire career.

"Always" has a very limited time frame for us.

She takes her time undressing me, and it's a real humbling moment when she crouches to remove my shoes, followed by my pants. I watch as she goes to my dresser, pulling out a fresh pair of boxers for me to wear post shower.

She turns to leave, but I grab her hand, pulling her back to stand between my spread legs and finding her mouth with a soft kiss.

"Can I steal some toothpaste?" she asks.

"Yeah." I kiss her again. "You need it."

She scoffs in faux horror, smacking me in the chest. "If you're telling me I have bad breath, you can take full responsibility for that. I did have your dick in my mouth, after all."

"Oh, hell yeah, you did." I pull her down and kiss her again. Harder this time. "I changed my mind. Don't brush your teeth. I like knowing my cock was the last thing in there."

Her head falls back in an easy laugh, and God, is it fucking beautiful.

"Mmm. And you still taste like my pussy."

"For fuck's sake, Ken. I already came in my pants once tonight. Can you not say 'pussy' so casually like that without any warning?"

She's off and sauntering her way into my bathroom, but not before she looks over her shoulder and mouths the word *pussy* as she disappears.

A burst of energy hits me and I'm off the bed and following her.

"Don't brush your teeth until I'm done with my shower."

"What?" she asks with a laugh. "Why?"

I drop my boxer briefs to the floor and my smile beams like a fucking glowstick from the way her eyes follow me.

"Because," I say, stark-ass naked, "it sounds like something domestic as hell I'd like to do with my wife."

My shower is quick, just a rinse to get the day off me, but I watch her watch me through the glass the entire time. I'm out, toweled off, and in my fresh pair of boxers in less than five minutes, because apparently, I've gotten to the lovesick phase where even a glass wall is too much distance to put between us.

That's probably going to be a big fucking problem for me when she flies out to California tomorrow.

She grabs my toothpaste from the cup by the sink, her opposite index finger stretched out as if she were going to use it as a makeshift toothbrush.

"Hold up," I tell her, rifling through a few of my drawers. Tucked into the back of my second vanity drawer, I pull out the toothbrush I bought for her weeks ago. "This is for you."

She freezes with the still packaged toothbrush in her hand.

"Is that the right one?"

From what I remember, it's the exact one I bought her the first night we shared a hotel room. Soft bristles. Purple handle. Well, at least, the cashier told me it was the purple-handled one.

"How long have you had this in there?"

Pulling my toothbrush out of the cup, I attempt the whole nonchalant thing when I say, "I bought it when we got home from that trip. After we went to dinner and you asked me to teach you some things, I thought there might be a night where you would stay over here." I find her reflection in the mirror. "I had hoped, at least."

Her expression completely melts, the sometimes-cold Kennedy not even attempting to hide how she feels. "I should've stayed the last time I was here."

I pop my shoulders. "I followed you home anyway."

"What?" She bursts a laugh. "You did not, you stalker."

"You really thought I was going to let you leave my house in the middle of the night without making sure you got home safely? I drove by, watched you get inside, before I came back here to deal with my three drunk friends. All the while, my mind couldn't get rid of the memory of how hard you made me come and how much I liked seeing you in those little lace panties and matching bra."

She opens her new toothbrush and I squeeze a line of toothpaste on it before doing the same to mine. We both face the mirror, her standing in front of me as we brush our teeth.

"A little sexier than this outfit, huh?" she asks over a mouth full of suds.

"Oh fuck no. This . . ." I circle my finger in her direction. "This is going in the spank bank reserve."

She giggles with her mouth full, and I swear to God, if I could bottle that sound, I would.

The rest of the two minutes is silent. Us brushing our teeth like the domestic, married couple we're pretending to be.

She smiles up at me anytime she catches me watching her in the reflection.

I hold her hair when she goes to spit into the sink, then bend over her and do the same.

I want this. These simple, normal moments that couples have, but I only want them with her and I want them to be real.

"Let's go to bed," she says, putting her toothbrush in the cup next to mine. "You're exhausted."

I didn't want to assume, but I was so fucking hopeful on the drive over here that when she asked to sleep at my house tonight, she meant for me to sleep next to her.

The martyr in me would offer to take the couch. Wait until she clearly states she wants me to sleep in the bed with her, but I'm too fucking tired to act the martyr tonight.

I want to sleep in my bed with my wife.

I follow her out, turning off the lights behind me. Kennedy slips under the covers to the same side she used the last time she was here, and I round the bed to mine, standing there.

There's a part of me that's waiting for her to change her mind. After all these weeks of me sleeping on the floor, I'm anticipating her to tell me to do the same tonight.

"What are you waiting for?" She's got this playful smile on her lips. "Aren't you going to teach me how to cuddle or something like that?"

"You're a dork. You know that?"

I slip under the covers with her.

"You love it."

She's got the sheets held up to her chin, beaming grin on her mouth, like she's far too giddy about this sleepover, and honestly, so am I.

"Yeah," I exhale, sinking into my pillow and facing her. "I do."

"Thanks for letting me stay over. After sharing the same room with you on the road, my apartment has felt a bit lonely lately."

"You can stay here anytime, Ken. You know that."

"Okay."

I scoot closer to her, my feet wrapping over hers under the sheet. "Okay."

Her hand slips out from under the blanket, cupping my cheek, her thumb dusting over the bone there. "You're tired."

I nod, leaning into her touch.

"Are you going to be okay?"

Her eyes bounce over my face, searching for my answer.

"I don't know," I tell her truthfully. "But I'm feeling good right now."

A soft tilt lifts her lips. "Has anyone ever told you that you're a lover boy?"

With a chuckle, I shift, laying my head on her shoulder, and in equal time, she wraps both arms around me while mine goes around her middle.

"I don't think anyone else has seen that side of me much, but yeah. You have no idea."

Leaning down, her lips meet my hair. "I think I'm starting to figure it out."

A few silent minutes pass between us and I'm close to sleep, this overwhelming calmness washing over me that in this moment I've got everything I've ever wanted.

But that's the problem, my anxiety screams. *It's only in this moment.*

"Kenny," I whisper. "Will you still be here when I wake up?"

"Of course." Her voice is sleepy. "I'm not going anywhere."

25

Kennedy

I woke up with a giant 6'4" man sprawled on top of me. His legs were between mine, his torso pinning me to the mattress. His head was tucked into the crook of my neck, and his arm was wrapped under my back.

I was a human pillow for Isaiah Rhodes, and I've never slept better.

When I went to use his shower this morning, I came out to a copy of today's *Times* with the crossword puzzle pulled out and already folded for me. It was accompanied by a coffee and a couple of toasted Eggos.

He almost lost his shit when I told him I had never had an Eggo before, but even more so when I mentioned I wasn't sure if I had time to eat before work.

My childhood home had a live-in chef, so fun, frozen food was never an option. And neither was skipping breakfast today. Isaiah has an odd affixation with feeding me and I think it might be my newly unlocked love language. Because it does things to me every time.

And now, here I am in his car on the way to the airport, leaving what I think might be what I've always been looking for.

Before batting practice, we went to my apartment so I could pack and change into clothes that weren't his, and once again, I left my car at the field and opted to ride passenger with him. But he's been silent most of the ride, entirely in his own head.

We haven't kissed today. We haven't touched. It's clear that neither of us knows where we stand in the light of day, and it didn't help that once we left his apartment, we were at the field all morning for Sunday batting practice, unable to really talk about things before leaving for my interview.

"You have everything you need?" Isaiah finally asks.

One strong hand on the wheel, sporting that backwards baseball hat that has me imagining all sorts of things I'd like him to do to me while wearing it.

"It's only a couple of days," I remind him.

He keeps his eyes on the road. "A couple of days could change a lot."

"Or I might not get the job at all."

And I shouldn't be entertaining that option. This is everything I've wanted. A position I've dreamed of. A city I would love to live in.

He shoots me a quick, deadpanned glare before refocusing on the road ahead of him. "You've got this, Kenny." His tone is full of encouragement, as if that's what he thinks I'm looking for. "In case you don't already know this, I'm so fucking proud of you."

My throat instantly feels thick. Impossible to swallow.

No one has ever said that to me before. I got a high score on my MCATs and my mother asked me when I was setting a wedding date. I thought I got the position I wanted in Chicago and Connor asked how many times a year he was expected to visit.

My voice is embarrassingly small. "You are?"

"Hell yeah. Even when I didn't know you, that first day I heard you with Dr. Fredrick, I was so impressed by you. I don't have to tell you how few women there are in professional sports, and you're doing it, Kennedy. In case you haven't figured it out yet . . ." He laughs to himself. ". . . I'm kind of a huge fan of yours."

Isaiah pulls his car up to the curb outside of terminal two, setting it in park. Finally, he undoes his seat belt and fully turns to face me.

"Go in, show off that big brain of yours, and be yourself. There's no way they're not going to love you the way that I l—" He stops himself.

My eyes go wide and his mirror them.

"Llllive, laugh, love you," he finishes. "The way I live, laugh, love you."

He says it so confidently the second time, but it still makes no fucking sense. Regardless, I can't help but burst a laugh.

"You live, laugh, love me?"

"God, so fucking much."

The car fills with our mutual laughter, and there's a part of me that wants to stay here all day, in this bubble of just him and me. Not thinking about my career I've worked hard for, not dwelling on the fact that this marriage is fake, and not worrying that regardless of anything different I might be feeling, next season I won't be working for the Warriors.

Because those are the facts. Whether or not I get this job, my time in Chicago is done. Isaiah agreed to fix our drunken mistake for the span of one baseball season. Not for eternity.

"Are you going to do your crossword on the plane?"

"That's my plan."

"You know, I've always wondered, but never asked. Why do you do those every day?"

I shrug. "When I was younger, I didn't get a lot of attention from my parents. I was an only child, and I was bored out of my mind most days. But my father, he'd get the *Times* delivered each morning to read the business section, so I started stealing the crossword to keep myself busy. Felt less lonely when my mind was occupied, you know?"

Isaiah's brows crease as if he hates that answer. "And you still feel that way? You do them because you're lonely?"

"I suppose so." I huff a dry laugh. "But I guess it says something that I haven't finished one in weeks, huh?"

His smile turns proud.

There's a knock on my window that startles us both.

"Keep it moving," the security guard says.

Cars are dipping in and out around us and it's time for me to go.

Isaiah's expression changes once again, and something I appreciate about him is that he's easy to read. He wears his emotions on his sleeve, and it's clear he doesn't want me to go. But regardless, he knows I have to, so he gets out of the car, pops his trunk, and pulls out my suitcase. I join him, standing on the curb with him on the asphalt. It still does nothing for our height difference.

"So, I'll see you soon then." His words are even, emotionless, nonchalant.

I can read right through it. He doesn't want to get hurt.

"Couple days."

He lifts his hat, running a palm over his hair before replacing it. "Have fun. Be safe. Drink water."

"All right, Mom."

"Don't forget about me," he adds with a spark of humor, but his teasing grin quickly falls.

I couldn't if I tried.

"Tomorrow before the game, if Sanderson is the one taping your wrists, make sure he does it the way I showed you. Because sometimes he does it too tight. If you need to, Facetime me pre-game, I can walk him through it—"

Isaiah's teasing smirk is back.

I have yet to miss a game or practice since I started with the Warriors, and I'm having a serious case of apprehensiveness, knowing that tomorrow's night game will be the first without me.

"I'm sure he'll do fine," I correct.

"He's not you, that's for damn sure. You'll be missed, Kenny, and not just by me. The boys will miss seeing you at the clubhouse tomorrow too."

"Don't forget about me," I repeat his words.

"I couldn't if I tried."

"Hey! Let's go." It's the same security guard as before. "This is a drop-off zone. Get your car out of here."

"I should . . ." I throw a thumb over my shoulder, gesturing towards the baggage drop off.

He nods in agreement but doesn't say anything.

"Okay. So I'll see you soon then?"

He nods again. "Couple days."

The silence is awkward, neither of us knowing what to do, so I turn on my heel and walk towards the entrance, towing my suitcase behind me.

I might not have any concrete answers as to what's happening between us, but it sure as hell isn't this.

When I turn back, Isaiah's head is dropped, hands in his pockets, rounding the car for the driver's side door.

"Isaiah!" I call out to stop him.

When he lifts to look at me, it's with so much hope.

"You know what I've never done before? One of those long, sweeping goodbye kisses at the airport."

He tries to hold back his smile. "Is that so?"

"I'd like to knock off another one of those firsts if you don't mind."

He tosses his head back and forth in faux contemplation. "I don't know."

"C'mon, Rhodes." My tone is teasing. "Play along."

His head falls back in a laugh before he jogs towards me. I meet him partway, abandoning my suitcase for him.

Hands cupping my jaw, his lips crash down on mine in a slow, all-encompassing kiss. Soft lips, but firm and commanding. I'm entirely under his spell when my mouth parts, allowing his tongue to slide against mine.

That's when I moan against him. *In public.* I lean into him. *In public.* I'm arching and bending as if there were a way I could get closer to him. My hands bracket his face, pulling him into me.

One of his arms snakes down to my neck, wrapping around, while his other hand glides down to cup my ass. Right there in front of the airport.

And with full control of my body, he leans down, dipping me like we're in some kind of goddamn Lifetime movie, and still his mouth never leaves mine.

We straighten, never losing contact, and when my arms are around his shoulders, he arches back, lifting me right off my feet. When my fingers slide up into his hair, Isaiah's hat falls to the ground, but still that doesn't stop us.

I think someone whistles next to us, but I'm not paying much mind. My main focus is on this man that I'm going to miss more than a healthy amount in the next forty-eight hours. The man I thought I couldn't stand for most of the time I've known him.

I couldn't have been more wrong.

I'm possessed by him. I had barely touched Connor when we were together, and never in public. And here I am, going at it like some uncontrollable horny teenager with the guy I drunkenly married in Vegas.

"Goddamn," someone says next to us.

That finally breaks the moment, our mouths separating. We're both short of breath and trying to catch it when our attention shifts to the side, finding that same security guard watching us.

"Let me guess," he says. "Newlyweds?"

"Yeah." Isaiah laughs. "Something like that."

He sets me back on my feet. Back on my platform Vans, and when he bends down to retrieve his discarded hat from the ground, he taps them, silently teasing me for constantly wearing the shoes we got married in.

"You're going to be great, Kenny. Don't miss your flight." He positions his team hat on my head. "This is so you don't forget me."

I secure it so it doesn't fall off. "Couldn't if I tried."

"And this is the weight room."

Immaculate, state-of-the-art equipment lines the wall. Towels are neatly folded and ready for tomorrow. San Francisco's logo paints every free surface, making it impossible not to know whose team this room belongs to.

"There's a sauna and a steam room attached back there," Josh says. "Everything we have is for both the team and staff to use, so when you officially get out here, make yourself at home. Upper management is good to their employees here."

Josh was a travel coordinator with Dean's team in Atlanta, but now works for San Francisco. I remember Dean mentioning that he'd be happy to show me around, but I didn't plan for my stepbrother to coordinate him also picking me up from the airport.

"Everything is so . . . beautiful. Is that a weird word to use when talking about gym equipment?"

He chuckles. "Not at all. I fully agree. The owners built this arena less than five years ago, so everything is practically brand new. Anything you need, they'll get it for you. If a piece of your equipment goes out, they'll have a replacement for you the next day. It really is a top franchise to work for. People leave other teams and take demotions just to work here."

Josh leads us out of the weight room and into the medical training room.

It's utter perfection. A medical staffer's wet dream. Organized and clean, stocked with anything I could possibly need. My eye snags on the office in the corner. *Dr. Tran* is printed on a nameplate attached to the door, with his title— *Head of Health and Wellness*—below it.

"And that'll be your new office," Josh states.

He doesn't say, "it might be."

He doesn't add on, "if you get the job."

He speaks about it as if I've already been offered the position.

"Is Dr. Tran hands-on with the players, or does he mostly do office work and consult when needed?"

It's something I need to know before my interview tomorrow. I'm not sure if I could accept the position if there isn't flexibility that still allows me to do what I love.

"Oh, he's barely in there. He has an office manager who does most of his paperwork duties. Candice is great. She'll take care of the managerial duties for you, but yeah, Dr. Tran is super hands-on in the training room and out in the dugout during games."

"The way you talk about him . . . He sounds like a beloved doctor."

"He is. He's been here twenty-six years, and he's going to be missed. But I know he's excited to meet you tomorrow."

"I'm looking forward to meeting him. Will he be in the interview?"

"Yeah, he's been in them all. From what I've heard, you're the third and final one."

There's a part of me that wants to get the inside scoop about the other applicants from Josh. He seems like he knows a little bit about everything that goes on around here, but I refrain. I know what I have to offer in both my experience and education, that if I *don't* get the job, it's because I wasn't the correct fit.

Which has me asking, "Does Dr. Tran and the rest of the hiring committee know that I'm a woman?"

Josh halts in his steps, utterly confused. "Of course they do."

Relief floods me.

"Come on," he says. "I want to show you my favorite view of the whole stadium."

I follow him to an elevator and down a few hallways. We pass the clubhouse again, which is the most beautiful one I've ever seen. The team logo is centered in the middle, and the locker stalls are individually illuminated. The players' gear is already waiting for their game tomorrow, regardless that they only finished playing today's game a few hours ago.

He holds the door open for me again, and as soon as I step into the room, I fully understand what he means by it being the best view in the house. It might be the best view in all of San Francisco.

"Holy shit," I hear myself say, utterly mesmerized by the sparkling water of the Bay behind the bleacher section.

Boats line the marina, and the scoreboard . . . Jesus, I never thought I'd be speechless because of a damn scoreboard. The sun is starting its descent, casting a warm amber and pink glow across the water.

I could get used to this. I could imagine working here, spending most of my days here. This has to be the most beautiful stadium in all of baseball.

But it doesn't have the history of the stadium in Chicago. It doesn't have the iconic hand-turned scoreboard, or the infamous ivy-covered brick. It doesn't have the red marquee outside or the best fans in the world. And don't even get me started on the hot dogs.

San Francisco doesn't have the people—the team, Miller, Monty, and most of all, it doesn't have Isaiah. But on the upside, it also doesn't have Dr. Fredrick.

And what it can offer me other than a stunning stadium and state-of-the-art facilities is the job I've spent my entire adult life working towards. Opportunities like this don't come around often, if ever, and I'm not going to throw it away because I suddenly realized I have feelings for my husband.

"Are you ready for your interview tomorrow?" Josh asks from my side.

"I think so. I'm a little nervous though. The last time I came in for a job, it didn't exactly have the best outcome."

"What do you mean?"

I brush him off. "Long story."

"Well, you have no need to be nervous. You're practically a shoo-in. The medical team has been talking about you all week, and you're the only application that Dr. Tran handpicked."

That earns my attention. "Really?"

Josh's smile is genuine. "Really."

Nodding, I refocus on the stadium in front of me. I can do this. Everything I've ever wanted could be mine tomorrow.

He clears his throat. "Apologies if this is forward. I noticed the ring on your finger. Dean gave me the impression that you were single, so I was hoping to take you to dinner tonight, but . . ."

I didn't think about the fact that I wouldn't have to wear my wedding ring if I didn't want to. There's no one here I need to convince of anything.

"I'm married," I say simply.

"Again, I don't want to come off too forward, but is it serious? With you moving across the country and all."

I raise my brow and he lifts his hands in surrender.

"Too forward. Got it."

I chuckle to break the tension. "Not too forward, but I also don't know how to answer that. And even if I were single, the last thing I should be doing as the only woman on staff is going on a date with a potential new coworker, but I am flattered that you asked."

"I understand. When I took this job and left Atlanta, my ex-wife and I both knew it was over. It was a way for us to create distance and finally call it. So, I wasn't sure if this was the same for you."

I shake my head no. I don't know what's going on with our situation, but I know it's not that.

"And by the way," he continues, "you won't be the only woman here. I couldn't even tell you how many women work on staff here."

I perk up at that. "Really?"

"Oh yeah. Good luck getting into the women's restroom on the clubhouse level. There's a constant line."

26

Isaiah

"Mills just texted." Kai sets his phone back in his locker stall. "They're in the hall."

I grab my hat—a different one than I sent with Kennedy—and follow my brother to the hall off the clubhouse.

Zanders, Stevie, Ryan, Indy, Miller, and Rio are waiting for us.

"Hey, guys. Thanks for coming," I say, approaching the group.

Zanders puts his hand in mine, the other going around and tapping the back of my shoulder. "Big bro announces his retirement, we figured we better get to as many games as we can."

We say hi to everyone individually, before Kai stays put with Miller, his arms folded around the front of her shoulders.

Other than Rio and me, everyone is paired off.

I fucking hate it.

I've gotten so accustomed to having Kennedy by my side, especially here at the field. All of this is a preview to next season. But my brother won't be in his uniform. He'll be visiting, just like the rest of these guys.

"Is Kennedy going to come out, or is that dickhead doctor keeping her too busy?" Indy asks.

"No, she's not here actually. She's in San Francisco."

"Oh, that's right!" Stevie says, so much excitement in her voice. "How'd her interview go?"

I hesitate, because the truth is, I don't know yet. I've been too afraid to ask.

My eyes flit to Miller's, silently begging for her help.

"Kennedy said she'd fill us in when she got home," she says in rescue.

"Sunday night family dinner," Ryan reminds me. "About time you brought her, don't you think?"

"There's my girl." Monty steps out of his office into the hallway, eyes on Miller.

"Hi, Dad."

He holds his arms open for a hug, but Kai doesn't let go of her.

Monty's attention shifts to him. "Really?"

"What?" My brother's tone is entirely too innocent as he holds his fiancée captive.

"I have no problem benching you tonight."

Kai huffs a laugh. "It's my first start after announcing my retirement. I don't think that's going to go over too well with the fans."

"Ask me if I give a shit?"

Kai playfully rolls his eyes and releases Miller.

"Where's my grandson?" Monty asks as he hugs his daughter.

"Emily from the bakery is babysitting him and Taylor tonight."

Rio's head shoots forward from the back of the crowd. "Emily from the bakery, huh? She single?"

"Please stop." Zanders' tone is exhausted.

Monty says hello to our friends. "I gotta get out there." He smacks me on the shoulder. "Same for you too. I want to win quickly. There's a bout of rain coming in later and I don't want to get stuck in a rain delay. Love you, Millie. See you after."

"Bye, Dad."

Stevie whips her head around to Miller. "Excuse me?"

320

"What?"

Indy is looking at Miller as if she can't believe what she just saw. "Your dad is hot."

"Gross." She physically grimaces.

"Oddly enough . . ." Rio lifts a brow. "I agree with her."

"You've got a hot dad, Miller," Stevie chimes in.

"Make it stop."

Zanders shrugs. "They're not wrong. I'm straight as a fucking arrow, but that is one good-looking man."

"Annnnd this conversation is done." Miller turns back to Kai, giving him a kiss. "Love you. Good luck."

"Love you, baby."

She hugs me. "Love you too, just a little bit less than him, though."

"Always keeping me humble."

"Someone's got to." She keeps an eye down the hall as the rest of the group heads out of the hallway, and when Kai turns for the training room, she turns her attention back to me. "Have you not talked to her?"

"Of course I have. I just haven't asked her how her interview went."

"And why not?"

"Because I know she killed it and I'm in denial. But I'm happy for her, I truly am. I just want to celebrate her when she tells me in person because we all know I'm not celebrating right now. Until she gets home, I'm going to wallow like a little bitch in private."

"Did she tell you that Dean basically set her up with his friend who picked her up from the airport?" Miller tries to hold back her giggle. "Bet you loved that."

"Yes, she told me. That fucking prick. As if I didn't already hate the guy enough."

Miller tilts her head to the side. "I know the guys have given you shit for years over your crush on her, but I see it,

Isaiah. I see the way you look at her, and I see the way Kennedy practically glows when she's with you. Your marriage might be fake, but the rest is so obviously real. Don't give up hope, okay? Maybe she won't even take the job."

"She better fucking take the job."

Miller chuckles, smacking me on the arm. "Go help your brother get a win on his start record by hitting a couple of bombs, yeah?"

"I'll do my best."

I did do my best. Or at least the best I had to offer tonight. But the only time my bat ever connected with a ball was when I skimmed a few fouls or when I hit a weak grounder and was out long before I made it to first.

I was struck out twice, and I couldn't tell you the last time I was so shit at bat. But I swear to God, every time my walk-up music played it was like the entire stadium was taunting me, singing our wedding song, while my wife is on the other side of the country landing her dream job.

That spot of rain Monty was worried about turned out to be a whole-ass summer storm.

Regardless of my shitty game, the boys pulled off a decisive win, ending it in regular innings, so I got home with plenty of time before the bad weather really started. As did my friends who came to watch the game, as well as Cody, Travis, Monty, Miller, and Kai.

I know this because I've checked on each and every one of them.

The only person who I haven't heard from is the first person I called.

Seven unanswered calls now going through to voicemail, and I still have no idea if Kennedy made it home. If her flight landed. If she got in a rideshare to her apartment or to the stadium where her car is. And I have no idea if she got home before this shitty weather hit.

I try Miller instead.

"Have you heard from her?" I ask as soon as she answers.

"Not yet. I tried to call but she didn't pick up. I know she landed because she texted to check in on how the game was going during the eighth inning."

"And then what? Did she get a rideshare to her car at the stadium? Or did she go back to her apartment?" My tone is frantic. "Why would she not be answering?"

"Maybe she's driving."

"Miller."

"Shit," she exhales. "Wrong thing to say."

"I'm calling her again. Let me know if you hear from her."

I hang up before she can respond and try Kennedy for the eighth time.

Once again, she doesn't answer.

A loud, thunderous boom shakes my apartment building, the rain hitting so hard and so fast against the windows I can hardly hear myself think.

The anxiety winds through my every nerve, making me unable to stay put in one place. I pace my living room, kitchen, in and out of my bedroom, rolling my eyes at every stupid fucking sign I pass that I don't have the capability to laugh at right now.

Phone ringing in my hand, I quickly turn it over, hoping and praying that Kennedy's name is on the screen.

It's not. It's Kai.

My thumb hovers over the green button to answer, but I can't. All I can think about is the tone in his voice and the look on his face when I was thirteen years old, when he came in and told me our mom died in a storm that looked exactly like this one.

I can still remember the smell of the pizza we ate that night. The sound of the front door closing as police officers left. The laundry I had piled on a chair in the corner of the room that my mom told me to fold before baseball practice but I didn't.

And I remember the exact tone in Kai's voice when he told me what happened to her.

For that reason alone, I don't answer.

Call it irrational all you want. I know it's not logical. Anxiety doesn't produce rational thoughts. It creates worst-case scenarios and acknowledging that still doesn't change the fact that anxiety takes over my entire body and mind, making me unable to focus on anything else.

Kai calls again and this time, I muster up the courage to answer.

"What's wrong?" is the first thing I ask.

"Nothing. I was just calling to check in on you."

A burst of light flashes through the windows as another strike of lightning hits the ground.

I find a seat on the couch, knees bouncing. "What the hell is wrong with me?"

"Nothing. Nothing is wrong with you."

"Kennedy isn't answering."

"Did she land from her flight?"

"Yeah. She texted Miller while the game was still going on that she had just landed."

"Okay. Do you want me and Miller to drive by her apartment and check on her?"

"No! Don't get in the fucking car."

"Okay." His voice is soothing. My brother, the caretaker. Always looking out for me when I can't do it for myself. "Call her one more time."

"It's been eighteen years, Kai. Why can't I just get over it?"

He sighs on the other end. "You'll figure out how to change your thought process, Isaiah, but no one who knows you would ever tell you to just get over it. If Mom died in a plane crash, no one would think it odd if you didn't like flying. If Mom died by drowning, no one would shame you for being afraid of the ocean. So how is this any different? Stop being hard on yourself, and give your mind a bit of grace, will you?"

I notice my heel creating the same, continuous pattern on the rug, as if the rhythmic movement could distract me, soothe me.

"I'm trying."

"I know in my gut that Kennedy is okay and probably left her phone somewhere out of reach. I know it's a simple answer, but it's all right that your mind isn't letting you believe that yet. One day you'll figure it out, but it's okay that today isn't that day."

I nod, even though he can't see me. "Okay."

"I love you. Call me if you need anything."

"Love you."

I hang up and stand from my couch. While walking in a full and complete circle of my living room, I dial my wife.

Once again, she doesn't fucking answer.

"Answer the fucking phone, Ken," I mutter for no one to hear.

There's not a thought that goes through my mind to stop me, not a moment of hesitation that stills my hand when I grab my car keys off the kitchen counter and head for my front door.

I stuff my feet into a pair of shoes and swing the door open the same time the elevator down the hall lands on my floor.

My eyes immediately lift to her.

Kennedy is standing there inside, clothes entirely soaked through, hair stuck to her face as she huffs to catch her breath.

Those damn Vans are on her feet but dripping water all over the elevator floor when she looks up to catch me watching her from the doorway of my apartment, car keys in hand.

"Hi," she says between hard-earned breaths.

I exhale for the first time since this goddamn storm started.

A tsunami-sized wave of relief settles over me, my body physically slumping from the tension unwinding itself. But I can't move, stunned into place that she's here. She's okay, and it isn't until she jogs down the hall to me that I realize that all those anxious thoughts begin to settle and rationalize.

But still, there's nothing soft or sweet about the way I ask, "What the hell are you doing here?"

She's breathing heavy when she stops on the other side of my door, water soaking the floor around her.

"Did you fucking drive here?" I continue.

She shakes her head no, and that settles me for only a moment before she admits, "I ran here."

"That's eight fucking blocks, Kennedy."

"Yeah. I'm aware."

I can feel myself amping up again. Can feel the nerves sparking to life, fragile and raw. Does she not understand how dangerous it is to be out in weather like this? She's dripping from head to toe, probably going to get sick because of it, and she's lucky something worse didn't happen to her on the way over here.

My fear speaks for me through my raised voice. "Why the hell would you do that?"

Her shoulders are straight, no hesitation in her tone when she says, "Because I didn't want you to be alone."

Her words bring me down again, the constant spike of fear accompanied by the drastic come down is spiraling my emotions out of control. My eyes instantly burn. My throat constricts.

"Don't fucking do that for me, Kenny." My voice breaks on her name.

"I wanted to." She shakes her head. "I don't know why. I don't know when it changed. But you always tell me to do what feels good, and I've never felt better than when I'm with you."

I inhale a sharp breath, trying to calm myself down, trying not to let her see how much it means to me that even knowing I'm going to be at my worst, she's here. Even when my mind plays tricks on me, she validates my fears.

Even when others would call me irrational, laugh off a silly summer storm, she ran instead of getting in her car to check on me.

She reaches out, hand wrapping around mine to uncoil my fingers. They soften in hers, dropping my car keys into her palm.

"Why do you have these?"

"Because I couldn't get a hold of you, and I needed to make sure you were okay."

Her head tilts, her face softening. She slips my keys into her jacket pocket the same time she pulls out her phone. Water drips from it, so she wipes the screen, allowing it to display my endless missed calls.

"I'm sorry. I didn't hear it on my way over because of the rain."

"You scared me."

She shakes her head, brows furrowed as if she truly can't grasp the concept of someone being concerned for her well-being. That someone would care about her enough, miss her enough that they'd get in the car and check on her.

A rumble of thunder shakes my entire apartment, the subsequent flash of lightning exploding in streaks across Kennedy's beautiful face.

I try not to pay attention to anything but her, yet I can't help the slight flinch in my expression.

Kennedy reaches up, her small hand cupping my jaw. I cover it with my own, reveling in her touch, proud of how easy it is for her now.

"Let me distract you," she whispers.

27

Isaiah

Stepping into the hallway, I take Kennedy's face in both hands and press my mouth to hers, desperate to touch her.

Her teeth chatter when I pull away.

"God, you're fucking freezing, Kenny."

"I don't care," she pants against my lips. "I couldn't not see you."

Fuck me with that confession. She knew I was going to have a bad night, and still, she wanted to be here.

Bending, I wrap her wet legs around my hips and carry her into my apartment. I kick close the door behind me, but still I don't set her down. I don't care that there's a river of water in our wake. I don't care that I'm getting just as soaked as her.

Fingers threaded through my hair, she dots kisses up my neck as I carry her. Her lips are cold, sending little shocks to my system as if I weren't already amped up.

"Fuck, Ken," I exhale. "I missed you."

She pulls back to look at me, sopping wet hair glued to her face, brows narrowed in confusion.

I halt in my steps. "What?"

"I've always wondered what it would feel like to be missed."

There are not enough words to describe how much I hate that. That she has felt so disregarded by a select few that she doesn't believe anyone in their right mind would miss her. *Could* miss her.

If only she understood just how desperately I longed for her while she was gone. Fuck, I longed for her when she was still here. I haven't *stopped* craving this woman since the day I met her in the bathroom and she asked for my advice about a fucking job.

"And how does it make you feel?" I ask.

A shy smile makes its appearance on her lips. "Important."

"Yeah," I agree with a nod. "The most important to me."

She hides back into the crook of my neck as I continue to the bathroom.

"Isaiah?"

"Yeah?"

"I missed you too."

And I swear to God I'm living in an alternate reality because in what world do I get to hear that Kennedy Kay missed me.

"Oh yeah? Just how much did you miss me?"

"So much." Her lips meet my ear. "I had to touch myself thinking about you every night I was gone just so I could fall asleep."

Fuck. Me.

Keeping her up with one arm, I use my other hand to turn my shower on to the warmest setting. "And what exactly did you think about while you touched yourself?"

"I thought about your mouth." She presses her mouth to mine. "Your tongue." Her own licks a path across my lower lip, pulling out a deep, needy groan from me. "And I thought about how much I need you inside of me."

"*Fuck.*"

"Please tell me you will tonight."

I set her on her feet in front of the shower, arm still holding her to me, trying to keep her warm before reaching behind her and testing the water.

"I will, baby. You're not leaving my bed until you've been thoroughly fucked."

I push her wet hair off her face, bringing my mouth down to hers as I start to unpeel her layers. Her jacket first. It falls in a wet heap on the tiled floor. I lift her heavy, rain-soaked shirt up and over her head, and it's only for a moment that our mouths disconnect before she's pulling me back down to meet her.

She kicks off her shoes as I run a palm over her stomach, curving over her side, my single hand almost covering the entire length of her spine. She's freezing to the touch, her pale skin painted in goose bumps. With a simple flick of my wrist, her bra falls between us, and as pretty as it is, it's soaking wet and needs to go.

Her nipples pebble between us, and I have to pull away from her mouth, leaning my forehead on hers so I can look at her. Somehow, it's the first time I've seen them without the barrier of fabric covering them.

Fucking perfect, just like the rest of her. Soft, creamy skin, painted with countless freckles. Nipples peaked hard and begging for my mouth. I circle the pad of my thumb over one as we both watch me flick it, much in the way I'm going to do with my tongue.

Hand cupping her tit, I squeeze.

She arches into me, accompanied by this pretty little moan.

"How the fuck is every part of you so goddamn perfect, Kennedy?"

"You don't think they're too small?"

I pause at that, my hand still cupping her.

Sure, my hands are above average in size, and yes, Kennedy is short and most of her is small, but I couldn't give two fucks how big her tits are.

Before immediately dispelling her concern, I ask, "Do you feel that way, or did someone tell you that you should feel that way?"

She doesn't answer.

"Did he make you believe that?"

She shakes her head, trying to brush me off. "It was a quick conversation."

"That you and he had how many times?"

Her eyes leave mine. "A few times."

My jaw works, but even though my head is angry at her ex, my hands are soft as they continue to roam over her skin, trying to warm her up.

Don't even get me started on the fact he never helped her, never let her learn or explore or try. He never took the time to reiterate that she's wanted and worthy. He did, however, continually remind her that she was reluctant towards intimacy, and now I'm learning that he let this woman—who I view as the most perfect one in the world—believe that she wasn't.

"Kenny, I couldn't give two shits about what your body looks like, but just so you're aware, I have never seen someone so perfectly made for me. And if you're so concerned about the size of your tits, I have no problem putting you on your knees, making you hold them together, and showing you just how perfectly sized they are for me to fuck."

Her mouth slightly parts, her eyes lighting with intrigue. "Would you do that?"

"Yeah, baby, I'll fuck your tits, but tonight, I need to fuck this." My hand slides down her zipper, my fingers gliding along the seam of the denim, building friction right where her clit is.

A desperate moan escapes her, and that sound only grows when I cover her nipple with my mouth and suck.

"Oh my God." Her hands slide into my hair, holding me to her. "Keep doing that."

I twirl my tongue before slipping her nipple between my teeth and gently tugging.

She pulls my hair at that, and I memorize the information, finding another thing my wife likes.

With the water warming behind her, I drop to my knees, kissing across her chest to focus on her other nipple. My hands stay occupied by undoing her jeans. I pull them down, peeling the wet denim off her legs, and leaving her in only a pair of panties.

Hands on her ass, I pull her into me and drop my mouth to kiss over her pussy, right over the lace. She folds over me when I run my rough tongue along her slit, using the fabric to create a delicious friction.

"Need you," she begs, grabbing at the back of my shirt and pulling until it's up and over my head. "Please." She tosses it aside before urging me to stand with her. Kennedy shimmies off her underwear, leaving her entirely naked when she grabs my wrist and brings my fingers to rub against her core. "Please."

With one hand warm against her, tracing every fold of her pussy, Kennedy makes quick work of my pants as I rid my shoes. She takes it upon herself to tug off my boxer briefs, letting my hard and ready cock spring free.

She moans, this hungry, desperate sound, licking her lips as she looks at me.

I push a finger inside of her, stealing her attention. "Don't even think about licking your lips again while you're staring at my cock, or this is going to be over a lot quicker than either of us would like."

Instead, she wraps a firm hand around it, giving it a long tug.

"Jesus, fuck." Falling forward, I smack my free hand against the shower glass to hold me up. "Please, Ken. I need to make this last."

My hips fall right into hers as she strokes me, my thigh pressing up against her core. I move my hand and push my leg flush against her, watching the way my skin glistens in her wake as she rolls over it.

She kisses my chest, reaching up on her toes to latch onto my neck, continuing to stroke me. And God, I'm so hard already, it's a bit concerning what this woman can do to me so quickly.

I'm going to fucking come if I don't do something to stop her.

With the steam billowing from inside the shower, I throw an arm around her waist, pick her up, and carry her inside.

She shivers as soon as she's under the warm stream, as if the change of temperature was too quick, but soon enough her body adjusts, calming and melting as the water runs over her.

She tosses her head back, letting the water wash over her face, letting it flow over her pretty hair. Kennedy's still holding my forearms for support, and I can't keep my eyes off her.

The way the water rolls over her curves, even the ones she thinks are too small. The way she tightens her thighs together when she hears me hum my appraisal. The way she pulls me into her, as if she doesn't want me to be too far.

I step under the stream with her, into her arms, my palms gliding down her back and over the curve of her ass as I map a path of warm kisses up her neck and behind her ear.

I bite it.

"What the hell kind of spell do you have me under, Kenny?"

She shakes her head as if she has no idea, her now warm body molding to mine. She lifts her seeking hips, finding my cock, and rubbing it against her.

"I want you," she says, folded up with me.

"Yeah?"

"More than I've ever wanted anything or anyone."

I swear my cock grows harder at her confession, and when my hand smooths over her ass, my middle finger slipping between her cheeks, and down to stroke over her center, I can feel just how truthful she's being.

I coat myself in her arousal.

"More than you want to come right now?" I tease.

"I want you . . ." she repeats. "To *make* me come."

Chuckling, I reach behind her, pulling the showerhead off its bracket.

Maintaining the water on her in hopes of keeping her warm, I flip her around. Arm slung heavy around her waist, I hold her back to my chest, my cock slipping between her ass.

She grounds back against me.

"Kenny." My tone is full of warning. "I'll fuck that one day too, but what did I just say?"

She arches again. "That you need to make this last."

"Exactly. So let me get you off before I come all over your back."

"That'd be fine by me. We both know how quick your response time is. At least you're not wearing pants this go around. That'd be embarrassing."

I playfully nip at her neck. "Little brat."

She laughs but it quickly dies when I nudge her feet farther apart and slip my hand between her legs. I give her pussy a couple of taps before spreading her open with my fingers, keeping her that way when I bring the showerhead down to pound against her swollen clit.

"Oh," she moans, her head falling back to my chest.

I keep her held upright, adding a finger against her clit, adding to the pressure of the pulsing water.

Her chattering teeth are back but this time they're accompanied by buckling knees and white knuckles as she holds my arms in place.

"How many times did you make yourself come while you were gone?"

"Three," she pants.

"And you didn't think to call me? Facetime me? Do you understand how fucking pretty you are when you come, Kennedy?"

"It didn't last long," she says, head thrown back, eyes closed. "Every time I pictured your fingers instead of my own, I came."

I rub languid circles over her clit. "Is this what you were picturing?"

She nods frantically.

"You're going to have to come three times tonight to make up for those times I didn't get to see it."

She nods again, a soft whimper escaping her.

I bring the showerhead closer, making sure the rhythmic pulsing hits exactly where she needs it, and when I drag my thumb down to add to the friction, I feel her entire pussy flutter against me as she comes.

I'm obsessed with this girl, that's fairly obvious, so it's probably no surprise that I'm obsessed with the way she comes—with my fingers on her clit and my name on her lips, chanted like a pleading prayer.

She slumps in my arms, her wet hair sticking to my chest.

I always wondered how dark Kennedy Kay Auburn would get when it's wet.

Wondered what it would look like threaded through my fingers.

Wondered what it would look like draped on my lap.

And soon, I'm going to find out exactly what it looks like sprawled over my pillow as I fuck her.

Replacing the showerhead to its rightful home, I keep a possessive arm around her, careful not to let her fall. I don't trust her knees at all at this point.

Taking a few steps back, I drag her with me to sit on the

ledge in the back of the shower. Enough of the water is still able to reach us, keeping her warm, though I'm fairly certain her orgasm is keeping her plenty hot judging by the temperature of her skin.

"Such a good girl for me," I whisper against her neck, decorating the slope of her shoulder with kisses.

"Are you going to be a good boy for me?"

I chuckle, remembering that day at the field when I told her she could call me a good boy while she straddled me naked.

"You let me inside of you and I'll be such a good boy for you, baby."

To my surprise, Kennedy stands from my lap, turning around, her beautiful naked body on full display. She uses my shoulders for support, setting one knee at a time against the bench to straddle me.

I almost come when she drops onto my lap, her pussy rubbing slow circles against my cock.

"Do that again."

My head falls back to the glass behind me when she rolls her hips, her arousal coating the tip of my dick.

She slips a hand behind my neck, urging me back up, bringing her mouth to crash down on mine. I focus on her warm lips, her hot tongue, her hips creating tight little circles, building the friction.

"You feel so good," she cries, her hands falling down to roam against my chest.

"Fuck. I love the way you touch me."

She whimpers at the praise, her face falling into the crook of my neck, and it's then I remember—she's never touched anyone the way she touches me.

I feel real possessive over that fact.

Her tits bounce and her thighs flex as she rocks against me. Back and forth. Back and forth, and every time she lifts her hips, the head of my dick nudges against her clit.

Until finally, it slips, notching at her entrance. We both still. Every muscle in her legs and abdomen are wound tight to keep her from sinking down.

I speak against her damp skin. "Do you want to fuck me, or do you want me to fuck you?"

If she wants to be in charge, I'll happily watch her sink down on my cock, right here in the shower. But if she wants me to fuck her, I need to take her to my bed where I can do it properly for our first time.

She pauses, contemplating as the steam billows around us. Her handprints are etched on the glass walls and my dick is poised at her entrance.

"I want you to fuck me," she finally decides.

That's all I need to hear for me to pick her up, turn off the shower, and carry us both to bed.

We're soaking, water running off us, but I couldn't care less when I cup the back of her head, protecting it to lay her back against my mattress. Wet hair, flushed skin. Legs spread and glistening between them.

Fucking angel.

I stand there, watching, trying to figure out what I did to get so lucky that I ended up in this position. If you would've told me three years ago that Kennedy Kay would be laying naked and spread on my mattress, I probably would've fucked my hand to the idea, but I definitely wouldn't have believed you.

"What are you thinking about?" she asks.

I shake my head, climbing on the bed to sit between her legs, heels to ass.

"What?"

I track every inch of her. "God sure did take his time on you, honey."

Her smile turns soft and a bit shy.

I kiss a path up her stomach, my hair dripping water onto

her belly, her chest, her neck until I'm draped over her, holding myself up on a single forearm.

"What are *you* thinking about?" I ask, my lips pressing to hers.

She runs a hand up my bare spine, hooking her leg over my hip. "I'm thinking it's about time we consummate this goddamn marriage."

My cock jumps at the idea and I huff a laugh, this bright smile reflecting on Kennedy's lips.

Rain pounds against the windows of my apartment and another rumble of thunder drowns out our panting breaths, but my sole focus is on this woman beneath me. I'm so consumed I could almost forget about the storm.

She pushes my hair out of my face, her thumb dusting over my birthmark by my eye before her hand follows the path of my arm, my side, my ass, until she wraps a fist around my dick.

I push into her hand. "I have condoms in the nightstand."

She doesn't make a move for it, continuing to stroke me, so after a beat of silence, I reach over her to grab one.

"I'm good without one," she says to stop me.

It works. I halt right there, arm halfway to my side table.

I would never in a million years consider going without one. But as always, Kennedy is my exception. She's my wife, for fuck's sake. If she's good without a condom, so am I.

I don't have to explain that I've been tested, seeing as she has access to all my medical records and already knows. And as of last weekend, she's also aware there hasn't been anyone else for a long fucking time.

"I'm good too."

She nods against the pillow, bringing my lips back to hers.

We kiss for a while, our bodies writhing against each other, our hips frantically looking for friction. Kennedy runs her thumb over my slit, pushing the precum down to coat my shaft.

Lips disconnecting, we hold eye contact as she lines me up with her entrance. We stay there for a moment, the tension thick, the anticipation heavy in the room. I watch her, this beautiful girl who I haven't been able to take my eyes off for years.

And it's no different now.

I rub myself up and down her slit, coating me in her before I press my thumb down on the head of my cock, curl my hips forward, and push into her.

Slowly. Torturously slowly. Inch by fucking inch.

My tip is hardly past her entrance and I'm on the verge of losing it. She's so goddamn tight. So fucking warm.

"More," she pleads, but it comes out like a cry.

I pull back and push in again, watching more of my length disappear inside of her this time, but I quickly meet resistance.

Her entire body is wound tight when I'm only halfway in.

"If it hurts, tell me to stop, and I'll stop."

"No. Don't stop. I can take it."

A smirk lifts on my lips. "Yeah, you can, but you've got to relax for me, Kenny."

Her brown eyes are begging for me to help her.

Leaning in, I kiss her, distract her. Let my tongue focus on hers for a while as I slowly work myself inside her. Kennedy stretches around me, her clit pulsing against my thumb as I circle it, hoping to make this easier on her.

"You're doing so good for me, baby. Taking me so well."

I feel her body relax into the mattress, her hands freely roaming my back when I slide the rest of the way home.

Holy. Fuck.

My pelvic bone is flush with hers, Kennedy's legs spread wide to accommodate me. I've never felt anything so tight, so warm, so fucking wet that I swear to God, I'll be lucky if I give her three solid pumps before I'm coming inside her.

She dusts her fingertips up and down my spine. I slowly kiss along her jaw and down her neck as we both adjust.

When she pushes her heels into my ass, urging me to move, I shift my hips and pull out partway before pushing back in again.

She fucking moans and I almost lose it once again.

Breathing through my nose to hold back, I focus on the way I disappear into her, my pace slow and cautious at first. But when I start to feel less resistance, I pick up speed, keeping my chest flush to hers, rolling over her entire body with each pass.

"Yes, Isaiah," she cries, her nails digging into my back.

"God, Kennedy. That feels so good. Look at you right now. Fucking unreal."

I hover above her, using my arms on either side of her to prop me up. I take her left hand in mine, lacing our fingers together and pinning it to the mattress. She wraps her other hand around my neck, pulling my lips to meet hers.

We're fucking slowly, hands intertwined, tongues tangled.

And *shit*, if this isn't different than it's ever been. *Better* than it's ever been.

I knew it'd be different with her, but I didn't know it'd be like this.

Soft and intimate, and still so fucking hot.

She moans into my mouth as I thrust into her again, all while circling the pad of my finger over the stone of her ring.

She chuckles against me. "I know what you're doing."

"Oh yeah?" I pull away from her mouth. "And what's that?"

"You're trying to make me fall in love with you, fucking me like this."

A mischievous smirk slides across my lips. "Is it working?"

She nudges her nose against mine, a sweet smile gracing her mouth. "Don't make me answer that."

I'll take that response as a win, so I keep doing what I'm doing. Fucking her missionary, kissing her senseless, and holding her hand the whole damn time. She tightens around me, her pussy creating this delicious friction as I reach between us, working her clit in time with my thrusts.

"I'm going to come," she whimpers, breaths coming hard and fast.

"Please," I beg. "Please come on my cock. I need it. God, that's all I've ever fucking wanted."

Her lower lip begins to tremble as her orgasm takes over, and I have a front-row seat to watch it all. The fluttering of her lashes as she tries to hold eye contact. The marks her nails leave down my arm. The sweet way she says my name when she's able to find words again.

I'm fucking mesmerized by it all.

She holds me to her, so close I can feel every desperate breath she takes, every moan that escapes from the back of her throat, and I fucking love it.

This girl who was once so uncomfortable with even the simplest of touches is now holding me as tight as possible as she comes.

Once it's clear she's on her way back down, I note the way her muscles relax, pressing her back into the mattress. I slowly pull out, my cock dripping in her arousal, her soft whines like music to my ears when I leave her empty.

Without hesitation, I slide down the mattress to press my face between her legs.

"Isaiah," she cries. "I'm sensitive."

Fuck yes, she is. She's still fluttering against my tongue as I lick up every bit of her release.

"Shit," she curses, rolling her hips in time with my mouth.

Her legs shake around me, her thighs pressing against my ears. I could easily make her come again like this, but I can tell she can't take much more tonight, and I need to come with her just once.

Sitting up, I hook an arm around her waist.

"Come here," I say, even though I'm the one dragging her up with me. She's so fucking easy to toss around, to position where I need her.

And that's what I do, with my back against the headboard and my legs sprawled, I straddle her over my lap. She sits on my thighs, her body still rolling with the aftershocks of her orgasm.

She's so fucking perfect like this. So fucking undone. Wet hair, a tangled mess, lips swollen from mine.

Cock in hand, I stroke long, slow tugs, twisting around the head as I watch her.

Her brown eyes are locked on my dick, pupils blown when I squeeze a bead of precum from the tip.

Kennedy scoots back a couple inches on my legs before folding over, moving my hand out of the way and swallowing down my cock.

"*Fuck yes*, Kenny. You're so good at that." I gather her hair, my attention following the length of her spine down to her perfectly heart shaped ass propped in the air. I reach over and smack it. "Make me come, baby."

She bobs, taking me deeper, moaning with every pass.

"Yes. Yes. Fuck. So close."

Kennedy's mouth pops off my throbbing cock, giving it one more long lick before sitting up and crawling back over my lap. She wraps a fist around my length, propping herself up on her knees and lining us up.

"Come inside of me?" she asks.

I nod eagerly, head thrown back against the headboard, as I watch her sink down on me.

"Fuck, I'm so hard. I'm so close. I just need you to take it, okay?"

Nodding in agreement, she bends her neck, bringing her lips to mine as she rolls her hips. Once. Twice. Three times.

It feels fucking amazing, but my body has this overwhelming need to pound into her.

Hands roaming, I grip her ass, helping her find the rhythm I need.

She whimpers, her lips moving to my neck as I work us together. Bending my knees, I fit us even tighter together, fucking her from underneath as I hold her in one steady position.

She screams my name, head thrown back, pinching her own nipples when her third orgasm hits, and this time when she comes, I'm right there with her. I spill inside of her, telling her how perfect she is, how much I want her, how good she feels.

I hold her warm body to mine, our heaving chests expanding and contracting together. She kisses me the whole time we come down and I swear to God, I'm a different person after it's all said and done.

But she's the one who voices my thoughts aloud.

"I had no idea," she whispers between kisses, "it could be like that."

I run two palms over her back, trying to keep her warm. "Me neither, Ken. It's never felt like that before."

Pushing her hair out of her face, I stroke her cheekbone, before my eyes are drawn to where we're connected.

My cum is spilling out of her and dripping down her leg.

"I'm on," she exhales heavily, "birth control. I should've told you that. And I haven't been with anyone since—"

"Say another man's name right now," I cut her off. "I fucking dare you."

She smirks, pressing her mouth back to mine. "Possessive."

"You thought I was possessive before we fucked? I feel fucking *unhinged* now."

All sorts of possessive thoughts run through my mind. How I want to mark her. Keep her. Fuck her until she forgets about the idea of ever leaving me.

And just like that, the question I was supposed to ask when I saw her screams at the forefront of my brain, forcing me to speak it aloud.

I'm still inside of her. She's still rocking slowly in my lap.

"How did your interview go?"

Kennedy pauses, her accompanying sigh full of defeat. "It went . . . better than I could've hoped for."

Well . . . fuck.

28

Kennedy

Isaiah pulls up to an insanely beautiful house thirty minutes outside of the city. I know this house. I came here last year on a random summer night when I got drunk with Miller, Indy, Rio, and a sober Stevie.

Miller was just realizing she wanted to be with Kai more than she wanted to be on the road. Stevie was pregnant then, and Indy wasn't quite yet.

And I . . . Well, I was still stewing over the whole Connor thing and entirely annoyed that when I got back to Kai's house that night, his brother was sitting on the couch.

Little did I know, less than a year later, I'd be this fucking gone for the guy.

The summer sun is beginning to set in the distance, casting a warm glow over the property. I don't know how else to explain it other than it feels good to be out here. Like a goddamn hug, which tracks how welcomed I felt the last time I met these people.

Isaiah parks his car next to the handful of others and kills the engine.

"So, this is called Family Dinner?" I ask, undoing my seat belt.

"Yep. Happens every Sunday night at the Shay house."

"Do you come every week?"

"If we don't have a game, yes. I've been coming every week since last summer. There's a core group that's consistently here. Sometimes, the other guys will bring their teammates. Sometimes, Cody and Travis will tag along. I've been wanting to bring you ever since we went to your family dinner." Reaching across the center console, he squeezes my leg. "They shouldn't be like that. You should feel good afterward. You'll feel good after this."

Leaning back against the headrest, I smile over at him. "I've been enjoying doing things that make me feel good."

"Does that mean you've been enjoying doing me?"

"Very much so."

He huffs a laugh as he hops out of his side of the car and rounds the hood to the passenger door, opening it.

"You look so good tonight, Kenny."

I've got an oversized blazer on, a tight white tee and a pair of well-fitted denim. It's casual but structured and couldn't be more different than what he's seen me in all week. Which is either my work polo or my birthday suit.

I lean forward and quickly press my lips to his as a silent thank you before climbing out of his car.

It's been days since I've been home from California, and we've barely spent a moment apart.

We go to and from work together.

We pick up clothes from my apartment before bringing them to his, where I've slept next to him each night.

Every morning, he asks me to pick out his outfits to ensure they match.

We cook together, and Isaiah has yet to let up on the whole feeding me thing.

We fuck. A lot.

And we spend at least an hour talking in bed each night before we fall asleep, entirely avoiding any topic surrounding my interview.

I had no idea it could be like this. Perfectly imperfect, and the perfectionist in me doesn't mind the flaws and quirks that make us work.

The biggest quirk being that I feel like I'm dating my husband.

Hand on my lower back, he guides me to the house, but before we make it to the front porch steps, I reach behind me, slipping my hand into his.

Isaiah glances down to our intertwined fingers, and it's the first time he doesn't look around for someone from the team to invalidate what's happening.

"You okay?" I ask.

"Perfect." He gives it a squeeze. "I like holding your hand in public." He doesn't even try to lower his voice when he adds, "And I like holding your throat in private."

I smack him in the chest with a laugh. "Perv."

"When it comes to you? Absolutely. You should see all the dirty things floating in my head that I have planned." He holds the door open for me, switching to a complete gentleman. "After you, wifey."

But then that gentleman façade flies right out the window when he smacks my ass on my way inside.

"Back here!" someone calls.

This time, Isaiah is the one who leads me to the rear of the house, where a second living room is adjacent to the kitchen.

"Hey, guys!" Indy calls out from the couch. She's got her feet kicked up and her hand smoothing over her pregnant belly. "Kennedy, I'm so glad you're here!"

"Hey." I offer her a small wave and note the way her eyes trail to where my hand is connected with Isaiah's. "Thanks for having me."

"Ken, this is Zanders," Isaiah says, gesturing over to the kitchen.

He's tall, just as tall as the Rhodes boys, wearing a gold chain necklace and covered in tattoos.

"He's Stevie's husband and defenseman for the Chicago Raptors."

"And in that exact order," Zanders says, dropping the knife he was using to slice tomatoes before wiping his hands on a towel and rounding the kitchen island to me. I shake his outstretched hand, noting the endless gold rings that decorate them. "You can call me Zee."

"Kennedy."

Isaiah cuts in from my side. "And you can call her Mrs. Rhodes."

Zanders bursts a laugh. "I still cannot believe you pulled that off. Kennedy, this man has talked about you nonstop for months."

"Years," Indy corrects.

"Years," Zanders agrees. "Part of me thought you didn't exist and the other part of me feels like I already know everything there is to know about you."

I find Isaiah out of the corner of my eye, heat creeping up his cheeks. It's stupidly adorable when this cocky man is left without words to say.

Max comes barreling in from the backyard, wobbly legs bringing him right to me, but Isaiah scoops him up on his way and Max immediately folds onto his chest in a hug.

"There's my favorite of the Rhodes men."

I run a hand over Max's back. "Mine too."

Max giggles. Isaiah shoots me a scowl.

"Ken," Max says, pointing out his little finger until it connects with my cheek.

"Hey, what about me?"

Then he turns and does the same to his uncle. "Zaya."

He repeats that a few times, pointing between the two of us and saying our names.

"Where's Stevie?" Isaiah asks Zanders, adjusting his nephew on his hip.

"She's putting Taylor down for the night."

"Which is exactly what we're going to do," Kai says, coming in from the backyard. "Hey, Ken. Glad you could make it."

He bends to wrap his arms around me in a hug and I don't flinch or hesitate before hugging him back.

It's so strange for me, to not even second-guess myself, but it feels really good too.

"All right, Maxie boy. Bedtime." Kai takes his son from Isaiah.

Max sits up, looking around the house. "Mama."

"She's coming, Bug. Mills," he calls out. "You coming?"

Through the open back door, Miller comes into the house with an empty tray. I can both hear and smell the grill going in the backyard.

"Coming," she says. "Kennedy! Hi! So glad you came."

"Really?" Isaiah holds his hands out. "My own family and no one is going to say hi to me?"

"No," Kai quickly answers.

"Honestly, I see you plenty," Miller says over her shoulder as she follows Kai and Max to the stairs. "I'm much more excited to see my friend."

Two more people come in from the backyard. Rio, and a man, who if I didn't already know was Ryan Shay, it'd be fairly obvious by the similarities he shares with his twin sister.

But it's impossible to not know who Ryan Shay is, especially in Chicago.

"Hey, Kennedy. Good to see you again, I guess." Rio's voice holds no inflection.

Zanders bursts a laugh from the kitchen.

"Get it together, Rio!" Indy calls.

"So glad you could be here," he corrects before shooting Indy a deadpanned glare.

"What's that about?" I ask.

"Guy's a little sensitive about being the only one of us who isn't paired off these days." Ryan holds his hand out to me. "Hey, I'm Ryan."

"Kennedy."

"I've heard that name so many fucking times," Ryan laughs to himself.

"For fuck's sake," Isaiah mutters under his breath.

Ryan pats him on the back before adding another dirty tray onto the sink. Judging by the toppings that Zanders is slicing, it's burger night here at the Shay house.

"You need help with the grill?" Isaiah asks.

"I can help!" Indy calls out.

"Not you," Ryan quickly disagrees. "Stay inside, Blue. Kick your feet up and don't do anything."

She rolls her eyes.

"I got you," Isaiah says before turning to me, hand snaked around my hip. "Are you good?"

As I nod, he leans down to kiss my temple before following Ryan outside, Zanders and Rio following not far behind.

I make my way to Indy in the living room, taking one of the comfy-looking chairs across from her just as Stevie and Miller come back downstairs to join us. Stevie takes the spot next to her sister-in-law and my sister-in-law takes the chair next to me.

"You look great, Kennedy. I love that jacket."

"So do you, Stevie. Good to see you again."

Honestly, all the girls look great, in styles that are unique to them.

Stevie in a pair of loose jeans, flannel tied around her waist.

Indy in a lavender sundress and high-top Converse.

Miller in her signature overalls, sunglasses slipped on top of her head, and bare feet.

"So, Ryan is a little—"

"Overprotective," Indy finishes for me, pointing at her belly. "Tell me about it, but it took a lot for us to get here, so I let him be."

"I think it's sweet. He cares about you."

Out of the corner of my eye, I see the guys circled around the grill, chatting and laughing with one another. Isaiah lifts his hat to run his hand through his hair, listening to something one of them is saying, but I catch him looking through the window over to me out of his periphery.

He grins this boyish grin, his cheeks turning pink from being caught, telling me it's not the first time he's looked over here since he's been outside. He gives me one more sweeping glance before he focuses back on his friends.

That right there is another first. Having someone across the room looking for me, checking on me. It seems like such a simple act, but it's something I've always wished for and didn't think I'd have.

It didn't matter if there were two thousand people or only the two of us alone in a room, Connor never looked for me and I didn't look for him.

We were, in a sense, business partners for our families.

Isaiah and me, we're something entirely different. I don't know exactly what it is, but it feels good, and warm, and right.

"You look happy." Miller nudges her foot to mine, stealing my attention.

I give her a small nod in agreement. "I am."

"So when did you and your husband start fucking?" Indy blurts out.

My mouth drops open as I turn to Miller.

She holds her hands up in defense. "I didn't say a word."

"She didn't have to," Stevie says. "Anyone with eyes could tell."

"How's your vagina feeling?" Indy turns to Miller. "Miller, you're with the brother, it's probably comparable. How's she feeling?"

Miller tosses her head from side to side. "Sore."

"My God, after all this time." Indy laughs. "I couldn't tell you the last Sunday we had that Isaiah showed up and didn't say something about you. Either how you did something impressive at work or how you wore your hair that day."

"You're the only person he's ever talked about," Stevie adds. "And now look at you two. Accidentally married and purposefully in love."

I want to argue that we're not in love. We're playing a game and that's all this is, but I know that's not the case anymore. I don't know exactly what this is, but I'm also aware I have never felt as good as I have the last couple of months, and more specifically, than I have this week from finally seeing what was always right in front of me.

Once again, Isaiah catches my attention out the window when he holds up his wedding ring for his friends to see. Chest puffed, shoulders back.

I've never met a man prouder of a piece of jewelry than Isaiah Rhodes is of his wedding ring. Since putting it on the first time, I've yet to see him without it. The only time his finger is bare is when he's swapping his metal ring for the silicone one before a practice or a game.

But that's where the confusion lies. What are we doing?

Dating is one thing. Even getting into a relationship. But marriage? A *real* marriage? Neither of us signed up for that. Not when we were too many tequila shots in and not when we were scheming to save my job.

Just because we're sleeping together now and spending all our time with each other doesn't mean our fake marriage suddenly turned real.

"So," Miller says. "Tell us about the interview."

Then there's that . . . The potential job I have waiting for me two thousand miles away.

She knows the gist of it. That it went well. That Dean tried to set me up with some guy that worked there. That the city and the stadium were beautiful, but I have yet to give her more details.

"It went better than I could've hoped for. Everyone was friendly and kind and welcoming. I met so many people who worked for the team, and every person I asked said they absolutely loved their job."

"That's rare," Stevie says.

"Even more rare is that there are a ton of women who work for the franchise. And they're *happy* and *respected.* There are two other women on the medical staff alone. I've never had that. The stadium is stunning. The equipment is all brand new. And the interview itself, it didn't feel like an interview at all. It felt like I already had the job, and they were just excited for me to get out there as soon as possible."

"That's so amazing for you," Indy says with a smile.

Miller stays silent so I look over for her to add something, but she doesn't.

"What?"

She shakes her head. "I know I'm being selfish here, but I don't want you to go."

"Miller—"

"I know. I know." She holds her hands up. "You and Isaiah are both being so fucking weird about it, but things seem so good for you lately. You seem happy, and I want you here. I'm just wondering if it's worth giving it all up for a lateral move, career wise. I get that you'd have a new lead doctor to work under there, but . . ."

Miller, and everyone else in Chicago, has no idea that this *isn't* a lateral move. I'd become the first female lead doctor in the MLB. I'd gain some financial freedom that's mine and not accompanied by the Kay name. I'd be in charge of an entire department in a great city with a thriving sports scene.

But thankfully, the back door swings open before I have to answer.

"Well, damn." Isaiah lets out a low whistle as he drops something into the kitchen sink. "Don't you four look good."

"Flirt," Miller mutters.

"I'm a married man, Montgomery. I don't flirt." He bends over the back of my chair as I crane my neck up to look at him. "Except with you. I like flirting with you. You want cheese on your burger?"

"Yes, please."

"You got it." He pops a quick kiss on my lips then he's out to the backyard once again.

My attention swings back to Miller at my side. She doesn't have to say anything. She's silently screaming to add that I'd also be giving up Isaiah.

As if it's not the only thing I've thought about this week.

29

Isaiah

As the burgers finish on the grill outside, I catch the girls standing from their seats in the house. I can't hear them, but I can see them all laughing, mainly the short one with auburn hair.

Head tossed back. Pretty throat exposed.

I can't help but smile as I watch her.

Then I stop, right there with the spatula in hand, and watch my wife open her arms and take the initiative to hug Stevie first, then Indy. Indy towers over her and that just makes them laugh even more.

"You good?" Kai asks, as he steps onto the back patio from putting Max down for the night.

"Did you see that? Kennedy hugging them?"

My brother's brows furrow, eyes trained on me. "Yeah? What's the big deal?"

The big deal is that Kennedy, who is self-proclaimed unaccustomed and uncomfortable with affection, just hugged two women who she's only beginning to know.

And I'm over here watching like the world's proudest husband because she gave a couple of hugs.

The four of them make their way to the backyard, out to the patio where an outdoor table is set for dinner. The sun has almost entirely gone for the day, but the string lights hung over the table cast plenty of light for me to watch Miller throw an arm over Kennedy's shoulder as if she were her little sister, even though Kennedy is the older of the two.

Kennedy wraps her arm around Miller's waist before picking seats next to each other. My sister-in-law grabs a beer from the cooler, holding up a Corona to see if Kennedy wants one too.

She nods in agreement, and suddenly there are four beer bottles laced between Miller's fingers that she brings back to the table.

"How much do you want to bet that those beers aren't for us?" I ask my brother at my side as we both watch them, arms crossed over our chests.

"There's not a chance in hell those second ones are for us."

"That's your fiancée," I remind him.

"And that's your wife."

I can't help the small smile that creeps across my lips. It's my favorite thing to hear.

Zanders and Ryan bring the burger toppings and condiments to the table, while Kai and I bring the buns and patties, including a vegetarian one for Indy. Rio follows behind with the fries and a bottle of tequila.

"Who wants one?" he asks as I take the empty seat next to Kennedy. "It's a sipping tequila since you all are getting too old to be throwing back shots."

"Sorry we're not twenty-five anymore," Zanders says.

Stevie holds her hand up. "I can't. I get really sleepy from tequila."

"Really?" Miller asks. "I get really horny from tequila."

"Jesus, woman." Kai shakes his head. "You're a mother."

"Hell yeah, I am."

"I get really married from tequila." Kennedy holds out her hand for me to give her a high five.

I connect my hand with hers. "Hell yeah, you do."

"You guys are cute." Miller smiles at us from Kennedy's other side. "Ken, you're my favorite sister-in-law."

"She's your only sister-in-law," Kai adds.

"And Isaiah, I just freaking live, laugh, love you."

My attention darts to Kennedy sitting between us, biting that fucking bottom lip to keep from laughing. "You told her?"

She simply shrugs.

I bend to her level, keeping my voice low for only her to hear. "What happened to doctor-patient confidentiality?"

"It doesn't apply here."

I narrow my eyes at her, attempting to be mad, but I can't. I'm so fucking obsessed with the girl that the only thing I can do being this close to her is lean in and kiss her quickly.

"I'm going to use the restroom real quick." Kennedy stands from her seat as everyone else begins building their burgers.

"You remember where it is?" Indy asks.

"I do. Be right back."

As soon as she's in the house, I grab her plate and get her food situated for her so it's ready to eat as soon as she gets back. With a tomato speared at the end of my fork, I pause with it midway to Kennedy's plate because it's far too quiet around me. Looking up, I find every single one of my friends watching me.

"Yes?" I drag out the question, my eyes bouncing around to each person.

"You better fucking tell her you don't want her to go," Zanders says, leaning back in his chair.

"Yeah." I exhale a laugh before continuing to build Kennedy's plate. "That's not going to happen."

"Why not?" Stevie asks.

"Because the whole point of us staying married this season was to keep her in good standing, so when the time came for her to interview for this new position, she wouldn't have a termination on her work record."

"But things have changed," Indy cuts in. "That was before"—she waves her hands, gesturing between me and Kennedy's empty seat—"this."

"Would you go with her?" Ryan asks.

My attention immediately falls to Kai. He holds my eye contact for a moment before dropping his attention to his lap.

"My life is here."

The words don't taste right as they come off my tongue, because when Kennedy goes, so much of my life will go with her. But Kai, Miller, and Max are here. As are my friends. As are my teammates. As is the team I play for.

"What do you think, Rio?" Miller asks. "You've been quiet over there."

Fucking troublemaker. We all know the only thing Rio has to say is—

"I just don't get why I'm the only single one left. It's not right."

The table echoes with laughter.

"I'm serious. You know how long I've been looking?"

"You're twenty-five," Zanders laughs. "It can't be that long."

Indy cuts in, "I think the hardest part for you will be finding a woman secure enough in your relationship that she'll be okay knowing you'll always be more in love with my husband than with her."

Ryan shakes his head.

"Damn straight." Rio points at him.

"Honestly, Rio," Stevie says. "Is there anyone you wouldn't be open to? You seem fairly open to everyone."

"Thirsty, Vee," Zanders cuts in. "He's fairly thirsty towards everyone."

"That's not true," Rio says. "There is one person I'd never give the time of day to." He allows the statement to hang in the air. "And it's not like I want a girlfriend just to have a girlfriend. I'm looking for something serious, and all Isaiah had to do was get drunk in Vegas and he gets a wife. I've tried that. It didn't work."

Kennedy opens the backdoor slider, rejoining us at the table. I leave her plate in front of her seat before beginning to build my own.

She takes a seat, but doesn't reach for her food, simply staring at it instead.

"What's wrong?" I ask quietly while the rest of the table is too busy chatting to hear me.

"You put fries on my burger."

"Yeah. That's how you eat your burgers."

Big brown eyes look up at me. "How did you remember that? I had one once with you."

I huff a laugh. "I remember every single thing about you, Kenny. In case you haven't figured it out already, you're my favorite subject to study."

She snakes a hand over my lap, hooking to hold on to my forearm. Her voice is quiet when she leans on my shoulder and says, "Thank you."

"You're welcome, baby."

Sitting up, she uses both hands to pick up her burger, fries tucked under the bun and all.

She pauses with it partway to her mouth. "Hey, Isaiah?"

"Yeah?"

"I live, laugh, love you too."

30

Isaiah

"I think my dick officially fell off." Cody's teeth chatter through his words as he suffers through an ice bath. "Kennedy, is my time up yet?"

She doesn't even look up from her computer. "Six more minutes."

"C'mon, Ken," he whines. "I want to have children someday. This can't be good for the swimmers."

Her mouth slightly hitches, her attention still locked on the laptop screen as she sits crossed-legged on top of a training table.

"Rhodes," he calls out. "Tell your wife to stop being so mean to me."

I'm on the floor, stretching out my hip flexor over a foam roller, not bothering to look up at him. "Sorry, man. I like her mean."

She and I find each other at that, and I don't miss the way her lips slightly part when she looks at me. Holding myself up on my forearms, I roll my body again, moving in a way that looks awfully similar to the way I fucked her last night once we fell into bed after a long game that went into extra innings.

My voice is all tease. "You doing okay over there, Doc?"

She swallows hard. "I hate you."

"Those aren't the words you used while you were riding my face this morning."

"Gross," Trav groans. "We're at work. You two can stop eye fucking now."

It's my two best friends and my wife, doing extra post-game therapy in the training room with no one else around. We're barely at work.

"Can't help it, Trav." That's Kennedy speaking up. "Have you seen the guy?"

I pump my brows across the room at him.

He groans. "Literally the only thing keeping his ego in check was that you didn't like him, Kennedy. What the hell are we supposed to do now?"

"Is my time up yet?" Cody calls out.

"Four minutes."

The door to the training room swings open, and Dr. Fredrick stills in the threshold when he spots us. "What's going on?"

"Ice bath," Cody grits out.

I don't respect him enough to look at him when I say, "Stretching out still."

His attention swings to Kennedy. "Why didn't you tell me there were still players in here? You were supposed to have the room emptied out and cleaned up an hour ago."

She opens her mouth to answer, but Travis speaks up first. "We asked her to stay back and keep the room open. It's our fault, not hers."

Dr. Fredrick's jaw tenses, attention on Kennedy when he speaks. "Well, since you like being in here so much, you can go ahead and be the one to mop the floors and deep clean the equipment when they're done. Supplies are in the closet."

Kennedy silently nods in agreement.

He looks at all three of us, then turns on his heel to leave without giving Kennedy a second glance.

I watch her shoulders loosen as soon as he's gone. For her, I can't wait for the day she doesn't have to deal with him ever again.

"Sorry, Ken," Cody apologizes.

"We'll help you," Trav cuts in.

She doesn't answer, just shakes her head, and continues to scroll on her computer.

Standing from the ground, I find my way behind her, hooking an arm over the front of her shoulders and placing a kiss on top of her head. "You okay?"

"He's such a fucking prick."

"I know," I soothe. "But soon, you won't have to deal with him anymore."

Once again, she doesn't answer.

"What are you researching today?"

She shuts her computer, turning around to face me, her legs open on either side of mine.

Her smile is cautious, her voice hushed for only us to hear. "Actually, I was chatting to an old friend of mine from undergrad. She's a psychologist now."

Kennedy lets the word *psychologist* hang in the air as I take a seat next to her on the table, our backs to my friends.

"Chatting to her about what?"

Her eyes roam over my face, her tone apprehensive. "I was hoping she might have some techniques that could help you when . . ."

When I can't think straight because my anxiety is telling me about the worst-case scenarios.

I swallow. "What did she say?"

"She sent some articles over. Some research about cognitive behavioral therapy that she's found to be helpful for her patients when they're having bouts of anxiety. I was just typing it up for you in a more digestible way."

I chuckle. "Dumbing it down, you mean."

"No." She smiles. "But the last thing I want is for you to have to rifle through medical research when your mind is playing tricks on you."

Fuck, I love this girl.

"It could be helpful. You've said you wanted to work on it, and I thought maybe I could use my connections to help." She's so unsure, overexplaining herself. "But I didn't want to bombard you with it, so it's here, on my computer if you ever want it, but seriously, no pressure either way. I just—"

"Kenny."

Brows furrowed with concern, she looks up at me.

"Thank you." I run a palm over her hair. "That means so much to me. I've been meaning to make it a priority, maybe even go talk to someone. I'm going to use it. And thank you for simplifying it for me. I know you love your medical shit, but that's not my thing."

Leaning down, I press my lips to hers.

"If you ever did want to talk to someone, and you don't have to if you're not ready, but she said she'd be happy to meet with you over a video call anytime. Or even get you a referral if you want to see someone local to Chicago."

"I love you."

The words are out of my mouth before I can overthink them, but fuck it. They've been true for a long time already.

Her wide eyes shoot to mine, her lips slightly parting to say something in response.

"You know I do, Kenny."

"Kennedy Kay Rhodes, whatever the fuck your name is these days!" Cody yells from the ice bath. "Is my time up?"

"For fuck's sake, Cody! We're in the middle of something."

"Shit." She looks at the time on her phone. "Yeah, you're good."

Just then, as we're staring at her phone screen and sitting in the tension of my confession, a call comes in.

With a 415 area code.

From San Francisco.

"Answer it," I encourage.

Her attention darts from me to the phone, back to me again.

"Answer the phone, baby."

She hops off the training table, leaving her computer behind and heading straight for the exit. Just before she pushes the door open, she answers the phone and brings it to her ear.

"Hello?"

After that, there's nothing. I can't hear her conversation. Can't listen to her reaction when she's offered the job. All I can do is watch through the small glass window as she paces the hallway with the phone pressed to her ear.

She's smiling into the line as she talks to whoever just called her.

Her eyes find me, watching her from the same spot where I just told her I love her, and before I can watch anymore, she moves away from the door and out of eyesight.

"You okay, man?" Trav asks.

Through chattering teeth, Cody answers, "Cold as fuck and I can't find my testicles, but I'll be all right."

"Not you, dumbass. I'm talking about Isaiah."

"No," I answer simply.

"Was that about the job offer?" Cody realizes.

They both cross the room to stand in front of me. I can feel them watching me with concern, but all my attention is stuck on the hallway outside this room.

I laugh to myself, but it holds no humor. "I don't know why I thought I had more time with her."

"Maybe they haven't decided yet, and they're just calling to let her know they're not ready to make a final decision. Maybe they'll wait until after the season is over."

"They're not." I don't even try to convince myself otherwise. I know in my gut what that call is about.

Trav pats me on the shoulder and Cody leaves me to stew during what feels like the longest five minutes of my life.

While she's figuring out a timeline to move out of her apartment and catch a flight to the West Coast, I'm glued in my spot waiting for her to come back and tell me it's over.

With my friends still somewhere in the room, the door finally opens.

That pretty auburn hair, those painted freckles I'm going to miss.

Kennedy stands there in the doorway, only looking at me when she says, "I didn't get the job."

31

Isaiah

She didn't get the job.

In what fucking world did she not get the job?

It's the only question I've been able to ask myself over the last twenty-four hours.

I mean, did they not meet her? Notice how fucking smart that brain of hers is? Realize what an overachiever she is? How hard she works? She was so close to everything she wanted, and just like that, it's gone.

The past twenty-four hours have been . . . *strange*. Between a day game today and watching Kennedy pretend she wasn't upset while at work, to processing the outcome from that phone call and contemplating what that means for us in the future.

I barely slept.

On the other hand, she was out like a light, sleeping like a fucking baby on my chest last night. But I guess she just accepted her fate quicker than I did. Either that, or she's never been allowed to show her disappointment growing up, and now doesn't know how to.

I'm at a loss for how to wrap my head around it. It was never a question of whether Kennedy was going to move away. The only question I ever had was how I would survive when she did.

Everything we did was for this opportunity. The marriage, the acting that wasn't really acting on my part. The months of being forced to share the same hotel room while waiting for her interview. The time we spent together that allowed me to really get to know her, to fall in love with her.

And I do. Fuck, do I love that woman.

And now she's, once again, stuck working for a sexist lead doctor with no light at the end of the tunnel for getting out from under him.

Our marriage was a game, a stepping stone to better things for her.

We had a plan.

Then there's the selfish part. My first reaction to the news and the silver lining constantly repeating itself. Contradictory to the disappointment I feel for her, I've also been racked with overwhelming relief.

Kennedy is staying in Chicago. *I'm* in Chicago. Nothing has to change between us. We can keep doing exactly what we're doing now.

If that's what she wants, I mean. I think that's what she wants. I think she wants me.

No, she didn't say anything in return when I told her I loved her, but that's not why I said it in the first place. Besides, Kennedy has always been a few steps behind me in this relationship. I fell for her three years ago. I'm perfectly happy to wait for her to catch up.

But just because she doesn't get to live out these new life experiences in a new city doesn't mean I can't keep giving them to her here. And even if she won't admit it, I know she's got to be upset and my specialty is making people smile. Her, specifically.

Knocking on her door, I wait for her to answer. I assumed the woman at reception would call up and let her know I was on the way, seeing as I had to be cleared by Kennedy's list of approved guests.

Her building is bougie as fuck. White marbled floors. String music playing over the speakers in the lobby. An escort who walked me up to her floor.

"Who is it?" she calls out from behind her apartment door.

"It's me, Ken."

Utter confusion is the first thing I see as she opens the door. "What are you doing here? I was just packing a bag to bring to your place for the night."

"Can I come in?"

Her eyes track my face and I watch her slender throat work through a swallow as she opens the widening into her apartment, allowing me inside.

It's spotless, minus the handful of unfinished crossword puzzles discarded on the entryway table. As if every time she came back here, she realized she had been too preoccupied to do one so she tossed it aside, only for her to never pick it up again.

"Is everything okay?" she asks.

"Yes, but are you okay?"

"I'm fine," she brushes me off once again. "I don't want to talk about it."

She hasn't once wanted to talk about it.

"Okay."

"Am I not coming over tonight?"

"Of course you're fucking coming over tonight. You think I can sleep without you at this point? Probably not, but I don't want to test the theory either."

Her face softens with amusement.

"I thought maybe you'd like a distraction tonight. I was going to see if there was another first I could check off your imaginary list. Ever had the chance to catch Fourth of July fireworks over the Navy Pier with your husband before?"

Lips pressed together, I watch that smile grow. "I can't say I've had the chance to experience that very specific scenario."

Stepping into her, I slip my fingers into hair, tilting her head back slightly. "Want to?" I drag my thumb over her smile. "But just a heads-up, the whole team is going to be there."

She doesn't hesitate when she nods against me. "Sounds perfect."

Kennedy's apartment building overlooks the Navy Pier, so the walk doesn't take more than a few minutes to get there. In fact, judging by the picture out her windows I caught while she was changing, she'd have just as good of a view of the fireworks from her place as she would down here.

But after losing out on the job she so desperately wanted, I need her to have some fun with all the people who are going to be stoked to hear she's staying.

Her hand is tucked in mine, and she's wearing that hat I sent her to California in. Simple grey tee, cutoff denim shorts, and those high-top Vans. It's plenty humid still tonight, even with the sun beginning to fall. A perfect summer night in the city I love, with the girl I love, hanging out with the team I love.

Lucky. I feel so goddamn lucky that she's staying.

Weaving through the crowd, my brother is the first one I spot, towering over the rest of the patrons. Leaning back against the metal railing, with his back to the water, he holds his hand up to get our attention.

"There they are."

"I can't see anything," Kennedy says, attempting to find our friends through the mass of people, leaning up on her toes and everything.

I try my best to bite back my knowing smile.

It doesn't work. She smacks me in the chest. "Shut up."

"Hey, guys," Miller says as soon as we make it to them. She's got Max in her arms, leaning with her back to my brother's front.

"Zaya."

"Hi, Bug."

"The boys are by the wheel." Kai nods in that direction.

I pop a quick kiss on Max's cheek when Miller puts him on the ground, before finding Kennedy's hand so I don't lose her in the crowd.

My nephew seems to have the same thought when he takes my wife's other hand, then his mom's, standing between the two of them with so much pride.

Kai chuckles to himself as he throws an arm around Miller and the five of us are off to find the team looking like one big happy family.

"Maxie boy!" Cody calls out, crouching to his level.

My nephew runs—if you want to call it that—to him before Cody scoops him up, and the team's attention immediately shifts. Some of them have dates with them, some of them came alone. It doesn't matter, each of their focus zeros in on Max, giving him high fives or trying to make him laugh.

It's something I love so much about these guys, the way they fully accepted Max when he came into our lives. There was never a complaint about a baby traveling with the team last year.

They all rallied around my brother to make sure he felt their support.

They're good ones, and I feel incredibly blessed that I get to have them as my teammates.

Miller slips her arm under Kennedy's, pulling her away to one of the concession stands and leaving me with Kai.

"She seems to be doing okay."

"Yeah," I agree, watching her in the distance. "Better than I thought she'd be."

"How are you feeling about it all?"

"Happy." There's no hesitation in my answer. "I'm stoked she's staying."

"And long term? Because you thought this was a temporary fix. Are you wondering what this means for you guys?"

My head whips in his direction. "Well, fuck. Now I am."

Kai chuckles, throwing his arm around me and pulling me to join the rest of the team. "Word of advice, little brother. You should probably think about asking your fake wife how she feels about being your real girlfriend now that she's staying."

Thankfully, that conversation ends just before arms wrap around my waist from behind.

"They have airbrush T-shirts here," Kennedy says, her cheek resting on my back.

"Are you thinking what I'm thinking?"

"That we should get Max one with his name on it?"

"Oh." My lip curls. "No, I was thinking we should get couples shirts. You wear my name. I wear yours."

"Why do I feel like you probably already had those made?"

"We're up," Travis says from the front of the line. "We can take Max in our gondola. There's room."

"Are you sure?" Miller asks. "You don't mind?"

"Do you want to go with the boys, Bug?" Kai directs his question to his son.

Max nods excitedly, clapping his hands as Cody carries him into their gondola.

The rest of the team disperses into multiple others, and Kai and Miller take their own, as do we.

As soon as the door closes, Kennedy takes the initiative to slide onto my lap as we face the window. "I've never been on a Ferris wheel before."

"What?" I laugh. "Yes you have."

She shakes her head no, watching as we slowly inch above the Chicago skyline. It takes me only a moment to register who I'm talking to. Sometimes, I forget that Kennedy didn't have a normal upbringing. That there's no way her pretentious mother would take her to the local fair or an amusement park.

"I got close once though."

"Oh yeah? How so?"

"My parents had a house in the Hamptons and one summer while I was home, we were going out there for this big party my mother had planned. I think I was eleven or twelve, and I didn't want to sit around while a bunch of older people faked that they liked each other. So, while the car was being packed up for the weekend, I ran away, got on the subway determined to spend my weekend at Coney Island. There was an old Ferris wheel there. It looked fun and I had never been on one."

"You did not."

She huffs a laugh. "I did."

"Okay, rebel. And did you make it?"

"Nope. I did, however, make it to Brooklyn before one of the family drivers scooped me up and drove me straight out to the Hamptons. My mother didn't even reprimand me when I got there. Even me trying to run away couldn't get her attention." She settles back into my chest. "A lot of people were impressed by my last name, but it wasn't much fun growing up as a Kay."

I slip my arm around her hip, finding her hand folded in her lap to run the pad of my thumb over her ring. "I don't care what your last name was, Kenny. I only care what it is now."

She chuckles. "You do know my last name isn't actually Rhodes, right? Just because we're married doesn't mean I automatically took your last name."

"Well, we should probably do something about that."

She doesn't respond. Just like she didn't respond when I told her I loved her.

And that's okay.

"When was the last time you talked to your mother?" I ask.

She shrugs. "I haven't. Not since that dinner in Atlanta."

"At all?"

She settles back against me again. "She tried to tell me that my *attendance was mandatory* at Connor and Mallory's wedding, but Dean and I decided we weren't going to go. I haven't talked to her since, and I have no plans to. I'm tired of trying to be perfect for them. They don't care anyway, so I'm trying to focus on what makes me happy instead."

Fuck, I love that.

"Proud of you, Ken."

A small smile tilts on her lips. "Me too."

"Speaking of Dean, can I just express how much I hate that you two are staying at your place while he's in town for this upcoming series."

"Three quick nights. You won't even notice I'm gone."

That's a goddamn lie and she knows it.

The wheel takes us up to the top of my favorite city. The sun is just setting off in the horizon, casting a warm, golden hue over Lake Michigan. The buildings' reflections are clearly outlined on the water.

"I love it here," I say to her quietly. "Chicago."

She simply nods her agreement.

"Do you?" I ask, because that's what I really need to know. Can she stay here? Can she be happy here even though staying wasn't her first choice?

"I didn't think much of it before, but it's grown on me recently."

"Are you talking about me or the city?"

"They go hand in hand, in my opinion. It's kind of a package deal."

32

Kennedy

Tonight has been fun.

I enjoy being around the team, and it's been nice spending time with them both in and outside of work. I used to be so afraid of getting in trouble for it, trying to be the perfect employee. But now, I just don't care.

If Dr. Fredrick was going to fire me, he would've done it a long time ago, but he knows he can't because I've done nothing to warrant it.

Well, other than marrying one of his players.

And blowing said player in the restroom at work.

God, that was fun.

"Ken!" Max yells, pointing down at me from where he sits on his dad's shoulders. He has no idea how loud he is, thanks to the giant earmuffs he's got on to protect his hearing from the fireworks that are about to start.

"Are you excited, Bug?"

He just smiles at me, unable to hear anything I have to say, and I smile right back.

A kiss lands on the top of my shoulder as Isaiah braces two hands on the metal fence in front of me, caging me in. "Hi."

"Hi."

"I like when you smile, Ken."

"Me too."

"Just for clarification, I think you're stunning all of the time, but happy looks real fucking good on you."

375

Leaning back, my head hits the middle of his chest as we wait for the fireworks to start.

Maybe no one has ever let you feel safe and that's why you're not affectionate.

I remember those words so clearly. He said them that night we went to dinner when I asked him to teach me how to be better with physical closeness.

I didn't know then, but he was right.

Hands sliding down his biceps, I pull his arms in to fold over me just as the first firework travels into the air. There's a collective wondrous gasp as red light illuminates the dark Chicago sky.

"You are, right?" he asks low in my ear as the show begins to build. "Happy."

Tilting to see him, the concern is evident on his face.

Of course I'm happy, but he's referring to how I feel about not going to San Francisco, and I don't want to talk about that right now.

I don't want to talk at all.

"Come with me," I say, taking his hand in mine and pulling him to follow me down the pier.

"Where are we going?"

"I have a different place I want to watch the fireworks from. Some place where I can show you just how happy you make me."

The door to my apartment isn't even closed before I toss his hat I'm wearing to the floor and slip my T-shirt over my head.

"Well, fuck," he drawls.

"Exactly. That's exactly what I want you to do. Fuck me." Crossing the living room, I throw open the curtains, allowing them to frame the fireworks show that's still going on outside.

"Right here."

Kicking off my shoes, I slip my shorts down my legs, leaving me in only my bra and underwear, standing right there in front of the window. Looking like the needy woman I am.

I'm so fucking desperate for him, it'd be embarrassing if I didn't know exactly the way he felt about me.

Across the room, Isaiah closes the door without looking away from me, his tongue darting out to wet his bottom lip as he stares.

Slowly, deliberately slowly, I reach behind and unclasp my bra.

"Close the curtain."

"No."

His jaw tics. "Kenny, I could give two fucks what the view out there looks like, but I'm sure as hell not sharing this view of you with anyone else. Close the fucking curtain."

A rebellious smile hitches when I allow my bra to drop off my shoulders.

"Kennedy."

"It's a one-way mirror, caveman. We can see out, but they can't see in."

A beat passes before he huffs a laugh, but it's dry and without humor. Isaiah crosses the living room, right to the bar where some too expensive whiskey sits in a decanter. He pours himself a glass, leans back against the counter, and slowly brings the whiskey to his lips.

"You want me to fuck you?"

Hands palming my breasts, I lightly squeeze, needing hands on my body, even if they're my own. "I thought that was obvious."

His eyes are glued on my fingers as I tweak my nipples. He takes another slow sip. "Show me."

"What?"

"Show me where you want me to fuck you."

My cheeks go warm as he sits back for his own personal show, the fireworks exploding in light behind me.

My hands are still roaming over my breasts.

"Your perfect tits," he says. "I'll fuck those tonight. Anything else?"

I run a single hand down my stomach, letting my middle finger glide over my underwear, over my pussy, lightly teasing my clit.

"I can't see what you're touching, Ken."

"I'm touching this." Using the waistband at my hips, I pull my panties up tight, letting the fabric slip between my pussy, but still not showing him everything.

"Tease."

My body feels his appreciative stare from across the room as it starts to move and sway on its own accord. His eyes are glued, focused on only me, not paying attention to the show just outside. No one has ever looked at me the way he does. I've never been worshiped the way he worships me. Have never had to question him because he's so steadfast in his feelings for me.

I keep my panties on, but push them to the side.

"Lose them," he says before taking another swig.

So, I do, right there in front of the window, I kick them off and leave myself fully naked while Isaiah stands across the room still fully clothed.

My fingers find my clit again, and his eyes bounce from mine to between my legs and back again. Smiling at me like he knows a secret, like he's proud of me for standing naked and fingering myself for him.

"You love to do whatever I tell you to do when you're like this, huh? Needy and desperate for it."

My nod is frantic.

"Then put that finger inside that perfect cunt of yours and show me exactly where you want me to fuck you."

So, I do, slipping my finger inside. Slowly at first, just to the first knuckle.

He shakes his head. "More."

Second knuckle and it has me rocking into my hand with a whimper of a moan. My other hand grabs my tit and squeezes.

"Fuck." It comes out like a breath of air before he throws back the rest of the drink, discards the empty glass by tossing it on the couch, and stalks across the room. In three predatory steps, he has me pinned to the window.

Ass cheeks pressed to the glass, and finger still in my pussy, I thrust in and out. It's far too easy. I'm far too wet.

Isaiah watches between us, using his foot to nudge my legs apart. He uses a single index finger to glide up my inner thigh, gathering my arousal.

"Pretty," he hums his approval, and just as I think he's going to slip that finger into his own mouth, he instead presses it to the seam of mine. "Open."

I do.

"You need to taste this for yourself, maybe then you'll understand why I'm so far gone. You taste like fucking heaven."

He guides his finger into my mouth, and I don't hesitate to lick a long line before sucking myself off him.

When he pulls his finger from my mouth, it's with a lewd pop, and immediately my hands slide to his waistband.

"I didn't tell you to stop fucking your finger, Kenny."

I still for a beat before sliding my finger back inside my pussy, only to quickly add a second.

"Goddamn, you're so good." He makes quick work of his shoes and pants, leaving only his shirt on. "So fucking smart. So fucking sweet when you want to be. So fucking mine."

"Yes," is all I can say, head thrown back against the window. The loud pops of fireworks are dulled from the pounding orgasm that's begging to release. My two fingers aren't enough.

My eyes are glued to his cock, the way it works in his fist. Fuck, he's hard already.

Isaiah flips me around, tits pressed to the glass. "Watch the show, baby. That's what you wanted to do."

I moan, rolling my body against the window, one hand bracing myself against it, the other working myself.

But then he pulls my fingers out of my cunt and instead, slides them up to my clit. "You don't stop touching yourself, okay, Ken?"

He helps me circle my clit, using the pads of his fingers to press into mine.

My exhale is hot, leaving a foggy film over the window, but that's nowhere near as filthy as when Isaiah slams his hand against the glass to brace himself, smearing my arousal for both of us to see.

"Arch that ass for me, baby."

I don't hesitate and just as more fireworks soar into the sky, Isaiah notches the head of his cock at my entrance, and when the resounding boom echoes around us, he pushes himself inside.

"*Fuck*," I cry out.

He pulls out and pushes back so easily. I'm so wet, so ready to come.

I don't even realize when my fingers stop moving. I'm so focused on the way Isaiah's cock buries itself in me, stealing my breath from me.

"What did I say? Keep rubbing your clit."

So, I do, in quick, tight little circles because I'm already so fucking close.

"Do you know how lucky I am, Kennedy?"

I whimper against the glass.

"Do you understand how smart, how capable, how fucking special you are?"

His words have me clenching around him. I know what

he's doing. He's trying to boost my ego after that phone call.

It's working.

"I have waited, and fucking waited for this. You're my answered prayer. You know that?"

My fingers move frantically as he fucks me from behind.

"You want to know what my favorite part of the last couple months is, other than getting to fuck this cunt that was made for me? It's getting to watch you come alive. You know that, Kenny?" He thrusts deep, continually hitting me right where I need him. "The way you smile. The way you laugh now. Fuck, I could come just thinking about it."

His knuckles turn white as he flexes his hand into a fist against the glass, his other hand digging into my hip, fingertips sure to leave bruises there for me to find tomorrow.

Bending over me, his mouth meets the crook of my neck. "God, I love you."

That's all it takes.

"Isaiah," I cry out, clenching around him.

I've never had someone say those words to me before. Not a single person. Never even had someone try to pretend they meant them.

But there's not a question in my mind that he does. It's what allows the blinding orgasm to rip through me, writhing into the glass, the fireworks outside looking real inconsequential compared to the ones racking my body.

"Fuck me, you're pulsing," he says, still buried deep inside of me.

I ride it out, and once I'm done, he slowly slides out of me.

"So beautiful," he whispers, fingers threaded into my hair when he gently pulls to turn my face to him.

He kisses me right there, freshly fucked and slumped against the window.

I hardly notice when he turns me around and guides me down to my knees. I'm too focused on the aftershocks of my orgasm, but I sit up on shaky, spent legs, my hooded eyes locked on his glistening cock.

His lips tilt with mischief as he looks down at me. "It's about time you get on your knees for me. I've spent the last three years on mine for you."

I hold my head high. "I fucking love being on my knees for you."

"Mmm," he hums, finger and thumb keeping my chin up and my attention focused on him. "And don't you look pretty down there."

He keeps his eyes on me as he uses a single hand to slip his shirt off, tossing it somewhere in the room.

"Remind me again what you didn't like about these tits." He tests the weight, his thumb circling my peaked nipple.

"They're small."

"Hmm." Crouching for just a moment, he slides two fingers against my sensitive pussy, gathering my cum. "And why do you think that?"

Because I was constantly told so.

But I don't dare say his name while kneeling in front of the man I'm married to, still riding the post-orgasm high.

"You're not going to tell me?" he asks as he stands, using my cum to paint my chest. He admires it as if he just created the next artistic masterpiece. "That's fine. I have no problem proving you wrong. Now push those pretty tits together."

Once again, I do as he says and when he steps forward, he slips his cock under my breasts, and thrusts upward into the tight channel.

Holy shit.

A bead of precum tempts me to lick it, each and every time his tip slips through my hold.

"Fuck, this is going to be quick."

I've never seen anything like him. So unhinged, so wildly desperate as he watches the way he slides between me.

"Do you want me to turn you around?" he asks through hard-earned breaths. "You're missing the show."

With my back to the pier, I look up and say, "This is the only show I want to watch right now."

"God," he exhales, palm sliding over my head. "The best girl."

"Your only girl," I correct him.

"Damn straight you are."

Shoulders back and putting myself on full display, I let him fuck me.

It's hot. It's so fucking hot to the point where I don't see how it's possible for me to ever be insecure about my tits again. Anytime I question myself, I'll remember the way his cock throbbed against them, the way he gritted his teeth just before he came. The way he moaned my name as hot white ropes decorated my neck and chin.

His jerky thrusts still, his cock twitching as he comes. And the sound he makes, God I'll never forget that deep, guttural groan.

Arms crossed over the glass, Isaiah drops his head on his forearms, chest heaving as he towers over me.

"Fuck, that was hot," he breathes against the window, eyes peering down at me.

Holding eye contact, I gather his cum from my neck and bring it down to circle my nipple, rubbing myself as he watches with hungry brown eyes.

"Jesus Christ, Kenny. I swear if I wasn't already, I'd fucking marry you."

I tuck my lip between my teeth in a smile. "That makes two of us."

33

Isaiah

"If it's still hurting you tonight, I can rub it out later."

My brows quirk with interest as I sit upright on the training table.

"Get your head out of the gutter, Rhodes." Kennedy stands between my open legs, wrapping the plastic wrap diagonally across my torso to keep the ice pack secured. "If your shoulder is still bothering you when you get home, I can come over and work on it before bed."

"And what about if my dick is still hurting when I get home?"

"You've got two hands."

Mouth popping open, I wrap my hand around the back of her thigh and pull her closer.

"We get it," Monty grumps. "You're into each other. What happened to keeping it professional at work?"

"Clearly they're not great at following that rule." Reese walks into the training room, high heels and pencil skirt in full force today. "Emmett, I need to speak to you in your office, please."

She walks right past him, into his office, blonde hair bouncing with each step. Monty stands there, arms crossed over his chest as if he has the option not to follow her. He takes a deep breath through his nose before remembering he wants to keep his job, and follows her into his office, closing the door behind him.

"What's that about?" Kennedy asks.

"I'm not sure, but he's been in a shit mood lately. Said that Reese has been constantly reminding him that he's up for contract renewal next year."

"They wouldn't get rid of Monty. Your guys' record since he became the field manager is good. Great even. And everyone loves him."

"Everyone besides her, and starting next year, her opinion is the only one that's going to matter."

Kennedy puts the plastic wrap roller away, a small smile tilting on her lips as she does.

"You're excited about that, huh?"

"Not about her not liking Monty, but I am looking forward to her taking over. If we're looking at the positives here, I get to work for the first ever female team owner in the MLB."

And she was supposed to be the first female team doctor.

There's that contradicting feeling again. Yes, Kennedy is staying here. We get to keep doing what we're doing, but the person I love lost an opportunity she's waited for her entire adult life.

"Rhodes," Sanderson, the other athletic trainer, calls out. "Someone is out in the hallway to see you."

I look back to Kennedy in confusion.

"Who is it?" she asks for me.

"It's uh . . ." Sanderson hesitates. "Dean Cartwright."

I burst a laugh. "Yeah. Hell no."

"Isaiah."

"Kenny, I didn't get into it with him during the game today. I still have to deal with him for two more in this series. You're not sleeping in my bed because he's here. What else do you want from me?"

"I want you to talk to him."

She stands firm, holding my eye contact.

I'm already annoyed that she stayed at her place last night to hang out with him, and now he wants to talk to me?

Every part of me is wanting to scream no. Fuck that guy. But I truly don't know how to say no to this girl. Never have.

"Fine," I huff. "But I'm only accepting sexual favors as a thank you from you."

A little grin on her lips, she shakes her head at me as she leaves to go work on another one of my teammates.

With only an ice pack and a pair of shorts on, I leave the training room to find Dean leaning against the hallway, waiting for me.

"What?" I ask, staying on my side of the hallway, closest to the door, so I can leave as soon as he says some stupid shit I know I'm not going to like.

He clears his throat. "I need to apologize."

That has my head whipping in his direction, single brow lifted.

"Kennedy chewed me out. She found out the details of our little childhood rivalry."

She did?

I try to act nonchalant. "Well, I didn't tell her anything."

"Wouldn't have blamed you if you did." There's a heavy pause, Dean's focus locked on the carpet under his feet, clearly uncomfortable. "The truth is, I was a little shit back then."

"Still are."

His eyes shoot to mine in warning. "Still am, *sometimes*, but I was angry as a kid, and I took it out on you. So . . . I'm sorry."

"How'd those words taste?"

"Pretty fucking terrible."

"Well, I don't really care anymore, so it's whatever."

"Yes, you do," he says. "And you should. It was messed up. I fucked with you because I could, and it made me feel better when just about everything else in my life made me feel like shit."

From across the hallway, I watch him, looking for any sign of bullshit, which is the only thing that comes out of Dean Cartwright's mouth.

Only this time, he seems . . . sincere.

"Jesus," I huff a laugh. "What the hell did Kennedy say to you?"

"Yeah, she's fucking pissed. Told me she was more than happy to cut off our relationship if I didn't apologize, so here I am, apologizing."

I brush him off. "You're good. I'll let her know that you did."

I turn back to the training room, but he stops me.

"I am though," he says. "Sorry about it. I know you probably won't believe me but I'm not that guy anymore. Well . . ." He tosses his head from side to side. "Unless my father is around. He tends to bring out the worst in me."

"Yeah, your family sucks."

"Tell me about it. Other than Kennedy, they're all the fucking worst. And I didn't understand how my life was shit and yours wasn't. You had everything I wanted, and I hated you for it."

"Me?" I ask in disbelief. "I had nothing. You were the one with all the best baseball gear. New cars. Fuck, you even took every girl I had ever liked. I showed up to games on a city bus. I shared gear with my brother and half the time it didn't even fit."

"You had a brother who cared about you. Who would do anything for you, and you'd do the same for him. People loved you."

I could try to argue the fact, but he's not wrong. Kai and I would do anything for each other, and I've always had the desperate need to make myself enjoyable to be around for other people. From Dean's perspective, I was a naturally likable guy, but he didn't know I spent my entire life making myself easy to digest. Always bringing the fun and laughs even when I didn't necessarily want to.

"My dad threw his credit card at me to make up for being absent," he continues. "And the one and only game he ever came to, we played against you guys, and he didn't have a single thing to say about me afterward, but he fucking raved about you. I hated you for it. I took it out on you for a long time and I'm sorry for that."

Across the hall, Dean holds his hand out for me to shake.

"Damn. Kennedy really did a number on you, huh?"

"I've never seen her so mad."

For her I want to forgive him, but even more so, for myself. I just don't care anymore, not when I feel like I finally have everything I've ever wanted.

So, I shake his hand.

"Just how pissed were you when you found out about us?" I ask, amusement lacing my tone.

"Oh, don't even get me started. I finally had someone in this fucked-up family who I enjoyed being around and she goes and marries you of all people." He huffs a laugh, shaking his head in disbelief. "I was livid. And not just because it was you, but because of what she went through, only to end up married to someone else she didn't want to be with."

"I get it."

"But you don't, Rhodes. I don't know what she's told you about growing up the way she did, but I had to sit back and watch it all. In the early years, when our parents first arranged for her to marry Connor, she used to cry herself to sleep at night. I'd hear it through my bedroom wall, then each morning, she'd act as if nothing happened. Once we got close enough, she finally admitted how unhappy she was, but in the same breath would also say she didn't know what happiness even felt like. How fucked up is that?"

She's happy now, I try to remind myself.

Sure, she didn't get the job she dreamed of. Didn't get the fresh start she wanted. Didn't get to try her hand at dating.

But she has me, and she seems happy.

Right?

"One day," Dean continues, "she got the courage to beg her mother to let her out of that arrangement, and she's such a perfectionist, you know. That includes all those years she spent trying to be the perfect daughter, so you could imagine how difficult that was for her to do.

"I've never seen someone get verbally berated the way she was. She was called selfish, ungrateful. The list goes on. And of course, I felt guilty because the only reason she was in this predicament in the first place was because of me. I didn't want to take over the family business, so she had to marry someone who would."

My stomach churns at the visual of that little unhappy auburn-haired girl.

She's happy now, I repeat to myself.

"I can't explain how relieved I was when he ended things," Dean says. "She finally got a bit of freedom to go do whatever she wanted, whatever would make her happy. She finally had the space to figure out what happiness looked like for her, and for the first time in her life, she was allowed to make her own decisions. So, you could imagine how furious I was when I found out you guys got fucking married and all of a sudden, Kennedy was trapped in another relationship she didn't want."

His words hit me square in the chest.

I did that. I trapped her in a relationship she didn't want. I wouldn't give her the annulment she wanted. I came up with the scheme to save her job. And for what? She didn't get her dream job and now she's stuck working for that piece-of-shit doctor again.

The past few days I've been selfish as fuck, basking in the idea that I get to have it all. Her, this city, my family.

And what does she get?

"From what she told me, she wanted to start over in a new city, get the job she deserves, and someday, hopefully meet someone. So, yeah, I was pissed when I found out that once again, it was all taken away from her. But I was wrong. Clearly, she doesn't feel trapped. Clearly, she wants to be with you."

"I don't know about that." My tone holds no inflection, my eyes fixated on the floor. I'm standing here like a zombie as too many realities I didn't want to see are sinking in. "Maybe she just doesn't have another option."

"What are you talking about? She turned down that job offer in San Francisco to be with you. She had another option, and she didn't want to take it."

My attention comes back to life. "What are you talking about?"

"The job she didn't take. They called last week and offered her the position. Wanted her to start shadowing the current team doctor right away. She turned it down."

That can't be true.

"What day was that? Tuesday?"

He thinks back for a second. "Yeah, I think so. She said she was in the training room with you when they called."

What the actual fuck?

In what fucking world does she get to turn down an opportunity like that for me. From the moment I met Kennedy, it's all she's ever worked for, to become a lead doctor. Fuck, even to become a second doctor. Anything to get out of the current position she's overqualified for. Anything to get out from working under Dr. Fredrick.

She can't make that hasty of a decision out of nowhere. I'm the impulsive one. She's the planner. She's been planning this move all year.

And what? She's staying because of me?

Holy shit. I told her I loved her right before she answered that phone call.

I'm always worried people won't stick around once they see the real me. How many times did I tell her that?

She's trying to stay for me.

"Shit," Dean curses. "You didn't know."

Without looking at him, I slowly shake my head no. "I do now."

34

Kennedy

"Good evening, Ms. Kay. Welcome home," the woman working at reception in my overly expensive apartment building greets me. "Are you staying in again tonight? Would you like me to set up a dinner delivery for you?"

With my keys dangling in my hand, I don't stop to talk as I cross the hall to the elevator. "Not tonight, but thank you! Just grabbing a few things and I'll be on my way."

She gives me her best customer service smile. "Of course. Please let us know if you need any assistance with your things."

"Thank you!" I blurt out just as the doors to the elevator close.

The lobby staff are all kind and over accommodating, which makes sense, seeing as this is one of the most expensive buildings in the city. But I can't help wondering what they think of me coming in every other day to grab clothes before leaving for Isaiah's minutes later.

Other than the past few nights Dean has stayed over, I can't remember the last time I slept here. This place doesn't feel like home anymore. It never has, I suppose, but especially not now that both Isaiah and his apartment feel like the closest thing I've ever felt to home.

Most of my stuff is there, but we haven't had a conversation about making that a permanent situation. Up until last week, I wasn't even going to be living in Chicago, let alone with him.

But now, now things are different. Now I'm staying, and neither of us has had the courage to initiate that talk. Now that our little game is over, what are we doing?

And then there's one more massive conversation we need to have. Something I need to tell him. That I was, in fact, offered the lead doctor position in San Francisco, and I made the decision not to take it.

I had been stewing over the option for days. This offer was everything I had ever wanted, everything I thought I was looking for. A new city with a chance to meet new people. The opportunity to figure out what kind of happiness I could discover with my newfound freedom.

But I didn't need to go to a new city to find what I've been looking for because all these years, it had been right in front of me.

When Isaiah told me he loved me, I knew I had found it. He didn't say it with an expectation to hear it back. Didn't say it with the hope it'd change our outcome when that call came in.

But it did.

For the first time in my life, it wasn't hard to believe that someone could feel that way about me, because he had spent months showing me. His words were simply a reminder of what I already knew.

Isaiah loves me.

So much so that if I would've told him that I got the job and turned it down, he wouldn't have let me stay. So, I didn't give him that option.

Before him, loneliness was comfortable. It was the only thing I knew. Entertaining myself any way I could find. Trying to convince myself that I was okay with going through life that way. And now I have a chance at a future where maybe I'm not so alone, and I don't want to mess that up.

So, I turned down the job.

For him. But for me too.

I haven't seen him as much as I'd like the last few days. Atlanta's team has been in town for the series against the Warriors, and Dean has been staying over at my apartment, but tonight is the night I get to go back to Isaiah's.

Unlocking the front door of my place, I toss my keys on the entryway table, heading straight for my room. With a duffel bag open on my bed, I pack. Underwear, socks, whatever else I might need, and I take enough with me that I won't have to come back here for a while.

It's quiet here, in this massive penthouse with big windows overlooking the city, and marble floors that echo the silence.

I hate it.

I want to be warm in Isaiah's bed, or hanging out with Miller at family dinner, or listening to the guys give each other shit in the training room.

I want to be somewhere that makes me feel good and it certainly isn't in this apartment my family owns.

Continuing to pack, I turn on the TV for some background noise, hoping it can drown out the silence until I can get out of here. The station is set to the same one I left it at last night, which is an MLB network that continually runs game highlights throughout the day, peppered in with a bit of commentary from baseball analysts.

That's what's on now. Four guys are seated around an arched desk going over the possible outcomes with the looming trade deadline in the league. They speak about the non-playoff-bound teams offloading guys that will reach free agency in the off-season. They go over what some of the playoff-bound teams are looking for.

Then they say a name I never expected to hear.

"This just came across my desk," one of them says. "And who knows how true it could be, but rumors are circulating that Isaiah Rhodes from the Windy City Warriors is interested in a trade."

I freeze right there, with a pair of socks dangling in one hand and clean leggings in the other.

"There's no way that could be true," another one suggests. "No way would the Warriors let him go. He's working with a career-high batting average this year, and they're currently sitting in a fairly secure postseason spot."

"And he's playing with his brother."

"Right. But Kai Rhodes is retiring in the fall, and Isaiah has a player option next season. Maybe he's looking into different clubs, wanting to get out of Chicago. I doubt he's going anywhere mid-season, but there's a possibility he could go somewhere else next year if the right offer came along."

"Again, nothing is confirmed, but there's been some noise going around the league over the last twenty-four hours and typically, where there's smoke, there's fire."

I'm stuck frozen in my bedroom.

What the hell is going on?

They keep talking on the television screen, but I don't listen. All I can hear is the ringing in my ears and the doubts creeping in.

He doesn't want to leave. There's no way.

And if these rumors are true, *why* would he want to leave?

All his friends are here. His family. His brother. He loves playing for Monty.

And me.

I stayed here for him.

Shit.

I stayed here for him, but all season, we both thought I'd be leaving. All this time, we knew our marriage was temporary. One day our game would end.

But I stayed, and now he's trying to go.

Yes, I know Isaiah loves me, but he didn't sign up for forever. He signed up for now.

So many intrusive thoughts are seeping into my mind and instead of letting myself believe them, I fall onto my bed and pick up the phone to call him.

He doesn't answer.

I try again, and as it goes through to voicemail, texts begin flooding in.

Miller: *What the hell is going on?*
Kai: *Where's Isaiah? He's not answering.*
Cody: *Are those rumors true?*
Miller: *Kai is freaking out.*
Travis: *Have you heard about what's going on?*
Kai: *Ken, I need you to tell my brother to call me right now. He's not answering his phone.*

My hand is shaking as I read the incoming messages. Clearly, there's enough truth behind what was said that even his brother knows something is wrong.

I think I might throw up. And why the hell isn't he answering his phone?

I go to call him again when there's a knock at my front door. I'm off my bed and jogging to swing it open, knowing exactly who I'm going to find on the other side.

35

Isaiah

The door swings open in one frantic, swift move.

Kennedy's eyes are wide, her breathing heavy.

"What's wrong?" I quickly ask. I take a step into her apartment, and she instantly retracts, maintaining distance. "What's going on?"

"Is it true?"

"Is what true?"

"Are you going to explore free agency when the season is done? Or ask for a trade? Or whatever the hell they're talking about?"

Fuck.

My wide eyes mirror hers, my lips parting without words to say.

"Oh my God." A single trembling hand covers her mouth. "It's true."

"Where did you hear that?" Pulling my phone out from my back pocket, I find countless missed calls and texts. From her, my brother, and my teammates. "Shit."

"It was on the TV. They were discussing trade rumors and your name came up."

Closing my eyes, I exhale a long breath. "My fucking agent doesn't know how to keep his goddamn mouth shut."

I called him only yesterday about the possibility of me joining free agency next season if the right offer came along.

But he also knows he's going to get a massive payout from

the next contract I sign, and he couldn't keep that news to himself for even twenty-four fucking hours.

Dropping the manila envelope I brought with me onto her entryway table, I attempt to step into her space again. "Ken—"

She flinches. "Don't touch me."

My stomach dips with those words, with the way she reacted. It cements me in place.

This is going to be so much harder than I pictured. She's the one who lied about the job offer and now suddenly, she thinks she can't trust me. "I wanted to be the one to tell you, to explain it to you."

"Are you breaking up with me?"

What the actual fuck?

"What did you just say?"

"Are you wanting to leave Chicago because of me? I know this was only supposed to be temporary and I was the one who was supposed to leave, so if you're doing this because you don't want to be with me—"

"There's no way in hell you're questioning whether I want to be with you. No fucking way."

"I just—"

"Don't even think about trying to justify some ludicrous situation about me running away from you. I don't want to hear it. I love you. You know I love you. I will continue to love you whether you're in San Francisco or some other city. That's not going to change, but you're sure as hell not staying in Chicago, Kennedy."

She stands there, stunned speechless. Kissable lips parted in confusion.

"I'm not going to San Francisco. I didn't get . . . What are you talking about?"

"Yes, you did!" I toss my hands up. "I know when they called you, they offered you the job, and you turned them down. But you're going. I can't let you stay here because of me."

Nervous eyes bounce over me. "How . . . how did you find out?"

My shoulders slump at her admission, my breath leaving me in a whoosh.

So it is true.

"Dean."

"Goddammit, Dean." Eyes closing in frustration, she begins to pace the room. "I thought his conversation with you would last two minutes. I thought he'd be completely disingenuous, and you two would go back to hating each other soon after. I never would've told him if I knew he was going to tell you."

"And thank God he did! What are you thinking, Kennedy?"

"I'm thinking that I don't want to go! Okay? I didn't tell you because I knew you'd react like this."

"You're damn straight I'm going to react like this! I'm not going to let you throw away everything you've worked for without even thinking it over." Stepping into her, I take her face in both my hands, not allowing her to be hesitant of my touch. "Kenny, since the day I met you, this is the one thing you've wanted. That first conversation we had, you asked for my advice on whether you should take the job in Chicago. Well, I'm giving you that same advice now. Take the goddamn job."

Her expression softens, as if my words are finally sinking in and reminding her of who she is and what she's worked for.

I run a thumb over her cheekbone. "You can't stay here, baby."

"And why not?"

"Because you're worth more than how you've been treated the last three years, and I love you enough to make sure you know that. I love you enough to make sure you start living up to your potential."

I watch the way her eyes bounce between mine, cataloging every shitty thing that Dr. Fredrick has done or said to her over the years.

I watch the realization dawn.

Watch the acceptance take over.

It's both relieving and devastating to see.

"You have to take that job, Kenny. I don't think I could live with myself if you didn't."

Dropping my hands from her, I take a step back, giving her space to think clearly without me interfering.

"Everything between us changed so quickly." *For her*, I want to add. Not for me. I've always known how I felt about her. "You're a planner, but you didn't plan this. And I need you to take a moment to think about it. *Really* think about it. Think about *us*."

Her eyes are beginning to gloss over, my sometimes-cold girl who is so fucking warm with me.

But I can guarantee what I'm about to say is a thousand times more painful for me to get out than it will be for her to hear. They're words I never thought I'd catch myself saying.

"When we started this game, it was for this exact ending. We got there. The game is over, but I haven't been playing for a long time. This is real to me. I love you. You're the person I want to be with for the rest of my life, but I know that night in Vegas, you didn't mean to choose me." My throat goes tight with the admission. "Then the game changed, and it was all about you feeling ready for what came next. It was never supposed to be me, Ken. You never wanted it to be me, and that's okay."

"That's not true anymore." The first tear falls down her freckled cheek, and I mirror her with one of my own.

"I don't want to trap you," I continue.

"You're not!"

"Kennedy," I exhale calmly. "You have never gotten to choose your person. Not with him, and not with me. I need you to have a choice."

I grab the envelope off the table.

Her eyes track it before finally she asks, "What is that?"

"You know what this is."

"Isaiah—"

I offer the manila envelope to her, but she refuses to take it.

"I need you to have an out. This was always the plan, and I won't hold it against you if you sign them. You never wanted to be married to me in the first place. I need you to understand that whatever you want to happen next, you have that option. If you want to go to San Francisco by yourself and start the life you've been so excited for, sign these. If you go and you want us to stay together, great. I'll happily deal with the distance. And if you want to go and you want me to come with you, I will try my fucking hardest to make that happen. That's why these trade rumors are going around. I called my agent to tell him I'd be open to an offer from San Francisco next season if that's what you wanted. But I'd only go where you are and only if you wanted me there."

Tears are fully streaming down her face now.

"You've never gotten a say in your own life, and the last thing I'm going to do is take that away from you again. Every option is yours, Kenny. Whatever you want to do, I will be your biggest supporter. But I couldn't live with myself if I didn't allow you the space to fulfill your goals, to live up to everything you've worked so hard for."

Her bottom lip is trembling through the tears, and when I step into her space again, she meets me partway, pulling at my shirt to bring me down to her level.

She kisses me. And I mean, she *kisses* me.

Deeply, and with everything she's got. Either as a thank you or as a goodbye, I'm not sure, but the idea that it could be the latter has my fear speaking for me, unable to hear her decision in this exact moment.

"Take the weekend," I whisper against her lips.

She shakes her head no.

"Please, Ken," I plead. "Play along one more time for me. Take the weekend."

"I don't want to."

"I know, but you need to."

She hesitates, using the back of her hands to clean her face before she offers the slightest nod of her head.

Every part of me is screaming to remind her that I love her once again, but the last time I told her that before a big decision, she based that decision on me.

This time, I need her to choose for herself.

It's what has me pressing my lips to hers one more time before leaving the divorce papers on the table and closing the door behind me when I leave.

36

Isaiah

I knock and wait, hands braced on the edges of the door-frame because my body feels too heavy to hold itself up. I tried to go home, but as soon as I pulled into my parking garage, I backed right out and came here. I didn't want to be there alone.

I did the right thing with Kennedy. I know I did, but it doesn't make it any easier, knowing I gave her the option not to be with me.

Typically, I hide the bad moments, lock myself in my apartment so no one sees them. Shit, hiding in the women's restroom while I was having a bad day is what got me here in the first place.

But I'm tired of it. I'm exhausted from trying to convince others that I'm unbreakable. That I'm the fun one who doesn't get too worked up about life, doesn't take anything too seriously.

I am breakable, and I'm currently at my breaking point.

So, I came here instead of hiding away.

"Hold on. Someone's at my door," I hear Monty say before he cracks his door open, phone pressed to his ear. He takes a moment to look me over before exhaling a sigh of relief. "He's here. I'll call you back." He hangs up the phone to give me his full attention. "What the hell is going on, Isaiah?"

"Can I come in?"

He looks me over, most likely noting how fucking wrecked I am, before fully opening his door to allow me inside. I barely make it into his entryway before he's cupping the back of my head to pull me into a hug.

"You good?" he asks.

"Not exactly." I smack him on the back a couple of times, hugging him in return before pulling away.

With a hand outstretched on my shoulder, I can feel him trying to read me, trying to figure out what's going on. "Come on," he says, nodding towards his couch.

I fall into it, letting my heavy body sink into the cushions. Monty heads to the kitchen, grabbing me a water, before settling in on a chair across from me.

"Care to explain why my phone has been blowing up all night due to trade rumors about you?"

"Sorry about that." It's my automatic response whenever I feel like I'm making someone's life more difficult than it needs to be.

"I don't need you to apologize, Isaiah. I just want to hear from you, not some random TV analysts, that one of my players, who I view as part of my family, is possibly asking for a trade."

I take a long drink of the water, letting it cool my burning throat. "It wasn't supposed to get out like that. I was going to talk to you as soon as I told Kennedy, but then my fucking agent opened his big mouth. He's wanting to build some noise around it, I guess. Get it on other teams' radars."

The hurt is so fucking evident on Monty's face. For being this solid guy who comes across as a hard-ass unless you know him, he looks devastated.

"So you are," he states. "You're trying to leave."

"No." Head hanging low, I keep my eyes glued to my lap. "Not necessarily."

There's a heavy pause, a clear indication that Monty wants me to keep talking.

"I'm only going to leave if Kennedy wants me to go with

her. I'm not going to shop offers or anything like that. The only teams I'm willing to play for are either Chicago or the team she gets a job with. San Francisco, in this case."

His brows furrow in confusion, shaking his head as he tries to understand. "I heard she didn't get an offer from them."

"She did, though. She only said she didn't because she was trying to stay. For me."

Understanding washes over him. "And you don't want her to."

"Hell no. Fredrick has gotten out of hand with her. I'm tired of it. I've watched him treat her like shit for years, and now she has an opportunity to get away from him and have the career she worked so hard for. I'm not going to be the reason she doesn't take it."

Monty doesn't say anything, so I look up to find him watching me.

"What?" I ask.

"I wish you would've said something before. I've seen bits of it, but nothing big enough to bring to upper management. But if it really has gotten that bad, you need to file a formal complaint so we can handle it."

I can't do that, and she won't do it for herself. Years ago, I promised her I wouldn't say anything, and regardless of Dr. Fredrick getting reprimanded over his treatment of Kennedy or not, the real issue is her current job title.

"When does she have to decide?" he asks.

"I don't know. It's already been over a week since she turned them down so I'm hoping when she tells them she changed her mind, the position will still be hers. They wanted her out there as soon as possible to train under the current . . . medical staff."

"And they won't let her stay until after the season is over? That's almost unheard of to ask for that kind of commitment from a junior position."

Fuck.

I hate lying to Monty, but I've held Kennedy's secret for so long. I'm not going to spill now. Besides, everyone will find out as soon as she leaves.

Folding forward, I lean my elbows on my knees, hands laced together. "I just don't want you to be upset with me if I explore free agency. The last thing I want to do is disappoint you, Monty. I know we're not like you and Kai, but you've been a massive part of my life since you came to Chicago, and I don't want you to think you have anything to do with me leaving."

"Isaiah," he sighs. "Our relationship isn't like the one I have with Kai because you are not your brother. He makes it pretty fucking obvious when he needs my help, even if he doesn't directly come out and say it, but you . . . you act like a little shit half the time because that's what you want the guys on the team to believe, so I play into it. But I know that's not you. I see who you really are, and whether you like it or not, whether you *leave* or not, you will always be part of my family. You *and* your brother. I feel blessed that you two have let me fill a role that someone else left, you know?"

Fuck, I love this guy.

"And I'm not disappointed in you. Furthest thing from it. I'm proud of you. It takes a real selfless man to give up what you're offering to give up, to make sure the person you love finds what makes them happy."

I try not to think too far into everything I could be giving up. My brother is here. My nephew. My teammates. My coach. The list goes on.

I'll spend my off-season in Chicago, be able to see everyone then. But the one person I can't give up is Kennedy, and I just hope she's not planning to give up me.

It's with that thought that Monty's door flies open and Kai comes storming into the room.

"What the fuck is going on, Isaiah?"

"Sit down. Chill out." Monty's tone holds no room for argument. "Let the guy explain himself."

And so I do. I tell my brother everything I told Kennedy. Everything I explained to Monty. I watch the frustration on Kai's face begin to melt away, replaced instead with a bit of sadness, but mostly understanding. I watch as the anger he had turns to sympathy for my situation.

"Well, fuck," he exhales, sinking into the couch next to me.

"Don't be pissed at me."

He shakes his head "I'm not, Isaiah. All I've wanted my entire life is for you to be happy. And I know that's why you fake that shit-eating grin sometimes because you don't want me to worry about you." He pauses with a sigh. "But just because I'm not happy about this doesn't mean I'm not happy *for* you."

"It's just . . . you did a lot for me. You gave up a lot for me, and I don't want you to feel like I'm leaving you."

"I made a decision about my career that's best for my family. I can't blame you for doing the same." He smacks my leg. "And shit, I'm retiring. You know how much time I'm about to have on my hands to come see you? We'll make it work. You never have to worry about that."

I nod in agreement.

"You two hanging here for a while?" Monty asks.

"Is that okay?"

"Of course. I'll order us some dinner."

Monty's off the couch with his phone in his hand, leaving my brother and me alone.

There's a heavy silence before Kai speaks up again. "Mom would be proud of you."

I nod quickly, clearing my throat to unclog the emotion stuck there.

"And I am too."

Monty orders enough Chinese takeout to cover his dining room table. The three of us spend the night hanging out, eating dinner, and watching today's game highlights from around the league. We don't talk about the possibility of me leaving. We don't talk about Kennedy, but for the first time ever, I also don't pretend I'm okay.

I spend the entire evening without a smile on my face, and it's nice in a way, to not be okay. Freeing, even.

But regardless of the distraction, there's only one question repeating in my mind and that's me wondering what the hell I'm going to do if Kennedy doesn't want me to go with her.

There's no rain tonight.

Just the rumblings of thunder and the flashes of accompanying lightning.

It's a dry thunderstorm and if it didn't freak me the fuck out, I might be able to find the beauty in it. Purple streaks paint the sky. Bright light beams behind the iconic buildings of the Chicago skyline.

But it doesn't lessen the anxiety. Like some kind of switch, it revs me up, forcing my heart rate to jump, encouraging my nerves to fire.

As much as I love this place, maybe leaving the Midwest wouldn't be such a bad thing. I wonder if Northern California deals with random summer storms like these.

It's part of the reason I didn't go to family dinner tonight. I knew the storm was rolling through, but even more so, I knew her absence would've been impossible for me to ignore. It's hard enough going to sleep each night, knowing she's not in my bed, let alone sitting around a dinner that finally felt complete because she was there.

It's been two nights since I've seen her. Been two nights since I've even *heard* from her.

We had the entire day off from the field yesterday, so I didn't get the chance to run into her in the training room. Today though, today she called in sick to Sunday morning batting practice.

She's never, not once, called in sick to work.

And that scares the hell out of me because I know she's not.

She's in that apartment, packing her bags, and I'm just sitting around waiting to find out if I'm going too.

I know I told her to take the weekend, but there's a huge part of me that didn't believe I wouldn't hear from her for two full days. And the more time apart, the more I fear that the decision she's coming to is the one that doesn't include me.

I felt sick to my stomach getting those divorce papers drafted, but that will be nothing in comparison to how I'll feel if she actually signs them.

Yes, I want her to have a choice, but that doesn't mean I'm not entirely desperate for her to choose me.

Another boom of thunder rattles my windows, and it takes everything in me not to reach for my phone to call her. To call Kai. To call each and every one of my friends.

But I told my brother not to check in on me tonight. I need to challenge myself and I'm not going to get any better if I continue to allow either of us to enable my anxious thoughts.

But fuck, if it's not difficult sitting back and simply hoping that Kennedy isn't out driving tonight.

I grab my phone, but not to call anyone. I scroll through my pictures instead, hoping for the distraction. There are some of Max, some of the stupid shit my teammates have done around the clubhouse, and an unhealthy amount of her.

She likes to call me a stalker and fuck, I think I am.

The first is recent, her laying on my chest in bed, smiling up at the camera as I snapped our photo. Another of her eating a bowl of pasta I made her, a single spaghetti noodle hanging down from her lips to the bowl. One of my favorites is of her and Miller with their arms around each other, crouching with Max between them, all three of them with beaming grins. And lastly, there's another of her trying to use a folded-up newspaper, her crossword no doubt, to cover her face and hide from me, but when I play the live version, you can hear her laughter clear as day.

When I keep scrolling, I come across older ones. Photos from last season. She's in the background of some that were taken around the field.

I have a photo of Cody flipping me off while taking an ice bath. She's off to the side, wearing her team polo shirt and a frown.

There's one of Max sitting on the dugout bench, grinning up at me. She's in the background, sad eyes blankly staring at the field.

Another of her and Miller from last year when they first met. Kennedy's arms are crossed over her chest, her entire body stiff as she bends in an attempt to get her head close enough to Miller's and in the frame. But her body language is so uncomfortable and the desperate look on her face screams that she wishes she wouldn't be.

So much has changed these last couple months, and if nothing else, I can bask in the knowledge that through our time together, she learned how to be comfortable in her skin. She learned that there are people out there who love her. And she learned that I'm one of them.

I get back to the more recent photos and the screenshot I took of the cover of the *Chicago Tribune*'s sports section.

It's the morning we got married, neither of us having any fucking clue what we were in for. Her in her white dress and denim jacket and me holding her heels above my head.

Yes, I was infatuated, but it was nothing in comparison to the love I have for that girl now.

A hit of thunder rolls in a loud boom, and I close my eyes, trying to drown out the sound, when my phone dings in my hand.

With a text from Kennedy.

The Mrs: *Hi.*

My chest settles.

Me: *Hi.*
The Mrs: *Are you okay?*
The Mrs: *I know you told me to take the weekend, but if you need me to come over, I'll be there.*

It takes everything in me to keep from calling her up right now just to hear her voice, but I don't because I told her to take the time to think.

I don't call her because we both need to know that I can get a handle on my anxiety without her help, whether we're together or not.

Me: *I'm going to get through this one on my own, but I fucking miss you.*

There's a long wait before the next text. Gray dots dance along the screen before they disappear and reappear.

The Mrs: *I'm proud of you.*
The Mrs: *And I miss you.*
Me: *Did you eat today?*
The Mrs: *Don't act like you weren't the one who had food delivered to my house three separate times today. Yes, I ate.*

The Mrs: *And thank you.*
Me: *You weren't sick today, were you?*
The Mrs: *I just needed some time away from there.*

Away from me? I want to ask, but I refrain because she sends another text.

> **The Mrs:** *My laptop is there. It's sitting on the dresser in your closet.*

Her laptop with the CliffsNotes version of the research her old peer had sent over. Techniques derived from a specific type of therapy, rewritten in a way for me to understand.

> **The Mrs:** *Call me if you need me and I'll be there, but Isaiah, you're a lot stronger than you let yourself believe.*

And so I do it. I get through the night without allowing my anxiety to check in on anyone, without calling her for help, because she needed to know that I could do it on my own.

37

Kennedy

Pure determination radiates off me as I park my car in the employee lot. I'm running a little late. The pep talk I gave myself in the mirror today took a little longer than I had planned.

But I'm here and ready.

I haven't been to the field since Friday, and granted it's only Monday, but I couldn't tell you the last time I spent two days away from the team during the regular season, other than my interview trip to San Francisco.

I called in sick yesterday because I refuse to spend another day working for Dr. Fredrick, and Reese wasn't back to work until today for me to tell her. I sent her a frantic email on Saturday night, asking for a meeting, and Monday afternoon was her soonest available time to chat.

Locking my car, and with that goddamn manila envelope tucked under my arm, I head straight for the clubhouse.

Isaiah is a lot of things, but if he could stop trying to be a martyr, that'd be great. Two days with these fucking papers sitting on my kitchen counter. Two days of thinking things over.

I didn't need the time, but the one thing this solo weekend did accomplish was allowing me the space to decide that I will never work for Dr. Fredrick ever again. It took being away from the players I enjoy working with. It took being away from the one person I'll miss working with the most, sharing hotel rooms on the road and getting to be a part of his game days here in Chicago.

The halls are busy with players and staff getting ready for the game tonight, and for the first time in three years, when the first pitch is thrown, I won't be on this side of things. I'll be out there in the bleacher section, watching just like any other fan.

Without hesitation, I swing open the main entrance door to the clubhouse. I'm not about to start knocking now when I've never knocked before. Besides, anything I might come across, I've already seen, and I've got too much adrenaline coursing through me to slow down.

"Kenny." My name comes out like a breath of relief, and it doesn't take me long to find him. Standing in front of his locker stall, Isaiah is so clearly worn out, the lack of sleep evident in the bags under his eyes and the slump of his shoulders.

My sweet, fun, thoughtful, idiot of a husband got divorce papers drafted. I get that he wanted me to have a choice, but I'd already made my decision. Those papers sat on my kitchen counter all weekend, so it's his turn to deal with them.

Crossing the clubhouse, I feel the whole team watching us, but mostly I catalog Isaiah's stare, watching as the realization hits him that I'm not in my team gear.

Because I'm not working the game tonight and won't be working one ever again. At least, not here.

"I signed them," I say, holding the envelope out to him.

His lips part, words evading him as he stares at me in disbelief.

I push them in his direction. "Just take a look at them."

He slightly shakes his head as if he were trying to shake the image away of me holding our divorce papers out to him, until finally, he takes them from me. But still he doesn't open the envelope.

Instead, his attention bounces to my left hand to see if I'm still wearing his mother's ring.

"Just look them over, okay?" I check the clock on the wall. "I have to go. I have a meeting with Reese. We can talk after."

There's a combination of defeat and pride in his tone when he asks, "You're meeting with Reese?"

"Yes. Right now. I have to go."

Turning, I jog towards the door, still feeling all eyes on my back, watching me go.

"Ken," he calls out.

With a hand on the door, I look back over my shoulder at him.

He offers a smile. Not the fake Isaiah smile that he forces out even when he's upset, but a real, genuine one. "Proud of you."

That seems to be our favorite thing to tell each other lately.

I hitch a grin right back at him. "Me too."

I don't let my eyes deviate to the training room when I pass it, don't let myself check to see whether Dr. Fredrick is sitting back behind his desk the way he always is. Head up, shoulders back, I walk straight to Reese's office.

Well, Arthur Remington's office, but he's rarely around these days, and next year, it'll officially be hers.

"Hi, Denise," I say to Arthur's secretary, the same one who called me the day after I got back from Vegas. "I have a meeting with Reese."

Her smile is bright. "Perfect timing. They're waiting for you."

"Oh, is Mr. Remington here today too?"

"Why don't you head on in. Good luck, Mrs. Rhodes."

My body doesn't recoil the way it did the last time she called me that. No, this time, I have to bite back my grin from hearing the name.

But that smile drops when I open the office door and find both Reese and Monty waiting for me.

"Come on in," Reese says from behind the desk.

Monty is sitting in one of the chairs opposite her, the same one Isaiah sat in when we found out that our drunken decisions were going to be made public. I take the chair next to him.

"Are you here because of Isaiah? I promise I didn't ask him to consider leaving. I'd never suggest that."

Monty shakes his head. "This has nothing to do with Isaiah."

This is strange, partly because Monty is in this meeting when it was supposed to only be with Reese, but mostly because the two of them are in the same room and they're not arguing.

"You called this meeting," Reese says, hands folded together on the desk. "What can I help you with?"

I try to remember everything I rehearsed in the mirror today, the same things I told myself all weekend.

Crossing one leg over the other, I sit up straight and begin.

"I know you and I haven't worked together long," I say to her. "But I have loved working for this organization the past three and a half seasons. The team, you, Monty"—I gesture to him—"have been highlights when I look back at my time here, but as of today, I'm no longer going to be working for the Warriors."

Reese quickly looks at Monty, but neither of their expressions change. Clearly, Isaiah filled them in already.

"Any specific reason why you're quitting?" Reese asks.

This. This is the part.

"Yes." I clear my throat, swallowing the nerves. "When I came here three years ago, it was under the assumption that I was going to be the team's second doctor. Because that was the position I was qualified to do."

Once again, neither of their expressions change, but this time it's more surprising. I really didn't think Isaiah would ever tell anyone. He held that secret for so long.

"I'm an M.D., specializing in sports medicine," I continue. "And Dr. Fredrick hired me to be his second-in-command, but when we met in person for the first time, and he realized I was a woman, the position that was offered instead was athletic trainer."

That finally gets me a small reaction when Reese's jaw flexes, as if she were grinding her molars together.

"And don't get me wrong, I have loved my job, but I can no longer allow myself to be treated the way he's treated me all these years. I think there was a part of me that stayed in hopes that he would see my capabilities, but that was a silly pipe dream. He didn't care.

"When I went to San Francisco a couple of weeks ago, it was to interview to be their new Head of Health and Wellness. They offered me the job."

"Did you end up accepting it?" Monty asks.

"No." I turn to face him, hoping to assure him. "You don't have to worry. Isaiah isn't leaving Chicago because I'm not leaving Chicago. I'm going to interview with some local universities while I wait to see if a team doctor position opens with one of the other pro teams in the city. But my life is here. I can't leave it behind."

Monty's smile is knowing. "Kennedy, this isn't about Isaiah. This is about you. I completely understood him offering to leave for you."

That feels good to hear. I've been so afraid that Kai and Monty were going to be upset with me even though I wasn't the one to suggest Isaiah explore free agency next year.

"Thank you for saying that." I turn back to Reese. "And thank you. Your family has been great to work for and I'm looking forward to watching you take over next season. I think you're going to do great."

Hands on the armrests, I go to push up from my seat to leave when she slides a folder across the desk to me.

"What is that?"

"Your employee file."

"Okay." It comes out as a question. "Am I taking it with me?"

"No, it's for in-house use only. But it does list your work history, including your education and previous experience. I got that from human resources on Friday night."

Lips parting, I swing my attention to Monty then back to her again. "You already knew? Did Isaiah tell you?"

"No."

"Emmett suspected something was going on. He called me on Friday after Isaiah told him you were leaving, and I did some digging. I wish you would've said something sooner. My grandfather, God bless him, is a sweet man but can be a bit checked out and unaware at times. I've noticed the way Fredrick has been treating you this season. It's been on my radar. I was watching, and I would've believed you if you told me the truth."

Holy shit.

I open my mouth to speak, but nothing comes out.

"I should've seen it sooner," Monty cuts in. "But my attention has been on running an entire team. It's difficult to see the ins and outs of everything that goes on in the clubhouse."

"No," I disagree. "No, I kept it quiet on purpose, and I never let Isaiah say anything either."

"Well, plenty of the other players spoke up on your behalf," Reese says. "Word got out that we were looking into things, and by last night, every single player had filed a formal complaint on your behalf, giving firsthand accounts of the things they heard Fredrick say to you. He was terminated this morning."

My entire body rears back as if the words slapped me in the face. In a way, they did.

What?

Reese chuckles at the expression on my face. Wide unblinking eyes, mouth dropped open, internally repeating her words again to make sure I heard them correctly.

"Really?" My voice croaks.

"Really."

"Well . . ." I stutter, trying to collect my thoughts, trying to find some words, but I can't. *What the hell is happening?*

Reese speaks before I can. "Looks like I'm in search of a new Head of Health and Wellness."

This cannot be happening. I came in here with the intention I'd never walk these halls again and now . . . Oh my God.

"I can't." I shake my head. "Will. That job should go to Will. He's the second doctor and was here first. He's next in line."

"He wasn't here first. You were. Which is exactly what he said when I spoke to him this morning. He agrees with me that the position should be yours."

"He said that?"

"And he wasn't surprised at all when I told him about your qualifications."

"None of us are," Monty says. "Kennedy, you're impressively good at your job."

My eyes burn. "Thank you."

Reese sits forward. "So, what do you say? As the first female team owner, it'd be my honor to have the first female team doctor."

I can't believe this is happening, but before I answer, my attention swings back to Monty and as if he can read my mind, he dispels my concern once again.

"This isn't because of Isaiah," he repeats. "This isn't to keep him here, it's to keep *you* here. I'll happily trade him if you need proof."

A laugh bubbles out of me. "Please don't do that."

His grin goes soft.

"So . . ." Reese urges. "What do you say?"

"On one condition."

"Oh, she's making demands now." Her tone is teasing. "Go for it."

"I want an office manager. I don't want to be doing paperwork all the time. I want to be hands-on in the training room and on the field."

"Done."

Well, shit. That was easy.

"One more thing."

Reese nods for me to continue, trying to hold back her laughter.

"My previous position will need to be filled. I want to be the one to hire my replacement."

"Well, that is part of your new job description."

Holy hell, it is.

"So, is that a yes?" she presses.

My smile blooms so wide, my cheeks pinch. "That's a yes."

"Perfect. I'll get your new contract drawn up. And Kennedy, I know my grandfather set some archaic guidelines, saying that if you and Isaiah ended your relationship, one of you would have to go." She shakes her head. "I don't care about that. If you don't want to be with him, you're not going to lose your job over it."

"I appreciate that, Reese, but that's not going to be a problem."

Her lips purse in a knowing grin, like maybe she's known certain details for a while now. "Okay. Good to know, but um . . ." Her eyes trail down my clothes. "Any chance you could work the game tonight? I'm short a doctor."

"I think I can do that."

Monty stands from his chair. "I got to get ready for tonight, but Kennedy, we're all glad you're staying."

"Thank you, Monty . . . for everything."

"Don't thank me. That was all you. But I need a win tonight, so you should probably go tell your husband that you're sticking around."

38

Kennedy

I'm in a complete daze leaving Reese's office. My vision is fuzzy and zoned out, focused on nothing in particular when I close the door behind me.

What the hell just happened?

How did that all happen?

Well, I guess I know the answer to that, so the real question I'm asking myself is how did I get so lucky?

"Kenny."

The voice snaps me back to reality, my focus zeroing in on a frantic Isaiah as he jogs towards me.

Speaking of lucky.

How lucky am I that I get to call him mine?

Isaiah is wearing his baseball pants—only his baseball pants. His perfectly disheveled hair looking like his hands haven't stopped running through it all morning.

He's got that manila envelope, holding it up when he stops in front of me, heaving chest and desperate, pleading eyes. "Look," he begins. "I know I gave you a choice. I wanted you to make your own decision, but I've got to be honest here, I don't totally love this one."

My face softens into a smile.

How was there ever a day that I wasn't completely and utterly gone for this guy?

There are a lot of things I learned in our time together, but the biggest lesson my husband taught me is what it feels like to be loved for the first time in my life.

I'll never be able to thank him enough for being unwavering in his feelings for me, but I'm going to spend the rest of my life making sure he feels as safe and secure with me as he's made me feel with him.

"Maybe let's hold off on this part," he continues. "I don't know that we necessarily need to file these right this second—"

"Isaiah," I cut him off with amusement. "Did you not look at them?"

There's a heavy pause as his throat works a swallow. "I couldn't do it, Ken."

My sweet, sensitive husband. Words I never thought I'd use to describe him, but Isaiah's soft edges are one of my favorite things about him. He only allows certain people to see that side of him, and I'm not only one of those lucky people he chose to trust, but I'm also the one he chose to love.

Staff members busy the halls, getting from one place to another while the two of us stay locked in a standstill in front of Reese's office. We're on full display for anyone to see us, and Isaiah is holding our divorce papers in his hand.

"Come with me," I tell him, taking his hand and pulling him behind.

Outside of the clubhouse, we slip into the same restroom where we first met.

"Open them," I urge.

He shakes his head. "Don't make me do that here of all places."

"Isaiah," I chuckle. "Trust me. Open the envelope."

Confusion is clear as day on his handsome face, looking at me like I'm attempting to torture the man in the place where we've had so many of our big moments.

We met in here. We exchanged rings in here. We've argued and made up in here.

I get to tell him I love him in here.

Leaning back on the sink, he carefully lifts the metal prongs, opens the flap, and pulls out the stack of papers.

His eyes trail down the first page before flipping to the second, looking for whatever it is I'm so adamant about him seeing. I don't rush him. I allow him the time he needs to take it all in. But soon enough, the obvious defeat takes over as he reads the papers *he* had drafted for us.

That is, until he flips to the final page, where our signatures should be.

Isaiah didn't sign them when he dropped them off at my apartment, as if he couldn't bring himself to do it unless he had to—unless I signed them first.

His eyes go soft as they bounce over the words, following the path of the pen I used to ink each letter on the signature line.

"Kennedy."

"I do."

I chuckle a bit at those two words that got us here in the first place.

"Really?"

"So much, Isaiah."

He finally takes his eyes off the page to look at me.

"I love you," I tell him, using the same words he found written on the signature line of our divorce papers. "It may have taken me a bit longer to allow myself to open my eyes and see it, but there's no doubt in my mind that I love you. Every part of you. The parts you show everyone and the parts you show only me."

His eyes trail over my face, his lips parted without words to say. So clearly stuck in a state of disbelief.

So I repeat myself. "I love you, Isaiah."

That mischievous smile is back. "One more time for me, Kenny. Don't think I quite caught that."

Taking the papers from his hand, I set them on the sink behind him, getting them out of the way so I can move to stand between his legs, hands slipping around his neck, needing to touch him.

"I love you."

He bends his arm back behind his neck to cover my hand with his own. Then he circles the ring I've never once taken off since he gave it to me. "God, after all this time, that feels unreal to hear you say."

His words come out like a breath of relief, as if he can finally tell me how he feels, knowing I'll say it right back.

His forehead falls to mine. "I love you, Kenny."

Do what feels good.

This right here, this feels good.

It feels *right*.

All this time, I wanted to practice, plan, and schedule how it'd happen. I wanted to be perfectly ready for love when the time came.

But falling in love with Isaiah wasn't a big, planned event. It was buying toothbrushes and providing food when I was too busy to eat. It was his mother's ring and eating dinner together in a booth at Chili's.

It was his patience and unwavering commitment to show me my importance in his life.

How lucky am I that I get to love and be loved so effortlessly?

My thumbs dust over his cheekbones as I begin the other speech I rehearsed this weekend.

"I have spent my entire life looking for validation, seeking attention, hoping for just a bit of acknowledgment that I exist, and you . . ." I shake my head. "You waltzed into my life and never left me alone."

He huffs a dry laugh.

"Thank you."

His fingers draw languid circles on my lower back, urging me to continue.

"I never had to beg for your attention, and I'm not sure you'll ever fully understand how safe that became for me, knowing you were giving it to me willingly. I never had to ask you to see me, to understand me, and I'm sorry that I haven't allowed you to be able to say the same. But I promise you, Isaiah, now that my eyes have been opened, I can't keep them off you."

His smile blooms, this devastating grin that lights up the whole room.

That's him, though. He's all good. Contagiously bright.

Bright enough to shine light on my untouched, undiscovered corners. The parts of me that no one else took the time to look for. He gave me the confidence and the security to come alive with him, to never once have to question his sincerity.

It's not lost on me how rare he is.

"I um . . ." I clear my throat. "I feel like I don't deserve to be as happy as you make me."

He exhales a sympathetic breath of a laugh. "Oh, Kennedy."

"I just feel really lucky."

"It's not luck, baby. The good things in your life are there because of you. You are good and smart and capable and so fucking deserving, Kenny. Yes, I've known all that for years, but I think for the first time ever, you're finally seeing it for yourself."

He leans in and kisses me, softly pressing his lips to mine. So unhurried, so patient, as if we have all the time in the world.

And we do. Only he doesn't know that yet.

"When do you leave?" he whispers against my lips. "How much time do we have?"

I run my hands down his torso. "I'm not."

"Kennedy—"

"You said I had a choice. And I choose to stay. I choose you, and I will continue to choose you every day after this one. There. Done. I made a choice, and it was the easiest decision I've ever made."

Hands cupping my cheeks, he holds me as if I could slip away. He looks at me as if I were his everything. "Kenny, you can't."

"Dr. Fredrick was fired this morning."

Isaiah rears back at that.

"The entire team filed complaints this weekend on my behalf."

He drops his head back, Adam's apple exposed as he looks towards the ceiling. "I fucking love those guys."

"And Reese just offered me his position."

"Shut up."

I quickly shake my head in disbelief, a beaming grin spreading on my lips.

"Shut the fuck up, Kennedy."

"I didn't say anything," I laugh.

"Well, you better have said yes."

"Of course I said yes. I went in there with this whole plan. I was going to quit, apply to some local colleges, and wait for one of the other pro teams in the city to have an opening. But now . . . now I don't have to."

He exhales in disbelief and I get to watch as every realization dawns on him.

"You're staying here."

"I am."

"We get to work together. Travel together."

"We do."

"And you love me."

"So much."

That grin grows.

"But I swear, Isaiah, if you ever bring me divorce papers again, I'll be real tempted to sign them with something other than an *I love you*."

We both know that's far from the truth. Even though this marriage was supposed to be temporary and I wanted to separate as soon as we woke up that morning in Vegas, I couldn't imagine that idea now.

His smile turns sheepish. "Is staying married really what you want though? We can start from the beginning, rewrite our story. We can still be together without being married. I can call you my girlfriend if you're not ready to be my wife."

"Can't I be both?"

"What?" he says with a laugh.

"I don't want to rewrite anything. I want to date you while already loving you. I want to learn about you while already knowing you're the one. I know we skipped a few relationship milestones, but there are no rules that say we can't be married while we go back and check them off."

"Yeah. I like that idea." He drapes his arms over my shoulders. "There's been a certain milestone on my mind lately. We're married and you still don't live with me."

"That is a big one."

His eyes go soft with a smile. "What do you say, wifey? Will you move in with me?"

There's no question regarding where we should live between his place and mine. His has felt like home since the moment I first walked through the front door.

"Yes," I agree. "I'd live, laugh, love to."

Chuckling, he brings me flush to his chest, lips dusting my forehead when he speaks.

"Thanks for marrying me, baby."

"It was the best mistake I ever made."

The bathroom door swings open, instantly shifting our attention. Reese walks in, eyes cast down on her phone, heading straight for a stall.

We look at each other, wondering what the hell to do, before Isaiah clears his throat to get her attention. Apparently, it only took the man three years to learn to make his presence known when he's busy hiding in the women's restroom.

"Oh," she startles, her attention bouncing between Isaiah and me. "I'm sorry. I'm clearly interrupting something."

"We'll go," I suggest, pulling out of Isaiah's hold, both of us headed for the door.

She's halfway into a stall before she stops and turns, looking right back at us. "Sorry, but this is so strange, seeing someone else in here. I usually come down to this bathroom by the clubhouse for privacy. All these months of it being empty, I started considering it mine."

Isaiah and I share a knowing look, stupidly mischievous smiles on our lips.

"By the way, Kennedy," Reese continues. "I was going to come find you. I requested a name change on your new office door. It should say Dr. Rhodes by the end of the week."

"Dr. Kay," Isaiah corrects. "It should say Dr. Kay. She did that all on her own, long before me or my last name came around."

I squeeze his hand in mine. "Actually, Dr. Rhodes is perfect."

Reese offers me a sweet smile, slipping into a stall.

We leave the bathroom before Isaiah asks, "Are you sure?"

"Positive." I hold his attention. "Like you said, I don't care what my name used to be. I only care what it is now."

Epilogue

Isaiah

Two years later

It's the worst day of the year.

At least, it used to be.

I used to connect this date to loss, but now I can't help but think of everything I gained on this day over the years.

My nephew was born four years ago on this date. I met my wife five years ago, and today, I get the privilege of remarrying her on our two-year anniversary.

Yes, I lost my mom on this date, but she spent the last twenty years sending her sons the greatest gifts in her absence, and it's become impossible to think of this day with anything other than overwhelming gratitude and love.

"How are you feeling?" my brother asks from behind me as he helps me slip on my suit jacket.

"Excited. I'm looking forward to remembering everything this time around. Her walking down the aisle. Listening to her say 'I do.' Coherently, might I add."

He laughs to himself.

Kennedy didn't want to deviate too much from the details of our first wedding, but the biggest difference with this one, other than the lack of tequila in our systems, is the intention behind it.

We're getting married because we love each other, trust each other, are each other's closest friend. We spent the last two years learning each other, dating each other, and supporting each other. And even though I'm stoked to create some memories this time around, I can't help but be grateful for that drunken night in this same city two years ago.

I don't know if we'd be having this wedding without that one. It gave us the opportunity to see the other for who they really are, and we haven't been able to take our eyes off each other since.

Kai smiles to himself through the reflection in the mirror as he smooths the fabric of my jacket over my shoulders. "Who would've thought, huh? We were just a couple of kids trying to get by on our own and look at us now. Who would've thought we'd be as blessed as we are?"

"Crazy to think we spent all those years just the two of us, and now look how many Rhodeses there are."

"Well, there could be seven Rhodeses if you and Ken ever decided to give Max and Emmy a cousin."

I burst a laugh. "I swear, you and Miller have tried to slip that into every fucking conversation we've had since Emmy was born."

"And I have no plans on stopping."

The truth is, Kennedy and I haven't thought too much about having our own. We love being Aunt and Uncle to my brother's kids, but we're also having a blast just the two of us, working together, traveling together.

One day, when I retire from professional baseball, maybe we will or maybe we won't. Life is real fucking good either way.

There's a knock on the door of the bedroom we're getting ready in.

"It's us," Miller calls out from the other side.

"Come in."

The door is only open a crack before my nephew comes barreling in wearing his best suit.

"There's the birthday boy!" I hoist him into my arms, holding him at eye level. "How old are you today? I can't seem to remember."

He very carefully holds four fingers up.

"What? There's no way. I thought you were still a little baby."

"No. I'm four." He giggles, pointing over my shoulder. "Emmy is a baby."

I turn to find my sleeping niece in Miller's arms, the little girl with her mom's green eyes and her parents' shared dark hair. Named after Miller's dad and our mom, Emmy Mae Rhodes was born shortly after my brother retired, and any doubt or hesitation I had about him leaving the game for good was dispelled the moment I saw how centered he was at home with the three of them.

It's been a full season without playing next to him, the second starting just next week, but the combination of having Kennedy with me and knowing Kai's favorite job is away from the field has made the transition easier.

But that's not to say that he hasn't missed being around the sport. We were hardly past spring training last year before Monty hired Kai as one of his pitching coaches. He's not there every practice or game, by any means, but he's still around and it's been a fucking blast.

"Thanks for sharing your big day with me and Auntie Ken, Bug," I say to my nephew. "We're going to have a big birthday cake tonight, huh?"

"Auntie Ken looks pretty."

"Did you get to see her?"

His blue eyes go big, his smile just as massive as he nods his head.

"Lucky guy. I can't wait to see her. Tell me everything. How is she wearing her hair? What does her dress look like?"

"Hey!" Miller cuts in. "Don't try to use my son to get information. You'll see her soon enough."

"I don't want to wait any longer. This is torture."

"Jesus, Isaiah," Kai laughs. "It's only been a few hours since you've seen her."

"You don't get to say anything," I argue back. "You were far worse on your wedding day."

"It was different. Miller was pregnant. I needed to check in on her before the ceremony."

Miller bursts a laugh. "I was perfectly fine, and you knew it."

Kai smiles to himself before leaning over to kiss her, following that with a press of his lips to his daughter's head. "My girls." He turns to me and his son, taking Max from me. "And my guys. You've got a big job today, Max. You ready?"

He nods enthusiastically. "I'm gonna carry Auntie Ken's ring."

"Heck yeah, you are," I encourage. "Do you know whose ring that was before Kennedy's?"

His smile goes wide. "Grandma Mae."

The room goes silent. We've been teaching Max about our mom for a couple of years now, so it's not shocking to hear him say her name, but today, on the day she passed, on the day he was born, on the day I get to marry the love of my life, it feels important to say her name out loud.

"Yeah," I exhale. "She would've loved to be here."

Kai puts a hand on my shoulder. "She is here."

My brother and I look at each other for a moment, silently saying all the things.

"Well," Miller pipes up. "I'd offer you a wedding day shot, but we all know how that turned out last time."

The room shifts to laughter, Miller's specialty.

"Thanks for that, Mills."

"Come here," she says, opening her free arm for a hug, and I wrap mine around her and Emmy.

"Is she doing okay?" I quietly ask.

"She's doing great. Excited to see you."

"Thanks for being such a good friend to her."

"Well, thanks for marrying her. How lucky am I to get to grow old with one of my best friends?"

She rubs a hand down my back as we separate.

"I'm gonna run to the bathroom before we leave." I throw a thumb over my shoulder towards the door. "Be right back."

In my wedding suit, I close that bedroom door behind me, stepping into the living room of the massive house rental we're staying in for the weekend. It's outside of the Vegas strip and big enough to house all our friends and their kids. The past few days have been a blast, all of us hanging out here. Days at the pool and nights making dinner together, playing board games, and staying up to hang out after all the kids are asleep, only to wake up to do it all over again.

"There he is!" Cody calls out from the couch, dressed for the ceremony, beer in his hand.

The room cheers so I give them a spin, showing off my wedding suit.

Zanders and Stevie, Ryan and Indy, Rio, Cody, and Travis all boost my ego as I cross the living room to one of the guest bathrooms. Only when I get to the door, my attention is immediately pulled to the room Kennedy and I have been sleeping in. The room she's in right now, getting ready for our wedding.

Looking over my shoulder to make sure no one is watching, I quietly make my way to the door, softly tapping it with my knuckles.

"Who is it?" she asks, and just hearing her voice has my shoulders settling, has a smile sliding across my lips.

"It's me, Kenny."

"Isaiah? You can't see me."

"Please," I beg. "Fuck, I miss you."

She giggles this sweet laugh that has my forehead falling to the door at the sound.

"It's only been a few hours," she reminds me. "We weren't supposed to even sleep in the same bed last night and we did. We weren't supposed to see each other this morning and you still made us breakfast to eat together."

"Well, if I don't make sure you eat, who's going to?"

Her laughter is soft.

"Please, baby. I miss you. Let me just see you."

She cracks the door open slightly, only enough to allow her freckled hand to slip through the crack—her left hand with her bare ring finger because for the first time in two years, she took her wedding ring off so I could put it back on later today.

I offered to get her something new, something that was strictly hers, something we could add to signify us doing this the right way today, but she only wanted my mom's ring. And this time when I slip it on her finger, it won't be as a ploy to save her job, it'll be as a promise to love her for the rest of my life.

"Hold my hand," she says from behind the wooden barrier.

I intertwine my fingers with hers, palm to palm, instantly feeling centered with her.

"You're not supposed to see the bride before the wedding."

"But—"

"C'mon, baby. Play along."

I huff a laugh. "You can't keep saying that to me."

"And why's that? It's been working for me for years."

"Exactly. That's the fucking problem, Ken. I've never been able to say no. Not before you took my last name and sure as shit not now. It's something I need to work on."

"That's okay. Let's keep it going that way."

I squeeze her hand in mine. "I can't wait to marry you . . . again."

She squeezes right back. "I love you."

"I love you. I'll see you there?"

"I'll be the one in white."

"Wow. Okay, maybe throw out a spoiler alert next time."

She chuckles. "There won't be a next time. This one is forever."

Pulling up to the little chapel we tied the knot the first time feels fucking surreal.

I don't have many clear memories from that night, and I'm looking forward to changing that this time, but the exterior is so sharp in my mind. Maybe it's from that picture that was blasted in the *Chicago Tribune* or maybe it's a true memory from the night my life changed forever, I'm not sure.

The entire group spills out of rideshares, getting dropped off right out front. My whole team is here, some staying at our house rental, some staying at their own. This preseason bonding trip looks a little different than our typical ones, but I'm thankful to have them all here for our wedding redo.

Kai carries Emmy in her car seat, and Max slips his hand in mine as we make our way inside.

The door handles are two halves of a heart that connect when the door is closed, the entryway has a partially burnt-out neon sign flashing the name of the chapel, and a goddamn Elvis impersonator greets us at the front desk.

It's perfect.

Monty is already waiting for us inside, going over some notes of things he's planning to say while he officiates the ceremony as the rest of my teammates and friends find seats, piling into the tiny wooden pews that flank either side of the aisle.

I can't help but laugh to myself knowing that we chose to get married here, not only once, but twice. But it just feels right. I'm sure growing up, Kennedy assumed she'd have some massive ceremony hosted somewhere like the Plaza in New York City, with her engagement publicly announced in the *Times*.

Instead, we're doing it here. In this little run-down chapel with plastic flowers hot-glued to the pulpit for décor. The lighting is fucking awful and the red carpet runner spanning the aisle is tacky as hell.

But I wouldn't change a thing, especially now that our closest family and friends are here to witness this time.

Speaking of family, Dean is the last to arrive, walking through the front doors minutes before Kennedy is due to appear.

The entire room of my teammates turn in their seats to look at him.

"My bad. Flight got delayed." He nods towards me. "Hey, man."

Hand in his, I throw my arm around him, smacking his back a couple of times. "Glad you made it, asshole."

"Thanks for the invite, dick. Sorry I'm late."

"Perfect timing. Kenny is on her way. Any word from your family?"

He shakes his head, careless expression on his face. "Nah. They're too busy trying to find Mallory a husband to celebrate Kennedy being happy. You know how they are."

I do know how they are, though neither my wife nor I have had to deal with their bullshit for almost two years. Her mother rarely attempts to contact her, and Kennedy has not once reached out since the night I met them.

Which seems to be for the best. The only thing those people ever did is make Kennedy question her worth, and over the past two years, I've done my best to make sure she'll never question it again.

Ironic, really, that the only reason Kennedy and I got married in the first place is that she was feeling petty and hurt over her ex-fiancé marrying her stepsister. But time would show everyone's true colors. Connor and Mallory never even made it down the aisle because, according to Dean, they constantly fought about their lack of trust in one another.

I guess that's what you get when you get together by cheating. You're always going to be worried about it happening to you.

"See you after," Dean says, taking the front-row seat on the side closest to where Kennedy will sit.

"They're here," Kai says, holding his still-sleeping daughter against his chest.

Monty stands front and center, facing the crowd, and I take the spot just to his left with my brother behind me.

Monty places a hand on my shoulder. "You ready?"

I'm bouncing on my toes with excitement. "Yep."

"Max," he says to my nephew standing at my side, hand slipped into mine. "Are you ready? You remember what to do when your mom gets here?"

Blue eyes sparkling up at his grandpa, he nods enthusiastically.

Elvis gives Monty a thumbs-up from the back of the room, and the doors are opening.

Miller is first, bouquet in her hands. She lines up at the end of the aisle, smiling at her dad, her son, her husband, then lastly me.

Max runs to her, high fiving my teammates along the way, before Miller hands him our rings and directs him back down the aisle to us. The boys cheer for him, and I'm fucking dying over how flushed his cheeks are, how wide his grin is. These guys are good at a lot of things, but they are excellent at making sure Max knows how important he is.

When he makes it back, he hands the rings off to his dad and Miller starts her walk.

It wasn't all that long ago that the roles were reversed. I was Kai's best man, and Kennedy was Miller's maid of honor. Monty officiated that ceremony too and Max hung out up front with us the entire time, the same way he will today.

Miller's got her attention locked on my brother the whole time and shoots him a wink when she stands opposite him.

"Fucking obsessed with that girl," he whispers for only Monty and me to hear.

"We know," we say at the same time.

Speaking of obsessed . . .

The door opens one more time, and the first thing I see is that color that caught my attention the first time we met— Kennedy Rhodes Auburn.

The air from the door closing blows her hair, allowing it to drape around her face, and I swear to God she looks like a real-life angel when it settles.

A bouquet of flowers held in her hands. Yellow, I believe. Chosen because it's my favorite color, after all. Creamy white dress, constructed for her body. Unlike her last one, this one skims the floor, fabric molding to every dip and curve. Simple and understated, allowing her to be the star of the show. As classic and elegant as she is.

And that smile. That goddamn, earth-shattering smile she shoots me. It steals my breath with how grounded, how content it is. Like she knows, just as I do, that this is where we belong.

Hi, she mouths from down the aisle, red carpet runner ahead of her.

Hi, I return. I shake my head in disbelief because in what fucking world did I get it so right that I get to have the privilege of being the one she's walking down the aisle to?

If I thought deeper into it, I could probably give a few hundred reasons as to why I'm not good enough to have this moment, but I'm a selfish man. So instead, I just hold eye contact with her and count my blessings.

The music shifts, not to the original song she walked down the aisle to, but something a little more classic. The crowd stands, and that's when she takes the first step towards me.

She's stunning and confident, no question or hesitation in her movements, and I know for a fact it's an image that this time I won't be able to forget.

Especially when she takes a step towards me and the toe of her shoe peeks out from the hem of her dress. There are no heels on her feet, just a pair of black sneakers I bought her when I was desperate for her to be comfortable enough that she might be willing to spend a bit of time with me.

I can't help but laugh to myself, and when my eyes make it back to that beautiful, freckled face, she's laughing with me, her steps never faltering.

Fuck, I love her.

I can't wait to marry her again.

The backyard of the rental house is packed with our family and friends. Food, dessert, and drinks cover every table. There's a makeshift dance floor in the middle of the yard, and string lights illuminating the Nevada night sky.

Our wedding reception is in full swing, and it's been a fucking blast.

We've mingled, we've eaten, and Kennedy has changed into her reception outfit, which was a surprise specifically for me.

That white mini dress, platform Vans, and denim jacket from our first wedding. Only this time, she had Indy embroider the back of it. *Mrs. Rhodes* is stitched in white thread and that's where my eyes are glued, watching her dancing with Max on the dance floor.

He's got his hands in hers, his feet resting on top of her shoes, smiling at her like she's the prettiest girl he's ever seen.

440

He's not wrong there.

I fucking love my family.

"Man of the hour." Travis stands behind my chair, hands on my shoulders, before he and Cody take a seat on either side of me, all three of us looking out to the dance floor.

"You did the impossible. You got that girl to fall in love with you," Cody says, connecting his beer bottle to mine. "How's it feel?"

I take a long swig. "Fucking fantastic."

"Wish me luck to do the same," Travis adds.

Cody and I burst a laugh.

"Not a chance in hell," Cody says. "Natalie would never."

I shrug. "You never know. She might."

Natalie is the new athletic trainer that Kennedy hired as her replacement last season. Trav's had a crush since her first day. I can't say I envy the guy getting that constant rejection, but I can relate.

"Last time I saw her, she told me my glutes felt tight. You know what that means."

Cody shoots him a deadpanned glare. "Not what you think it means. It only means that you're a catcher and your entire lower body is fucked."

"It means she was looking at my ass."

"Dear God, you sound like Rhodes."

I tilt my beer bottle to the dance floor. "And look where that got me."

Natalie is still new in the sports medicine field, which is part of the reason Kennedy hired her. She wanted to help guide her and give her a positive experience right out of the gate. She's loved having another woman on staff, and just as they did with Kennedy, the guys don't treat Natalie any differently than the male medical staffers.

Well, other than when Travis tries his best to flirt with her.

There's been a shift since Reese has taken over as team owner and Kennedy has become the Head of Health and Wellness. So much of what Kennedy wanted to accomplish was to simply prove there was space in sports for women, and she's done just that.

Reese has hired quite a few women in other departments and Kennedy has split the medical staff equally. Two guys. Two girls.

It's been a nice change, and I'm proud of her for being the beginning of that shift.

The song she's dancing to with my nephew begins to fade, so I stand from my seat, leaving my beer on the table.

"I gotta go take care of something," I tell them before I go.

Stopping by the DJ booth, I request a song, then make my way to the dance floor to steal my wife.

I catch her attention as I cross the dance floor to her, soft smile on her lips, hands still holding my nephew's.

"Excuse me, Bug, but I need to steal my wife from you."

He looks up at me as if I've lost my goddamn mind to take the pretty girl in the white dress away from him.

"No."

I startle with a laugh. "Max, it's my wedding day."

He points to his chest. "My birthday."

Well, shit. He's got me there.

"Hey, Bug," Miller says, crossing the floor to us. "How about you dance with me for your birthday instead?"

He quickly appraises his mom before agreeing and swapping Kennedy's hands and feet for Miller's.

It feels like a sigh of relief when I slide my hand against Kennedy's lower back, pulling her against me. She melts into my touch, her cheek resting on my chest, one hand wrapped around my waist, the other holding mine out to the side.

"Missed you."

She chuckles. "It's been two songs."

"Do you think that matters?"

There was once a time Kennedy questioned what it felt like to be missed, but she'll never have to wonder now. There's not a day goes by that I don't miss her. If she goes into another room, I miss her. If she leaves for work before me, I miss her.

And I'm sure to tell her each and every time.

I catch the DJ's eye and give him a nod of approval just before the song Kennedy walked down the aisle to the first time comes on.

Mariah Carey's "Obsessed" overtakes the speakers and Kennedy's head instantly falls back in laughter.

"You didn't."

"Of course I did. I'm still counting this as our wedding song."

The guests around us cheer for the song they all know as my walk-up song. I haven't changed it in two seasons, and I have no plans to change it in the future.

"I still can't believe you picked this that night."

She shrugs, this sweet knowing smile on her lips. "Was I wrong?"

"Not even a little bit. Not then and not now."

My hand slides down over the curve of her ass, and it's strange to think there was ever a time that she'd flinch at my touch. Or when she didn't hug her friends, or when she felt uncomfortable at the prospect of holding my hand.

Now, Kennedy initiates physical contact as much as I do, whether that be a quick kiss at work or taking my hand when we're walking next to each other. And there's not a day that goes by when she doesn't hug Miller or Indy or Stevie when she sees them.

"Are you happy?" she asks, looking up at me.

"Do you even have to ask?"

"No." Her smile is soft. "You wear it. Just like you always have."

"So do you, Ken. I've never seen happiness shine quite as bright as the kind you've worn the past two years."

"I think that's because I was the opposite for so long, you know? Before us."

Leaning down, I kiss her, pressing my lips to my wife's on our wedding day, dancing to the song she once walked down the aisle to, wearing the outfit she first said "I do" in.

"I told you so."

"Shut up," she laughs.

"I did, though! I always knew."

"You're annoying." She kisses me again. "But I'm glad you were persistent enough for the both of us."

There's not a whole lot that's changed between us in the two years since we first said I do. We fell deeper in love. We moved in together and recently bought a house close to my brother and Miller. We dated, continuing to check off any firsts Kennedy hadn't experienced.

I started bimonthly therapy to deal with the trauma response to my mom's accident, learning to control my thoughts and not relying on Kennedy to settle me down. Now, when a storm hits, I find the rational part of my mind to walk me through the steps I've learned instead of instantly grabbing my phone and dialing those closest to me.

We stay and dance for the entirety of the song, slow dancing to a tune that isn't exactly meant for that. But neither of us cares as we slowly sway under the string lights.

"I love you," she whispers up at me as the song fades out.

I'll never get over hearing her say those words.

"Love you, baby." I nod towards the bar. "Want to do a celebratory shot with me?"

She laughs, her eyes crinkling with a smile. "Tequila?"

"Obviously."

Her hand in mine, we find the makeshift bar set up in the corner of our reception.

"Congratulations, you two. What can I get you?" the bartender asks.

"Two shots of tequila, please."

He pours the clear liquor, topping the shot glass with a slice of lime.

Kennedy holds it up to me in a cheers. "To getting it right the first time, even if it was an accident."

I connect her glass with mine. "To forever."

"Forever."

Leaning down, I kiss her before we each throw back our shot.

Zanders, Stevie, Ryan, Indy, Kai, Miller, and Rio are all seated around a table just off the dance floor. We join them, taking the last empty seat, where I pull Kennedy onto my lap.

"Congrats, you two." Indy sits forward, elbows on the table and chin in her hands, beaming at us like the romantic she is.

"Thanks, Ind," Kennedy says, wrapping an arm around my neck. "We're so glad you all could make it and help us recreate our first one."

Zanders looks between us. "Wouldn't miss it."

"I've got to know," Ryan says. "Was the Elvis impersonator there the first time?"

"Couldn't tell you," Kennedy and I answer at the same time.

"Guys. Look at them." Stevie nods towards the dance floor beside us.

All our attention swings to the completely empty dance floor minus the four little ones dancing together in a circle they've created. Max is the oldest and most coordinated so far, holding Taylor Zanders' hand in one and Iverson Shay's in the other. Iverson's got the hand of his sister, Navy, on the other side and she's connected with her cousin.

They're fucking cute out there in their little suits and fancy dresses.

"That will be you one day too, baby girl," Kai says to a sleeping Emmy on his chest.

Miller's got her head on his shoulder, her fingers toying with the ends of his hair as she watches Max with his friends.

"Cute tiny humans, we get it," Rio says. "But let's make this about me for a second."

I can feel Kennedy's silent laugh against my chest as she sits in my lap, head resting back on my shoulder as our wedding reception begins to wind down.

"Seriously, when is it my turn? Look at you guys." Rio gestures around the table. "You're all wifed up and I'm over here, twenty-seven and still looking."

"Four out of five," Kai adds. "One to go. It'll happen soon, Rio."

"Well, they better be fucking great, making me wait this long to meet them."

"What if it's someone you've already met and you have no idea?" Ryan asks.

"Nah," Rio brushes him off. "I can't think of a single person I already know that I'd be remotely interested in."

Zanders shakes his head. "You are the pickiest guy I know while also being the thirstiest. It's the strangest combination. It's no wonder you're single."

"This is the year. It's happening. And Cody and Travis just need to stay in their lane and be single because I swear to God if I have to attend another wedding without a date . . ." Rio shakes his head. "Well, then I just won't come."

"Wow," Indy laughs. "Very threatening."

"You all *should* feel threatened. You'd all be bored as hell without me around."

The conversation continues, but I'm not listening. I'm focused on the auburn-haired girl currently curled in my lap.

I press my lips to the skin under her ear, feeling her shiver against me.

I hold her tighter before my eyes meet Kai's. One hand holding his daughter, the other holding a beer, resting on Miller's thigh. He lifts his beer to me across the table.

I nod, the two of us having a silent conversation acknowledging how fucking blessed our lives have turned out to be. What was once just the two of us is now this massive family, some blood-related, some not.

Most important to me is the one on my lap, wearing my mother's ring.

Leaning my head against hers, I whisper, "Thanks for marrying me, Kenny."

It's been a common phrase I haven't been afraid to voice over the past two years.

She turns to look at me, warm brown eyes tracing my face before running a fingertip over the birthmark by my eye. "And which time are you referring to?"

I press my lips to hers. "Both."

THE END

Acknowledgments

The first and biggest thank you is to you all—the readers. If it weren't for you taking the time to read, review, and share your love for this fictional world, I wouldn't be where I am today, getting to spend my life telling these stories. So, thank you from the bottom of my heart for allowing me the space to do what I love. It's all because of your unending support.

I am more grateful than I could put into words for all of you.

Allyson—I think my favorite part of this job is getting to do it with you. You're not only one of my best friends, but such a stellar sounding board when I'm needing help with plot points and storylines. I'm so grateful for your friendship and your willingness to listen to an hour's worth of voice memos in order for me to straighten out the ending of a book or tell me when I'm being dramatic on those nights I'm convinced everything I type is literal garbage. I can't wait for what the next chapter looks like for us. Love you!

Sierra—I am so thankful for you! You're such a massive help to me in areas I don't have the capacity for. Thank you for all your help and for being such a great addition to the alpha reading team!

Megan—book three together! Thank you so much, as always, for all your help with alpha reading. Isaiah, my golden retriever boy, is all yours. You deserve him.

Erica—book four together! I am so grateful to have you in my corner, as not only my editor, but also my friend. Thank you for your patience with me on this one.

Jess—thank you for being my wonderful agent! I appreciate you and everyone at SDLA for all the hard work you put in for me.

SJ—my author bestie. I'm not sure this book would've come to fruition if it weren't for our constant midnight sprint sessions and plot chats. It really was such a game-changer for me on this one, when finding writing time was tough. Also, I'm just like your biggest fan, so there's that.

Samantha—my wonderful PA! Thank you so much for taking on the things I can't. I appreciate you so much!

Marc—another book. Another playlist. Cheers to accidentally making this one a banger.

We've got one more trip to the Windy City. Rio's turn is up next. Stay tuned for Windy City Series book five!

And until then, make sure you've read all the other books in the series . . .

Starting with book 1, Stevie and Zanders story. An athlete and air hostess enemies-to-lovers romance . . .

Then it's time for Ryan and Indy's story. A forced-proximity, fake-dating, best-friend's-brother romance . . .

And make sure you've read the third book, Kai and Miller's story. An enemies-to-lovers, forced proximity, single dad and the babysitter romance . . .